FEAR of HOPE

Upal Chakraborty has been a student of Presidency College, IIT (Kanpur) and IIM (Bangalore), and has spent around 35 years in senior positions at various corporations such as DLF, Pepsi and Reckitt Benckiser. Presently he works as an external consultant for Corporates and a teacher at management institutes like IMT (Ghaziabad) and IIT (Delhi). He has contributed numerous articles and short stories to both print and digital media. He can be reached at upalcy@gmail.com.

Sanmay Mukhopadhyay is originally from Kolkata and now lives in America. He studied physics in Presidency College, Kolkata, and then eventually moved as a technocrat to the US. He worked or consulted for Dunlop, CESC, Unisys, Yamaha, Microsoft, GE, Sun Microsystems, Los Angeles superior court and County of Los Angeles. He retired from his tech executive job to spend time with yoga, ayurveda and spirituality, and to promote Vedic culture. Though he has other publications (Prentice Hall, Handspring), this is his first novel. He can be reached at Dryogi4all@gmail.com, Facebook, Twitter @dryogi4all, .and Instagram @sanmaymukhopadhyay.

FEAR of HOPE

An Indian–American Saga

| UPAL CHAKRABORTY | SANMAY MUKHOPADHYAY |

RUPA

Published by
Rupa Publications India Pvt. Ltd 2023
7/16, Ansari Road, Daryaganj
New Delhi 110002

Sales centres:
Allahabad Bengaluru Chennai
Hyderabad Jaipur Kathmandu
Kolkata Mumbai

Copyright © Upal Chakraborty, Sanmay Mukhopadhyay 2023

This is a work of fiction. Names, characters, places and incidents are either the product of the authors' imagination or are used fictitiously and any resemblance to any actual person, living or dead, events or locales is entirely coincidental.

All rights reserved.
No part of this publication may be reproduced, transmitted, or stored in a retrieval system, in any form or by any means, electronic, mechanical, photocopying, recording or otherwise, without the prior permission of the publisher.

P-ISBN: 978-93-5702-053-4
E-ISBN: 978-93-5702-042-8

First impression 2023

10 9 8 7 6 5 4 3 2 1

The moral right of the authors has been asserted.

Printed in India

This book is sold subject to the condition that it shall not, by way of trade or otherwise, be lent, resold, hired out, or otherwise circulated, without the publisher's prior consent, in any form of binding or cover other than that in which it is published.

CONTENTS

1. Waking Up to Dystopia — 1
2. Trapped Under a Veil of Ice — 6
3. The First Experience at Los Angeles — 14
4. Just One of Those Days — 19
5. When the Candles Cost More than the Cake — 24
6. Down Memory Lane — 34
7. A Baby is Born — 52
8. A Precursor to the Weekend — 57
9. An Evening at Home — 72
10. The President's Tantric — 81
11. The Narrative Unfolds — 87
12. Trauma — 100
13. 'The Worst Part of Memory is the Holding of Pain' — 109
14. Crawling Back to Normalcy — 132
15. The Ugly Face of Racism — 137
16. Satyen Has His Way — 145
17. Knowing a Wife's Mind — 152
18. Building a Perfect World — 156
19. Walking Through Fire — 164
20. Replacing Cracked Panes — 176
21. The Closely Guarded Secret — 201
22. The Wind Blows, But I Feel Not the Breeze — 209

23.	Quietly Remembered Days	226
24.	The Magic of Fresh Chapters	239
25.	Waking to Reality	251
26.	A Conflict Within	255
27.	Santiniketan	262
28.	Breaking the Fast and Facing the Music	272
29.	A Long Lost Sweetheart	275
30.	That Fateful Day	283
31.	Sorting Out the Mess	295
32.	Lalbazar	305
33.	Turning a New Leaf	325
34.	The Aftermath	333
35.	The Conversation	342
36.	Tying Loose Ends	350
37.	Catching Up	372
38.	An Unscheduled Visit to Kolkata	377
39.	The Closure That Never Took Place	386
Epilogue		399

WAKING UP TO DYSTOPIA

From an Undisclosed Location

December 2019

Samir woke to the aria of birdsong, to a night-smitten dawn, glimmers of sun curving around the edges of the soiled, torn curtain which covered the singular window in the room. The shadows of darkness dotted the thick foliage with shades of emerald-green, and a forest of white and orange flowers limited his view of the horizon. The ethereal stillness added to the seduction of the fading night. Gentle sounds of a flowing river resonated from a distance, but he was doubtful about whether it was truly a river. The bird perched on the windowsill sang an eerily familiar melody.

The atmosphere inside the room presented a stark contrast to the peaceful and uplifting scenery outside. It was bare and dank, the plaster was peeling and its shades of dark olive had faded to a light amethyst, the spores of dust had been there for ages. The duvet and bedsheet had not been washed, possibly since the day they had been acquired.

Going back to sleep seemed like a safer option—his eyelids were heavy and memories faint.

The loss of perspective concerned him. He did not seem to know either the sequence of events that had led him to this alien location, or, more worryingly, his identity as an individual. It seemed prudent to let the dawn pass, to wait till the sun appeared resplendent in its orange hue. He had no clue how long it would take; he was not accustomed to it.

The nap that followed was nightmarish—haunted by a raucous mob, chased down a narrow lane, hearing the staccato of bullets, smelling a pervasive scent of gunpowder and the sight of gore. He could also hear a faint whisper in the background, in the midst of dark solitude.

When he woke up for the second time, he seemed to slowly regain his awareness. His left arm felt heavy and as he started to recollect the events, he noticed his watch. It was past ten in the morning. The sun had covered the planet with a fierce mid-morning intensity. Pangs of hunger and thirst manifested.

An elegant, dark green, opaque bottle—out of sync with the surroundings—was placed by his captors on a side table next to the bed. Once the water flowed through his veins, releasing pent-up energy, it prompted him to scramble out of the bed and rush towards the door. It was locked from the outside, but the bang he made was loud enough to attract the attention of his captors.

A bearded man with squinting eyes, wearing a banyan and lungi, opened the door and was followed conspicuously by a gun-toting man. Both were tall and erect, one carried a slight limp. The bearded one was carrying a tiny plate with four pieces of bread and a cup of black tea. The bread was probably nibbled by rodents—it had a number of holes in it.

'Who are you? Why am I here?'

'We have been ordered to limit our discussions to your physical needs.'

The voice was gruff, the tone impolite and crass.

'Tell me why I am here. Who are you?'

The tight slap threw him off-balance.

'*Chup Banchot*, do not repeat yourself, bastard. Just shut up! We obey orders from our boss scrupulously. He will be here by late afternoon and disclose whatever details you need to know.'

The whack had stunned him. At sixty-five, he was used to being treated with age-appropriate respect in social and professional circles, and the humiliation felt damning.

They escorted him, with a colt revolver at his skull, through a massive courtyard to the bathroom. The two men waited outside while he performed his ablutions. A leaky tube of toothpaste, a cake of dirty soap and an unkempt, used toothbrush were stacked inside. It was futile to ask for a razor.

The events of the previous evening flashed before his eyes—the walk through the desolate park, being accosted by three ruffians, asked to reveal his name, then gagged with a smelly scarf. He had resisted with all the strength he could muster, but had lost consciousness within minutes.

There was nothing else he could remember.

But why had they targeted him—a harmless and neutral old man? It could be a case of mistaken identity, and after their boss realized the mistake, they would release him. Nevertheless, they may be apprehensive that it would be dangerous to do so and may opt to finish him off instead. Something like that had happened long back to an acquaintance of his. Or was he being held for ransom? But he was hardly a stinking rich NRI (Non-Resident Indian). Just an ordinary OCI (Overseas Citizen of India) with modest savings to speak of.

The heat and humidity stifled him, and once he was back in his isolation, he noticed that there was no fan in the room. It was surprising that it could feel so hot within what appeared to be a forest. He pushed hard against the door but it did not budge.

They had snatched away his mobile, and there was no newspaper or reading material around. His only option was the practice he had been cultivating for many years. Meditation helped him steer the mind. He could move into alleys frozen in time, buried inside the subliminal consciousness, each path converging into a rich warehouse stacked with sixty-five years of bitter-sweet memories.

He remembered that his wife had once shot a video of him meditating on the sly, revealing a mosaic of cartoonish expressions. He had explained to her that the experience was spiritually liberating; he enjoyed decrypting, contextualizing, analysing gobbets of encrypted secrets, peeling them like layers of an onion. The expression on her face had expressed incredulity.

The mind always existed for him as a separate entity—not a component of the brain as his materialist friends asserted. Yoga and meditation helped him transcend the material world. Not that he had attained transcendence so far, but he was confident of achieving it one day.

Today, he was finding it difficult to meditate. His mind was untamed. He desperately recalled those rain-soaked mornings, meandering his way through the back alleys of the surrounding run-down locality to his elite school, Don Bosco, the mind switching to the sultry odour of the beaches of Puri. The rhododendron, neem and peepul trees on stormy afternoons, animated by the fragrance of the aguru perfume emanating from his mother's clothes. He remembered the sweet scent of the plumeria flowers planted in their miniature garden, smoldering incense sticks inside their puja room bedecked with tiny figurines. The putrid stench of corpses as the funeral cortege of his father approached the crematorium; the sweet taste of patali gur and jaynagarer moya during winter months and the images of a fountain pen, an ink pot, a Remington typewriter and a 45 RPM vinyl record swept past his mind. Childhood days were just wonderful.

But these were just flashes.

As he flipped through the pages of his life, invisible hands froze on the page of his sixtieth birthday weekend—peppered with epiphanies and encounters. It had been a tumultuous weekend; a weekend that had changed his life, redefined his relationships, accelerated his career and culminated in the serendipitous discovery of a long-lost friend.

TRAPPED UNDER A VEIL OF ICE

15 May 2014

On an uneventful Thursday afternoon, the sky was overcast and the morning had not gone his way. Samir Chattopadhyay was sulking and the ominous dark clouds on the western horizon added to his hopelessness.

He was desperate to discipline his wayward mind before driving down a highway notorious for accidents.

The weekend had not officially commenced, but Samir habitually started feeling the soft touch of the weekend by the time Thursday rolled around. It also happened to be his sixtieth birthday. The family was keen on celebrating the day with pomp, but sixty was just a number for him. If at all it meant something, it was a milestone. It reminded him of fading autumn and a dreary winter cooling its heels at the sidelines. He thought of the pain in his knee, frequent recurrences of bronchitis, restrictions on gluten, fried food, red meat and milk products. These were symptomatic of this phase in his life.

The reason for his gloom lay elsewhere—a distaste for hedonistic, bibulous parties. Once a party animal, Samir despised wild parties these days with a vengeance when he was made the centre of attraction. He had been caught unaware ten years back on his birthday. He was looking forward to a dinner at his favourite joint, as agreed with the family, but on reaching home, the door opened to a roomful of boisterous friends with mischievous faces, massive balloons, streamers, candles ensconced inside a mammoth cake and a cartoon skillfully etched on its top. A collage of photographs from progressive stages of his life were pasted on a clipboard, and he had tolerated the rancorous music that defied permissible decibel limits.

They had celebrated their silver marriage anniversary in this manner too. Thanks to his enthusiastic friends who forced them to replicate the rituals, including the seven rounds undertaken by the bride. Standing on a rickety platform, the bride circled the groom and exchanged garlands symbolizing the formal stamp of marriage. His friends overruled his staunch objection to such a frivolous exercise.

Getting into the car at the basement parking lot followed by a brief conversation with his boss, Mike, he chucked his laptop brief on the rear seat. He scanned the dashboard for warnings on critical parameters crossing their threshold levels, switched on the DVD player and zoomed past the sparse Thursday afternoon Los Angeles state traffic. A soft Tagore-devotional song permeated the interiors: 'Where are you, my Lord? Guide this desolate being who has lost his way.'

He had personally planned on celebrating his sixtieth birthday by relishing the charms of meditation, followed by a peaceful dinner with his wife Neelanjana, nicknamed Neelu, at a Thai restaurant around the corner. It was one of the best in Orange County.

On other days, Samir's mind would drift into the past like it was a gentle stream, but on days like this, it resembled boisterous waves relentlessly lashing the beach on a rough day. It was noisy, threatening and portentous. It usually commenced with acrimonious feelings against his overbearing 'helicopter parents'. He introspected, yet could not answer whether it was their obsessive love or a desire to bask in his reflected glory later in life that had led them to dominate every aspect of his existence during his teenage years.

He remembered the few discordant notes in childhood's otherwise smooth and pleasant tunes. One day, sometime during the mid-sixties, he had returned early from school and happened to overhear his mother boasting to a neighbour about the enormous resources they had invested into his education. They had admitted him to a good English medium school and spent lavishly on his expensive private tuition, despite struggling to meet both ends. On the contrary, he believed that they had not offered him enough other than supporting him in academics. His cousins had trained to develop their talents in music, tennis, photography, cricket and so on.

As the metallic brown Mercedes ML-350 branched into the highway, memories of his childhood friend, Subroto, cropped up from obscurity. A classmate from the first-standard, whose parents were renowned doctors, Subroto continued in the English-medium elite school that Samir quit after nine years. He had scored twelve points for his school-leaving Cambridge exams from a school that regularly boasted five-pointers. On the other hand, Samir ranked fourteenth at the state level in his board exams from the famed Bengali medium school—Hindu School. Both of them had qualified for the leading Indian Institute of Technology (IIT). Samir was offered the coveted Electronics and Communications while Subroto had to settle for Metallurgy.

Samir returned home after two months to obtain admission in the aspirational college for a career in Physics. The Oxford of the East they used to call it. During the first eight weeks of the 1970 summer he spent at the IIT, Subroto and he would travel together on Saturday mornings to spend the weekend in Kolkata. Standing next to their imported Chevrolet, Subroto's parents were religiously spotted at the Cab Road of Howrah station as the train chugged in. The car was gigantic, especially by the standards of an era when only two or three oddities were licensed to be manufactured and sold in India. They offered him a lift because they lived close by. Subroto's embarrassment was palpable. It manifested into an irritable behaviour on the journey back home. Sometimes, he would land in Kolkata the previous evening without informing his parents about his sudden change of plan.

After completing his MBA from Stanford, Subroto—based out of Toronto—joined the leading global consultancy and had recently been promoted as a partner there. Samir and Subroto were not in touch, but a professional acquaintance who knew him kept Samir informed. They had last met eons ago, when Samir had visited Canada on a short project. After being picked up from his guesthouse on the last day of his stay, he expected an invitation from Subroto to stay back for the night, but was offered a drive back, and even refused to apologize for arriving an hour late. Samir had laughed it off, commenting that Subroto was yet to forego his Indian habits. That pompous evening soon turned intolerable, battered by incessant hatter on his professional accomplishments and haute brands, including a thousand-dollar watch. Full of himself, he did not even bother to express a cursory interest in his friend's life or career. Subroto's Canadian wife (six-months into the marriage) dropped by for a while, retiring after a series of uncouth yawns. On returning home, Samir had buzzed Subroto to express gratitude for the evening and was promised a call-back, which never materialized.

Samir's initial stint as a techie witnessed a meteoric rise after spending the first few years with startups in a rural Midwest location with country yokels. He had honed his skills through successive stages in the evolution of technology, moving into the modern era from the good old days of massive computers and roundish magnetic tapes capable of storing a few thousand characters and eighty-column punched cards. Every moment, he regretted that he could not grow in sync with technology. The only consolation at his ripe old age of sixty was a comfortable financial situation—attributed to the *right* investments at the *right* moments, rather than fabulous sums earned at work. He had laid his dreams of a cottage by the seashore and a Ferrari to rest long ago.

Samir had moved to Cincinnati in 1977 from India. Starting as a programmer, he started taking lead roles in projects and became a project manager within a couple of years. His flare to convince people on technical as well as business issues in a non-formal setup made him a natural choice and he was accorded the responsibility to manage projects both in Cincinnati and elsewhere. He decided to continue working with IT companies to sharpen both his technical and business skills.

His first opportunity with a large IT organization based out of Orlando in 1990 in a global role enabled travel to diverse countries like South Africa, China, Vietnam and Argentina. The parting from this company was sweet. They made promises of an enviable career path thereafter, but he declined to withdraw his papers when he was selected for a consumer goods manufacturing organization as a Chief Information Officer at Los Angeles. At his age, the prospect of heading the systems department of a hundred-million-dollar entity was an offer to gloat over. He was offered a strategic role with opportunities to design business processes driven by transformative seminal technology innovations, presented as case studies in elite business schools, exuding wisdom yet disruptive, in harmony with his 'illustrious' past.

In one of his initial presentations to the Leadership Team, his inability to communicate in an intellectually convincing manner had been starkly apparent. The same President, the one who had bent backward a few months back to ensure that his financial demands were not just met but exceeded by a few percentage points, did not bother to disguise his exasperation. In Samir's earlier roles, jazzy presentations were the prerogative of the sales team; the technical experts were rarely encouraged to climb the podium. Catapulted, suddenly, into the role of an internal salesman to solicit funds and approvals, his inability was self-diagnosed as a teething problem destined to disappear once he got used to the bunch of stern-faced, cynical honchos.

A candid pronouncement came from the counselor who did not believe in mincing words. Although he did not rule out marginal improvements, a total transformation would elude Samir. It was in his DNA; the panacea lay in a mutation of the genes.

An alternative perspective emerged while discussing the topic with his CTO, an African-American gentleman by the name of Frank, an individual with impeccable credentials and a friendly disposition. 'It's the cultural bias, boss. As you face that race, your tongue ties, the brain stops, paranoia grips you,' he explained. Samir's smiles vanished, like fairies of his childhood dreams, revealing undisguised pain and anger. 'You got to be cocky in this country! It's tough for folks from your cultural background to perceive the phenomenon because you never faced discrimination in your country.'

The movement to Los Angeles had taken place in 1993. By that time his family had grown, and he wished to focus more on his kids and a tad less on his career. Life was less tense there and the atmosphere less stifling and racist. California offered more opportunities—career, premium universities where his kids could go to and, of course, the soaring real estate prices.

Caught in a web of confusing arguments, he decided to shift gear and look into a verse from the Bhagavad Gita, taught by his father early in life.

Karmaṇy-evādhikāras te, mā phaleṣhu kadāchana
mā karma-phala-hetur bhūr mā te saṅgostva karmaṇi

(You have a right to perform your prescribed duty, but you are not entitled to the fruits of action. Never consider yourself the cause of the results of your activities, and never be attached to not doing your duty.)

In this verse, Arjun was not willing to fight the epic war, Mahabharata, but Krishna persuaded him to perform his duties. 'Your right is to the effort, not to its fruits. Do not make your actions be attached to the outcomes, nor let your attachment lead to inaction.'

However, the cold comfort proved evanescent as bitter memories churned through Samir's mind, and he soon found them rocking like the gusty winds raging outside on a turbulent afternoon.

Like frames of an avant-garde movie, thoughts flashed through him in rapid succession, starting with thoughts of the old lady who wished to sell her dwelling in Orlando. He had set off with an estate broker one morning, contemplating purchasing a modest town hall to prove his financial prudence. The first one failed to meet his expectations and he had offered a lowball price out of courtesy, but the response had rattled him.

He next thought of the aggressive behaviour of the bus driver at LA, who had screeched his brakes after a round of desperate gestures: 'You dope! Go back to wherever you came from.' Controlling his rage, Samir had settled for an inoffensive piece of rhetoric: 'Where the hell is that?' Samir had complained to the highest authorities thereafter, and the transportation company profusely apologized through an email, but the incident left a bitter taste. It had happened only a month after Obama became the President and Samir was still audacious enough to dream of a less turbulent future.

Hope, hope, hope. The missing word in Samir's dictionary. Nothing seemed to have changed. 'I am always on the receiving end,' he thought, as he took a quick lane change, perhaps a bit rashly.

THE FIRST EXPERIENCE AT LOS ANGELES

1995

Friends had told him that LA boasted a far more professional environment and his problems would be far less here. Yet, a few years later, he found himself pounding the massive brown table in the boardroom, yelling at the 'tough' Project Manager appointed by the vendor facilitating a business transformation project. The lady had been overbearing, churlish, was long past her prime and wore thick spectacles, but Samir decided to be respectful from the day he had been introduced to her. A few days later, in a mood to flaunt his advanced project management skills, he had pleasantly requested, 'Judy, I wish to be presented with a detailed activity plan populated with the expected dates at the task level.'

Strolling past him as if he did not exist, she had casually pronounced in a soft tone, 'Can provide a high-level plan, but you don't need a detailed plan for a six-month project.'

'Judy, I do need a detailed plan with a list of activities planned for the week, updated to a status report every Monday. Please understand that we follow standard practices here. I will send you samples.'

Wrinkles appeared on her forehead; her eyes turned bloodshot. 'Reporting at a detailed level would delay the project. This is the era of agile projects. Let me speak to Bryan tomorrow and sort this out.'

THE FIRST EXPERIENCE AT LOS ANGELES

Samir was surprised at his assertiveness. 'Bryan happens to be my boss, but I am the project director here. Can you please stop walking away? Small courtesies, you know.'

She had nonetheless slipped into her office without uttering a word.

In an uncharacteristic display of hostility, a steering committee meeting was convened the next day with Bryan and the entire project team to resolve the issue. Judy threw a tantrum, questioning Samir's basic understanding of the project, while the other committee members received due respect from her. Bryan and her boss defused the situation by crafting a compromise suggesting that she provide the details Samir had requested only for activities lying on the critical path. Nevertheless, they failed to censor her impertinent behaviour.

His Operations Manager, Paul, openly sided with him that day. 'Judy, may I remind you of the racist comments you made the other day at the cafeteria?'

'What the hell are you referring to?' she had shouted.

'Come on, Judy, don't tell me you suffer from amnesia. Just a few days back, you displayed your contempt for Indians. You said, "They are habitually lazy, emit a nasty stink, their turmeric-stained nails and undergarments stick out, they emit a burping noise while eating, are connoisseurs of goat meat, their dames are frigid" and used a slew of expletives which I would not like to repeat here. Many of us were present in the cafeteria the day you took off on Sam, several witnesses can be summoned if you desire.'

The tension in the room manifested while numerous eyes rolled, and the few fixed on Samir communicated that they were not on his side.

'Well...'

A visibly shaken Judy was cut short by Peter and requested to hang on. For Samir, it was a maiden experience. They called him after an hour to inform him that she would no longer continue in the project and a suitable replacement might take a while. They seemed eager to appease him, but he cared not to respond to this Pyrrhic victory since her manner had a brutal impact on him, shards of his self-esteem spattering across the conference room. And he also believed that they had taken corrective steps out of fear of the law.

The toxic scowl from Judy when they bumped into each other later during the day remained etched on his mind for months.

Vice Presidents from the vendor organization were spotted in multiple discussions inside closed rooms for the next few days, even as Samir waited patiently for a formal apology from the vendor for the racist utterances of their senior Project Manager. He knew they were scared as strict laws against racism at work could disqualify their contract. Judy was in clear violation. But why were they taking so long? What were they trying to cover up?

He was reminded of Bryan's 'nostalgic' remark in the corner coffee room about being back home in South Africa. Before Nelson Mandela had taken over, speaking to an Indian on a one-on-one basis used to invite dirty looks from passers-by. He was apprehensive that they would make him walk on a plank on the ground and claim that he lacked teamwork skills. Apprehensive of the outcome, he narrated the incident to his wife at night, expecting a few words of advice and encouragement, but after the brief conversation, he wished he had not broached the topic. She instead laid the blame on his door for not integrating enough with the Americans.

The final stab came a month later, sugar-coated with a gentle European touch, couched in typical corporate jargon. Bryan called him into his office to state that they would 'hate to lose Sam, but things were not working out'. Promised a silver handshake with six clear months to hunt for a suitable opening and see the project through, 'adding a feather to his feather-strewn cap'. Not a soul would ever know the real reason for his departure and Bryan would even grant a laudatory letter of reference.

However, Bryan did not forget to add that if Samir was unable to obtain a job, he could hang on for a few more months but that would not be in his interest. The message was clear, and it was obvious to Samir that Bryan was unable to dismiss him because of certain provisions in his contract and because he was scared of facing backlash for behaving like a racist.

They stuck to their promise, but Samir obtained another opening after six months. He was emphatic that he felt 'unwanted' in the organization during the exit interview. The HR person conducting the interview requested that he elaborate, but he believed that no one would record or listen to his version.

Friends and well-wishers advised him not to pursue the case in a court of law because it would be tough to establish the racial bias, and, after all, as a professional, negative publicity would not be in his interest. He did speak to Paul, who had stood by him that day, but he chickened out and was unwilling to testify before the court of law.

◆

Samir's agitated mind strayed to a horrendous account of explicit racism, a gory incident he had faced at Memphis, an incident of physical assault. He felt an impotent rage and slammed the steering wheel. The panic-stricken expression on the guy in the adjacent car stimulated a feeling of vicarious victory and he was able to regain his concentration only after branching into the arterial road.

'*Anuloma vilom*,' the yoga technique taught a year back by his guruji was his lifeline at an age when memories catch up with a brutal vengeance.

A few more incidents flashed. He thought of them all, but realizing the risk of losing his concentration on a treacherous highway, resolved to introspect instead on the day's happenings.

JUST ONE OF THOSE DAYS

15 May 2014

The IT Strategy and Budget for the quarter were to be presented before the Board. He was called in at half-past eleven, thirty minutes behind schedule. The Chairman, Alan, and three non-executive independent directors could be spotted at the conference table, apart from Mike, the CEO, and Bill, the Finance Director. Reminded of whispers flying thick and fast across vending machines, corridors and washrooms, Samir was able to conclude why the Sales Director, a member of the Board, was not to be seen. He was disappointed because the gentleman was genuinely fond of Samir.

The Board members were effusive. Their boots were perched on the table and empty food packets were scattered around them. Entering right in the middle of a crude scatological joke cracked by the florid Chairman, the below-the-belt narration offended Samir's refined tastes. He was requested to relax for a while, but he could not fathom the exuberant mood in the room since rumours doing their rounds suggested that business was not going great. After proving to be a patient audience member, when requested to connect his laptop to the projector, Samir noticed that they had purchased the latest model.

Taking off his presentation with aplomb, he hit hard at the pitcher. The first half flew like a hurricane despite the unwavering, intense gaze of the recently inducted non-executive Director, Colin, seated at the furthest corner, bearing an arrogant expression. His dense eyebrows expressed visceral disgust, but

Mike had cautioned Samir that Colin had to be listened to as he had hooks to financial institutions.

As he started to think that he was on top of his audience, disaster struck! A baritone voice reverberated in the room, a voice that was capable of terrifying strong personalities. Colin was speaking.

'You are reinventing the wheel, and a software already exists for the App you recommend we develop in-house'.

Familiar with emerging technologies and an avid reader of the latest publications, Samir knew Colin was talking bollocks. The first App was a year away from release, and the beta-testing had not even begun. Nonetheless, Samir was unable to muster the courage to confront him head-on. He paused and gazed at his notes. He could counter Colin. However, he could sense his mind blanking out and his confidence evaporating.

Colin, nonetheless, continued relentlessly with his attack.

Ultimately Samir muttered. 'Sure, sure. Will revert to the drawing board on this.'

'But why don't you present a comparative cost-benefit analysis?' It was Bill, the Finance Director, who spoke. He disliked Samir and had chosen the right moment to wake up.

'He has not even considered the alternative, Bill,' Alan interjected. 'Sam is fixated on developing the tool in-house.'

The nasty grin revealed Bill's satisfaction at Alan's snide comment. Like a rabbit caught in the headlights, the red ray of the laser pointer in Samir's hands moved to the glum faces across the room. He felt the pincer attack from all three directions, entwining him like the claws of an octopus.

Mike intervened at this stage. 'During the latter half of the budget session scheduled a week from now, we will squeeze in an hour for IT. Sam, we need to send the numbers to finance for compilation; so please present some decent stuff the next time.'

The comment stung him like a bee, his forlorn voice and downcast look betrayed the state of his mind.

'Sure, Mike, sure. Will do so.'

His downcast manner did not escape the eyes of Jenny, his admin assistant and a keen observer of human behaviour. She was immensely fond of Samir, and her audacity was of the affectionate kind.

'Didn't go to your satisfaction, Senior?'

'Cool, but it was inconclusive.'

What followed was a comment accompanied by a wink. 'Don't take it too hard, Sam,' she said. After having interacted with him for several years, she could discern when he was not being truthful.

'Jenny, I have to leave. Planned to reach home by early afternoon.'

'Happy birthday, once again. Hope you remember that I am on leave tomorrow. See you on Monday and have a good one.'

It was past one when he reached the parking space reserved in his name. Mike's tall, athletic frame and smiling face was visible from a distance. He usually travelled home during lunch hours to settle his kids after they returned from school. The genial expression failed to inspire Samir because Mike seldom scowled and was known to sack employees with a reassuring smile, deceiving the victim that he was pulling a fast one.

'Cheer up, Sam. The presentation was awesome, but you stumbled. A word of advice. If someone needs to be told on his face to take a walk, please practice the art of doing so. I am certain you would have proposed the alternative if it was feasible and I would have stood by you, but you failed to take him head-on.'

'But, Mike, you told me the guy has hooks with financial institutions.'

'Sure I did, Sam, but does that mean you grovel before him?'

'Well, I guess, that was what constrained me.'

'My analysis is that you are a great guy, but mild-mannered to a fault. It is a rat race out here, every guy looking for an opportunity to stab the other. You got to be assertive and aggressive, Sam. Now, my advice is to perform a serious weekend study. Will take a hard look on Thursday morning.'

He had shrugged.

Mike continued. 'No big deal. See you. Hey! Many happy returns of the day! It slipped my mind in the morning. Have a fabulous weekend, and do take your beautiful wife to an upmarket restaurant.'

Mike was an amazing man, a leader capable of motivating his team. Samir placed him on a pedestal. Nonetheless, he dismissed the pronouncement that Mike would have stood by him with buckets of salt. His hands were tied in a corporate structure that reeked of racism, and Mike was unable or unwilling to upset the applecart. He was reminded of Wharton-qualified Gaurav, who had been condemned to pass vendor invoices and provide cash projections for the following quarter.

Jenny, who handled the payroll for his department, had let the cat out of the bag, informing him within a month of his joining that, his team-member, Harry, earned more, despite reporting to him and being less experienced. Perhaps he should have bargained harder, but how on earth would he have known that he was being offered less than his subordinate? Harry's contempt towards him manifested through acts of insubordination. Like the day he refused to travel to their Virginia office instead of Samir when Neelu had been down with a bout of flu.

As Samir meandered out of the basement, he remembered the term, 'implicit biases'. Associating positive qualities with folks in similar racial or social categories, the individual is unaware of his deep-rooted prejudice because long-standing biases are entrenched deep.

The gentle streak of happiness when he reached home within forty-five minutes was short-lived. The neighbour had crept into his parking space yet again. Samir was in no mood to spoil his birthday arguing with a person who, like many others of his ilk, had taken South Asians for granted.

WHEN THE CANDLES COST MORE THAN THE CAKE

15 May 2014

He glanced at the façade of his house for a few moments, distracted. Picking up the loose papers strewn untidily across the front seat, he dumped them into the leather brief, ensuring that his priceless Mont Blanc and the key to his steel locker were safely tucked inside its interior pockets. Samir was fastidious about the key. It opened a locker that was embedded inside the closet in their bedroom, which contained not just important documents and certificates but a precious object that had been lying in his safe custody for forty-two years. Returning it to its rightful owner was a mission he hoped to accomplish someday, despite having failed to do so for many years now.

As he gently opened the car door, a stream of raindrops greeted him. He would avoid sprinting the short distance—his knee had popped while driving. The doctor had recommended a knee replacement surgery three months back and, although confident that yoga would cure him, on some days every step sent a high-voltage electric current of pain. 'Que sera sera, whatever will be, will be' was the facetious response for Neelu whenever she broached the topic. It rankled her, despite her years of familiarity with his lackadaisical nature.

He was reminded of the mellifluous voice that had glided through a roomful of guests, ten years back. The cacophonic chatter had melted into an awestruck hush as Neelu's nimble fingers struck the piano. It took a while for the crowd to erupt into applause. Laura had remarked, 'Wow, your wife is a maestro!' and it had evoked a coy smile, along with the unmistakable twinkle in a corner of his eyes, betraying his unentitled pride.

He stumbled twice while climbing the flight of peach-coloured stairs; the stumble was an evil omen hovering above his sixtieth birthday. Instantaneously, he was reminded of the black cat that had darted across the road on his fifty-eighth birthday after a similarly frustrating day at work. Samir's superstitions were inherited from his mother.

Opening the wrought iron front door with a mild squeak, he was startled by the unmistakable buzz of the landline. The ringtone reminded him of childhood in Kolkata. It seldom rang, retained in case long-lost acquaintances wanted to get in touch.

He was concerned about the water dripping from his hair. He let go of his brief on the floor and paused for a while on the landing that overlooked their sprawling family lounge. Although he knew he was susceptible to bouts of common cold, and needed to take care, he waited, staring pensively through half-drawn curtains at the gently swaying trees in the backyard. The torrents had gathered intensity, drenching unwashed clothes left to dry in the open. The drier required fixing—Neelu had sent a couple of text reminders in the morning. The thought of the inevitable frown on her face evoked a wicked smile, which soon disappeared at the thought of perishing vegetables and dispersed leaves spattered across the swimming pool. The disgusting squeaks from the French doors prickled his fraught nerves despite the streaming aroma of petrichor from his fifteen-year-old cozy nest.

He felt relief once the phone stopped ringing. Adroitly balancing his Joseph Abu jacket on the railing of the short staircase that led into the lounge, he impulsively squat on the steps and massaged his bare skull, once resplendent with a dreamy crop of silky hair. Although the phone recommenced its buzzing again, he sat transfixed, like a wax statue enjoying languid moments, with no intention to respond to the call, change into a comfortable pair of boxers or rush downstairs to salvage the wet clothes.

There was another reason he had returned early today. The complex polling process for the Indian general elections had ended only a couple of days back. Samir was keen to catch up on the plethora of analysts pontificating on the exit polls on Indian television. A clean sweep was predicted for the nationalist party, led by Narendra Modi, and Samir was, by now, an unapologetic admirer. Neelu's friends and relatives were aghast at Samir's transformation. A staunch supporter of the centrist party, Congress, that had ruled for the past ten years, Neelu was as perplexed as his children, for whom the leader was the embodiment of right-wing bigotry. His children were actually disinterested in Indian politics, and they found Indian television debates to be cacophonous. What they were puzzled with was his advocacy for the Right in India, while retaining his liberal stance in the USA. He countered with reticent responses whenever they quizzed him on the apparent dichotomy.

As a late convert to spirituality, Samir was convinced that Modi was capable of restoring the glorious tradition of the Vedas and Upanishads, concomitantly carrying the nation on his shoulders towards modernity and progress, while countering sinister threats posed by religious terrorism and a hostile neighbouring country. His son, a self-declared liberal Republican, interpreted the conundrum as a disingenuous attempt to substitute a 'moth-eaten' ideology of the past with restorative nostalgia for a cultural tradition he was proud to belong to.

The incessant chatter from the bedroom was weird because his wife was not expected home at this hour. She taught Economics at a local school and seldom returned before 4 p.m. The caller refused to give up, but what still fazed him was the murmur from inside the house and even though he called Neelu's name loudly and repeatedly, he failed to obtain a response. Yet there had been this distinct murmur emanating from the house.

He had an unpleasant thought. He would walk out if she had organized a bash today. The meditation he planned to do brought an inner calmness and reconciliation and he decided not to trouble himself with the voices. They had, in any case, subsided by then.

'Pratyahara' was a yogic tool that enabled Samir to experience his inner self and attain a state of bliss. It insulated him from raging storms of the material world and he felt like a tortoise drawing its legs in. His tryst with spiritualism had begun a few years back, under the avuncular guidance of his guru, Swami P, a ninety-four-year-old globetrotter who ate once a day and slept for three hours on indulgent nights. The claim sounded dubious until Samir witnessed it first-hand on a trip to Trinidad, a trip that had transformed him from a dilettante into a committed practitioner.

He had once upon a time desired an escape into nothingness, inspired by a verse composed by the fourteenth-century Kashmiri mystic Lalleshwari, popularly known as Lal Ded.

Knowledge dissolved into consciousness
When consciousness dissolved nothing remained
Nothingness dissolved into nothingness...

His friends had persuaded him with psychedelics. He remembered his vision oscillating between a frog in a pond and a celestial star. He had regained his normal state of mind after a couple of hours, and the perilous journey into an apocalyptic, sepia-tinged world had been a nightmare. It held him back from further experimentation with drugs. Withdrawal symptoms were mild. Nonetheless, he was advised to smoke pot sometimes as a compensatory activity, which was a habit he managed to rid himself of only after a year.

Spirituality was a tool to assert his identity. Despite his sincere efforts to assimilate into the diaspora, in a liminal state of existence, he had failed. He possessed a keen understanding of Western culture and its idiosyncrasies, acquired from a missionary school background, but he soon realized that the much-touted salad bowl was, in reality, a cauldron. He had not spared any effort—the challenge lay in his reluctance to sacrifice his identity in a genetic sense. Like a mobile phone with a pair of SIM slots, he desired that his facets—Indian and American—would operate independently from each other and on an equal footing. But he grew disillusioned after a while. He was regularly stereotyped as a pagan goat-eater from a nation where snake-charmers and dancing bears can be spotted across cosmopolitan cities, where gods are worshipped at street corners, and love marriages are looked down upon.

The contempt he faced often mutated into multiple forms of covert biases, allotropes of brazen violence, but they were no less toxic to his identity.

To Neelu, his growing symbolic protests against assimilation were shambolic. He refused to register as 'Sam Chat' at the local Starbucks outlet, proclaimed the ethical superiority of vegetarianism out of context, and stressed perspectives of his heritage at get-togethers and official parties. Once, on a homeward journey, she declared that such behaviour demeaned him. Despite having sparse knowledge of psychology, she pronounced it to be an obsession, mania and cognitive dissonance rolled into one, and, although he had not believed a word of her, the statement stimulated introspection upon reaching home about whether the roots for his discontent lay elsewhere—perhaps back in India, planted in the turbulent months before leaving the shores of his native country?

Although he had quit alcohol a year ago, he sauntered towards the wet bar in the lounge, arguing with himself that a bit of indulgence on the sixtieth birthday was par for the course. Most of the bottles were bereft of liquid; they had been consumed by friends and, occasionally, by his son, Apu. Stocks had not been replenished since his conversion as a teetotaller. Still, the silver peg-measure, the burgundy and bordeaux glasses, exquisitely crafted beer mugs and the minuscule liquor containers evoked memories of a bygone era when he could claim to be a connoisseur of exclusive tastes, hosting celebrities like a celebrated Indian classical maestro. Excited to locate an uncorked Balvenie Doublewood, gifted by a colleague a few years back, leering at him from an obscure corner, he pulled it out and poured the liquid neat before settling on the couchette, which had the right ergonomics for his favourite Savasana. The sneaking feeling of guilt was suppressed with some effort.

He gazed for some time at the collages, expensive oil paintings and the framed photographs on the mantelpiece of a handsome young man with bushy hair and a twinkle in the eyes next to a stunning beauty with an enticing dimple on her cheeks. He closed his eyes and inhaled a bout of fresh air, held it for six seconds, then exhaled gently. After repeating the act several times, he could feel a throb—activating his dormant memory cells like jagged flashes of lightning. Random thoughts hurtled across the misty zone of nirvanic release, gliding into a typical April evening ten thousand miles away, oblivious to the unconsumed whisky in the glass, to the rooftop of their once-modest dwelling, to the kalbaisakhis that raged during the summer months of April and May with an unfailing regularity on alternate evenings. As a youngster, he had loved spending hours on their terrace in the maelstrom of the tempest, fascinated by the trees bearing red and yellow krishnachura flowers as they bent sideways to hold on to each other, like beaus locked in a promiscuous embrace. The mellow storms would be accompanied by intermittent streaks of lightning, rumbling thunder, the sweet harmony of pattering raindrops and cacophonic howls from stray canines, which cascaded with the subsiding storm. A trail of broken branches and a few uprooted trees and electric poles would be left behind as detritus on rare occasions. The gentle storms resembled the docile folks from his hometown, as opposed to the hurricanes and tornadoes experienced later in Florida and Cincinnati.

'You scared me! When did you arrive, Apu?' A full-throated welcome from Samir's son Apratim, lovingly called Apu, interrupted his stupor that had barely begun. The boy's casual T-shirt and boxers indicated that he had arrived a while back. The elder one of the two siblings, Apu settled for the insipid life of a techie at Apple—despite being desirous after grad school for a literary career (peppered with poetic enjambments, travelogues and whodunits). Taller and fairer than his dad, he was well-built and only their cherubic faces bore a resemblance to each other. Pockmarks on his rectangular face and a bony torso failed to disguise his sociable personality. He was a thoroughbred epicurean, and rarely missed out on the good things in life, like spending happy Friday evenings at the pub next to the office. His sagging muscles conveyed he had been avoiding the gyms for a while, focusing more on pubs and restaurants. The name Apu was also ensconced in the Bengali psyche because of a famous movie directed by their iconic director, Ray, wherein Apu was the name of the protagonist.

Samir gave him a long hug, a kiss on the forehead and gently fondled his wavy locks, but was interrupted by a thinly veiled frown.

'Baba, please don't mess up my hair.'

Samir responded with a casual wink. 'Just making sure you

do not turn into your dad by forty.'

'That will not happen. I am confident. I take good care of them. Anyhow, I arrived by the early morning flight to surprise you and have booked a special restaurant tonight. Don't say no. Here's wishing you many more happy returns.'

'Thanks, Apu. Your mom and I planned to visit Charn though.'

'Come on! Enough of Thai food, let us have classy stuff tonight, it's your sixtieth.'

His son was interrupted by Samir's clenched palms, a salute he had picked up as an activist in college. It now indicated concurrence.

'Hope you guys are not planning a boisterous party,' Samir said. 'One joker spotted other than the four of us and I walk out. Do me a favour. Send a message to Ruplu and request her to join.'

'She's in her room upstairs! Another surprise!'

'What? She's already there?'

Samir's calm demeanour vanished instantly.

Apu's mischievous eyes and a shrug of his shoulders led to more discomfiture. Nevertheless, he waited for a while. 'Cool it, dad, it is so damn easy to pull your legs. There is no party planned today. We respected your wishes but can we not pull off a surprise? Ruplu has bunked school and is resting in her room. Ma will drop in at the patisserie for a cake on her way back.'

A sigh of relief followed. 'That explains the chatter.'

'Shall I call her?'

'Let her rest, she looks so overwhelmed these days.'

His daughter was pursuing a PhD in Political Science at UCLA (University of California, Los Angeles), and she often dropped in on weekends with a truckload of dirty clothes, returning to the school on Monday morning. She took with her untainted dresses and sufficient rice to last the week, along with a few bowls of her favourite tarka-dal packed in ziploc bags.

'Why did you guys not respond to the buzz of the landline?' Samir asked.

'Did it ring? Lot of gossip to consume after a gap of two months, Baba. The ring tone is also unfamiliar, the damn thing wakes up once in a blue moon. Look at you! It seems like you are in a mood to doze off. Please rest, it will take a couple of hours for Ma to return.'

Samir smiled indulgently. He was relieved that he had at last solved the mystery of those spooky voices emanating from the room inside.

'I will respond to a few urgent emails. The next release is just twenty days down the line.' Apu sounded serious.

Familiar with his son's penchant for pomposity on official matters, he was not too impressed when Apu self-importantly glanced at his watch.

Failing to regain his concentration, Samir gently dozed off to sleep.

◆

From an Undisclosed Location

December 2019

Woken from a trance by the incessant buzz of mosquitos, Samir glanced at his watch. It was around 1 p.m., but the guys had not bothered to serve him lunch. He was not hungry, but was apprehensive about a bout of acidity, a medical condition that was a constant companion since adulthood. Long gaps between meals led to excruciating pains in the stomach, and the thought itself was scary because he was sure that the guys would not maintain stocks of antacids.

He banged loudly on the door.

'Need to go to the bathroom?' the man asked.

'Yes, but more importantly, lunch. I suffer from acidity if there are long gaps between meals.'

'Food is cooked at another location and will take another hour or two to arrive. You are a greedy pig. We served you a heavy breakfast.'

'I never said I was hungry. I said I needed to eat for medical reasons. Anything will do.'

'Do you wish to be slapped once again, son of a bitch? Do not disturb us unless you need to attend to nature's call. Come along.'

It did not take long to resume his trip into the secret alleys of his mind—some of which he did not even know existed. It was replete with countless anecdotes. The pathway that occupied his mind now emanated from his wedding, meandered through four years of unstable equilibrium, the nadir of his married life. But why was the mind insisting that he transport to a period in his life thirty-five years ago? Travel down its winding alleys when those traumatic days were now well behind him? Enigmatic were its ways indeed.

DOWN MEMORY LANE

December 1981–May 1985

The concept of arranged marriages had intrigued Samir from his childhood. His parents and uncles narrated stories of their first encounters with spouses. It went thus: respective families converged at the bride's place, indulged in small talk, and by the end of the afternoon or evening, agreed to tie the knot if the chemistry worked out in the eyes of the seniors in the family. It was only of late that it was necessary for the boy and girl to concur as well. The concept of two individuals sealing their fates based on a brief encounter seemed primitive to him, and he had not imagined in his wildest dreams that he too would pass through a similar experience.

Breaking convention, Neelu's family had trooped into their home.

A tinge of disappointment had flowed in his veins when he noticed a gulf of difference between the lady in flesh and blood and the photographs they had sent earlier. He spent the first fifteen minutes solemnly conversing with her parents, abruptly turning towards her after some time, attempting to draw her into the conversation.

Her parents burst out in peals of laughter when he did so.

The girl he had turned his attention to was the sister of the svelte and sophisticated girl who last entered the room. Neelu was wearing a light purple saree. After brief introductions and a few minutes of inane discussions about the weather in Cincinnati, he protested when his aunt requested that Neelu render a favourite number or recite a poem. A little later, a brief one-on-one conversation followed in an adjoining room. When quizzed on his favourite author, the reply, 'Albert Einstein', had stumped her. Although he was disappointed by her dismal sense of humour, he had let it pass, floored by her stunning beauty by then. He was baffled by her quip to his goody-goody statement that he drank only on social occasions, 'So, no minor vices?' But the edge was tougher to camouflage when her dad barged in unobtrusively to poke fun at him: 'Lots of girlfriends then?'

Their future was sealed by the time they completed dinner; destined to be entwined like creepers for the rest of their life. There were still three weeks before he left for the States, and Neelu's father expressed desire for dinner at their place to introduce Samir to their relatives. Theirs was a joint family; they lived under the same roof and shared a kitchen.

Samir had felt on top of the world, but was unable to fathom why. It was not love-at-first-sight, nor could he sense any irresistible force of attraction. She was more of a trophy, a showpiece, with an optimal mix of intelligence, beauty, affable behaviours and family background—not to undermine the middle-class penchant for her fair Aryan skin.

Tension commenced after a week—a week spent gallivanting with friends. He was rudely disturbed at the stroke of dawn by bright rays of sunlight that streaked through the windows and the incessant chirping of swallows, and he suddenly realized that the week had passed by without hearing from Neelu's family. The wall clock, which his father had received as a retirement gift, had the irksome habit of chiming every fifteen minutes. He had hung it in his son's room for some unknown reason, and Samir did not have the heart to ask him to take it away.

The topic was broached at the breakfast table.

'I have a distinct feeling that they have backed out. It occurred to me that she was not the type to leave her parents for a distant land,' his father began. 'Never mind, two gentlemen are chasing me with their daughters. The girls are equally good-looking and the families are cultured. Let me contact them today.'

'But don't you think you should call Neelanjana's family once?'

His dad was egotistic on such matters. 'Why should I? It is her father who said he would get in touch after three or four days—did he not say so?'

Even after many years, Samir couldn't fathom what had led him a few hours later to stroll towards her college, not far from his home, bang opposite a massive park he had spent his young days playing soccer and cricket. It was a vast expanse of green, wilted with time and lack of care. The park where he and his friend, Adesh, used to play once upon a time, where Adesh taught him a few mysteries of life, the same park where Adesh was shot dead.

He remembered Neelu mentioning that their classes ended at 2 p.m., and she usually proceeded home immediately afterward. It was not a co-educational college, and boys were not allowed inside without a valid reason. He actually had no wish to demean himself to that extent, so he parked himself on the sidewalk opposite the college at 1.30 p.m. and consumed a few cigarettes, staring back at amused passers-by to counter their indiscreet glances.

The exodus of students happened around ten minutes past two. Some were in twos, some in larger groups, absorbed in animated conversation, soaking in the joys of youth, excited at trivial, inconsequential matters. Then there were the habitual loners. He was sure that she would be trudging all by herself, an assessment based on the few hours they had spent together. Peering intently with a pair of strained eyes, he was soon exasperated by the constant stream of cars that obstructed his vision and her delay. Perhaps she was unwell, or he had not noticed her? Was she planning to devote a few hours at the library?

He could have missed her since she looked so different without make-up. She appeared wearing a pink salwar-kameez. Hurriedly crossing the road, he noticed her stopping short of a light blue Ambassador car to hand her notebooks to an unctuous driver. Samir was swift, briskly walking past her while she lazily climbed into the car. There was no way she could have spotted him.

Abruptly turning around, he gently waved.

'*Aarey, tumi? Ki khobor?*'

'Passing by after a round of adda with old pals. Noticed you suddenly.'

'We were discussing you just this morning. *Aar bolona*, a goof-up by parents. Rather, a communication gap. Baba had to fly out on official work at a short notice and he thought he had asked Ma to contact your mother, but she maintains he did not. He returned this morning and must have contacted your dad by now. Are you guys free tomorrow?'

Samir was not willing to concur so easily. 'I am a free lark, on a holiday, but unaware of their engagements.'

'You still have a couple of weeks before you go. An alternative date can be worked out if they are not available.'

She claimed later that the relief on his face was perceptible.

They met the following evening, surrounded by her curious relatives who landed up by the dozen to steal a look at Neelu's fiancé—as if he were a curio at the museum. The conversation bordered on the puerile. He was relieved when the date was finalized and the forgettable evening sputtered to a close.

A few days later, the betrothal was completed with a bit of ceremony before he left for the States. He convinced her to watch a Hollywood flick with him surreptitiously, challenging the taboo on secluded interactions for couples in arranged marriages. There was a valid reason for such a rule—it was not rare for potential grooms to back out after a few months of intense companionship on the grounds of incompatibility. Neelu and Samir also had a quick lunch where discussions were focused on the best tandoori chicken in town and a comparative evaluation of the acting prowess of the Bollywood superstars, Amitabh Bachchan and Rajesh Khanna.

Many years later, she had let the cat out of the bag at a weak moment. She had been in two minds about him till that morning, and had consented to the marriage after persuasion by her mother. The reasons: she had not gelled with him that night; she hated the manner he dressed and was not too impressed with his conversational skills. He did not care to ask her whether the story about the goof-up by her parents was concocted that very instant or earlier—he did not give a damn by then.

Like other Indian weddings, theirs, too, was a visual treat. Vedic rituals were followed, and the celebration was steeped in years of tradition. They wedded amidst a riot of colours, decorations, frolic and mirth. Formal celebrations commenced with a bridal shower on the wedding-eve to commemorate the bride's last supper as a young maid. It was not customary for the groom to attend the event, but in an impulsive moment, he decided to be there with his friends, much to the consternation of her conservative grandfather and a couple of aunts. Her maternal aunt was sarcastic. 'Could not wait for a day to see her? He seems to be in deep love with Neelu.'

It was smartly dealt with by her mother. 'Good for her!'

Her aunt refused to give in and referred to Samir as a diehard American.

They then proceeded to an old friend's place, whom he had not seen for eleven years, since college. A power cut provided the perfect opportunity to strike a conversation. They were in the middle of an endemic malaise in a city besotted with systemic issues that had caused corporate houses to move shops to greener pastures and factories to close down, all of which made the infrastructure crumble like ninepins. The city had turned into a gasping belt on the banks of the Hooghly, resembling the 'rust belt' of USA. The only person in the room with an experience of the world outside, Samir, took off on a condescending note, criticizing the parliamentary left that was in power after their thumping victory in 1977. He blamed their lack of vision. Erstwhile friends from the ultra-left—some having emerged after completing their terms in penal confinement, unconditionally released by the elected government and inclined a shade towards them—were rankled by his pompous tone and decided to rake up his betrayal of the movement at a crucial juncture. A heated debate ensued, reminding him of the heady days he thought he had left behind. Samir was tense because he expected several piercing questions about his disappearance from the country, but thankfully, the topic never came up.

Six large pegs were downed in quick succession. It was disastrous for an individual habituated to a couple of sundowners back in USA. Perplexed by the rather unusual phenomenon of a groom passing out at a friend's home the night before his wedding, they tried to get in touch with his parents and succeeded only after repeated attempts. He apologized the following day for being the cause of a sleepless night, but his father, Satyen, with a straight face, reminded him of his last few days as a student in Kolkata.

After consuming a liberal dose of antitoxins, he reached home before dawn, just in time for the ritual dodhi mangal—an edible mash of sweet curd, rice flakes, banana and sweets. As the almanac, house astrologer and priest dictated, the wedding was scheduled late for the evening, permitting him to take a power nap in the afternoon.

As they proceeded to the venue in a convoy of cars, the

one he was travelling bedecked with white flowers, he felt like a prince. Neelu appeared, looking stunningly gorgeous, adorned with golden jewellery, an expensive red Banarasi saree and copious dollops of cosmetics (unavailable in the insular India of the eighties). The soft, melodious music of the shehnai, a classical Indian flute and sweet ululations was soothing to the ears. Still, the noises emanating from conch shells blown by her aunts and grandmothers irritated him. These were blown on religious occasions and ceremonies to propitiate goddesses, but his religious sensibilities failed to rise to the occasion.

While her relatives carried her around through the mandatory seven-rounds, punctuated by boisterous outbursts and hilarious comments from the assembled crowd, a queer thought kept pestering him. Had he taken the right decision? There was no immediate reason for it to bother him, but the question stuck to him like a leech. It stayed till Neelu regaled the audience at the nocturnal 'Bashar ghor' with a mellifluous mélange of musical numbers, ranging from Rabindra Sangeet to Western country songs. At least the lady was culturally inclined, he had thought to himself.

A couple of days later, the massive gathering at the lavish reception party emerged as the talk of the town. Samir offered to bear the lion's share of expenses, despite a contrarian convention. His father's objections were overturned by the intrinsic strength of the dollar. People he had never met, all relatives, flocked like pilgrims; they were introduced to the bride and groom simultaneously.

Satyen had visited all of them in person. The metaphoric expression '*Golayey gamchha diye nemontonoo*' translates to 'to invite humbly with a towel around your neck', and was a tradition followed by and large in Bengali families those days. A very Bengali way of inviting friends and relatives.

When it came to arranged marriages, the initial years required intrepid charting of unknown territories for the deracinated wife. Ritualistically, girls bid their parents and family adieu to join their in-law's families the day after the ceremonies. The tears continued as the wife struggled to establish a communion, not just with his family but with the partner himself. In arranged marriages, this situation was unavoidable.

It was cruel for Neelu after the marriage, habituated to bonhomie in her joint family consisting of parents, grandparents, uncles and cousins, with the freedom to retreat to her private space whenever the need arose. She had appeared for her undergraduate exams a month before the wedding and was sailing through a period famed for its ennui, the university taking six months to publish results. The ordeal was compounded as she was compelled to spend the intervening time with her in-laws, waiting for the coveted visa, a concertina wire barricade separating the applicant from his spouse.

Her in-laws were not garrulous by nature, and the relatives and family friends who dropped by were not her type. Intrusive neighbours freaked out on prurient curiosities that, in her opinion, revealed their social class. The food habits of the two families were like chalk and cheese, and she missed the eclectic continental and Chinese dishes her mother had learned to make at cookery classes. It was tough to swallow the bony varieties of fresh-water fishes Samir's family swore by. The red-oxide floors and the walls painted in aqueous pastels were in stark contrast to the luxurious finishes of acrylic paints at their house. Mosquitoes, flies and cockroaches were ubiquitous; Indian-style toilets were tough to endure.

On his first visit back from the States, Samir had not understood Neelu's passionate outpourings. The passion on the night before his departure was, in reality, an encoded message to rescue her from this hell-hole as soon as possible.

The interviews at the consulate office were humiliating. Neelu was reminded of a distant cousin's word of caution that life as an immigrant bore its share of insults, requiring a thick skin. The interviewers talked down to her as if she had entered their country latched onto the tutelage of an aircraft. As if she were not an individual married to a green-card holder, demanding her legitimate rights. His tech-industry background, however, helped. It only took a year, faster than most applicants.

At the international airport of Cincinnati, the stern expression on the officer's face sitting inside a cage-like structure was disconcerting, but she ignored his nasty frown while he stamped on her passport, winking at him coquettishly with a rare display of chutzpah.

Neelu was delighted on spotting Samir waving from behind a glass partition. It was June 1983. The peak of summer. Her arrival could not have come at a more appropriate juncture. He had been recently promoted as the Project Manager. And now Neelu had joined him within a few months.

Floating on cloud nine, the initial few months in the US were a joie de vivre. Evenings were reserved for shopping, fine dining or forays to the club next door. She attained finesse in table tennis, billiards and the piano, viewed the latest Hollywood flicks and Broadway plays and met up with Indian friends on Saturday nights to compare notes on their stints. Sundays were for fancy drives. His distant relatives at Cincinnati—the warm mashima and meshomoshoy—were a constant source of joy. The newly-weds were driven to cities like Nashville, Columbus and Tennessee and entertained at tony restaurants; they too wished to reciprocate such largesse but were constrained by their meager means. Not that it mattered to the other side.

They looked forward to the homecoming of the older couple's

daughter from Boston. Supriya, closer in age to them and married to an American guy, Samir and Neelu bonded like the sides of an equilateral triangle. The topic of Samir's crush on Supriya as a bachelor was discreetly avoided, although the vestiges of such feelings had been safely buried under the sands of time.

Neelu's life turned brighter by a thousand lumens. Attaining proficiency in cooking, she experimented with novel delicacies, purchased the choicest clothes from shopping complexes around the corner, kept the house spick and span, and ensured that Samir's needs were catered to. He had no reason to crib, but the longing for a free and capricious life, one he had left behind, sharpened by the day. In his previous avatar, holidays were reserved for bridge sessions in the afternoons and teeing off in the morning. He was now compelled to settle for a lazy round of table tennis or billiards. He was coaxed to switch from the news channels he loved to devour HBN for some god-forsaken movie. Her topics of interest were quotidian, like Mills and Boon's novels, tough to engage beyond a point since classics and non-fiction were his choices. Her obsession with banal perfection at home was like an 'obsessive-compulsive desire', a disease of the mind.

Coincidentally, pressures mounted at the office when the project he was assigned to lagged months behind schedule, contributing to the irascible behaviour at home. He began to jump into bed after a quick dinner, face the wall and plunge into deep slumber before she could even attempt a conversation. Her repeated attempts to reach out through the intervening layers proved exercises in futility; her sensual touches were neither reciprocated nor acknowledged. The alienation transformed into indignity on the night she was told to desist from 'nyakami' (a colloquial expression for coquettish behaviour).

Her excruciating loneliness refused to mitigate even after the situation eased on his professional front, even after the client agreed to stretch the deadlines. His relief found outlets in seminars, books, rounds of bridge, weekly golf and moonlighting, as he turned to an autonomy left by the wayside the day Neelu had landed in the States.

Back in Kolkata, friends, relatives, and parents would have been there to support her during those moments of angst, but here there was no one. The folks they socialized with were Samir's friends, and she was not inclined to share her sob stories with them. She found solace in nostalgia, fondly remembering her unmarried days when solitary hours were the occasions she looked forward to because she could engage in conversations with her inner voice, engage in literary pursuits and compose poems. Her thoughts were ominous in Cincinnati, dragging her on sweat-inducing, humid journeys through creepy winds of deafening silence.

Then, that fateful spring Sunday morning came. In Kolkata, the transition from winter to spring was seamless despite innumerable odes to Basanta composed by a flurry of poets, ranging from Tagore to budding rhymesters in Samir's neighbourhood—like Shyamal. He was a guy whom Samir and his friends avoided like the plague, paranoiac that he would burden them with another freshly composed poem.

In Cincinnati, on the other hand, the transformation was sudden. Samir was soaking in the bright morning sunshine, resplendent with pinkish-red hues of Japanese maple leaves visible from his patio. It reminded him of the stint at Toronto and Algonquin Park with its red and yellow leaves opulently hanging from aspens and red oaks.

The sullen mood inside the apartment was incongruous with the bright spring morning outside. Neelu, atypically, refused to probe deeper when he announced his golf tournament in the afternoon. Pretending disinterest, she descended to mundanities—

the plumber was due at four and needed a gentle push, the cupboard door had to be yanked as it was hard to open and the liquid soap in the guest washroom required a refill.

Unable to fathom a reason for her behaviour, he escaped to the patio. The corner plants usually reminded him of a teenage couple in the joys of adolescent love, but today they appeared like cadavers laid to rest in a cemetery. The one that towered majestically above the cedar railings was on the verge of extinction. Instead of clinging amorously to its beau, the pruned plant leaned on the other side, weeping profusely—not that she was herself in pink of health. Rushing indoors, he could not locate Neelu in the bedroom nor obtain a response to the gentle knock on the washroom door. Strange, did she step out? It was as if she had transformed and disappeared into thin air. It did not strike him that she was refusing to respond to him, and he decided to focus on the newspaper.

She appeared after a while with dark patches around her eyes.

Pretending not to notice them, he shot off sternly, 'So you were inside, yet refused to respond?'

She walked past him as if he did not exist.

At a loss for words, he focused on news items from various corners of the world while she persisted with her household drudgery, not in a mood for banter. His patronizing remark, 'Dress up by 7 p.m., we shall go out for dinner,' failed to have its desired impact.

It was not that Samir was proficient at golf, but his performance that day was particularly dismal. He was in no mood to honour his commitment, smug at the thought that the condescending act of picking up a few of her favourite dishes from the local Bangladeshi restaurant would mollify her. While entering the compound, the weird sight of a frail silhouette against the fading twilight was not surprising. She was an animist after all. The tree she was peering at was paler than their neighbour's, covered in new outbursts of red, gold and orange.

When the reason for her mood finally dawned on him, he was confident that a bit of promiscuity and the ziploc bags with her favourite delicacies would melt the glacier. Yanking her towards himself, he made an attempt at dry humour. 'I'm appalled by your choice of a lover, the ugliest one of the lot.' It fell flat. He kissed her at a sensitive spot and gently lifted her by the waist, but she broke into fragile but loud sobs. The tears sparked memories of kaal baisakhis back home, storms accompanied by heavy downpours. A rare occurrence in their tranquil conjugal life, despite the subterranean currents that eluded him.

A week later, Samir dropped her off at the airport. She felt that she needed a break to escape a nervous breakdown and a possible suicide attempt, the logical outcomes of snowballing depression. Repeated persuasion failed to dissuade her from leaving, although she did appear a tad cheerful on the morning of her departure. By evening, her poker face had resurfaced, and as the faint figure disappeared into the security enclosure, he realized that she did not care to wave back.

He rushed to the men's room. By god's grace, not a soul was there at the late hour.

The initial days of separation were painful. Nothing seemed to taste right. No conversation seemed to interest Samir. Television programs, like the evening news and the quiz-time he was addicted to, sounded insipid. He could not concentrate on his work. She called him after a week, conversing nonchalantly as if the departure had been an ordinary event. He found her behaviour strange but he still called her twice a week, appalled by her non-committal reply when he queried about when she planned to return.

The frequency of calls made dropped in direct proportion

to his growing stoicism. Samir did not enjoy his situation, but gradually learned to take it in his stride. He made lame responses to his friends about her absence, and they were polite enough to not probe. It was evident to him that they could perceive the messy situation he was in.

Mashima was circumspect. Her long stint in the States had taught her to draw lines around private spaces, but he was apprehensive that Supriya, a close friend, would not care for niceties. Fortunately, she did not visit the city during those months.

One fine morning, pondering after his first cup of coffee, he arrived at a weird diagnosis. He realized he was polyamorous by nature, which lay at the root of all problems. It appeared clairvoyant when a friend's wife buzzed an hour later as he was about to leave for office.

'Hi, Samir! How's life?'

His response was daft. 'Couldn't be better. Why?'

'Gosh, you just told me that you are enjoying your alone time? I'm surprised. Tapan had to rush to Kolkata yesterday since his father is scheduled to undergo a cardio operation. He suggested that I visit your place to help tidy your house. He believes it to be a complete mess. Was planning to drop in for an hour in the evening tomorrow.'

The response was instantaneous. 'Not that it is in a mess, but you are always welcome. Stay back for the night. Why plan to return home so late? I'm sure you will love my cooking.'

Samir did not notice the sudden alteration in her voice, nor the shock, the bewilderment before she hung up. He woke up on a cheerful note the following day, humming a favourite tune. The cheer was short-lived because she called to say that she would not be able to make it.

'Cool, how about tomorrow?'

'Not possible. Something cropped up and I will remain busy till Tapan returns after the operation.'

It did not strike Samir that there was anything else to it. Not that he may have been leading up to cheating not just on his wife but also betraying a dear friend.

A few weeks later, at a get-together, she remarked. 'Samir, the gesture of tidying your house was at Tapan's insistence. I thought I told you so. There was nothing more to it. Did you honestly believe I was dying for a night out with you? And is Tapan not a friend of yours?'

His face grew ashen in the presence of an assortment of friends and their spouses, each looking askance at the other. He had not been just presumptuous but rash and stupid, unable to conjure up a decent riposte for the simple reason that he had not realized that she had backed out because of his misdemeanor.

A few days later, Samir was woken by a call from his father early in the morning.

'Congratulations, Khokhon!'

The line was crackling, and he was too dazed to comprehend what the man was driving at, relieved at the same time that there was nothing serious at the other end. A deep voice boomed through the wires, 'Come on Khokhon, what is there to be so coy about your impending fatherhood?'

'What? This is news to me, Baba!'

After a few seconds of stunned silence, his father responded. 'What the hell is going on? Her mother rung up Sulekha last night with the news that the report from the diagnostic centre came a couple of days back, and you are still not aware?'

Yes...yes...but I was busy with official work, Baba.'

'But she was the one who had to inform you, and she is relaxing at home. It does explain a lot of my misgivings. I smelt a rat the day she landed here. She visited us a few times and has been polite, but the reason offered for the sudden arrival and the reluctance to stay back at our place for the night struck me as strange. We were relieved last night on hearing the good news. And now this!'

'Nothing is seriously wrong between us, Baba.'

'I have no desire to intrude upon your personal life, but my advice would be to tackle the issue head-on instead of sitting on it in your characteristic manner. Smell the coffee before it is late.'

Excusing himself, Samir then dialed Neelu's number, beginning the conversation with an accusation.

She responded calmly.

'Samir, I planned to ring you today. The reports were collected the morning I left the States. Three months now. Managed to suppress it from my folks due to lack of visible symptoms, although I suspect that my grandmother sensed it.'

'But why would you not wish to disclose it?'

'I did not want to say anything till the trajectory of my life became clearer to me. It still lacks clarity, but a friend convinced me not to abort the baby because it amounts to a surrender to patriarchy.'

'My, my, my... I never realized you are now a card-holding feminist. I am dying to meet your friend. Quite a personality if she could influence a conservative woman like you. My only request is that the news I am entitled to hear directly from you should not reach me through a third person.'

Their situation, indubitably, had reached a point of no return.

◆

It was a Saturday afternoon, a few days after the call. Samir was sulking, looking forward to the evening at his friend's place to mitigate the persisting stress. He had skipped both breakfast and lunch, and slept through the day. He was perched on the sofa around 4 p.m., helping himself to a cup of coffee and a can of pretzels, when his eyes strayed to a thick layer of grime on the side table. Habituated to dusting the furniture every Sunday morning, he had not felt the need to do so after Neelu had left. With some time on his hands, he rushed for the duster.

On the mantelpiece, beneath the portly Buddha, he noticed a pale-yellow envelope. It had been kept there arguably in the hope that he would spot it. Inside were a few sheets of fancy yellow paper and an epistle composed in flawless handwriting. He had always felt that she lacked flair in her mother tongue but was surprised at the subtlety of this letter. It was evocative, sprinkled with short poems—a few of them self-composed, the others quotes from renowned bards, like Tagore and Jibanananda Das. There was unmistakable romance, sprinkled with pangs of unrequited love and optimism. Although insensitive by nature, he felt moved, heard the strains of a sitar strumming unfamiliar notes. It caused him to pause, detach himself from his surroundings, ponder for a while and dump the duster on the floor. Slumping on the sofa, he hurriedly consumed half a dozen cigarettes, extinguishing each one on the floor. The decision to call Neelu was impulsive, although he was not sure whether the desire was a result of his suppressed emotions, the news of an addition to their family, the pangs of loneliness experienced lately, or the letter's tone.

It was early in Kolkata, and her dad was offensively rude, agreeing to wake her up after a couple of desperate pleads.

Her voice was understandably drowsy. 'All okay, Samir? It's 4 a.m. out here.'

'I know, but I just discovered the note you left me. Believe me, I dusted the furniture today for the first time after you left. Neelu, I genuinely miss you...and I now realize my mistakes. I have an earnest request to make. Please agree to another shot at making the damn marriage work.'

Bouts of silence, punctuated by soft sobs and incoherent utterings. The call remained inconclusive, culminating in Neelu making a request for a few more days to mull it over.

He absently chucked the duster into the kitchen bin and rushed for a hot-water bath. There were a couple of hours before the party, and he settled for a cup of coffee and chicken sandwiches at the café, forgetting to lock the main door.

Only after a few days did she express her concurrence—on the condition that she be allowed to stay back at Kolkata till the third or fourth month after the baby was born. That was a clear nine months, but he reluctantly agreed, desperate to repair deep gashes.

Desire and agony intensified by the day. For Samir, her silhouette appeared in dreams, at work, as he was driving down to work or playing golf. He slept on her side of the cot to inhale the residual body odour left behind with a trace of the fragrance of patchouli. He was on the verge of a breakdown when a six-month deputation to Wisconsin on a project came like a whiff of fresh air.

He had applied for leave many months in advance to be present in Kolkata for the most momentous event of his life.

A BABY IS BORN

May 1985

Reaching home on a Sunday afternoon, he was greeted by his mother. She shared the news that Neelu had already been admitted to a nursing home. Samir was groggy and planned to visit her the following day, but he grudgingly agreed to his father's orders.

At the hospital he saw that her eyes were heavy, and her skin was notably pallid, bursting at the seams, drained of her innate beauty and charm. She did not seem like a normal mother-to-be. A pleasant smile greeted him, and it appeared to be welcoming, but something in the air bothered him, despite the animated conversations that followed. He shot off a few instructions to the man who entered to clean the room and, turning around, noticed her intensely staring at the tube light on the wall, as if decrypting a complex code. She made no attempts to turn her gaze away till the doctor on his rounds arrived abruptly to examine her and pronounce that the delivery was expected within a day.

He left it there. Relieved to be back home, he settled for an early dinner and jumped into bed, to be rudely woken at 4 a.m. It was from the nursing home. Neelu's birthing pains had begun, and the doctor had to be picked up and brought to the site.

It was one of those nights. It was raining cats and dogs, almost as if a deluge had decided to drown the city of Kolkata. Most roads were flooded in knee-deep water when Ashim kaku came to their rescue. His chauffeur luckily resided inside his apartment and his car was a sturdy model that could boast of withstanding waterlogged roads. By the time Samir and the others landed at the nursing home, dawn had broken through and a faint flickering of light peeped from behind layers of dark clouds.

A couple of hours later, Samir, his parents, and in-laws were spotted anxiously strolling outside the labour room. Then the doctor appeared with a disgusted look on his face.

'I am sorry to say this, but she just refuses to push. I will try for another fifteen minutes, and then call for a C-section.'

Her mother took Samir aside after a while.

'Samir, there is something I have wished to tell you for some time but never got the opportunity. We realize that we have pampered Neelu more than we should have. She was unprepared to venture out into the wide world. Bear with her for a while. I am certain she will turn around. We have counseled her. She has a heart of gold.'

Aware that he was primarily to blame, the words sounded vacuous, a desperate attempt to repair a fragile marriage. Nonetheless, he preferred to be discreet, relieved when the nurse barged in to announce that the process was finally over. The baby's cries were audible from a distance, loudly proclaiming its arrival into the world. Smeared in blood with the umbilical cord still in place, he could make out it was a boy.

The decision to name him 'Apratim'—meaning unequaled in Bengali—was instantaneous.

◆

A New Beginning

August 1985–May 1986

He returned to Cincinnati after three weeks, sticking to his promise and leaving both Neelu and Apu at Kolkata for another three months. Apu was still a giggling infant, and despite the usual hassles with a newborn, Neelu showed no signs of post-partum depression, surrendering to Samir on the nights he spent at their place, enjoying the flowering of passions after a year's interlude. However, her occasional stares into the distance continued to haunt him, and he started to believe that she was trying her best to convey a few thoughts that rankled her.

The day before leaving, he decided to be frank.

'Are you serious about joining me, Neelu?'

He was dismissed with a hearty laugh. 'Still in doubt after the birth of this one?'

'You have forgotten what your feminist friend told you?'

'That was an impulsive statement. I later realized that it would not be fair on the child.'

The jury was still out on whether the yellow envelope or Apu's arrival had somewhat repaired their cracked marriage.

Their starry-eyed romance after her return convinced him that the episode had been crafted by the Almighty. Their hearts resonated in unison, brought together like a tuning fork every night.

If he was stirred in the dead of night by an asphyxiating hug, he reciprocated each time with a faint whisper. 'Don't leave me, okay? Not again.' He followed it with a display of crude strength, a roll across the bed to crash land on the stained carpet after a brisk round of power-play. She relished the foreplay, despite the anti-climactic consummation. Advised repeatedly by her parents to focus on adjustment in her conjugal life, she decided not to make an issue out of it, forswearing the desire to experience orgasms, which she had only vicariously witnessed in blue movies with friends a few years back.

Instead, the inevitable wails emanating from Apu's cot when hungry or uneasy after soiling his nappies irritated her, playing spoilsport to their passionate night. Samir, a transformed man, offered to spend sleepless nights when Apu was unwell, disregarding her murmurs of protest that he had to go to work early in the morning. He was moved by her display of consideration, which he believed she had earlier lacked.

The ecstasy lasted for a few months, perhaps a couple of quarters, collapsing like a Shakespearean tragedy soon after, the fatal flaw destined to plunge the hero towards destruction.

Neelu was declared pregnant once again before Apu's first birthday. She looked forward to a fruitful career after enrolling for a post-graduate degree in Economics at a university offering distance learning. However, there was a difference—he was no longer indifferent and aloof, and made an attempt to remain cheerful and genial. She could discern the conscious attempt on his part and decided to ignore the vanishing passions and reconcile with the situation. With classes to take care of, assignments to complete, and two nurturing kids, life was not confined to gossiping with plants and bonsais. And why leave a cushy life behind?

Naively, Samir thought he had managed to successfully camouflage the state of his mind, and his intellectual pretensions led him to conclude that the state was traceable to gory incidents in his life. Yet, he refused to introspect or consult a specialist since their lives moved on, assisted by mothers who landed alternately from India to take care of the kids while Neelu doggedly pursued her own career.

◆

From an Undisclosed Location

December 2019

Samir could not understand why his mind constantly drifted towards such a forgettable episode in his life. He wanted to focus on his sixtieth birthday weekend—six years back. It had been a weekend to cherish.

It was well past 2 p.m. in the room, but there were no signs of his lunch.

Although it was cloudy and the temperature had come down, he was thirsty enough to gulp the remaining water in the bottle, unsure about when the next replenishment would arrive. Once again, he took control of his mind—a technique mastered through years of practice. Back from the distant past to his sixtieth birthday weekend.

A PRECURSOR TO THE WEEKEND

15 May 2014

Waking with a start, he pushed the button of the remote. The recorded session could not sustain his interest beyond a point, and he settled into a short snooze, woken an hour later by an exuberant crowd carrying a slew of expensive presents.

'How are you back so early?'

Neelu's endearing tone was a rarity.

Samir gave a shrug of the shoulders and a demure smile.

He was then smothered by hugs and kisses, to which he made the inane remark, 'Are we done?' That was met with bursts of raucous laughter.

Ruplu, the doting daughter, was the one who replied. 'Yes, for the time being. In the evening, we go for a sumptuous dinner at Laguna, la Brisas, and then it's story-time through the night!' She followed the remark with a tight hug.

Although her complexion was darker and features were not as stunning, Ruplu's mannerisms, curved lips and light brows resembled that of her mother. Her petite figure reminded Samir of Neelu on their wedding night. The figure, for Neelu, was the outcome of rigorous training as a classical dancer, relinquished after joining college. Ruplu was born on Valentine's Day, and at times, she seemed to be an epitome of love, but solipsistic at other times. She was short, with a husky voice and a fascination for the colour pink. She was chatty, focused on her career and liberal in her attitudes. The cargo shorts she wore outdoors on warm days were a constant source of friction between father and daughter.

He remarked. 'I am not a raconteur, kiddo.'

Ruplu responded with a reminder that she was only referring to the deal struck a month back according to which he had agreed to narrate a few episodes from his tumultuous days at the Presidency College. 'If you wish to avoid another grand party...' Ruplu could be very persuasive.

He acquiesced with a gentle nod, grateful that there would be no mob to disturb the equanimity.

Samir gave a lukewarm response to Ruplu's comment. 'Wow, looks like Yogi Baba is already on his whisky! A perfect setting for an exciting plot.'

It triggered an abrupt response. Ruplu was not happy to see dad's less than enthusiastic demeanour.

'Were you looking forward to a solitary evening to coax your thoughts? We could junk our plans then.' Her comment was accompanied with a naughty smile.

Despite feigning to be a doting husband to cover the absence of passion, his fondness for his children was unalloyed. They were the glue that held the family together. 'I surrender, guys. Work has been stressful of late. Nothing that a homely evening can't beat. I'm famished, so let us rush to wherever Apu plans to take us, and then we can marinate on my past while sitting on the lawn.'

'Touché.' The exclamation came from Apu, the perpetually cheerful person, as he gingerly pulled his father up. With a propensity for zany details and a typically Brit fondness for weather forecasts, he thought it fit to update them that rains and storms were forecasted through the night, prompting a sarcastic remark from Ruplu and disinterested chuckles from others.

As they walked down the luminescent pathway, a dash of fragrant oceanic winds smoothened Samir's fraught nerves. It had been a terrible day and a mess of unpleasant encounters with his past had made it worse.

Everyone was dressed to the nines, and in an alluring gossamer red gown, Neelu radiated sensuality. It had been an eternity since he had seen her like that. He was fidgety through the evening, sitting next to her on the table that overlooked the Pacific, but he desisted from a public display of affection. He remembered her strong views on the subject. Neelu had even refused to kiss him beneath the Bridge of Sighs during a visit to Venice, content at being the odd couple standing out amidst a gaggle of affectionate tourists.

Ruplu appeared elegant in a grey tuxedo with mascara-tipped eyes, and the dapper Apu charmed his way through in a dark lounge suit somewhat unsuitable for summer.

The delectable food failed to warm Ruplu. The promised stories held more charm than the extensive spread of burritos, salsa and tacos. The food did not satisfy her sophisticated palate either. Apu pretended not to notice her frequent glances at the watch. He loved the ambiance of the place, the restaurant had been his choice, and to top it all, he was paying! Despite Ruplu's efforts to hurry them, it took them a couple of hours to complete dinner, cut the cake, blow the candles, smudge icing on their faces and moronically smile to a melodious rendition of 'Happy Birthday' by the waiters.

In a spirit of resistance, Ruplu demanded to occupy the driver's seat and broke quite a few traffic rules on the drive back. Having arrived home sooner than they would have if Samir had driven them, the family settled on their sturdy but slightly worn garden chairs.

'Goodness, Ruplu, you are one crazy driver!' Apu noted and Neelu nodded in agreement.

Samir intervened when he spied his daughter gearing for combat from a corner of his eyes.

'Okay, okay. Can I begin?'

The clouds bowed to their wishes. Faint stars peeked through a sparsely overcast sky. It was Neelu's turn to shoot a question. 'Do you recollect the pejorative poem about Kolkata you were fond of reciting ad nauseam long back?'

Samir managed to recall only the last couple of lines.

'And, above the packed and pestilential town,
Death looked down.'

Apu was quick on the uptake. 'That was Kipling. Wow, your British accent was terrific. Englishmen fascinate me as a race.'

'I have always wished to ask you—how come when you have not even visited that country?'

'Guess from an overdose of literature,' Apu replied.

'A techie with a passion for literature!'

Ruplu, not entirely comfortable with the direction the conversation was meandering into, interjected. 'Can we now jump straight into the story?'

Ruplu was an enigma. Although she had gotten over the few jarring experiences of her childhood, he continued to keep her under constant vigil. The contradictions in her personality were glaring and inscrutable. After joining college, in the year 2004, her commitment to activism, debates and discussions manifested in multiple forums. Still, literature had never been her forte, and he found it strange because empathy for the downtrodden and verses complemented one another back home.

Her strain of radicalism differed from the kind he had witnessed in his youth—a manifestation of pent-up revulsion against dismal social, environmental and economic conditions faced by the deprived. Racism, misogyny, discrimination against the LGBT community and immigrants grabbed her generation's attention, but they rarely went beyond it.

She could boast of few good friends, predominantly of the same gender. She failed to make it to Harvard to pursue a career in Political Science because she had been rated low on personality traits, despite scoring high in the written examinations. In her opinion, it was an instance of blatant racism, and Samir was convinced of it as well. He had read a news item in the print media on this. A significant factor in her inclination towards the liberal faction of Democrats was the angst that expressed itself in activist forums from the first year.

He could never come to terms with her refusal to take a firm stand against economic inequalities, despite his current posturing, skewing to the right end of the ideological spectrum. Rather unkindly, he interpreted her feminism as stemming from insecurity as a woman in the USA, and her anti-racism as a Pavlovian response to perceived biases against the brown-skinned. It pained Samir when she glorified her mongrelized cultural identity as a manifestation of cross-cultural fertilization in the multicultural space of the United States, unwilling to consider it a product of hegemonic cultural dominance. She postured against social discrimination but not cultural dominion and was proud of her uniqueness, untainted by his own feelings of rootlessness.

Despite the great recognition she had been showered with by fellow Indians as a practicing classical dancer, she decided to quit dancing after entering college, attributed by Samir to a reluctance to identify with the Indian community. The rebellion displayed by Ruplu's generation was more *about* the self than a transcendental awakening of the self. Over the years, the 'we' disappeared, replaced by individualistic concerns, like 'what's in it for me?' which overtook the sheer passion in their collective agitations, interventions, debates and discussions.

Samir's generation desired to be a part of a collective whole, crusaders against the status-quo. Accusing fingers could be pointed at a minuscule section of anti-war activists of the '60s for exploiting the movement to dodge the draft, but the multitude participated out of genuine revulsion at the miasma surrounding their government's aggressive brutality in Vietnam. Identity politics was sprinkled with generous doses of liberalism manifested through demands ranging from a shared dormitory for all genders to the plight of the homeless. Over time, actual issues had been pushed to the background, and activism in itself acquired an autonomous identity, a spiritual awakening powered by empathy and compassion.

Belonging to a post-ideological generation, Ruplu rarely articulated the vision of a utopia or identified with the avant-garde. She was bothered with immediate issues, manipulated by social media into a tacky image of the real world and incapable of revolting in a meaningful manner against consumerism, destruction of the environment or inequities.

Samir's impression was dispelled to some extent during the next two days as the wide gap between two individuals (who never quite understood each other) narrowed while they sat down to discuss staid issues.

Apu, on the other hand, was uncomplicated. He felt as comfortable in the presence of his white, hispanic, black friends and colleagues as he was with his cousins back in India, or children of their friends. He was a keen worshipper of the free market and a critic of 'pseudo-liberalism'. His son fitted into Samir's present ideology, minus his fondness for the religious Right in India.

Both his children bore the stamp of the well-bred. They were affectionate towards each other and their parents at the end of the day. Despite Ruplu's self-centred attitude, she rose to the occasion whenever they needed emotional support through gestures that moved him. Their demure behaviour with their friends and relatives was remarkable, unlike that of their friends' kids. He had reconciled himself to Ruplu's occasional sarcastic remarks at his obsession with India's cultural heritage and spiritualism as good-humoured banter and nothing more despite Samir and Neelu trying to bring up the kids in line with traditional cultural and religious values—Bengali language at home, puja on Tuesdays and Thursdays, fasting on Mondays.

But was Samir entitled to criticize Ruplu and her generation with no bombastic pretensions of working for the underdog?

They huddled together. Just like childhood days.

'I wish to structure the narrative with the usual preface and introduction before I plunge into the main story since I need to explain my background and portray the zeitgeist of the times. Let me warn Apu that the entire episode may sound uninteresting to him since it relates to a period consigned to the pages of history. Although I was situated at the periphery, the experience I plan to relate tonight is spine-chilling.'

Neelu raised her eyebrows. 'More than peripheral involvement. Ruplu, do ask him why he sports that occasional limp for so many years now.'

He smiled with a flush. 'Yes, Neelu, that incident lies at the core of my tale tonight... Kolkata was teeming with disparities in those days. There were the rich and the poor, atheists and devotees, social reformers and conservatives, the emotional and the rational, smart cookies and idiots, educated and illiterates, all coexisting in a city glaring with its contradictions. Samir Chattopadhyay was the product of a synthesis of countless theses and antitheses pervading the era.'

The lexicon of an outdated philosophy failed to resonate in space. No heads nodded to Samir's interjection.

'At the cost of repetition, I was the only child of Satyen and Sulekha, nicknamed Khokhon. I had a pampered childhood. They were overbearing and stern at times, yet my memory of them is peppered with sweet remembrances. He sent a sidelong glance at his kids before he could complete his sentence. 'Yet, I grew exasperated later in life when excessive parental affection and control appeared unreasonable and intrusive, and was eager to get away from what I felt was a moronic existence.'

While the others preferred to be discreet, Ruplu's response was nonchalant. 'Baba, can we skip the grandpa and grandma bit? I've heard variations of this so many times.'

Neelu's amused look was palpable, even in the darkness but, determined to have his way, he pretended not to have heard his daughter.

'On this day, I am reminded of the birthday parties and the manner in which they were celebrated. No pomp and grandeur, balloons, festoons or fancy cakes; only homemade sweets and payesh, eaten among friends from the neighbourhood, with simple indoor games organized by your Dadu—that was it. At the end of the evening, Ma would hold my hand, circle the dia round and round, render a religious tune and bless me with grass and rice. No cakes, no music. Yet, so profound.'

The thought of those simple birthdays, whispers of a bygone era, kissed him with a tinge of melancholy. It reminded him of his parents, of carefree days, of the love and affection they had showered on him, of the simple food they had cooked with such meticulous care.

Samir's universe initially revolved around The Beatles, the Blues, cricket and soccer, cultural events, mandatory Bible and moral science lectures where Christian ethical values were projected as omniscient. He was suddenly transferred to a traditional vernacular-medium school of competent academic standards in the ninth standard, located far from home, bang opposite the college he aspired to be admitted into. The brighter ones majored in physics, economics, or chemistry. The college was called Presidency College.

Samir had never imagined that he would be compelled to quit

his education at this school before completing his eleven schooling years. He never wanted to be transferred. The image of walking down a broad road leading to an incandescent future was ensconced in his brain. The alternately verdant and patchy soccer grounds, indoor gymnasiums that dotted the corners, brightly painted classrooms, smiling teachers, the chapel and a massive auditorium where he acted in plays and participated in quiz contests, with the Belgian priests with over-flowing white gowns and stern faces that masked their intrinsic tenderness, and the bellboy who rang the bell at 3.30 sharp to trigger a burst of staccato were all integral components of his existence. It had been his second home.

It was in the year 1967 when he was transferred to another school. Satyen was requested to report to school to sign a few papers and collect the transfer certificate. As they trod their way home, he could detect the teenager's feelings as they briefly paused to purchase ice cream.

'Son, it is for your future' was all Samir's father could muster in a faint voice.

♦

The judgmental Ruplu flared up. 'But why did they force you to change schools? So damn inconsiderate of them.'

'The new school held the keys to academic success. The teachers were experts in predicting probable questions and the best manner to compose brief yet meaningful answers to satisfy the examiner.'

'You mean they fixed the exams?'

The interjection rattled his ego. 'No way, Ruplu. It was just experience and insight. Our school boasted of high academic standards. There was another reason. Your Dadu was keen on a foundation in Bengali culture, which was amiss at the previous school.'

Apu could perceive that Ruplu's comment about 'fixing' had not gone down well and waded in. 'Ruplu, don't you know how good Baba was in mathematics? It was tough in those days, not like our times.' He was prompting her to try and make amends for the faux-pas.

'Yup,' she responded. 'I also remember it was mandatory for us to speak Bengali at home as well. We have had to consume food satisfying the typical Bengali palate, and forsake the use of a spoon and a fork. Dadu was successful in inculcating the culture thingy in Baba.'

Samir felt the remark was intended to be sarcastic and decided to counter sarcasm with sarcasm. 'How can I possibly forget your embarrassment when we used our fingers to eat the rice the evening your friends were invited for dinner, Ruplu? We are digressing. It was initially tough to adjust to the alien environment at the school. Few spoke fluent English, although Shakespeare or Dickens were treated with deserving respect. John Lennon and Jimmy Hendrix were unheard of, soccer soared above cricket and academics was the be-all and end-all. The school did not have a proper playground, it availed facilities offered by the college opposite ours whenever it was available. Our core competence lay in topping board examinations, year after year.'

The budding sociologist in Ruplu intervened. 'Don't you feel class differences had a role to play in your perceived alienation?'

To think of it, what she stated carried a grain of truth. The landed gentry that belonged to the northern part of the city predominantly hailed from a different social category. Samir's roots, traceable to the upper-caste landed gentry who had migrated to India after the nation split into two, declassed into the salaried middle-class after migrating. Much later, lifestyles transformed, new jobs were up for grabs. Gated complexes, two or three-storied houses, small bungalows and cozy apartments (resembling art decos) had marked their appearances in the southern stretch. The former continued to boast of huge, but crumbling rococo mansions. The preponderance of the northern gentry in the school he moved to was a factor that never crossed his mind.

He was impressed by her keen observation since she visited Kolkata only for her vacations, and he sensed a bright future for her in the social sciences.

'Maybe...the incongruity of the bonedis and nouveau rich... though I discovered my muses there. At the coffee-house, a plebeian version of a French café, roadside bookshops and the famous, Presidency College across the road inspired me during those moments of despondency. The college, apart from its academic excellence, was the hotbed of a radical student movement.'

'Did you get involved with the same student movement in college?'

'Yes, Ruplu. The college resembled UCB (University of California, Berkeley) with its impressive gothic structures, clustered columns, a steep staircase, intricate sculptures of distinguished alumni, flying buttresses. A quaint clock resembled the Big Ben as well, but it rarely displayed the accurate time.'

'And what about the students?'

Not noticing the wink in her eyes, Samir fell into this well-laid-out-trap.

'It was not customary for girls to wear western outfits in those days, and their ubiquitous sarees—those diverse colours, wrapped around the waist with an exposed midriff, fluttering in the gentle breeze—was a sight I could barely take my eyes off from. I had lived a sequestered existence till then, and the experience was novel. I would religiously spend a few minutes beneath the impressive portico during the lunch recess to take in the mindset of a college student.'

'So you were there to ogle at the girls,' Apu said, prompting Samir to raise his fists playfully. '*Apu, ebar kintu tui maar khabi.*'

Ruplu contributed her bit. 'You found sarees sexy, Baba?'

'I never used that word, you crude American! Just that the inscrutable saree exposed and concealed simultaneously, tantalized and provoked my curiosity.'

The memories had emerged thoughtlessly, and Samir was oblivious to the audience. A faux-pas. The two siblings were embarrassed, and were unable to recall Baba discussing sensuous topics before. The prudish Neelu turned a shade of pink.

Ruplu was blunt. 'Seems like we are growing up, Baba.'

Uproarious laughter greeted Samir's pathetic attempt to cover up. 'I was just fourteen at the time, guys!'

'But now you are grown up, Baba! It is your sixtieth birthday today! Ma, I guess you need to purchase a truckload of sarees on your next visit to India.'

The whisky seemed to have taken its toll and he had to bring himself back.

'To cut a long story short, I was converted to the radical fold. Literature espousing the cause of a violent revolution found its way across the street, and many of us were inspired to sacrifice our lives for a better world, not merely free of hunger and deprivation, but one that offered a self-actualization for all. Best of times for young romantics. Students and working classes in France had occupied their universities and factories while valiant Vietnamese were fighting back against the most powerful nation in the world. Palestinians held on to their last inch of land, Dr King inspired the Civil Rights Movement, and Bob Marley and Dylan had taken American and European campuses by storm with their heart-wrenching numbers. Just a decade back Che, Fidel and a motley gang had conquered Havana, descending from the mountains of Sierra Maestra. The context of the era, guys!'

Reminded of Ruplu's uncharitable views on Che, Samir wished he had not mentioned the name since he was not in the mood for a controversy. She let it pass, stimulated by the very mention of Martin Luther King, a name that evoked the historic Selma-Montgomery march, a perpetual source of inspiration for her generation.

'You are on the right track. But I need more backdrop since my PhD thesis deals with similarities in social upheavals of the '60s and '70s around the globe.'

'Well, a large section the youth voiced their solidarities with the peasants of a tiny and nondescript hamlet called Naxalbari situated on the northern periphery of our state, and rose in ferment against oppressive feudal exploitation, sparking a prairie fire across swathes of the countryside. That was sometime in 1967. A section of the communist party parted ways with the mainstream party from the left who, like their counterparts in France and Latin America, believed in a more peaceful, long and seamless transition. Within a few years, the government brutally suppressed the uprising, and its leaders were hacked off or confined to prisons.'

The excitement was palpable in Ruplu. 'Was this the precursor to the Maoist movement today?'

Samir suddenly felt excited and got up from his chair. 'Remotely, but there is a discernible continuity. The embers glow today in the Maoist movement. Nonetheless, although I no longer adhere to their philosophy, it was a dazzled generation that I belonged to, a generation that printed its stamp on the sands of time, passing on residual vignettes for posterity.'

'So, you too were influenced.' There came the sarcastic taunt with an unmistakable tint of undisguised superiority from Neelu.

A small factory that her father, Jatin babu, had nurtured to a decent size had gone down the tubes due to agitations by labour unions. She had been repugnant when Samir first told her that he had once hobnobbed with adherents of a left-wing persuasion.

On the other hand, Samir remained smug in his belief that she had taken his stories in her stride. Her occasional curiosity was seen as an academic attempt to understand a leftist perspective at a juncture when the left was passé. The real cause for her inquisitiveness eluded him through so many years.

Like most of his peers, Samir had veered into a different ideological trajectory with age and experience. Passing through challenging transitions, the final shift occurred on a business trip to the once-iconic nation of Vietnam, where he was greeted outside the airport by young kids begging for a dime and soliciting damsels on scooters accosting him at the entrance to the hotel.

In his later years, despite the commitment to spirituality and yoga, because of a few brutal episodes, and a perpetually haunting discrimination—both of the implicit and explicit varieties—there were occasional reversals to these once-cherished beliefs, but ephemeral and episodic in nature.

Clouds thickened into layers of cumulus, prompting them to shift to the covered patio to escape the light precipitation. The darkness lent a freakish backdrop to their still-hung kitschy Christmas lights, not able to justify their raison d'être anymore.

The family sat cuddled on the antique sofa they had collected from a garden sale, and he noticed the bottle of Balvenie on the tiny centre table. The torrents that rapidly picked up in intensity succumbed to strong winds in the easterly direction. Oblivious to the lashings, his scattered mind wandered off to their terrace in Kolkata, until he was interrupted by a hard nudge from Apu.

'Baba, do not sleep here. You are not that young anymore, and you're not even wearing a jacket.'

He scurried indoors.

A deafening clang of metal emanating from the spookiness

of the dark house pierced the humid environment, sounding ominous at the late hour. The phone stopped ringing as soon as they entered the house, but it must have been ringing for a while because it had not been audible from the lawn.

'Neelu, hope all is well back home?'

'I spoke to Ma a few hours back. That reminds me—she wanted to wish you but I did not have the heart to wake you up.'

'You heard it ring in the afternoon, didn't you, Baba?'

'Thanks for reminding me, Apu. Quite a few times. Did not feel like responding. I have a feeling it must be one of those pestering salesmen from time-share companies.' Instantly, he realized the vacuity of his statement since unearthly hours were not meant for unsolicited calls.

The thought of a relative or friend in need perturbed him. He kept in touch regularly with quite a few people, and they kept him informed on finalized weddings, unpleasant deaths, and exams cleared with flying colours. At times, they came with requests for financial assistance. Relatives from his previous generation had expired, and the only individual whose demise would cause him immense grief was his father's friend, Ashim kaku, a father to him at the moment.

However, Ashim kaku had called in the morning to wish him.

'Apu, do you plan to stay through the weekend?'

'Oh, yes! Do you wish to resume the story tomorrow?'

The whisky, dinner and weather had been heavy, and he was looking forward to a good night's sleep.

Ruplu was disappointed but did not show it.

AN EVENING AT HOME

16 May 1985

The clouds cleared at the break of a day that passed peacefully. At the office, Samir planned to meet Mike for a few minutes to discuss his situation but the marketing presentation dragged through the day. He ultimately logged off as he witnessed the dreary sight of a deserted Friday evening workplace.

The fading sunlight and the first sighting of the glimmering stars in a darkening sky impacted Samir's senses on his way back home. It triggered excitement at the thought of spending the weekend with the family and watching the elections in India, the outcome fairly certain to him by then. He could not recall similar enthusiasm in recent times towards polls either in India or the US, barring Obama's first-time victory.

As he entered the lounge, the sight of Apu crunching numbers on his laptop was heart-warming. Neelu was focused on the Bengali novel she had picked up during her last visit to India. It was a novel that she seemed to be reading in perpetuity. The bright yellow chrysanthemums, polished vases and a quaint cuckoo-clock that he had received as a birthday gift from Apu had been placed around the room, making the room look different.

'Hi, guys, we have just two more nights together.'

'I plan to catch the early Monday flight. Ruplu wanted to pack by Sunday evening but I have persuaded her. She leaves with me early Monday morning,' Apu said.

'Great news! Allow me to take a bath. Would you care to pour the single malt with lots of ice, son, after I am through?

And help yourself too! But where is Ruplu?' Samir simultaneously requested and questioned Apu.

'With her friend. Upstairs. I have been asked to inform her the moment you arrive.'

Samir gestured with a gentle wave of his hands. 'I'm going for a bath upstairs, will knock on her door on my way.'

Ruplu had locked the door from the inside. He found it strange because she usually kept it open, even while she was sleeping. He heard peals of laughter, interspersed with what sounded like rhapsodic outbursts. Only after three knocks did he hear the gentle murmurs of shuffling bedsheets, muffled voices and hurried footsteps on the wooden floor, culminating in the sound of flowing tap water. At a loss to comprehend the situation, he decided to bang loudly.

It took a few more minutes for her to open the door. 'I'm dreadfully sorry, Baba. We drifted off to sleep.'

He did not bother to say that he had heard voices.

His own query sounded ludicrous to the ears. 'Your friend left for the day?'

'Nope, she slept off after a tough brainstorming session. We are due to present a joint paper on Tuesday.' Ruplu quipped.

'I'm heading in for a bath. I'll settle in the lounge after ten minutes. Take your time, there is no reason to rush.'

Ruplu's expression of guilt was apparent.

A while later, the plumpish figure that joined them in the lounge bore a sharp and innocent countenance, capable of standing out in a crowd, exuding the carelessness of youth. Ruplu introduced her. 'Angela is from Argentina and we are research scholars under the same supervisor.'

'Hi, Angela.'

Her smile was gracious and demure. 'Ruplu tells me it's story-time tonight,' she said.

'You can join us if you wish to.'

The bout of laughter that followed seemed weird to Samir. The statement had neither been funny nor had he intended it to be so. It was merely a desperate attempt to correct an awkward situation.

'Nope got to reach home,' she hurriedly said.

He had decided to bury bizarre thoughts that had kept surfacing through his bath, sincerely hoping that he would not have to jump through more hoops at this stage of his life. It would be okay, he thought. Ruplu was a good girl.

'Righto. Off we go. How do you guys want me to structure the narrative?'

'I would like you to start with the manner in which you were indoctrinated.'

'Ruplu, your basic premise is counter-factual. I was not indoctrinated, they convinced me through a clear stream of reason. However, the point I wish to emphasize now is different. Please do not cut me off whenever I bring in references to your grandparents.'

'Come off it, Baba. We loved Dadu and Thamma as much as you did. It's just your annoying habit of repeating the same stories over and over again.'

The innocent roars of laughter kept him alert.

'At the outset, let me start with a date that remains etched in my mind. 1 May 1969. As I mentioned yesterday, I was not enjoying the new school. The cultural differences were stark and I missed my buddies at every moment. Novelties like the roadside bookstalls, the coffee-house and the sherbet shop at the corner, the sweetmeat joints, and the college across the road kept me stuttering along. There were other stimulants. The loud sloganeering, for example. I heard fiery speeches, intoxicating choruses from young leaders, and I often saw the stretch in front of our school paralysed for hours at the drop of a hat. Shopkeepers, passers-by, and passengers inside cars and buses curiously listened with deadpan faces to haranguing student leaders. Cops cracked down after a while, greeted with powerful explosives intended to scare and not hit, and the crowds dispersed. Life limped back to normal. It was more entertaining than scary.'

'Reminds me of France in 1969. Just last week I watched a movie on the students' movement at the film club,' she said.

Samir ignored her and continued.

'The movement in our city did not spread like a bushfire nor extinguish like a spark. It continues to smolder fifty years after, the rebels still waging a fierce insurgency in isolated pockets. Conflicts have left more than ten thousand dead and hundreds of thousands displaced. There was another reason for my interest. Other than my friend Utpal, most of my classmates avoided me, and I needed to demonstrate some interest in a shared topic.'

'Utpal... the warm uncle with a cherubic face and a protruding tummy we met at the Calcutta Club last year?'

'Spot on! Although he did not remotely look like that fifty-odd years ago. He was short and lanky with a sociable temperament. The only friend to take me under his wing the day I joined the new school. He was the guy who kindled interest in their literature. The authors were of course bright, perhaps one of the best in the country, and their articles and poems churned the fire in my belly.'

'You still maintain you were not indoctrinated?' Neelu asked.

After so many years, Samir failed to understand why Neelu continued to make such squeamish comments about his short-lived dalliance with radicals.

He continued. 'I believed what they said was reasonable. It is not the same as indoctrination. Do you not feel the same in this country when you witness biases, subtle discrimination, poverty and exploitation? Don't Ruplu and Apu feel the same? Was she not unfairly deprived of her Harvard seat? Come on, at that age, you are prone to rebel, Neelanjana.' He shrugged.

'Fine, then admit you believed in violence.' Her comments were often shallow digs, not what one would expect from an economics post-graduate.

Ruplu jumped to his rescue. 'That's a topic for another day, Ma. Let us stick to the story now.'

'Thanks, Ruplu. To pick up the thread, 'May Day 1969' was a historic day. A new party was launched with an inaugural bash at a site earmarked for public rallies. It was situated near a historical monument named after Sir David Ochterlony, a distinguished commander of British East India, its name altered to Shahid Minar to rid it of its colonial legacy.'

'You took us around once. Remember, the phuchkas in the park facing the monument?'

Samir refused to be distracted. That day had been one of the most important days in his life.

'I was persuaded by my friends to accompany them. I had been growing bored with my bi-weekly visits to the coaching centre and the few hours I spent at school, and so I decided to join them for a thrilling experience.'

'But what are these coaching centres? I have heard you mention them before,' Ruplu egged on.

'Somewhat like the tutorials here, but conducted outside school and college. I got away with a fast one, told my parents that our tutor, Ashu babu, wished to conduct a special lecture.'

'You cheated your parents?' Neelu asked.

Why did Neelu have to intervene so often? Although convinced that their relationship had stabilized over the last thirty years, he suspected a deep grouse within her on occasions like this.

'Can you place your hand on your heart and swear that you never lied to your parents? What do Apu and Ruplu have to say on this?' He slyly winked at them.

The frown on his face disappeared only after a round of guffaws. The kids were smart and knew exactly how to defuse a tricky situation.

'Walking into the maidan of Kolkata with its expanse of green could feel like a breath into a pair of lungs. A tram ride through the luxuriant surroundings during the morning or the twilight hours was always a pleasurable experience. The Shahid Minar corner, of course, was more of an eyesore. There were chaotic hawkers, magicians, tricksters and acrobats scattered all over the place. Nonetheless, it was an enchanting and memorable Sunday afternoon in May when the sun gave way to a mild drizzle. The trees were swinging, set against a towering monument in the background, and the entire locality was bedecked with half-drenched colourful flags. Soprano-tinged songs were blaring and a few thousand spunky youths, sporting coloured caps, unmindful of the persistent drizzle, were marching on. For me, individual identities merged into collective indistinguishability. The keynote speaker focused on concrete plans for the future, followed by a young student leader from the college I aspired to study in, a trade union leader, and a down-to-earth gentleman with a thick, unkempt mustache who had led the peasants' revolt. It was a surfeit of rhetoric and hyperbole—nonetheless, it was a magical experience for a fifteen-year-old.'

On his way to the bar to pour another drink, Apu placed his outstretched palms on Samir's shoulders. 'Was it a total conversion on that day itself?' he asked.

'I was sold. But today, when I introspect, I believe that the conversion happened due to a combination of factors. I was convinced of the necessity for a revolutionary change, but was also overwhelmed by the desire for a romantic embrace with an intangible cause, and I must admit, there was also a selfish need to be accepted by reticent classmates for whom I remained an anglicized oddity from an English-medium school. What ultimately sealed the marriage with the ideology was inexplicable. Perhaps it was an urge to unite with the infinite.'

Samir was himself amazed by the spiritual slant he brought to his stint with left-wing militancy. He dismissed it as a vain attempt to link two unconnected entities, but it soon appeared like a continuum in his life as he closed his eyes to pause and focus on the sights and sounds of the past, linking them to the present.

As the three of them exchanged glances, Neelu was the one to interject. 'I recall you mentioning that your Baba discovered your escapade...'

'Yup, not something I bargained for. A gentleman from our locality happened to be there, and he had identified me from a distance. As I approached home, I spotted my parents pacing the road outside. I was surprised because I normally reached home from the coaching class by eight after a round of chit-chats at roadside teashops, and it was not even seven that evening. The first thought that struck me was of a mishap in our extended family.'

'Isn't the chit-chat called adda?'

'Yes, Ruplu. I am glad you have, at last, picked up the nuances of your mother tongue. It is like salons here. Dominated by meaningless gossip, but at times deeply insightful.'

'Gosh!' Apu said, 'your parents must have locked you in and started accompanying you to the tutor—Ashu babu, or whatever his name was.'

'Surprisingly not, Apu. Baba adopted a smart, tactical line instead and struck a deal he believed I would adhere to, promising not to intervene after I joined college if I offered to withdraw from activism in school. I agreed since I was not really involved then, had achieved my objective of forging friendships with quite a few classmates, and college was just a year away. Well, I stuck

AN EVENING AT HOME

to my side of the deal but he failed to honour his.'

'Was your dad, by any chance, a leftie? I thought he was more inclined towards the spiritual aspects of life,' Ruplu asked.

'Radicalism and the gods co-habited inside the inner recesses of his mind like many Indians of his generation, Ruplu. I was reminded of him the other day while reading of a left-wing chief minister of another Indian state calling himself a proponent of the Upanishads, a component of our Vedic scriptures.'

'Tell us what happened afterwards. I'm curious.'

'He locked me in my room. I was seething in fury because he had slapped me in public, but the rage faded after I perused through the literature obtained at the rally. I was soon humming the numbers sung that afternoon. The two that I recall even today are the ones in honour of Paul Robeson and "We shall overcome."'

Ruplu interjected with a wink. 'It is my favourite. Bet it will sound sweeter than what you sang that night.'

'Are you aware of its origins? It used to be a gospel song from 1900, which evolved into a protest number thanks to Pete Seeger somewhere during the '40s. In tune with altered lingo, the *will* was altered to *shall*.'

Ruplu nodded. 'I heard Pete singing it at Central Park in New York to a rapturous audience. During my summer assignment at Columbia!' She turned introspective, looking askance at Apu, who lowered his gaze, puzzling Samir.

Samir proposed they render the number in a chorus to ease the situation, loud enough to pull the neighbour's house down.

Traces of despondency disappeared when the number ended. Ruplu then coaxed him to render the Bengali version of the ode to Paul Robeson—an African American actor, singer and civil rights activist.

'Wow! We discover a hidden gem now and then, Baba.' Apu said after he had finished.

'*Pabey, pabey*. There are many such.'

'Oh, come on. He was being polite!' Ruplu yanked him heartlessly from the pedestal he thought his son had placed him on.

'Can I resume the story? I have lost track.'

'You were locked in your room.'

'Yes. I was woken before dawn by pangs of hunger, and scrambled to the kitchen hoping for some food. I discovered a plate of rice, vegetables, a couple of chilies and the ubiquitous Bengali fish curry arranged neatly on a plate with meticulous care. Micro ovens were yet to hit the market, and it took a while to locate a matchbox to light the gas stove. The old man suddenly appeared with bloodshot eyes. The maudlin melodrama that followed offended my sensibilities more than the slap on the road.'

'Heralding a brief interlude to your torrid affair with the revolution?' There it was. One of those sarcastic comments that Neelu specialized in.

Ignoring her, he immersed himself in a thought experiment. He attempted to connect two independent events—a dismal performance in the boardroom the previous day with his radical politics forty-five years back. He believed that, like quantum twins, every incident on life's journey is entangled with its twin, situated at a distant point in time. It had sounded outlandish the day it had been discussed in physics class in college, but was re-engaging his attention after his conversion to spiritualism.

Puzzled by his sudden silence, the siblings glanced at each other, but Neelu requested them to hold on with a gesture of her fingers.

THE PRESIDENT'S TANTRIC

March 1982

This was not the first time she had experienced the phenomenon, and she decided to observe him closely. Although she had made her peace with Samir's yoga and meditation, it bothered her whenever he broke off in the middle of a conversation.

It was not as if it was the first time that he was disclosing the episode. She distinctly remembered the night by the levees of the Licking River in Cincinnati, dark memories standing out in stark contrast to whispers from the gently flowing waters.

It was clear that there was no love lost between them, but after living under the same roof for thirty-two years, she felt she owed him this much.

A spectre often haunted her—Samir heading towards insanity, abruptly reminding her of her cousin's Biology teacher in Kolkata who had almost turned raving mad under the influence of a sect called the 'Tantrics'. They followed a practice that traced its origins to the first millennium after Christ. A hybrid of Hindu and Buddhist traditions, the practice was in recent times perceived as a set of perverse rituals that played on the weaknesses of vulnerable individuals through a potent mixture of cannabis, sex and hypnosis. Who knows—one of them may be sitting right here in LA. They were also devotees of Shiva and would gel with Samir.

The spine-chilling incident that shook her once kept haunting her memories whenever Samir behaved strangely.

'Tantra is a powerful spiritual tool but had been hijacked by some people,' Samir had responded after hearing the story about the man who created mayhem for her cousin's tutor. 'Did you know that a tantric once came to the USA and became one of our Presidents' advisors?'

She remained unconvinced. To her, they were a bunch of frauds.

A few months before her wedding, during the summer of 1982, Neelu's maternal cousins had been pestering her for a treat, and they had settled on the Amber restaurant, famous for its tandoori chicken. Reaching around 1 p.m., the manager had requested that they wait for fifteen minutes. The restaurant was massive, yet chock-a-block on a weekday afternoon. While waiting in the lounge, they noticed an old man with a few incongruously dressed white devotees. The old man appeared to be a weird guru, with his characteristically unkempt hair. He was sporting a rudraksha necklace and was dressed in saffron.

Her cousin Nibir turned introspective because the man was distinctly familiar to him. It came in a flash after they had settled in and helped themselves to cold glasses of mango juice and a plate of deliciously fried potatoes. Roy was a dangerous fraud whom Nibir had the misfortune of encountering three years ago in school. The episode had taken place on the day he had gone for Biology tuition at Sumit babu's residence. He was an outstanding teacher of the biological sciences and genetics, with an interest in literature and spiritualism and a favourite teacher at the school. As Nibir had started packing his books after the tuition, he had requested him to keep company for a while to a man squatting in the corner of the room pensively, gazing at the surroundings with a magisterial expression. Another guest had landed up, and he had to take care of him.

The man's flowing beard resembled Tagore's, and he was bare-bodied, a dhoti wrapped around himself like Mahatma Gandhi. Nibir soon realized that he was a loud-mouthed braggart who proclaimed himself as an avid connoisseur of poetry (with a few publications to his credit). His primary domain of interest lay in spiritualism and the Vedas, although he did talk about Kashmiri *Shaivite tantra* also. His voice was dense, capable of mesmerizing the gullible and he spoke with measured cadence. He made some outlandish claims that he could transport himself to the Himalayas within a few seconds and was even capable of communicating with microorganisms. Nibir was amused, nonetheless curious, and accepted his invitation to visit his home, despite finding his personality repulsive to more delicate sensibilities.

Roy's younger daughter charmed Nibir, and her parents never resented his presence even after frequent visits, although the elder daughter occasionally pierced him with nasty stares. Nibir was a nerd, confined to books and music, and the outgoing behaviour stoked suspicion in his father's mind.

After enquiring about his movements from their driver, Gora, Nibir's father had confronted him one evening.

'He is my teacher's master, a spiritual man. Why the cynicism?' Nibir had asked.

'Stop this nonsense, Nibir, and focus on your studies. Gora has told me he has two beautiful daughters. Whose legs are you trying to pull? Nor is this the time for you to play footsie with spirits. Do not forget that you are due to appear for your school-leaving exams next year.'

The frequency of his visits dropped thereafter, and he limited himself to occasions when his dad was not in town, availing public transport.

The last encounter he had was on a balmy afternoon, and upon arriving, Nibir was disappointed to hear that the man was alone at home. His lecture on an uninteresting and arcane topic was excruciating, too peppered with continued doses of gibberish.

'15th August 1985 is the day, Nibir, the day. Not what the Christians call "doomsday", but a Hindu version. A new world springs into existence that day. Those who follow us survive, others will be rendered extinct.'

He seemed to have transcended into a different world as his hands flailed, moving sideways, and his face turned apple-red. Nibir was petrified when the man squeezed his private parts, and he pushed the hand away.

'The experience will transform your life. Do not resist.' The voice was stern.

Nibir scrambled out of the house, regaining mental peace after resolving never to visit the man's house again. Sumit babu did not turn up at school for a few days, and it did not strike Nibir that there could be a connection. A few days later, the headmaster introduced a young substitute teacher since their regular teacher was indisposed and would take a few weeks to resume his classes.

On returning home, his grim-faced father confronted him. 'How do you explain this note?' he said, throwing an unsigned note dropped inside their letterbox on his face. 'Please do not allow Nibir to visit the kapalik's house anymore. Nibir is his next target.' He read out the note in a stern voice.

Nibir knew that kapaliks were a sub-sect within the tantrics, notorious for criminal acts. His father was furious, his mother alarmed. He promised never to visit the man again, which he had already decided in any case. A few days later, he visited Sumit babu. Their teacher had recovered, but he shocked Nibir out of his senses by narrating a terrifying episode. Using the force of hypnosis and other dubious methods, the man had attempted to cast a spell on his teacher, administering a concoction of drugs and compelling him into a compromising position with one of his daughters, photographing him on the sly.

His teacher had recovered but only after a few rigorous sessions with a therapist.

Nibir was requested not to discuss the matter with others as they had no intention to attract the attention of the social circuit. They had even desisted from informing the police. It was Sumit babu who had penned the anonymous note when he came to know that Nibir was a frequenter there.

'Good luck, Sir, let us wipe the incident off our minds,' Nibir had said.

◆

Nibir was sure it was the same man at the restaurant. On hearing his story, the cousins were determined to expose the guru, but as they were debating on the best manner to proceed, they spotted the bunch leaving. Fortunately, they had completed their meal and started following them after requesting Neelu and her sister to go home. A few of the devotees were spotted climbing onto a cab while the others were waiting for another one.

'Need help?' Nibir asked them courteously.

'No, we were just waiting for an empty cab to get to this shop in New Market.'

The cousins, too, hired a cab to head towards the market. It took a while to locate the shop they were in, an antique outlet facing the main road, its drapes swinging gently in the spring breeze. Nibir stepped inside, posing as a customer. The devotees were there—slumping at a far corner of the massive shop. One glance convinced him they were concocting a joint.

'Roy babu?' Nibir said. He could almost hear the man's heart pound, notwithstanding the long drag from an earthen pipe. His colours faded instantly.

The shopkeeper lashed out. 'He is not Roy. Kindly clear off, do not create mayhem here. Bloody loafers!'

'I know the guy; he is a crook.' The smell of cannabis had by then pervaded the environment.

One of the devotees tried to push Nibir out of the way, but his cousin, Sukanto, was smarter and rushed outside to explain the situation to passersby, requesting their assistance in handing over the fraudster to the police. Cops landed within half an hour and the entire gang was taken into custody, charged with smoking a contraband item. A few plastic packets were seized.

The cousins dropped in at Neelu's residence to celebrate the victory. Although confident that the crook and his sidekicks would have been let off after a warning and the exchange of a handsome bribe, it did not concern them.

The incident was reported in a major newspaper the next day. Another tantric had come to USA earlier at the President's invitation.

THE NARRATIVE UNFOLDS

16 May 2014

Samir's interrupted narrative resumed with a jerk. 'The year was 1970. My school-leaving examinations had got over. Between the last incident and my exams, not too much happened at school. I stuck to my promise, focused on my studies, and kept a safe distance from overt involvement in activism. I fared reasonably well in school-leaving exams, missing the top ten by a whisker. I got through to IIT Kharagpur, the leading national Institute of Technology situated a hundred miles away. They conducted their independent entrance exams and commenced classes before school-leaving results were declared. Baba felt I should obtain admission there as a stopgap measure. Although reluctant, I agreed since sitting idly at home was telling on my nerves. I was not committed to studies and rushed home every Friday evening to return by late Monday morning. I was being ragged by seniors there, unable to swallow the horrible food, and forced to mix with strange guys I hardly knew. I was focused on a seat in the Physics department of Presidency College.'

'You were obsessed, Baba! Was it for academics or activism? Indian students have always pined for admission to the IITs.'

'Both, Apu. Hankered for the best of both worlds, but there was also my lack of flair in engineering. I was bluntly told so by the assistant facilitating our technical drawing sessions, the only engineering paper taught in the first semester.'

'Yes, that may be true. You are so bad at fixing stuff.'

'There were other minor factors. Pursuing a career in

engineering was expensive, and although I was eligible for a partial scholarship, I wished to avoid burdening Baba further. I had qualified for the National Science Talent Scholarship, limited to students pursuing pure sciences, and was looking forward to a degree of financial independence. A guaranteed income and additional compensation to potential earnings from private tuitions I would conduct.

'One afternoon, late 1970, enjoying a cool siesta in my room, I was interrupted by loud bangs on the door at my hostel in IIT. First-year students had crowded in the recreation room surrounding a massive radio set. The top ten positions of our Higher Secondary examinations had been announced, and four of the names were from our school. Cables to Kolkata were jammed, and the official gazette was yet to reach Kharagpur. We desperately wished to gain access to the booklet, and a few of us rushed home by the first available train. As luck would have it, an accident on the tracks delayed our journey by a couple of hours, and I reached home by late evening. My relatives were scattered all over the place, some I could not remember at all. Baba had managed to lay his hands on a copy of the gazette only an hour back. I had missed the coveted tenth position by just seven marks. They were desperate to contact me, but the hostel offices had shut for the night, and the 24/7 number was jammed.

'The evening commenced with hugs and kisses interspersed with homemade sweets Ma managed to prepare within a short time, concluding with the traditional grass and rice used for blessings, the 'dhan dubyo' as we call it. The celebrations seemed to drag on till eternity. Fulfilling my aspiration was then a certainty, as I was only a few points behind the last person on the merit list, and the college's Physics Department had forty seats.'

'Before I move on to describe a chilly and fateful December afternoon, let me narrate another day. Aspirants were asked to assemble by 10 a.m. to complete admission formalities at Presidency. Baba, a stickler for arriving early, ensured that we stood there with an hour to spare. I was gaping with a glum face at the locked gates of the deserted college. Although Baba was generous enough to offer me a bottle of Coke, what I pined for at that moment was the stick that he puffed at—a ubiquitous brand called Charminar that had the punch of raw tobacco.'

He exchanged a sly look with Ruplu but it went unnoticed. He had once caught her smoking but had complied with her request not to divulge the discovery to Neelu, because she was scared that her mother's conservative mindset would not accept a daughter addicted to tobacco. Another secret he alone was privy to.

'The neighbourhood suddenly rattled with a loud blast, followed by two more in quick succession. The phenomenon was familiar to us, but it shook Baba. The stall owner perched on a platform assured him, I remember. "Don't get flustered, kaku. The college is reopening after vacation. *Eta to bauni*." The Hindi word 'bauni' literally stands for the commencement of the sowing season, metaphorically signifying the inauguration of an event.'

'What? Let me get this right. A college after vacation reopens with a series of loud blasts. Never heard anything similar before! What did Dadu have to say?' Ruplu prodded.

'Even today, I recall his tremulous voice. "Khokhon, your admission at IIT stands. Paying today's fees is not an issue for me, but do give it sincere thought."

The gates then flung open. The college was pulsating with the chatter of enthusiastic students eager to get a taste of their first day in college. Girls in colourful sarees and guys in dark shirts with parents or relatives scrutinized the forms and attachments to ensure no item was amiss. The buildings were littered with posters of Chairman Mao, Che, and the impending revolution. The guys who hurled explosives a while back were now assisting aspirants to fill forms with meticulous precision. It was a case akin to that of Dr Jekyll and Mr Hyde. Aspirants presented a contrast. Students from the upper classes came in chauffeur-driven cars, conversing in evolved English, flanked by those from the lower end of the spectrum in torn pants and soiled dhotis, chatting in an earthy vernacular, awed at the majestic surroundings like fishes out of water.'

'What was your initial reaction?' Apu asked.

'I thought it was an ideal setting for the class struggle.' Samir stated casually.

He broke out in full-throated laughter. His children responded with half-hearted smiles as the lingo sounded alien. Neelu threw an expression of intense disgust at him. 'Class struggle' was anathema to her, and it reminded her of her father when he was confined to the corner room of his factory for three nights, held hostage by the labourers. On the verge of a heart attack, Jatin was advised a fortnight's rest to ease his hypertension, which had manifested through symptomatic blood pressure.

Samir's next words were desperate to gush forth, as if waiting release from the depths of an aquifer. The happenings of a day he dubiously planned to project as the 'game-changer of his life.'

Like his father, Satyen, Samir was more spiritual than left-wing, but he had attempted to mask it from his friends, only to expose himself on numerous occasions, like when passing by the innumerable temples dotting the streets of Kolkata. He had lost control over his life, not realizing the moment he got swept off his feet, landing neck-deep in swirling waters. The irony was pronounced because, unlike his friends, he was never an uncritical follower. Satyen was honest about his dualism and withdrew early in life from the Party, continuing to remain a fan of Tolstoy, Pushkin, Turgenev, Gorky and Mayakovsky, the perpetual emblems of Russian literature. He had narrated Gorky's

Mother and Tolstoy's *War and Peace* to Samir in an abridged format during his childhood days and taken him along to witness Eisenstein's *Battleship Potemkin* during his teens.

Kaku, his father's younger brother, was more committed to the cause, presenting Samir with many preliminary, made-easy treatises on the philosophy at the age of fourteen. His views carried no weight those days, and he found the booklets missing on his return from school one day. The issue remained an apple of discord between the brothers.

A few days after joining college, kaku once again tried to persuade him to join the students' wing of the peaceable parliamentary left party. He was cannily selling it to his elder brother as a prudent move to mitigate the risk of getting involved with dreaded extremists infesting their college. Samir disregarded the suggestion and was quite candid in his refusal while the brothers sat in stony silence. His decision to support the revolution was a conditioned response to horrendous conditions prevailing in the country, not by a stretch flowing from a conviction in the philosophy. The mini-revolt was also an expression of protest against earlier acts of parental dominance. Satyen could not press his point when reminded of the agreement they had reached barely a year back.

The handouts and home-grown literature he had been exposed to were persuasive but not critical in shaping his opinion. The heart and not the mind had dragged him into a yawning abyss. Triggers were manifold. He was drawn to a Guevara-type romance, empathy for the underprivileged, a burning desire to integrate with indifferent peers, and the desire to avenge a friend's death—sincerely in the hope that the critical factor would remain buried till it was time to leave this world.

A day in his life, to be narrated to his family in the form of a white lie, similar to the Ashwatthama episode in the Mahabharata.

It was a smart act of subterfuge by Yudhisthira, the eldest brother of the Pandavas, intended to incapacitate Drona. Drona was an indefatigable warrior, an Acharya, a spiritual guru, and a war strategist in the battle of Kurukshetra. The news of his son's demise would be unsettling for Drona, and he would not be in his right mental frame after hearing that his son had perished. Yudhishthira was assigned the job whose ethical principles forbade him to utter untruths. He found a convenient way out. His brother Bhima slaughtered a namesake pachyderm, and the fact was communicated to Drona, ensuring that the last few words remained inaudible. The shenanigans were blatant, and Yudhishthira had to bear the consequences when his chariot got stuck in mud during the battle, and even had to visit 'hell' for a short while, which was actually an illusion for the real 'hell'.

Samir was similarly apprehensive.

If ever held accountable, the ploy of not exposing the siblings to another gory episode in his life would be dubbed unconscionable, although a couple of notches more acceptable than not coming clean to his life-partner long back. And unlike the Mahabharata episode, the story to be narrated tonight was not just a white lie.

'The entire state was reeling as the ultra-left declared war on the government, intending to encircle cities from the countryside, slaughtering oppressive landlords and their agents with impunity. They infiltrated into Kolkata to eliminate cops, and killed a majority from the lower ranks.'

'How come you were never arrested?'

'Well, I stuck to non-violent forms of protest like chanting pro-militant slogans in and around college, plastering walls with colourful graffiti, heckling authorities, boycotting classes at the drop of a hat. We did not violate any statute in the law, but the threat of an act that would enable authorities to apprehend recalcitrant citizens without a trial loomed on us. A minuscule militant group often hurled explosives from roof-tops with amazing panache, and the authorities were both unable to catch them red-handed and were under orders not to set an elite college on fire.'

'Wow, exciting, Baba. Carry on,' Apu said as Samir paused to pour himself another drink.

'I will now describe a day that altered the trajectory of my life. I forget the date but it was in May 1971, a few days before our summer vacations commenced. It culminated in being thrown out of the country by my parents.'

The subsequent sentences had been rehearsed in the morning. Samir wanted to create a dramatic effect.

'A series of deafening noises rock the hundred-year-old college building, and a streak of oblique sunlight pierces the dense smoke to emit a spectral hue on a misty and desolate afternoon. My school across the road is a mere speck. The ravens are cacophonous, foreboding worse things to follow. We are taken by surprise as audacious comrades decide to drop powerful explosives from the terrace to catch the Central Reserve Police Force, stationed on the road outside, unawares.'

'You were not part of the group that hurled those explosives?' Ruplu asked.

He replied after a momentary pause. 'No way. Did I not tell you that my activities were non-violent?'

A pungent mix of tear gas and gunpowder choked Samir. Unable to bear the toxic smell, he planned to perch himself closest to the principal's office, a safe sanctuary. At that moment, a tear gas shell lobbed by law-enforcing authorities from outside the college hit him straight on the thigh, the impact hurling him headlong into the wall.

His mind took on the murky quality of the tear gas.

He saw canisters that rebounded from the walls, accompanied by loud explosions reverberating across the locality. He lay down with his head covered. Students and professors ran helter-skelter, rubbing their watery eyes. Most darted to the safe confines of classrooms, the canteen, and the common room, with a few girls mustering the courage to rush towards him. They were no first-aid experts, and in a spate of confusion, one of them topped her water bottle from a leaking faucet and poured the water clumsily over his head.

He could hear his grandfather's deep voice in the background. 'Did I not ask you to be a doctor?' Samir wished he realized how it would have helped.

The very next moment, he was flown to a different planet with bluish rays, white roses, and seductive angelic figures in colourful robes. The vertiginous moment lasted a few seconds, passing through a wakeful semi-conscious state experienced during shallow slumber's REM.

Samir spotted Ruplu in an actual state of shock, and he had noted the furrow of her wavy eyebrows a while back. Neelu's inscrutable face bore no signs of emotion. Apu seemed more curious than rattled.

'Sorry, Ruplu, I should not have been so clinical. Let us skip this part of the story.'

'Certainly not. Continue, Baba, just the way you were.'

'Okay, guys if you insist. Let us strike a deal then... Only if you allow me another drink.'

'Come on, Baba, you just had one. I've never seen you boozing so much before. Give it a break.'

'Okay, I will obey your orders. But I insist you stick on till the end of my story even if it does not interest you. Even in Kolkata, only a few from your generation are aware of too many details of a period that shook our generation. It was like it was in France,

Latin America, or here—with the Black radical movement.'

'How come it was not publicized? The French student rebellion of 1968 is famous.'

'The leaders were perhaps not as stellar as Nelson Mandela, Bob Marley, Che or Daniel Cohn-Bendit, but the happenings were no less epochal than the Vietnam War or the 1968 student rebellion in France.'

'Well, then I spot an opportunity to develop my thesis.'

'Certainly, Ruplu. If you present it well. But you need to research it meticulously.'

'Give me the references you have.'

'I will.' He began again. 'The earth quaked with uncertainty, familiar structures were toppling in an anarchic fashion as autonomous units took their own decisions, redolent of Fidel and his band of revolutionaries holed up in the mountains of Sierra. It was not wishy-washy liberalism, but the articulation of a future socio-economic order—'

'Can I record this, Baba?' Ruplu interrupted.

'As long as you keep it to yourself.'

'Malcolm X was dubbed a communist and Martin Luther way out on the left. There are striking similarities here. Let us carry on. I see a lot of value in this topic for my dissertation.'

'With respect to Malcolm X, I agree. He was a radical activist assassinated by the establishment, but Martin Luther was neither a radical nor a practitioner of violence. Although they did not spare him either.'

His eyes wandered. Perhaps for the first time after joining college, she grabbed hold of him to render a passionate kiss on both cheeks before setting up the recording device.

'The mind soon descended to grim reality,' he continued. 'Thirty minutes back our chubby gatekeeper, 'Motu' as students affectionately called him, had ambled to the portico in his casual, lackadaisical manner to bang the huge brass gong with a hammer wrapped in a cloth. The gong had sparkled once upon a time.

'The day started as a normal day. Not a premonition of what lay ahead. Only a few minutes back, I was discussing a tough multivariate integration problem with a bright, young professor. He invited me inside the staff room to explain the concept better, but I had to humbly request him to postpone it for another day since I was getting late for the protest demonstration.'

'The trigger?' Ruplu asked.

'Sixteen unidentified young corpses were discovered early in the morning by a milkman cycling through a leafy lane in the northern peripherals of the city. Just a few of the martyrs who were dying by the thousands. We planned a peaceful demonstration demanding basic human rights for the activists, but the protest was hijacked by a few hot-headed buddies. They were driven by outrage because of the genocidal murders.'

Apu, the perpetually famished in the family, interrupted. 'Can we break for dinner? I am hungry.'

'Come on, don't be such a spoil-sport, Apu. Let's take a short break instead while Ma and I serve the two of you a little snack here.'

Samir would not have it. 'He's hungry. Let us proceed to the dining table for dinner.'

Delicious and pleasing to the eye, Neelu had cooked a sumptuous dinner of ilish maach. He soaked it in fried rice and ate it with the mustard-dotted succulent lobsters. Neelu was a lousy cook after landing in the USA, but she had acquired the flourish to reach out to his heart through his taste buds. Although unsuccessful, she gained an impeccable reputation among Cincinnati's Indian and Bangladeshi communities and was frequently offered contracts to cook select dishes for large parties, which she graciously declined each time.

He had never before seen his children complete dinner within ten minutes. While re-entering the lounge, it seemed like he could hear 'An ode to Joy'.

Images segued like an avant-garde Godard movie: the Physics auditorium at the Baker Laboratory on the other side of the college complex. Amal Raychaudhuri—lovingly called AKR, the distinguished professor from Princeton whose paper on black holes had been cited on numerous occasions by Roger Penrose and Hawking—was lecturing from the podium in his characteristic breezy style. The sprawling patch of green grass, maintained with immaculate care by the college staff, a patch that witnessed Samir being awarded a gold medal at the school annual sports day a few years back. After presenting the trophy, the headmaster had requested that he not participate the following year since it was to be his final year.

'We bank on your making it to the merit list to keep our flag flying high.' The headmaster had said.

Samir's mind flitted to the encounter with the same man in his chamber, a few days after the results were declared. He expected an admonition for not making it; what he received was a bear hug. 'You will go far in life, young man, but always remain a sensitive human being.'

Vignettes kept flashing through his mind. The playground, lecture hall, professors, the affectionate headmaster across the road delivering the last lecture of the day at that very moment. The gaping cavities in the college boundary wall that were surreal signifiers of the situation prevailing in the country. At a banal level, they provided an escape route to the adjacent Bhabani Dutta Lane, a narrow alley surrounded by a maze of narrower alleys bearing the legacy of a feudal and colonial Kolkata legacy. The area was run-down, squalid, bereft of gaps between adjoining structures, surrounded by open drains, and lower-middle-class in appearance. From there, hidden activists pounced on police vans, makeshift garages assembled homemade explosives like cottage industries and armed comrades roamed the streets as if they owned them. The clichéd sobriquet—'*Mukto elaka*' or 'liberated zones'—was borrowed from guerrilla warfare terminology.

'Adesh's face was a nightmare. He was my childhood friend from school. The cops once arrested him, pretended to set him free, and then shot at him, point-blank from behind. An "encounter death"—euphemism for premeditated murder in India.' No sooner had Samir made a mention of 'encounter deaths' than a primordial squeal pervaded the room. Samir and Neelu were stunned, not by the words that were uttered, but by the manner they were expressed.

Neelu sounded surprised. 'What were you trying to convey, Ruplu?'

Ruplu's reply was spontaneous. 'It happens here too, right here, in the USA.'

Samir intervened. 'Come on, you can't be serious.'

'It is getting scary for her, Samir. She is not habituated to such violence.' Neelu was not quite agreeable to exposing the kids, especially Ruplu, to bloodthirsty episodes, and the concern seemed genuine.

Samir replied in an apologetic tone. 'OK, OK, let me tone it down.'

Switching off her recorder, Ruplu wobbled to the bar cabinet, gulping down half a water bottle. 'Will be back in ten minutes. No sugarcoating, please. I'm good.'

Samir looked at Apu with a puzzled expression. 'What's going on, Apu?'

It took him a few minutes to reply. 'I believe memories of the trauma she went through seven or eight years back have surfaced.

At the mention of encounter deaths. None of you are aware of it...you were so absorbed in your hectic lives.'

'Why did you not tell us? As it is, the poor thing had two encounters during infancy.' Samir questioned Apu, a bit annoyed.

Memories of the traumatic episodes that impacted Ruplu as an infant popped up as Samir waited patiently for Ruplu to rejoin.

TRAUMA

March 1989

The telephone operator entered the meeting room with the news that Neelu had called. Irritated at being disturbed, Samir blurted out. 'Tell her I will call back later.'

'Sam, I'm afraid you need to take this. It's an emergency.'

It was Ruplu. She had dropped out of a slide in school and injured herself. He reached in record time after a bout of mad driving. The tension was short-lived since the fracture was not serious; the broken bones were plastered and expected to heal in a couple of weeks. Ruplu repeatedly asserted that a gang of kids had pushed her out of the slide. It tormented him.

After she had healed, it was tough to convince her to return to school, and Neelu had to take leave to hang on with her for a week.

The Principal had dismissed Ruplu's accusations casually. 'Children at this age are imaginative. Do not go by what she is saying. One of our teachers witnessed the incident. The slides were slippery after a couple of drizzles. We have decided to lock our playgrounds henceforth after rains and snowfalls.'

Neelu nodded graciously, but Samir remained sceptical. It had happened once before. Ruplu had gotten a deep gash from an "accidental fall". It reminded him of what the shrink had said of self-esteem of children disintegrating when they are pushed into a corner.

Then came the evening he would never be able to erase from his mind. He was convinced that Neelu still held on to it as well—one of her innumerable grudges.

It all started at an official party hosted by the chief of one of the organizations he worked for at Cincinnati. Neelu opted to stay back at home because they had no option. All his Indian friends had migrated from Cincinnati one after the other and mashima and meshomoshoy had gone off to Brazil on an assignment.

The Chief was scornful. 'Where's your better half, Sam?'

'At home. Taking care of the kids.'

'You could not get hold of a babysitter?'

'Actually...'

'You did not wish to spend the money? Guess that's the way it is in India. Grandfathers and grandmothers perpetually hanging around.' The words had perhaps slipped out, but Samir could sense his face turning crimson. Adding to his insult, he heard peals of laughter from half-drunk colleagues revelling at his discomfiture. It seemed to reverberate across the banquet room, drowning the cacophony of zany music. Tony, the only colleague who did not join in the bout of schadenfreude, took him aside to volunteer his services.

'Thanks, Tony. Do you employ a babysitter?'

'Not really, my kids are grown up—they should be able to take care of yours. Why suffer these insulting comments from pompous, racist pigs? There would not have been even a casual reference if my wife had not joined in tonight. These guys have these weird ideas that Asians do not like taking their wives along outside their homes. They stereotype you guys. You know something, they selected you for the post because they did not have a fucking white alternative. Heard them mention this many times. This city is infested with hicks. It's not that bad in coastal areas. Get out of here at the earliest. New York may be slightly expensive, but you could try Boston, New Jersey, or for that matter, any town on the West Coast.'

'Grateful for your offer, Tony.'

'Don't mention it. It took me years to get over this feeling of racial superiority, but guys from the Midwest belong to Harper Lee's era.'

At Tony's farewell lunch at the office a few months later, Samir brought up the topic light-heartedly. 'Tony, what will happen to my kids now?'

'Shit, that promise slipped my mind. We are moving town, otherwise, the offer would have stood. It would have been better actually because we would have taken care of them instead of leaving it to kids.'

'Oh, come on Tony, don't look so damn serious. At least not today. I can manage to get a nanny. Not an insurmountable challenge.'

A month later, the next party was announced to celebrate a huge contract that had been bagged by their organization. Samir disclosed the caustic remarks he had to endure on the previous occasion to Neelu. 'Let your boss go to hell, Samir. Do you get evaluated on the number of times your wife accompanied you to a party? What if you were single?'

'Guys here have a small-town mentality. You know that. And I thought you were planning to teach.'

'I have worked that out. Ma has volunteered to spend a few months every year here till Ruplu goes to regular school. I'm sure your Ma will also not mind filling in a few more months. A crèche for the remaining months.'

'There is no point needlessly arguing about this. Why would I subject myself to sickening comments from a bunch of morons? I checked out babysitters. It is around fifty dollars for the evening. Let's be pragmatic. Most folks at our office have utilized their services at some point or the other.'

The very appearance of the lady with a southern drawl pissed both of them off. They could not understand a word of what she spoke. The last thing they heard before stepping out the door was Ruplu howling at the top of her voice, although Apu was calm, perhaps able to accept the situation.

Neelu retained her composure throughout the party and played on with his flirty boss, dancing gracefully to even the raucous music.

'You have a pretty wife,' the Chief complimented as they made their way to the car.

On the way back, Neelu opened up. 'The guy made my flesh crawl.'

'Come on, you enjoyed yourself. I could see from a distance.'

'You have a jealous and dirty mind.'

'I just stated whatever I observed.'

An acrimonious argument followed. The car was surrounded by tiny snowflakes swirling across the windscreen, which they graciously wiped away. The snowfall gathered in intensity, a sharp breeze commenced and the flakes changed direction—striking the windowpane on his right. It was a relatively long distance to their house, and he had to drive at a snail's pace. Streetlights kept reflecting his eyes and the snow was dashing with savage intensity, the wind accompanied by a shrieking noise. All he could see was an expanse of never-ending white, and an indistinguishable mass soon covered the parked cars and trees.

'It's a blizzard,' shrieked Neelu.

Samir yelled at her. 'Please keep quiet. A single mistake could turn fatal.'

He could hear the deep exhales and inhales.

'Recite the Hanuman Chalisa, it will do us good,' he said to her.

They breathed a sigh of relief when their complex was visible at a distance.

The guard took a while to reach the gate, informing them that the basement was inaccessible due to the snow; they would have to park the car near the entrance. The walk from the parking lot was long, Neelu lost her balance twice and Samir barely managed to hold her at the nick of the moment. When they finally entered through the front door, their bodies were snow-covered and their hands were frozen. If they had entered through the back door, they would have noticed it unlatched.

They rushed to their bedroom, hoping to find the kids smug in bed, but the first glance of the house left them silent. Apu and the nanny were snoring away but Ruplu was nowhere in sight.

After checking the other rooms and the washrooms, he belligerently shook the babysitter out of her deep slumber.

'Where the hell is the younger one?'

'No idea.'

He flew off the handles. 'Were you not supposed to look after them? Why do you think we employed you? For your fucking face?'

Her accent was now intelligible. 'Lower your voice and don't you dare insult me. Firstly, you touched me, which is not permitted. Your wife should have woken me. I put your kid to sleep. Am I to blame if Indian babies sleepwalk? Now just pay me off.'

Neelu managed to hold on to Samir's lifted hands before he could make a costly mistake.

'Are you crazy? Do you wish to go to jail?' she shouted at him.

They rang their neighbours' doorbells. The majority seemed unhappy at being woken up or disturbed at an intimate juncture. Only the local church pastor volunteered to join them in the search. The cops arrived promptly, despite the weather. Ruplu could not have strayed out of the complex because the guards stationed at the only exit point had not seen a soul, and it was too long a distance for her to cover. The babysitter, meanwhile, disappeared—braving the inclement weather, opting to forego her wages.

A cop finally spotted Ruplu, attracted by her faint murmurs from below the tip of a crevice behind the casuarina trees. Samir and Neelu rushed when they heard him yelling. Luckily, there were only patches of snow there and the dense foliage had blocked her fall to the far off ground. Nevertheless, her hair appeared to have been brushed with white paint, and she was stuck inside a hole a few centimetres wide, unable to extricate herself. A faint squeal and a gentle movement of the arms indicated that she was alive. One leg was caught under a branch, while the other was bent at an odd angle. An elder child would have managed to climb out, but she was just a kid.

While they pulled her out, her murmurs conveyed neither despair nor relief. All Samir heard was a bizarre snort from an infant in deep shock.

Samir draped her in a blanket and rushed her to the hospital. She was in her nightclothes, not warm by a long shot.

The nurse was stern. 'She could have died of cold and shock. You are plain lucky. Pray to the Almighty and Jesus. Do you guys have any sense? Left a kid of her age alone at home? How did she manage to leave the house?'

'She was with a nanny who fell asleep. We have no clue how she got out, possibly the nanny had stepped outside and forgotten to close the door after coming back.'

'In the snow?'

'Perhaps she went out for a smoke. And it started snowing much later.'

'I will not rule out carelessness from one of you. You must have been eager to reach the party on time.' Samir recalled that he was the last to leave the house, disturbed at Ruplu's howling and a delay of fifteen minutes beyond the time they had planned to leave.

He was certain Neelu had already drawn her conclusions.

'Kids of her age are not normally left behind in these parts with unknown babysitters. We employed one only after our kid crossed his sixth year.'

The nurse was speaking to Neelu. She remained calm—the lady of the house bears the blame.

The X-rays showed a mild crack on the left foot and the CT scans indicated no visible impact on the brain. The hospital decided to hold Ruplu back for the night, under heavy sedation and palliatives, expecting an outbreak of pneumonia. It snowed through the night, and Samir and Neelu sat on a sofa beside the bed; Neelu kept up a stony silence while Samir was furious, eager to lay his hands on anyone in his path.

The doctor agreed to discharge her only in the afternoon. 'It's not likely that she will catch pneumonia. A tough girl, but psychological setbacks cannot be ruled out. She passed through a trauma. Consult a psychiatrist if you can.'

Samir carried her out. He held her tight, careful not to slip on the slushy road, remnants of snow scattered across. It was bright and sunny by then.

The psychiatrist sounded hopeful. 'You just need to treat her with kid gloves for some time. Keep hugging and kissing her. No scolding, not even for grave misdemeanours. Keep her on constant watch. A behavioural change might occur as she adapts.'

The change did not take long. The first symptoms of crankiness were diagnosed as 'separation anxiety' as Ruplu refused to be left alone even for a minute. Neelu could not even go to the washroom while she was awake. Other symptoms included the irregular movement of the bowels, lack of appetite and occasional violent acts. She would carelessly damage utensils and artifacts.

It was diagnosed as PTSD. The doctor recommended cognitive behavioural techniques in a secure environment. Friends insisted they sue the nanny, but Samir did not have the money for a legal battle. What purpose would it serve anyway?

The infant made a slow recovery. Neelu was grateful only to an undefined divine power she believed in, even as she persistently seemed repulsed by Samir. Her complex emotions were all stacked, one within the other, like a Matryoshka doll.

After a year, in 1990, the family migrated to Orlando. Samir obtained a new job and the family looked forward to the mild weather. The sad part was bidding mashima and meshomoshoy goodbye. They had stood by them like a pair of rocks throughout their stay. Cincinnati was not a city one commonly travelled through, and they invited the elderly couple to drop by at Orlando. They could not meet Joe and Supriya, as the latter was stuck in Boston with a pregnancy.

◆

In the lounge, Samir was perplexed. He spoke to his son. 'I would prefer you be around, Apu. If Ruplu agrees to speak about it.' Then he relapsed into a reflective mood, distraught at his imperfections as a father.

He felt relief when Ruplu finally appeared with a radiant smile. She switched on the recorder with nimble fingers.

'Baba,' she began. 'I wish to know more about your friend.'

'It seems like you are more interested in his friend than your injured dad!' Samir joked. The remark was in jest and evoked smiles, but the laughter was cut short by the unmistakable sound of the landline piercing the silence of the night.

'Must be a comrade from the past,' Neelu's wicked taunt left them in explosive laughter.

The pain in his right knee flared up as he briskly scampered across to reach the instrument in the guestroom. Slackening his pace, it took a while to reach the instrument situated at another corner of their mezzanine floor. The caller's patience held. It did not demand an instant response and Samir felt like he was hearing from one of those mellow, laid-back, and genteel souls from his childhood days.

It could be Utpal. It had not struck him yesterday. He was one of the few who did not have his mobile contacts since, entitled to unrestricted free calls on his official connection in India, Samir was apprehensive he would be disturbed at odd hours in the office.

The flash on the LED, however, indicated an LA number. Perhaps an old friend or acquaintance at work or on holiday in town. Having discontinued the practice of entertaining old-timers, the prospect of a long-lost friend held no particular attraction. His desire to catch up on lost days had eviscerated over time. He derived pleasure from meditation, soulful music, from surfing the news, sports channels and immersing himself in religious scriptures. These days, he would excuse himself from a chat after a round of polite banter, remaining steadfast through their insistence.

The last chat with Utpal came back to him. His son was due to visit LA for an orientation session with the parent of the US multinational that had offered him employment back home. The guy was so talkative!

The phone stopped ringing before he could receive the call.

Although he was unable to recognize the flashing number, he was not unduly worried since it was not from India. He stayed back for a while in case the caller decided to try again.

It did not strike him that the instrument stored the last calling number in its internal memory.

◆

'THE WORST PART OF MEMORY IS THE HOLDING OF PAIN'

16 May 2014

When he returned, Ruplu was desperately trying to focus on a book, Apu was tapping vigorously on his laptop, and Neelu was nowhere to be seen.

'Where's Ma?'

'In the kitchen. Who was it?' Apu asked.

'It was disconnected by the time I reached. Have a strong feeling it is Utpal's son. He was scheduled to be in town around this time.'

'You can dial back the last number. Someone is trying to call you since yesterday.'

'Did not strike me. I will do it later, maybe tomorrow. I promised Utpal I would ask his son over to our house when he's here. If it's any other friend from India in town, I will avoid him.'

'Why?'

'Meeting up with old friends disturbs my yogic concentration.'

'This is sophistry, Baba! Ridiculous logic,' Ruplu spoke up. 'I am reminded of that friend of yours. Do you recall the guy, from a rural background, on a study tour to California? The one who taught mathematics in some vague college in North Bengal? He could not hold a damn fork. Apu, am sure, will be able to recall our desperate attempts to suppress giggles. You had to leave the dining table on some pretext.'

'We were kids then, Ruplu. I realize it was improper.'

Her response was cursory. 'I guess so.'

Samir held up his fingers. 'And why would he need to learn to hold a fork, Ruplu? Your cosmopolitan disdain makes you sound like a brown memsahib. The racism you abhor manifests in other forms. These are our forks.'

The individual was a dear friend of Samir's. He was offended by Ruplu's statement that he felt exposed her Janus-faced personality. She could go on mighty processions against the oppression of blacks, immigrants, queers and hapless refugees from Iraq or Palestine but she barely had an organic connection to individuals. Samir was able to relate to her.

Apu, on the other hand, was not in the habit of sermonizing from the pulpit of liberalism, but he was more empathetic to human beings.

The phone buzzed once again. Loud and clear.

Both Samir and Apu jumped up.

'Now, now, old man, let me take the call. I will reach faster than you.'

'Hey, stop calling me old, I get an inferiority complex,' Samir responded.

His son was back in a few minutes. 'Ma received it.'

Neelu entered after ten minutes, reminding Samir of the years that passed by. She settled into the other corner of the room, and gazed at the painting on the wall. Sometimes her behaviour could be awkward, somewhat like his own...inexplicable and strange.

'Who was it, Neelu?' he asked her.

After a moment's hesitation, she said, 'You were spot on, Samir. It was a time-share company.'

'But it is past nine. How can they call now?'

'I have threatened to complain. Have noted the caller's name, number and the name of the company.'

'Forget it, the guy will land into trouble. Hopefully, if you have given him a piece of your mind, he will not call again.'

'Okay, okay. Can we resume the story please?' Ruplu asked.

'Yup. Back to the story. So where was I? Yes. Adesh was my best friend in the English medium school. We studied at Don Bosco School during the early years of our lives. I can recite innumerable stories about him till the cows come home. Stories about him throwing chalk at our Bengali teacher, because he was disgusted with his monotonous drawl, or about his constant scuffles with Kala, a senior bully, who he once challenged at a local park and locals forced to intervene to separate them. He was an intelligent and compassionate student, and he wore a perpetual smile on his face.'

Samir was drenched with nostalgia as memories flashed, one after the other.

'Ma harbored a fondness for Adesh, and would announce his arrival at the door. '*Shuncho, khokhon, Adesh eshechey.*' I will stick to just one incident about him, about the night his mother came over as we planned to retire after dinner. We were initially concerned about why she would be here at such a late hour and on seeing her distraught face. But we burst into squeals of laughter when the reason was disclosed. Adesh was insisting that their household employee be allowed to dine at the dining table. The practice in India, as you are aware, is for domestic workers to sit on the floors for their meals. His father refused to entertain the audacious request and he retaliated by refusing to consume dinner. His mother was keen that I try and persuade Adesh out of such inanities since she believed he valued my advice. I tried, but he had his way. Many years later, I remember him telling me that that one incident molded his convictions in life.'

'People like him don't exist these days,' Ruplu commented.

'Cannot say, Ruplu. I'm out of touch. We cannot judge Indians back home based on guys settled here.'

'Perhaps, but my cousins back home are more career-driven than I am.'

Samir laughed gently at her confession before continuing to speak. 'The events leading to his arrest will be narrated tomorrow, let's focus today on his brutal death in police custody.'

'It was a dark, moonless night, still a couple of hours for dawn to break. The police woke Adesh as he slept soundly on the hard cement floor in his prison cell. They ordered him to accompany them since they were under orders to release him, but Adesh was not a moron, and it did not take long to gauge what they planned to do. Prisoners, as a rule, were never released in the dead of night, and they had assassinated a top leader in a fake encounter only a few months ago. He managed to slip a one-liner inside his inmate's pocket. The hastily scribbled note, 'They are taking me away, comrade,' still bears testimony to the police's brutality.

'It found its way to his sister after the mate was released, and had been carefully preserved in the hope that it would serve as a valuable document to indict the police. The family, however, did not feel it worthwhile to pursue the case. The new government released the prisoners but was reluctant to initiate proceedings against oppressive police officers since it was dependent on them to maintain law and order.

'The van Adesh was in screeched to a halt near a park, setting his doubts to rest. It was where Adesh and I spent our afternoons playing soccer before Adesh moved up north. He was asked to proceed home and warned not to join the movement ever again.

'Displaying an incredible presence of mind, he raced down the road in a zig-zag fashion, dodging the first few bullets and managing to leapfrog across the rusted railings of the park. A notorious officer named Dhruva Roy struck him down with his semi-automatic. The roar "Fuck you, *maddarchod*, and your brother-fucked mother" soared above the volley of shots, tearing through the silence of the night. Adesh's legs shook for a long time; fingers grasping at the freshly minted mud cakes on the grass. The white shirt and green grass was drenched in blood and the sandal remained glued to his left foot. The paranoid cops took no chances and fired conclusive bullet right into his skull from close range before ordering menials to tow away the body.'

Ruplu broke the silence. 'But how did you come to know of this?'

'We befriended pavement-dwellers who slept in the park at night. They were reluctant to open up but sang like canaries when told that Adesh was no ordinary criminal but a person who had sacrificed his life for hapless folks like them.'

'What was the explanation the police gave?'

'Killed in an encounter. The corpse lay in a mortuary for fifteen days before they handed it to his parents, covered in a white sheet, tied with thick ropes. We never got to see his face at the crematorium. Adesh's father bore a deadpan expression, but his mother erupted into loud and hysterical wails, her daughter and relatives had to hold her tight. I stood tearless at a distance, resolving to avenge his death someday.'

He noticed Ruplu's tear-stained eyes. He had not expected it.

'Even after so many years, I remember the spectacle. A few unrecognizable teens, surfacing from nowhere to wrap their comrade's body in a red cloth and sing our anthem, the "Internationale", with clasped palms. They vanished into obscurity after removing the cloth before the body was wheeled into the crematorium. I tried to catch up for I wanted the flag as a souvenir, but could not trace them.

'There were no last rites or funerals, partly to respect Adesh's beliefs and partly to follow the conventions of their Brahmo family, a monotheistic offshoot of Hinduism that shunned traditional rituals. I could not sleep for a few nights after the experience at the crematorium.'

The pithy remark that followed from Ruplu stunned him. 'During any violent revolution, both sides lose precious lives, Baba. It has happened throughout history.'

This was not the Ruplu he knew. Indeed, they rarely discussed such topics, and the only occasion they had done so was the night they were returning from the theatre. They had just watched the anti-racist movie, *Boycott*. She had pronounced that racism was an integral component of the US's prototypical militaristic and hegemonic social structure. Samir had been sleepy that night, and not in a mood to engage with her.

But with her comment, he could sense his discarded convictions contending for space with well-ensconced ones, the heart churning like a propeller.

'Your friends believed in violence. Does that mean they were not entitled to a fair trial in a democracy?' Ruplu pushed further.

'Coming to think of it, Ruplu, it's the same story everywhere. Remember the Costa Gavras movie, *Missing*? Argentina, Brazil, Peru, Chile, Colombia and the genocide in Indonesia. Nonetheless, India has maintained a semblance of democracy and it is not fair to characterize it as a banana republic—except for those two scary years under the Emergency rule. In Kolkata those days, two opposing dispensations were reacting to each other, one brutally, the other in a knee-jerk fashion.'

The whisky had loosened his tongue. He was traversing backward through time, impersonating the lost persona of yesteryears, shedding his skin. Yet he was hardly in the Kolkata of his student days.

'Despite what I just said, Adesh represents the Malcolm X's of the world.'

A memory flashed. The image of an agile eight-year-old

resting on the branch of a mango tree, reaching his hand to pull him up. The two boys were adept at plucking fruits during summer holiday afternoons when their fathers were at work and mothers were engrossed in sleazy quotidian Bengali whodunits, desperately struggling to unearth the mystery behind a fictitious murder. The flirtatious and the adulteresses were the only ones visible on the roads—somewhat seductively dressed, wearing sunglasses to hide their identities from a hypocritical society.

The plucking of mangoes resulted in a round of hard spanks on the buttocks from the owner of the trees and harder ones from their mothers. From that day, Samir was not allowed to leave the house before afternoon playtime, although Adesh's mother failed to chain him.

'Let us go back to the story,' Samir said. 'I will lose my chain of thought. More on Adesh tomorrow.'

◆

Breathlessness subsided as the tear gas shells stopped being fired. A few friends reached out to Samir to nurse his wounds. Just when the situation had stabilized, the Central Reserve Police soldiers were again hit by a powerful explosive, seriously injuring a couple of them. The situation spun out of control. Booksellers deserted their stalls without locking their wares, pedestrians scurried for cover, street dogs scampered helter-skelter, and vehicles changed gear. Outraged cops again volleyed tear gas canisters in all directions. The adjacent lanes provided some cover to the friends still stuck inside the college. The naïve cops ultimately decided to break into the college and climb the terrace from where the students had hurled the explosives, but an improvised signal triggered below led smarter activists to position themselves innocuously inside classrooms on the second floor. Not able to locate a soul, the police ran amok—whoever stood in their way was pushed, punched, kicked, and stabbed. They primarily targeted students and young professors.

'The college had not witnessed a similar incident in living memory, ironically at the same spot where the iconic freedom fighter Subhash Bose once slapped an impertinent English professor for disparaging comments against Indians.

'I had managed to move into an upright position to inspect the injury. Blood oozed through improvised bandages but I was able to lumber up. I moved, aided by friends, and we proceeded towards the staff room in the administrative block, where first-aid assistance would be available. The soldiers spotted me and pounced on my body, throwing me to the ground with such intensity that the expensive books I had borrowed from the library and the meticulous class notes lay scattered, some at distances over ten feet.

'Then came the first punch. The police were bereft of any compassion, and they continued to batter me for a good half hour, pausing intermittently to discuss strategies among themselves. I had given up hopes of survival and wished to scream, but my lungs failed me as Adesh's image flashed in my mind. I didn't know if l would meet his fate.'

'You are really lucky to have survived this incident, Baba, to be able to sit and chat with us here tonight,' Apu said.

'Sure, I am, Apu. Some are born lucky. But as I look back, those few minutes—squirming with pain, limbs numb from the thighs till the tip of the toes, the drumming at my temples, the spasms all over the body—were minutes that transformed my life. It was an unexpected encounter with my creator that strengthened my belief in a superior power. And things turned for the better.'

He remembered the current that had flowed through his spine as he lay on the very spot where the famous national leader of India had once stood up fifty years back. The yellowish-white pillars and wooden shutters in plebian green witnessed in nineteenth-century sketches grew large in his memory, accompanied by faint echoes of slogans from fellow students. It all seemed light-years away. He had been a soft target. The soldiers lacked elementary human compassion. They had been like droids from *Star Wars*, culturally irreconcilable with mild-mannered Bengalis.

'I implored with them for my dear life. A steady crackle of high-voltage electricity singed me. "Don't kill me—I am not one of them", then in Hindi, *"Humko chodo"*, *"Mein unka saath nahin hoon"*, I was fortunate that my friends were not around to witness these outpourings of defeatism.

'They dragged me across the floor, yelling at the top of their voices. "Bastard, tell us who threw those bombs?"

'A feeble voice somehow managed to utter the words: "How would I know?"

'"Bloody liar, we saw you climbing down those stairs. Now tell us, asshole, where are they?"

'I could sense them planning to push me down the flight of stairs. And just then, a miracle. I could see through my hazy eyes. A plump senior police officer from the local force was sprinting up the stairs, sweating profusely. It would have been an amusing spectacle in normal times, but now it offered only relief. I suppose the state wished to avoid casualties within the precincts of our elite college, scared that this could result in unpredictable global repercussions. Our alumni were scattered worldwide, and I later learned that the officer was an alumnus of our college. Not that the local cops would be less brutal, it was after all they who killed Adesh, but they were sensitive to local nuances. Till that point in time, unwritten codes were meticulously followed by either side.

'Our explosives were symbols of protest, not meant to strike. They, too, honoured the time-tested convention of seeking the authorities' permission before entering a temple of learning. But that day in May was not a normal day. Photographs of fifteen young corpses stacked on the ground threw traces of restraint to the winds.

'As the police officer's eyes rested on mine, I discerned a glimmer of compassion, possibly moved by the pristine innocence in my eyes. The next I heard was a loud voice. "*Chodo usko.*" "Leave the guy alone." The CRP theoretically reported to him, and he was not just keen to exercise control but demonstrate his authority within his alma mater.

'"Did you spot him hurling explosives?" he asked the junior officers, who answered. "Yes, sir, I saw him climbing down the stairs."

'"*Kuttar baccha SOB*, does that prove that he hurled those bombs?"

'The constable was stunned.

'Just then a middle-aged Professor Bose dashed out of the staff room, managing to pierce through the police barricades. He was a former freedom fighter with impeccable integrity, and tales of his valiant encounters with the British colonial police in the forties resonated across the community. He had earlier expressed a desire to engage with us on the mindless killings and about us defacing statues of national icons like Rabindranath Tagore, Mahatma Gandhi, Swami Vivekananda, and Ishwar Chandra Vidyasagar. Displaying street-smartness, as soon as his eyes strayed to a bleeding student lying helplessly on the floor, he shouted at the top of his voice. "I know this guy. He is innocent. *Oder bolo o kichu kore ni – o aamar classey chhilo ektu aagey*. Tell the CRP men that he had been attending my lectures till a while back."

'The officer, an erstwhile student of the Professor, was aware of how they lionized the man across the community. Even though he believed what the constable had stated, his experience taught him that constables rarely lied on such matters before their superiors. "I have instructed them to let him go, sir." He then pleaded in the same breath. "Can I request a small favour of you? Is it possible to find out whether my brother is safe? Shivaji Guha, a graduate student in the department of chemistry."

'The professor took a few seconds to respond. "Yes, I saw him upstairs a while back, safe and sound. No need to worry." Many years later, when I bumped into the professor at the Coffee House, he disclosed the truth to me. "I knew Shivaji well. He was a person who would remain a thousand miles away from trouble."

'As the officer heaved a sigh of relief, the professor yelled, pointing at me "Take him to the hospital."

'And that is how the men in white were ordered to carry me to the medical college a few hundred metres away. Subsequent events remain a blur. All I recall is my flailing hands and legs on a stretcher, past emaciated patients and their anxious relatives, moving through a massive hall inside the public hospital that reeked of disinfectants and urine. There were two or three patients to a bed, some were even lying on the floor where stray canines roamed fearlessly, often stopping by to suck their wounds. I was asked to lie on a bed, and they ripped off my clothes in public view. Some had gathered to witness the sight—doctors and nurses made no effort to request them to display discretion. After washing my wounds with an antiseptic liquid and cleaning sensitive lacerations with an unpleasant smelling liquid, an anti-tetanus fluid was injected, followed by bitter-tasting tablets forced down my throat with salty water. Finally, they applied a sticky fluid to the incision without any word of comfort for the attendant pain.

'The treatment succeeded in stemming the bleeding but what followed was eye-dropping. They stitched my skull without applying local anesthesia. The cure turned out to be more excruciating than the wound, like tablets of quinine to cure malaria or chemotherapy to alleviate cancer.

'Glimpses of a familiar faces from college peeked from behind a door and that provided me with some relief, although I was not well-acquainted with the persons. One of them had poured water on my head to wash off the blood.

'The doctor concluded on an insensitive note. "This is a bad gash, and you are lucky to escape with a minor concussion. Not that internal hemorrhages do not flare up later, it depends on your constitution, so one cannot be too sure. You have to remain under observation for forty-eight hours, no assurances till then." I passed out of sheer exhaustion at this stage, although technically it was induced sleep.'

A few hours later, Samir recalled that he woke up lying face down on the rear seat of a car driven by a boy whose father, a leading luminary at the bar, could wriggle him out of any situation, including driving at an age he was not entitled to. It was customary for rich kids, pining for a slice of romance, to flirt with radicals. It was trendy, cool and safe since cops would not dare to touch sons of well-connected fathers.

A stained white sheet covered his bare body. Someone had discarded the blood-soaked shirt at the hospital. He felt none of the gentle cool pre-monsoon breeze since the windows were tightly shuttered. Somewhat embarrassed, he realized that his skull was perched on the lap of one of the girls he had spotted at the hospital, the one who had poured water on his wound. She was massaging his head gently with her soft fingers. Turning his head gently upwards, a pair of eyes crossed another pair of gimlet eyes, withdrawing the moment they met.

'How are you feeling now? Does it hurt?'

'Not too good. The headache is excruciating.'

'Don't worry, you'll be fine. We are transferring you to a private nursing home and should reach there any moment. Your parents are following us. The hospital authorities contacted them as soon as numbers were provided by college authorities.'

What followed was indiscreet and inexplicable, considering his physical state. Many years later, a doctor friend assured him that sexual fantasies were not unusual, even in extreme conditions. He sincerely hoped that the woman had not noticed the manifestation of his fantasies, but a barely audible snigger conveyed otherwise. It was a day of many first encounters.

She did not make any effort to move away as he gently placed his palms on her knee, although he could feel the stiffening of her muscles. He lay motionless for the remaining part of the journey, but he could sense a change within, as if someone had unlocked the locked door to a dilapidated house after many years. Despite the pain and the spasms, he hated it when the friend driving the car announced that they had reached the nursing home.

He was wheeled away in a mobile cot past manicured gardens, marble floorings, clean surroundings, and well-dressed doctors and nurses. A feeling of guilt sparked within him, tinged with resentment at his parents for stepping in. In a somnolent state, he could catch snatches of a conversation between his father and the receptionist, under strict instructions not to accept cash as advance. His mates volunteered to stay back for the night, but Satyen assured them there was no imminent danger. The resident doctor at the hospital had categorically pronounced so.

He was woken later in the evening by a gentle nudge from the nurse to change into night garments, and he spotted his kaku and mama whispering from a corner of the room. Even in that state, the irony of the situation intrigued him since the two relatives hailed from opposite political camps. Although the middle-class society valued social etiquette and were likely to put differences aside, adherents of opposing ideological viewpoints interacting in a civilized manner amused him at that particular instant. He could not spot his parents and was too exhausted to ask for them.

He was welcomed the following morning by a chirpy burst of bright sunlight filtering through the drapes, contrasting with the gloom. A loosely-fitted nightdress brought back memories of the previous evening. The painkillers ensured that the frisson of pain remained under control despite an odd twinge and a piercing headache. The bandages served as emblems to the harsh encounter.

The aged nurse greeted him with undisguised sarcasm. *'Ki, biplob holo, gunadhar khokha?'*—or, 'What is the stage of the revolution, delinquent young man?'

Samir responded with a hearty laugh.

'Give me a moment, let me call your mother. Poor soul spent a sleepless night bearing the brunt of her son's daredevilry.'

At his request, the drapes were pulled apart, revealing a lush green garden.

Sulekha was relieved to find her son wide awake. Nonetheless, her tenor was frosty. 'How are you feeling now?'

'Fresh after a good night's sleep but the headache persists.' He jumped out of the cot and triggered a shrill cry of alarm from the nurse who had briefly stepped out of the room. 'You cannot leave the bed until the doctor examines you.'

The sight of the bedpan was revolting, as were the bitter rounds of medicines that followed. The worst was the uncanny silence in the room, finally interrupted by Samir's faint voice. 'Is Baba at the office?'

'Are you crazy, Samir? How can he go to the office after what you did to yourself? Ashim kaku is expected at any moment. He owns this nursing home.'

'Oh! That's why they refused cash last night?' He said, immediately repenting the remark after she retorted. 'Your father is a self-respecting man and will not accept charity.'

Once upon a time, the tall, slim, and dark gentleman, his Ashim kaku, used to visit home almost every day. After acquiring fame as one of the country's leading neurologists, visits grew less frequent, although the friends who had migrated from Dhaka met up more regularly at Kwality restaurant in Ballygunge. Satyen and Ashim had been classmates in school and batch mates at Dhaka University before the partition. Ashim had pursued medicine, and Satyen graduated in mathematics. Their families migrated around the same time after the partition, a few years before Samir was born. Ashim remained a bachelor due to family commitments and considered Samir like his son. But that was once upon a time.

Ashim marched in with a large briefcase after a while, a stethoscope hanging from his neck. His demeanour made the doctors and nurses stand to attention. '*Sattarer dashakkey mukti'r dashak ey porinoto kortey cheyechili*? (Transforming the '70s into a decade of liberation?)' He was referring to the ubiquitous slogan that riddled the walls of Kolkata. His wisecracks were infectious.

Abruptly, the tone in the room changed. 'The State is all-pervasive, Khokhon. You guys deviated from the declared path of an agrarian revolution. Where is the mass upsurge, young man?'

Such unsolicited advice was not unprecedented in a city remorselessly tossing and turning at the vortex of a tempest, citizens waking each morning to an assortment of dystopic and unpredictable possibilities.

CT scans and sophisticated equipment were rare in those days, and accurate diagnosis depended on the subjective intuition of the physician. Ashim ruled out a hemorrhage. It was reassuring to everyone in the room since his expertise and skills were respected and famed across the country. On a note of abundant caution, Samir was advised to stay back at the nursing home for forty-eight hours since the time of injury. Stress and excitement were to be avoided and the diet was to be kept minimal. The nurse was instructed to raise a red flag if he felt nauseous, slurred or giddy and advised to avoid excitement.

It was a blessing in disguise, since the sticky topic was avoided between the parents and the son.

He was released from the nursing home after two days. Satyen threw a tantrum to compel his friend to bill him at a discounted rate.

While limping towards the cab, the pain was present but the drunken joy of existence was an experience to cherish. He felt like the trees soaking in the first drops of rain in summer, branches in perfect synchronization, gently swinging to the breeze. Samir loved Nature and could perceive the harmony of the surroundings. He was reminded of the long queues for water at the roadside slums that dotted his locality, the six-feet by eight-feet rooms infested with mosquitoes, flies and other insects, where emaciated children ran around half-naked during annual puja festivities when the better-off clothed themselves in their best attire.

Samir was pondering on the secret source of enjoyment that kept the wretched of the earth ticking. Here he had discovered the elixir of life, the lubricants that run the human engine. In the 'commons', he saw the myriad gifts that Nature had showered them with. Sunshine, birdsongs, the romantic glow of moonlight on a clear evening, the myriad shades of petunias, a clear blue sky on an autumn afternoon, the gentle tickle of the morning dew, blazing fire from raktakarabi flowers, somnolent walks by the lakes on a deserted night, chirrup notes of the sparrow, a melancholy hum from a radio interrupting the silence of the morning, orgasmic spasms of carnal excitement after a round of jerking. These were gifts from nature and every single living creature wished to enjoy them. To enjoy them one did not require wads of cash. But common spaces were shrinking under the pulls of an acquisitive society.

Still, existence was a divine privilege, and he planned to make optimal use of the second lease of life granted by providence.

Newspapers carried passing references of the day's events, tucked in obscure corners, limited to reporting on the powerful explosions that had rocked a busy part of the city. Satyen had earlier expressed surprise that the police had not registered his presence at the government hospital despite statutory guidelines. It was crystal clear now that they wished to erase the incident for posterity. He was to be an insignificant statistic—a seventeen-year-old non-entity, badly injured, precariously poised between life and death, with no special significance for the State and most members of civic society.

His sarcastic comment, 'A free press in the world's largest democracy,' did not escape Ma's ears, but she pretended not to have heard it, opting to silently observe him gulp a glass of cocoa-laced milk that he did not seem to enjoy.

'Baba joined work the next day. Stitches were removed after three days, revealing fading blemishes. According to the nurse who untied the bandages, it could take months, even years to heal. Except for the bruise on the forehead that paled after a few days, the scars were confined to unexposed parts of the body. Pain persisted a few more days, analgesics keeping them under reasonable control. Lackluster and feeble, I napped longer hours than the usual, but the drowsiness was accompanied by depression because not a single friend had turned up. It was impossible to contact them since not many boasted telephone connections. For the fortunate few, ensuring that it remained in working order necessitated frequent visits to the telephone office to grease palms. I was relieved after a few days when I realized that Ma had sent many friends away on the plea that the doctor had advised total rest. Kaku and mama and their wives dropped by during evenings to regale me with stories from my childhood. No other relative was informed since they did not wish the incident to be the talk of the town. It is common for relatives to emerge out of the woodwork and spread the news far and wide in such situations.

'It was only on the sixth day that Baba booked a table for a celebratory dinner at the Peiping restaurant, one of the few fine outlets serving authentic Chinese food those days. It was no-brainer that he chose the ambiance of a restaurant to broach the topic.'

'"What happened that day?"

'I had already decided that it was proper to disclose the truth since he had his sources and was aware of my ideological proclivities.

'"Khokhon. This is an ultimatum. It's either us or them." I attempted to jog his memory to the deal struck a year and a half back, but it failed to have an impact.

'"We, too, participated in college politics during the early forties, responding to the call of Gandhi. We ventured out of colleges to participate in the 'Quit India' movement and were drawn towards the left after the historic Soviet victory over fascism. The situation was different then. We contested elections, chanted slogans, called for strikes on issues global, national and local, fought for students' rights, debated burning topics of the day, donated blood for freedom fighters, and collected resources for victims of natural calamities. I remember visiting remote villages during the Great Bengal Famine in 1943, not sleeping for three consecutive nights. Not that Brits were incapable of brutality, but the times were different. Bombs exploding inside the campus were unheard of, and no street fights erupted between students aligned with opposing ideologies. The situation is far more ominous today. How could I possibly anticipate the turn of events the night I made the promise?"

'A promise is a promise, Baba,' I said to him.

'Oblivious of what I had to say, he rolled on. "Remember France a couple of years back? Anarchism at its worst. Collapsed in two months. Did you ever read about Che and his band of ten revolutionaries waging a ludicrous revolutionary war in Bolivia? Ashim was asking you, where is the mass upsurge? Have you ever visited the labour colonies a stone's throw from home? You would find out if you did that almost all of them remain with the mainstream left parties. You have not realized that the village of Naxalbari, a few pockets of Midnapore district, and isolated tribal areas in the state of Andhra can be compared to specks of sand in a vast desert. You guys are waging a futile war, Khokhon."

'Finally, the eternal parent surfaced. "Youngsters of your generation are so self-centred. You spare no thought for parents. Not that you are unaware that your mother was compelled to remove her uterus after delivering you and today you are our sole raison d'etre." It was a curious blend of autocracy and mawkish sentiment, but Baba had played his cards well.

'To cut a long story short, he visited the college and met our Principal the next day, requesting him to keep a stern watch over me, which the keen acolyte of the establishment readily consented to.'

Ruplu thundered. 'You accepted their dictum without a murmur of protest?'

A nebulous cloud hovered over Samir's mind. Did her choked tone stem from a love for the revolution that had failed to take off? Or was she overwhelmed by the clinical narration of a painful day in his life?

Struggling for words to reply to the unanticipated query, Neelu's narration of another anecdote diverted the attention of the room. Unwittingly, she had deflected the topic, perhaps setting Ruplu's query aside.

She told them about an incident a few years back, sometime

in 2012, when the couple had gone to College Street to procure copies of recent Bengali titles. The very sight of the place depressed Samir. Pavement shops with on exorbitantly priced handbooks that guaranteed sure success in examinations. Conspicuous by their absence were rare copies of a Mark Twain or a Charles Dickens, biographies of historical figures like the Nawab Siraj-Ud-Doula published in the nineteenth or early twentieth century, and texts on existentialism or books by Derrida. Wistfully sipping a mango juice at the famous Paramount restaurant across the road, he expressed a desire to visit his alma mater to find out whether it had managed to buck the general trend. The security supervisor informed them that admission to the college was nowadays restricted to students, staff and professors. The others, including alumni, had to procure passes, and were not allowed on holidays. One glance at the aged couple, however, convinced the supervisor to allow a quick tour, accompanied by one of the guards.

The college had, in the meanwhile, acquired the status of an autonomous university. Its premises appeared squeaky-clean, the buildings were freshly painted and not one indigenous breed of canine hung around. The stinking toilets of yore were cleaner, if not dazzling, Promodeda's canteen was brighter, the auditorium plush and the library colossal by their standards. While passing the spot he once lay, soaked in blood, precariously hanging on a slender thread between life and death, he had abruptly bent forward like a modern version of Sherlock Holmes, without the magnifying glass, to inspect the ground from close quarters. Out of sheer boredom, the security guard started scratching his crotch immodestly, compelling an embarrassed Neelu to proceed on a short walk down the corridor.

An ambivalent deist like Neelu failed to perceive the reason Samir had peered at the floor. He had wished to visualize the painful event with his inner eyes rather than indulge in a crazy and stupid endeavour to trace bloodstains after forty long years. Neelu remained silent, not inclined to enter into an argument at three in the morning, but Ruplu countered with a terse comment on the absurdity of his quest.

Apu's statement reflected his generic attitude to life. 'I think Dadu did the right thing. Coming to think of it, we would not be sitting here today if a deadlier incident had taken place later.'

Samir almost choked.

'Self-centred Republican brat!' Ruplu sneered at Apu. It was taken in stride as a banter, not requiring any meaningful riposte.

'Well, guys, this is the end of my anecdote. I had in any case planned to disclose it after you were both grown up. After filling up a bundle of forms, I got admission to the Imperial College in London. After going through my school-leaving mark sheet, one of my distant cousins, a lecturer at the college, assured Baba that obtaining admission would not pose a challenge, although he ruled out financial support. Baba sold off his landed property that had appreciated over the years, and I accepted his decision without a murmur of protest—eager to escape their clutches for an independent life.

'I was bundled into an Air India flight after a couple of months, and at an unearthly hour, leaving friends, college, professors, relatives, parents, and my city to fend for themselves. I recall weeping inconsolably at receding lights. The rest, as they say, is history.'

The narration ended with a triumphal expression. He was thankful to Neelu for inadvertently diverting the topic from Ruplu's innocuous query, which would have necessitated another yarn. Samir derived his values in life opportunistically. Like Yudhishthira, he was opposed to brazen untruths; but a few white lies were cool.

'Well, folks, have nothing much to add now. For Ruplu's sake, I will take an hour tomorrow on the sequence of events leading to Adesh's arrest, and the better part of the evening will be devoted to her.'

She was baffled. 'Are you kidding? What are you planning to devote to me?'

He shot back. 'I'm aware of bits and pieces of an incident in your life and please do not ask me how. Tomorrow, we would like to hear more about it.'

The silence lasted a while, culminating in a reluctant nod. It coincided with the cuckoo chiming thrice to penetrate the eerie silence of the night. As he bent forward to kiss her forehead, Neelu said something perplexing.

'Samir, tell me one thing, do you remain in touch with the friend who accompanied you to the nursing home?'

'The last time I remember speaking with her was when I was in college. Why do you ask?'

'Just curious. I would have considered her special in life, a friend to stick to for a lifetime.'

'We lost touch after I crossed shores. You forget there were no emails, WhatsApp, or Facebook those days.'

As they proceeded towards their respective bedrooms, Samir was in two minds about whether to switch on the television. He finally opted to catch up with the news in the morning and dedicate the following day to scholarly dissections by analysts and experts, accompanied by snippets of a victory that was, by now, a foregone conclusion.

The very act of recalling his days had been pleasurable, as if a load had been lifted off his shoulders. However, while tossing and turning through the night, Neelu's innocuous query occupied his mind, even as she slept soundly like a log. Since yogis desist from soporific pills, he tried his best to deflect the strong urge. Either it was the whisky consumed after a long time or the pervasive feeling of guilt.

The incident narrated this evening had neither altered the trajectory nor marked an inexorable discontinuity in his life. It could be compared with a border skirmish presaging a full-fledged war. He had left out another episode in his life, told a white lie like Yudhisthira. The day that was instrumental in his leaving his country and a day that he sincerely hoped would remain buried under the sands of time. Never to surface again.

There were a few concocted details in his narrative too, but not material ones. He vowed to come clean someday.

Samir descended into a deep slumber only after the first rays of ochre sunlight were visible in the horizon. He dreamt of his car's wheels stuck deep inside the heart of Los Angeles.

CRAWLING BACK TO NORMALCY

17 May 2014

The headache pierced through his skull the following morning. It was ages since he had experienced a crapulous morning and he had forgotten how one felt.

In two minds, whether to yell for Neelu or fetch the aspirin pills himself, he opted for the latter. 9.20 a.m. on the bedside timepiece. It was not too late. He had snatched a few winks but he struggled to recall the precise hour he had fallen asleep. Perhaps it was around six but, it did not feel like he had slept for just three hours. Dismissing the piece of detail as inconsequential, he opted to focus on the panacea.

He found a cryptic and carelessly scribbled note on a dirty piece of yellow paper. It had been carefully placed under a book on the side table. 'Off to Ralphs.'

There was also a cup of tea, bundled with two loaves of pita bread, a boiled egg, and a large slice of his birthday cake on a plate meticulously kept in a corner of the oven. It took a while for him to locate the aspirin bottle, and after gulping down a couple of pills, he opted to settle in the lounge after sneaking a peek into the kids' rooms. He did not expect to find them awake—their circadian cycles were longer during weekends.

The hangover did not take long to subside. Despite nursing a doubt on whether it was the placebo effect, his yoga instructor was accorded the benefit of the doubt. Usually, headaches took the entire day to subside, despite copious doses of aspirin, and he deserved a sumptuous meal at the earliest. After wasting a few minutes browsing through the novel Neelu was reading the previous evening, he was reminded of elections back in India. It triggered a rush for the remote. He was subjected to an enervating wait for the advertisements to end.

When the news crawler finally appeared, he was at a loss on how best to express the tsunami of euphoria building up inside as he impulsively leaped on to the divan. Oblivious of the potential danger to his damaged knee, he bounced up and down like a recoil spring, accompanied by the whoop with widely spread-out hands, transporting himself to the stadium of his childhood days, amidst the rapturous soccer crowds back in Kolkata.

Samir's family, hailing from the eastern section of Bengal, bore the moniker, 'Bangals' and were fanatical supporters of the East Bengal team. He had often gone to the stadium with Baba as a kid, retaining the habit even after Satyen stopped. Soccer was embedded in the zeitgeist of the seventies. Migrants who had been forced to flee East Pakistan slowly marked their presence after two decades of struggle at the margins. The opportunities they found were in the form of stable government and private sector jobs, teaching assignments, and options for entrepreneurship, although unemployment was still high. Repeated setbacks had toughened them, (like the African-Americans here in the US) and their effete counterparts from West Bengal proved no match inside the stadium. Emblematic red and yellow flags were perpetually visible across the city's southern suburbs, symbolizing the resurgence of their collective pride. A big match was an occasion to proclaim their group identity through full-throated roars rocking the stadium. More often, their team emerged victorious over their rivals, the Mohun Bagan Club.

An unkempt Apu rushed in almost immediately. 'What's going on? Have you lost your sanity? You scared me, Baba.'

'Take a look at the television.'

Despite Apu's modicum of interest in Indian politics under the influence of Samir, a Saturday morning was not the opportune time to get overly enthused, and his lukewarm response disappointed Samir. 'You are one hell of a supporter, Baba. Read it on my newsfeed early in the morning. Conveys mixed messages. On one hand, there is a threat of religious intolerance and on the other hand, it opens the doors to implementing long-awaited economic reforms. However, your somersault amazes me after the narrative you shared last night.'

Samir gave him an insouciant jerk of the shoulders and a dismissive response. 'I have moved on with age. That forty years back, the context was different, and the convictions emanated from another era. Whatever our views, we need to uncork the bubbly tonight. Can you ring Ma and request her to purchase a couple of Dom Perignon's on her way home?'

'Baba, I'm unable to come to terms with your softness to bigotry. It seems you have an innate inclination towards extremist ideologies, swinging from one pole to another. Were you not a victim of racial hatred in Memphis and Philadelphia? The core philosophy of the party you support today hinges on polarizing the nation,' Apu argued.

This was hardly the day to be reminded of the incident on his way to Philadelphia. Or worse, Memphis.

'Where is Ma?' Apu asked Samir after a while.

'Off for the week's purchases. Left early today, normally leaves around ten.'

'You must be in cuckoo land. Do look at the clock. It's nearing noon!'

'Gosh! I remember planning to get batteries for the bedside timepiece on my way home yesterday.' There was a distraught expression on his face at the thought of the battery and the drier. Despite leaving office early, he had forgotten about it. It concerned him, although Neelu had fortunately not mentioned it. Were these early symptoms of Alzheimer's?

Apu wore a bemused look. 'She is usually done by eleven. Let's buzz her.'

'Is Ruplu awake?'

'Yup, in the bathroom. I have to rush after speaking to Ma. Your Balvenie was strong, I dare say.'

'I realized it in the morning. Let's not blame the poor bottle since both of us lost count after a couple.'

'It is always an issue when you drink neat.'

'I diluted mine each time with soda and ice, and you were the guy who mixed most of them, scatterbrain!'

Neelu picked up on the first ring. She had stepped into Starbucks and was expected in half an hour. She had bumped into an old pal, and on hearing the news from Apu, Samir made a cheeky comment. 'Hope it's not a long-lost boyfriend.' It brought in the first hearty laugh of the morning.

'Absent-minded, insecure old man! She will join you in a while,' he said to his father.

'Next time you call me an old man, Apu, I'll...'

More boisterous laughter.

◆

From an Undisclosed Location

December 2019

The lunch ultimately arrived. The bowl of rice was sufficient for a ten-year-old, and a tinier bowl that sat next to it contained a handful of vegetables, floating in a watery liquid that smelt of kerosene. Samir was engrossed in a trance, and he had not noticed the man who had kept it there. A bunch of carefree chimpanzees outside were jumping dexterously across the branches. The green grass bore the stamp of freshness.

Dark memories of the dreadful night at Memphis flashed.

He was returning from a pub to celebrate the successful completion of the penultimate phase of a challenging project, feeling on top of the world because the project manager had officially acknowledged his contribution.

THE UGLY FACE OF RACISM

1980

Walking down Union Street, Samir had spotted a gang of plucky African American youngsters on the other side of the road.

'Salaam alaikum, bro, rednecks are out there!' they called out. He was unable to comprehend their accent, but he glanced over his shoulders long after they had passed by, a cautious habit he had acquired from his radical days back home.

They had just wanted to caution him.

The danger lurked at the corner before the final turn for his apartment—half a dozen well-built hunks, rippling muscles and six-pack abs, were reclining on the wooden steps of a house that appeared dilapidated from the outside. They were with a couple of giggling dames, who seemed euphoric like hunters spotting a game after a period of anticipation.

'There's a brownie for you, Martin,' one said.

With matronly gestures and a long hairless arm, the ruffian had the appearance of a malevolent bullterrier. His colourful baguettes and dandy shirt sparkled even on the dimly lit street.

A pansy voice called to Samir. 'Hey, what you doin' brownie?' It pierced the silence of the still night. He reeked of foul breath from alcohol and a familiar stink, one Samir was unable to identify.

Samir pointed towards his apartment with a straight face. 'Letting our hair down to celebrate success! I am on an assignment here and am putting up in the transit apartment around that corner.'

It was futile because they had not even cared to process his words. Before he could gauge the situation, a blunt object landed on his skull. He was face down on the road. A couple of twenty-dollar notes tumbled out of his pocket, and he gingerly picked them up before they could lay their hands on it. He sprang up and dodged them like a soccer centre-forward, confident of making it to the apartment, where the security guards would offer him protection.

The toughest one turned out to be swifter than Samir, grabbing him by the corner of his leather jacket. He managed to drag himself a few feet before falling flat on the face near a concrete wall—the familiar façade of his apartment visible on the horizon. Although they kept slapping at him mercilessly, he protected his skull with his bare hands.

Noticing the guy with the doggish face breaking a liquor bottle, it struck him that he had to get away, now or never. Mustering courage, he grabbed a protruding brick on the wall, staggered up, punched the one closest to him hard on the groin, and trotted a hundred metres through a gap, making a sharp turn into an apartment complex. This one had the stamp of affluence, unlike the one he was putting up in. Noticing a garbage bin staring at him from a corner, he bounced straight into it, the pole-vaulting skills acquired in school coming in handy.

A mild cut on the right finger drew his attention to a couple of empty beer bottles stacked in an untidy heap. He was startled out of his wits by the fluttering of a pair of pigeons, and Adesh's bright face appeared in a flash of memory. The image of a lifeless body covered in a white cloth, tied in position with the help of long, sturdy ropes. He could taste the blood oozing from the cut and he heard the illusory staccato of bullets reverberating. He managed some yogic breathing, a technique taught by his father at a young age, but it failed to calm him.

THE UGLY FACE OF RACISM

Just then, a sweet face triggered memories of another day and it inspired him to go down fighting. He would resist the ruffians with every fiber of his being. He crouched in pin-drop silence with a couple of beer bottles held loosely in his trembling hands, his face soaked in blood, and he recited a quick prayer to his lord, Shiva.

Apprehensive that this complex may have security guards, the bullies had halted at the gates. Although this complex had no sentinel, a few inhabitants—attracted by the commotion of heavy footsteps and wild screams—dialed for the cops.

Samir scrambled out at the sound of their loud chatter and loud hoots. At the sight of the spectacle of a man covered with blood, stale food and sticky tampons, there were humiliating peals of laughter.

Initially, it was difficult to convince the cops that it had not been one of those drunken brawls, but that the pungent odour emanated from the spirit the goons had poured over his head. Only when the occupants, incensed with menacing rednecks disturbing the peace and tranquility of the neighbourhood, spoke up for him that first aid was administered, an ambulance called for and painkillers offered at the hospital. The relief evaporated when the lieutenant, with a deadpan expression, arrived to escort him home.

He scrambled into the van, weighed down under the six stitches they had administered at the hospital, eager to go to bed.

The project manager contacted their headquarters in Cincinnati the next day. They stuck to the organizational policy and advised him to return to base. The project was nearing completion, and they could manage without him. Although they displayed concern for his safety, he was saddened since he earnestly wished to see the project through. Somewhat unfairly, he imagined that a fair-skinned colleague would not have been recalled home but provided with a car to commute to the office or shifted to an apartment downtown beyond the reach of those goons.

After so many years, what burrowed incessantly through his soul, the thought growing like termites, was the brutal reminder that the thugs had not bothered to grab his overflowing wallet. They were after him and not after his money—like they had been after the Mahatma who was dumped out of a train in South Africa, eighty years ago. To his white colleagues at Cincinnati, it was a criminal act not attributable to racism—according to them, a guy with fair skin would have suffered a similar fate. He had just been foolish enough to venture out alone during late hours in a city like Memphis, notorious for its criminality. An insensate friend even sneered, 'Come on, Sam, you are not Mahatma Gandhi.'

◆

The Incident in Philadelphia

September 2001

A junior colleague, Jenny, had joined him from New York on a late afternoon train to Philadelphia to attend a professional conference many years later. After the long flight from LA, Samir was dozing and found it tough to reciprocate her banter. She was one of the brighter members of his team and was based out of New York. She was intrinsically chatty and chirpy but to the cynical Samir, it seemed like a vain attempt to impress her boss.

A bunch of ragged-looking guys joined them after a while. Samir politely pointed out that a shoe was brushing his trousers, but the request triggered a flurry of offensive, racist and misogynist comments.

THE UGLY FACE OF RACISM

His colleague was terrified, but Samir decided to ignore their remarks about Indians who snatched call-centre jobs despite their hilarious accents and pronunciations. The conversation soon degenerated into snide comments on garlic-breaths, stinking armpits, and eating from the hands of white girls.

The hatred was partly racist and partly emanated from class inferiority. Since the other passengers preferred to sleep, read or gaze outside, he sprung out of his seat, located the middle-aged ticket collector, and fetched the tough man who threatened to throw the ruffians out at the next station. Although they remained subdued for the remaining journey, lewd comments resurfaced after they had grabbed their luggage to disembark.

Samir and his colleague later regretted the mistake of taking a break on the platform. As the train resumed its journey and the compartment passed them by, he was thrown off-guard when a cup of hot coffee was hurled his way, which he managed to duck at the nick of the moment. It was not the right move because she was standing right behind him. It was lucky that it missed her face, but her expensive suit was soiled with dark stains.

The comparison of this incident with the one in Memphis was facile. Outsourcing was not widespread during those days. Unlike the dark alleys of Memphis, it was broad daylight, and he was able to witness their venom-spouting faces, wondering whether they despised the wealthy 1 per cent who grabbed 70 per cent of the nation's wealth with equal intensity. He was also curiously sympathetic. They were not brutal goons like the Memphis gang, but victims of a cruel economic system where job losses were integral components of one's existence. Perhaps they had lost their jobs to outsourcing. He had experienced pangs of joblessness and knew what it meant to an individual. Lacking the qualifications and experience, they had probably been left high and dry.

He was in Philadelphia when 9/11 happened. A two-day professional conference was to be hosted there, and they were invited by a vendor who had offered to sponsor the conference charges and lunch, and their company had agreed to bear the lodging and travel expenses. The first two days passed peacefully, and the proceedings of the concluding day had barely commenced when the disastrous piece of news trickled in. Participants were devastated, milling around the massive television in the hall.

Samir was reminded of his pet topic. He loved waxing on the myriad temples destroyed in his country during the medieval era and he was overjoyed that it was now a collective war. He did not venture to express his feelings as he was uncertain about how the stunned crowd around him would react. Seeing the twin towers crumble on TV reminded him of the destruction of Nalanda University a few centuries back.

He had not noticed when Jenny came to stand beside him with a petrified look, shoulders shaking like that of a spaniel.

He was genuinely concerned. 'Did you call home?'

'Was not able to get through. The lines are jammed.'

'Tried texting?'

'Yes.'

'Why don't you send a mail? It should reach.'

'I don't know my dad's official email address. Mom doesn't have one yet.'

'Where do your folks live?'

'Miles away from the Trade Center, but dad goes to work only a couple of blocks away.'

'Please pray. I feel he is safe. But do keep trying.' Samir tried his best to assure her.

'If you do not mind, can I settle in your room for some time?'

'Sure.' He folded a warm blanket on her as she lay down in utter fatigue. He walked out into the lobby downstairs. The

THE UGLY FACE OF RACISM

conference organizers announced the termination of the day's proceedings, promising to mail the presentations in due course.

In California, Neelu, Apu and Ruplu huddled together. Their schools had let them go and they were desperately trying to get in touch with Samir. Only Neelu had a cell phone and got through after half an hour, requesting him not to move out of the hotel since they expected more attacks. There had been strikes on Pentagon. Samir said, 'Yes, we are watching that on TV,' he commented.

He could not resist a reference to his pet topic. 'Yes, we are watching it on TV, this is what India faced for centuries.'

Neelu did not seem too interested.

Good news for Jenny filtered in a couple of hours later.

The instruction from the HQ at San Jose was categorical: stay put at the hotel till further advice. The hours were primarily spent inside the hotel, and he ventured out only once for lunch. He could discern the menacing stares, some people spinning around with threatening looks. The entire city was riddled with national flags, and it sported a surreal appearance. How could it be the same Philadelphia where the Universal Declaration of Human Rights was signed and sealed?

She advised him to shave off his goatee and stick to the hotel.

The next few days, the country saw attacks on Asians of all kinds. One of his San Jose friends was manhandled.

They left the city two days later.

Luckily, they were situated more than two thousand miles apart.

Neelu put in her papers after a few months—the mail was curt and official.

◆

From an Undisclosed Location

December 2019

Darkness softly engulfed the surroundings, an hour early because of the dense clouds. The birds were retreating into their nests. Why was the human race different? Why are we always at each other's throats? Why are we the cause of so much unhappiness to fellow humans?

Was it ever possible to achieve utopia? The utopia for which he had been willing to sacrifice his life once upon a time, seemed to recede with every passing day. Why did he have to go through so much suffering in life? Why was he incarcerated in this jungle? Was it just a nightmare?

All of a sudden, Samir lost the desire to live.

SATYEN HAS HIS WAY

14 May–15 May 1971

In the evening at Peiping restaurant, Satyen told his son that he was hell-bent on requesting their principal to keep an eye on him. Dr Pratyush Mukherjee would likely agree. He was a well-connected individual, and the world was aware of his proximity to the powers that be. If he agreed to play ball, Khokhon could be kept out of harm. He was confident that he could be convinced to shy away from a showdown, unwilling to sacrifice a comfortable lifestyle in decent surroundings, affectionate parents, financial security and a bright future.

Satyen had to merely remain stern and uncompromising, initially utilizing his persuasion skills. He had succeeded many times before with Samir and with his comrades at the office.

There were three clear options before Samir: defy his father, unconditionally surrender, or continue activities on the sly. He was eagerly looking forward to more activism, and was fueled by a resolve to avenge a close friend's death, so the second option was not in his mind while returning home in a cab.

The third one was out of reach because Dr Mukherjee and his mini-Gestapo had their tentacles spread all over the college, assisted by a competent and avuncular Dipak da who maintained cordial relations with both authorities and students. He was a maverick of sorts and could boast of an uncanny ability to remember students who crossed the portals ten years ago by name and face, some by their roll numbers.

Samir tossed and turned on the cot and conjured up a fourth

alternative. He would surrender, but ponder on it for a month. An acceptable solution would surely emerge by then, although the silent voice at the back of his mind mumbled that he was fooling himself.

It was his seventeenth birthday, and the clock loudly announced that it was time for his mother to troop in with a bowl of payesh. A brand-new sling bag and a grey pullover with a price tag lay on the cot. Birthday gifts! A convenient carry bag, ubiquitous among the younger generation, a fancy item for women, capable of carrying a host of items ranging from books and notebooks to pens, pencils, tiffin-boxes, and even clothes for changes. There were ethnic varieties like his mother's one, embellished with embroidery and artwork. They came in shimmering hues, buttressed by stones, twigs, and beads in various sizes: small, medium, large, and extra-large. From a vehicle of convenience and couture, it had transformed into a signature item for bearded radicals.

Ma gave him his morning cup of tea and a bowl filled to the brim with payesh. 'Happy birthday, Samir, and wish you a long life. Do wear the sweater and check whether it fits you. Be careful not to damage the price tag. Just in case.'

'No need to, have noted the size. Thanks a ton, Ma. And for the jhola. Must have caused a heartbreak to lose yours, loaded with nostalgia.'

'By the grace of my goddess, we have got you back, Khokhon. I have no regrets about the jhola but I do want to make a sincere request to you to not let us down again.'

'Is Baba back from the fish market?'

'He's just returned, relishing his second cup of tea in the bedroom. You may speak to him.'

After accepting the birthday greetings and touching his feet, Samir conveyed his decision with a caveat. Their conversation would commence at nine. It was not a challenge since the Principal was known to reach the office by then, and the discussions were not expected to last more than half an hour. Few students would be around as classes commenced at ten.

'I'm game, Khokhon. Why would I desire to let you down before your friends? But have you realized that we have just got half an hour left to start the journey then?'

It took a heroic effort to take his eyes off the fateful spot. Perhaps the challenges faced by revolutionaries were not meant for namby-pambies like him brought up in a protective environment.

Dr Mukherjee was sifting through files with the assistance of his able assistant. They were greeted warmly as he rose from his seat as a mark of respect for the middle-aged Satyen.

His initial remark was directed at Samir. 'Welcome back, young man, I was planning to visit your residence this evening.'

Samir, like many others, bore an intense hatred towards the pompous gentleman with a glib tongue and a propensity for charades like his compatriots. He said nothing as the man continued. 'Hope you feel better now. I was out of station for a few days and returned the day before, planned to visit you yesterday, but your classmates informed us that you had been advised total rest.'

Samir could not resist a snide comment. 'Sir, none of my classmates visited me.'

The salvo misfired. Satyen corrected him. 'He is right, Khokhon. Many of them did land up at the nursing home, others dropped by at home. It was Ma who did not wish you to speak to them since the doctor had warned against excitement of any kind.'

His relief at the news did not escape the roving eyes of Dr Mukherjee.

'What took place can be denounced only in the strongest

of terms. I would have stopped the cops if I was in town and apprehended the rogues who hurled bombs from the terrace. Poor guy faced the brunt of a backlash. I am told the gundas promptly disappeared. Was sharing a drink last evening with Suprio who expressed his strong disapproval of what the cops did to Samir.'

Instead of appreciating the Principal's gesture, Samir felt like whacking him where it hurt most—on the forehead. He had a massive goose egg, popularly known as an 'aab' in Bengali, adorned his forehead, and some students had coined a pejorative nickname for the man: 'Aabu'. He had been singled out for his sycophancy to people who mattered. Suprio Roy was his batchmate, a central minister currently accountable for the state of West Bengal. Cynics felt he had climbed the career ladder because of Suprio.

Lighting his pipe to exhale fragrant rings of varied shapes, the Principal settled his eyes in the direction of Dipak da. However, the comment was directed at Satyen.

'Do not worry, Satyen babu, we shall protect your son to the best of our abilities. Provided he dissociates himself from those ruffians. In any case, the summer vacation commences within a week so there is some breathing space.'

Dipak da's nod confirmed his intention to help Samir follow through. The conversation lasted around fifteen minutes, and Satyen left after copious reminders to Samir to return home as soon as the day's sessions were over.

Samir felt the need to sensitize Dipak da. He was squatted inside his tiny cubicle with a pensive look, and when he saw Samir, the wise man immediately realized why he was there. His keen wit, sharp brains and colossal memory were frequent topics of discussion among students who commiserated with a genius of sorts who was wasting his precious years as a clerk.

'Do not worry, not a soul will come to know of our conversation today. Samir, I'll tell you what. I respect the ideals you guys stand for but am helpless since a government servant is tied to rigid service rules. Nonetheless, my sincere advice to you is to focus on your studies till you pass out, young man.'

'Dipak da, there is another reason I dropped by. I lost my books and papers in the melee and I desperately require a copy of the weekly timetable.'

'You lost nothing, buddy. I collected your belongings after they carried you to the hospital.'

As he opened the closet behind him, Samir noticed his jhola, his books, class notes and a blood-stained handkerchief. The man never ceased to amaze. 'I'm at a loss for words of gratitude. Ma will be thrilled since the jhola was a present from Baba a few days after their wedding, a souvenir from the past.'

Dipak da's amused look at the unrestrained statement left Samir embarrassed.

'Tumi khub saral, Samir. A naïve simpleton. Try to maintain this laudable trait for the rest of your life,' he said to him.

His eyes brightened at the sight of the timetable. After thanking the gentleman once again, Samir rushed towards the Baker building, where physics lectures were conducted. The first scheduled lecture was from AKR, a Princeton PhD and a doyen of Theoretical Physics. Even students not pursuing physics as a discipline were willing to donate an arm and a leg to attend a couple of them. Lumbering down the tall flight of stairs, he realized that the nagging pain had stuck like a leech and the chemist's shop opened only at eleven.

And then the encounter happened. It was a defining moment in his life.

◆

From an Undisclosed Location

December 2019

A momentous split second later...

Here was a sliver of time frozen in rigor mortis, encased subliminally like a diamond blazing in an underground coal mine.

◆

When Samir woke up from the deep trance, he felt exhausted, drained and petrified. Darkness had engulfed the surroundings, and not a bird sang, not a leaf stirred. Only the croaking frogs seemed to announce that there was life around him, that he was not alone in this vast universe.

It was naïve to expect the doors to be left unlocked. But still he checked. Criminals do commit mistakes.

The vegetables they had left was insufficient for him. It reminded of his stint at the night school. The poor of India survived on rice. Vegetables and pulses rarely covered a quarter of the plate and they compensated for it with a generous sprinkling of salt. Those were the underdogs whom Samir and his comrades had once resolved to liberate from the bondage of poverty.

The brutes had not bothered to visit him nor wake him up. He was certain that a request to warm the food would be met with a kick on his balls.

Hunger was all that seemed to matter and the cold rice and vegetable curry tasted like manna from heaven. He devoured it like a tiger feeding on a young deer. Needing a wash and a trip to the bathroom, he banged loudly on the door. The tall man carrying a gun entered.

Perhaps the other one had returned home to his family. Samir also had one, a family likely at their wit's end by now.

Should he land a solid kick on the man's scrotums and snatch away his revolver? Make such a desperate attempt? No, the moment had not yet arrived. There would certainly be a few of his compatriots around. And he was not even aware where they had dumped him nor did he have a clue about the path to the nearest village or police station. He was situated outside the boundaries of civilization.

'You said your boss was expected in the afternoon.'

'He is a busy man. Not an asshole like you, sleeping away.'

'What do you expect me to do? Masturbate? You did not even provide a newspaper or a TV set or a magazine to kill time with.'

'Shut up! Banchot! Do not answer back.'

Samir received a punch on the stomach followed by a tight slap on his face. This one was harder, and it flung him onto the cot.

'To answer your question, he is expected early tomorrow morning. One more word and I will bugger you.' The man continued. 'As it is, I feel horny. Have not visited my wife for a week.' Then he pinched him harshly on his cheeks.

'Accompany me to the bathroom.'

Samir wept bitterly. 'I am an innocent person. You guys have kidnapped the wrong guy. If money is what you are after, tell me. We are not very rich, although we live in the United States. But I will try my best.'

His peals of laughter were boisterous yet cruel, and they lasted for a few minutes. Samir smelt raw country liquor on his breath.

'Enough nonsense, *buro bhaam*. Old hag. Enough nonsense from you. Now, wear your slippers and follow me to the bathroom.'

KNOWING A WIFE'S MIND

17 May 2014

There was deafening silence at the dining table. A dour-faced Neelu responded brusquely to queries, reticent to express herself beyond singular syllables.

Ruplu had turned introspective, arguably for a different reason. Sensing the tension in the air, Apu found it tough to revert to his gregarious self, although he ultimately succeeded in tearing through the imbroglio.

'So, Baba, the Federal Appeals Court upheld Rajat Gupta's conviction. What do you have to say to this now?' Apu kept staring at his father.

Samir was equally assertive. 'Was desperately hoping they would reverse the judgment.'

The passion in Apu's voice was palpable. 'It is an open-and-shut case. Told you right at the beginning.'

Samir sounded like an attorney. 'I still maintain, Apu, that the colour of his skin was the clincher. Folks have been let off many times in the past on charges of insider trading. Nor do I agree with your opinion on it being an open-and-shut case. The causality was never established. There was no cash transfer to any of his accounts. Where is the pecuniary gain?'

Ruplu deftly managed to divert the topic from corporate honchos. She hated them all with her heart and soul. 'They dare not punish errant financial sector executives responsible for millions of job losses across the planet. Did you read Krugman's analysis today? The current pace of recovery is unsustainable unless it is accompanied by higher taxes and fiscal consolidation which the government is reluctant to do. Rajat Gupta is just a scapegoat.'

The last sentence sounded like a non-sequitur to Samir.

'A recovery is round the corner. IT companies have started hiring. Apple, I know for sure. And credible buzz is that IBM and Microsoft are also on a spree. Today's *Los Angeles Times* carries the cheer that retail sales are picking up.'

Samir was reminded of what Daniel had to say yesterday. 'High time we left the aftermaths of the recession behind us. A grim situation persists in the heartland.'

Apu was rearing to strike back at Ruplu. Her dogmatism was the expression of an egoistic personality, and he was determined not to allow her to get away. 'For Krugman, Keynes is the gospel of truth. Sufficient stimulus has been provided; markets now need to function in an unfettered manner,' he said to her.

He heard a barely audible mumble between her teeth. 'Market fundamentalist.'

It was countered immediately with a riposte: 'Pompous left-liberal.'

Samir enjoyed their academic barbs, but the non-responsive Neelu bothered him. The only trained economist in the family, she was in the habit of butting into any discussion straddling the subject in which she had majored. Although she was text-bookish in Samir's assessment and her knowledge was confined to silos. While conversing with Apu, he had once casually turned the gaze in her direction to catch the furtive glance at him, and she had been compelled to turn her face away in embarrassment.

Attempting to draw her in, he changed the topic. 'The ilish maach was fabulous. Both the manner of cooking and the quality of fish. Purchased from that Bangladeshi outlet?'

Samir's intense contempt for the community had diluted over

the years, but it occasionally surfaced with a vengeance. It was a trait acquired from his folks with roots in erstwhile East Pakistan who had been compelled to abandon their ancestral homes after the partition. Facing disapproval at home, he took special care to tone down disparaging comments these days. But deeply ingrained prejudices were tough to dislodge. Apu's comments about fundamentalism in the morning were still fresh in his mind, and he controlled himself.

Neelu rarely displayed uncivil behaviour, and he could only remember her refusing to respond to his queries when she announced her intention to leave him for a break. Proud of her upbringing, she loved to wear it as a badge of honour.

'A different one,' she finally said. 'Joyita mentioned the shop at Paromita's party last weekend when you men walked into the adjoining room. It's cheaper too.'

Then she grew quiet. The reason still eluded him; he expected a lot more talk from a lady in the habit of turning loquacious whenever Apu and Ruplu were around.

'What time do we assemble, Baba? I have tons of testing to do. And you need to catch up on sleep. You look weak.' Apu said. Ruplu added, 'I have a paper to submit by Tuesday and will be meeting my supervisor at a café a few miles away. Will be back by six. Can I take your car, Ma?'

Samir despised conversing on official matters at home but decided to make an exception. '*Aarey, aar bolish na*, there is this newly inducted Director who believes there are dozens of AI apps floating in the market. Must I waste my Saturday afternoon researching to prove him wrong? I doubt whether my constitution will withstand it. I must have slept for four hours last night, it was the whisky.'

Apu laughed. 'We have named such guys "compulsively erudite". They never let go, even without the faintest knowledge of a topic. Have scores of them at our office, predominantly the powerful ones who get away with throwing their weight around.'

Samir was disappointed that, for Apu, it was a personality trait—independent of parameters of nationality, complexion, or ethnicity, a mere manifestation of power-play. The youngster, a second-generation immigrant, was situated miles away from the glass ceiling and took a lot for granted. Not that tech companies were not different workspaces, but they too had displayed chunks of biases experienced during the early part of his career. At the same time, he sincerely hoped that Apu's experiences would turn out to be less painful than his own.

'I do not wish to be disturbed before seven,' Neelu explained. 'Could catch only three hours of sleep last night.'

Samir concurred. 'Let us assemble at eight then, Neelu. After completing my short anecdote on Adesh, it is Ruplu's turn all the way. Will try and close by eleven.'

He was confused by his wife's uncanny behaviour and unseeing looks and he suppressed the intense desire for a freshly brewed cup of Earl Grey. While dispersing, Samir was in two minds about whether to probe the cause of Neelu's sudden reticence, ultimately deciding against it. *The poor lady is stretched thin, and it is not an opportune moment*, he thought.

If only he were clairvoyant enough to visualize that the ability to seize upon opportune moments was out of his hands by now.

BUILDING A PERFECT WORLD

17 May 2014

Woken by a cruel jerk on the neck, he realized that he had dozed off. He was now determined to not keep his tasks aside for a Sunday, or to postpone it till a Monday or Tuesday. He thought of spending the following day lazily, skimming through books and magazines, browsing and watching Sunday shows on television. Lunch would be sumptuous. The kids might wish to be taken out for a drive, or he may feel drowsy.

The only solution available was to dress up, pack his laptop and drive down to Starbucks for a strong cup of coffee. He left a scribbled note on the side table.

On Saturday, with most people enjoying their afternoon siestas after five days of stress at work, parking was not a challenge. Neelu's car was parked right outside as well, since Ruplu had taken it. Here it was, Samir thought, an excellent opportunity to be introduced to Ruplu's supervisor. She had spoken a lot about the man, and his interaction with academicians was so rare these days, as he was a part of the corporate world.

He scanned the café. Just when he thought that the two may have decided to occupy a second-floor table; the sight from a corner of the room startled him. For a moment, he could not believe his sleepy eyes. He spotted Ruplu and with her was Angela, who he recognized despite her awkward posture. The same girl he had encountered for a few fleeting moments yesterday, unmistakably.

Angela leaned over the table and held onto Ruplu's in a tight embrace, her chin on Ruplu's shoulder, her eyes shut. He was not sure if Ruplu was enjoying the hug because it was tight and bore traces of dominance. Angela would not have noticed him; her eyes were shut.

Recoiling with horror, he retreated as if it was he who had committed a misdemeanour. The salesman behind the counter recognized him and caught up with him outside, unable to decipher the strange behaviour.

'Anything the matter, Sir?' he asked the retreating Samir.

He had gathered himself by then. 'Nope, nothing is the matter. Was expecting a friend here who claimed he was sitting inside. Unable to spot him, it struck me that he had mentioned another outlet. Signs of aging, Johnny, you better pardon me.'

They laughed heartily for a few seconds before waving goodbye.

The other Starbucks was not too far, and he would have taken a few minutes to reach, but it seemed to take an hour as myriad thoughts crowded his mind. He was now sure that his daughter was in a relationship with Angela. Would it be prudent to speak to her? But why should he? Would he not go down in her esteem if he displayed a regressive mindset about who she chose to be intimate with? She was leading her own life, and it was judicious to accept the harsh fact that she was different. Come on, they were not living in a district town of West Bengal, or a small town here. They were in the heart of California.

A rare tinge of compassion for Neelu engulfed his mind.

Not desirous of wasting time, it did not take long to get down to serious work.

When Samir commenced working, he could switch off and become oblivious to his surroundings. A friend long back had compared him with Valmiki, the legendary epic poet of ancient India, credited to have authored the Ramayana. A dacoit-turned-hermit, legend claimed that anthills over his body failed to interrupt Valmiki's literary pursuits.

As a teen, Samir would contemptuously dismiss such apocryphal fables which Satyen narrated to him, often offending his father. It was only during the last few years that he turned credulous towards quintessential components of a culture bequeathed by his motherland.

Delving deep into various AI options available in the market, it soon became clear to Samir that Colin had not spoken out of total ignorance but from hubris, powered by superficial knowledge, aptly described by Apu as 'compulsive erudition'. Colin had positioned himself as an expert on AI before the Board, blissfully unaware that existing chat-bots in the market were incapable of catering to their organization's requirements.

Samir had proposed that the in-house technical team be assigned the job to develop an application that would employ the principles of natural language processing to converse with customers who logged in to register complaints on products and services. Manual inefficiencies were galore at the company service centre, and they had been unable to recruit more executives due to cost constraints. Consequently, a flurry of customers grew dissatisfied with the speed and quality of service responses.

Mike had once planned to outsource to India, but their minuscule size of operations did not justify offshoring, and the Chairman was sceptical of Indian capabilities. In-house development of the tool, according to Samir, was not such a demanding option since analysis conducted by his team had established that a set of twenty-five customer issues accounted for 90 per cent of customer queries and complaints. Subsequently, a prototype had been developed and they now eagerly awaited his green signal.

Siri had been the first bold attempt to free the human mind of repetitive and tedious tasks. Apple, for unknown reasons, had shed its exotic features, and strategically confined Siri to trivia, like predicting the weather, auto-replying to emails, or scheduling meetings. Google Now was focused on AI for search engines, and Watson, developed by IBM's research team, concentrated on gaming and healthcare. Despite announcing the launch of interfaces with generalized natural language processing, the buzz was that they were still months away. Alexa, Amazon's AI, was a year from its scheduled launch, and he was unable to locate any other product that worked for their needs.

After scripting a comprehensive report within a couple of hours, he was satisfied with accomplishing what he had planned to achieve over the weekend. Clearing the check at the café, he reached home to stretch himself on the cot in a momentary gust of euphoria, erasing memories of Ruplu and Neelu's ominous stares at lunch. What soon occupied his mind was his disgraceful performance at the presentation in front of the Board. Perhaps it would have been proper to carry a detailed document and circulate it before the presentation to justify advocacy of an in-house developed tool, but was he not, as a senior official, entitled to more trust than what Colin and the Chairman were willing to accord to him? Colin had not only thrown a query at him, but also pronounced before a roomful of Board members that he was reinventing the wheel. It was a grave allegation against a Chief Information Officer, accusing him indirectly of wasting time and money and delaying the project. However, Samir's argumentative alter-ego kept insisting that it was his submissive persona that was at fault. Not one individual present in the room had stopped him from vociferously challenging Colin, placing his arguments on the table, educating the Board on finer technical aspects, and offering to demonstrate the prototype. It was he who chose to remain tongue-tied and to paint the reaction of the Board as a manifestation of 'racial bias' was a tad cynical—he conceded.

Thoroughly confused, he settled for a well-deserved nap in the lounge. Setting an alarm for half-past-seven would allow him a few hours of sleep, but the brain refused to fall in line. Despite his satisfaction, he kept thinking; it was not Ruplu but Neelu's grumpy face that popped up like an apparition. Her reticence at the table had been unfathomable. Was it due to lack of sleep? He found it weird that he failed to understand the companion with whom he had spent thirty-two years. There would be thousands of distractions in India, but as an expat, his life revolved around her and his two children, the interactions far more intense than couples back in India. Yet, his friend Utpal and his wife Srimati back in India, for instance, appeared so much more adjusted to each other.

The veneer of civility at home disturbed him. He often wished that Neelu would come clean about her negative emotions. She stored them within herself. Their dysfunctionality was apparent to the outside world, and Samir was reminded of Prince Charles and Diana before they had officially announced their separation.

He too bore equal responsibility for their lack of transparency. He was reminded of the days he had spent at a Starbucks outlet, hiding from his family. He did not wish to disclose a piece of news to Neelu, nursing a typically Indian stigma when it came to job loss. It was a stroke of luck that he obtained another job within a month, and the transition from Starbucks to the new assignment rolled over seamlessly.

That had been an unsavory episode in his career, and the bitter memories pervaded his mind after many years. It happened sometime in 1997.

◆

Two hefty individuals with eagle eyes were spotted one morning, strolling around his office. His boss, the head of finance, was accompanying them. It was a busy day, and he ignored them until he was asked to hand over the key to the server room. Samir presumed that they were one of those auditors who kept visiting; he let it pass, slightly peeved that his boss did not bother to introduce them to him. But that was his style of functioning.

As per the Data Security Policy, only Samir and the Data Security Officer were permitted to retain the keys to the server room. He had handed them in because he did not wish to offend his boss, not with the annual appraisal scheduled a month away.

However, a more professional boss would have pulled him up for violating the policy.

A colleague took him aside during lunch to inform him of whispers floating in the corridors that the hunks belonged to a data forensics organization. Samir's declared ignorance was taken with a grain of salt, interpreted as a scrupulous observance of the dictates of confidentiality expected out of the position.

The Data Security Officer reporting to Samir was an Indian man by the name of Vivek. He was a competent professional and a straightforward person. Around 3 p.m., the two of them were called to the boss's office along with their laptops. A copy of an email was lying on the table, which had been sent from the personal account of an unknown employee, and was addressed to the personal account of another unknown person—presumably a competitor—with crucial company data enclosed. The hard copy of the mail was shown to them; neither the contents of the attachment nor the soft copy were available. Anonymous complaints were usually thrown into the waste-paper basket, and the unsigned letter had arrived by ordinary mail.

This complaint, however, was being looked at differently.

He smelt a rat. Instead of picking their technical brains to solicit an opinion on the purported security breach, the boss asked them to surrender their laptops and leave the office. Vivek was grounded till further orders and Samir was instructed to report the day after, and go straight to his boss's office. The way they went about it was not just dubious; it bordered on skullduggery. The hefty guy, introduced as a retired FBI officer, specialized in Data Forensics and currently worked for one of the big five consultancy houses.

When Samir demanded more explanation, the reply was curt. 'Unfortunately, Sam, divulging more information at this stage is not possible.'

They met up the next day at a café. He was surprised when he spotted Vivek's wife accompanying Vivek, and they both appeared relaxed and composed. 'Sam, did you read the body of the mail?' Vivek asked him.

'No, I was boiling with rage, unable to concentrate. What did it say?'

'The note was from the competitor's employee who received the information. There was no clue about his identity. It was from a personal e-mail account. The man decided to mail a copy of the information obtained from a corporate spy anonymously back to his competitor, disturbed by rumblings of his conscience. Sounds like a fairy tale.'

'Fucking incredible.'

'It is a planned attempt to hang me. Maybe they do not like my face, or perhaps they do not trust an Indian in my position. Whatever!' Vivek said.

'Some other guy may be involved who wants you out of his way and the bosses are too thick to understand. Let us wait until tomorrow.' Samir tried to explain.

'For me, boss, tomorrow's outcome is a no-brainer. Have started applying for jobs, obtaining one should not be tough.'

As expected, after scanning Vivek's laptop for deleted files, they detected incriminating stuff. He was summarily dismissed and Peter, his assistant, requested to take over with immediate effect. Samir's views carried no weight, nor was he offered a copy of their findings. His boss was convinced; that was all that mattered.

For the first time, without any compulsion, Samir offered to resign. He felt that he had no option. It was not just an insult to his intelligence, but continuing in the position would be equivalent to compromising with evil forces. Although he had made compromises on several occasions, this was an extreme situation. And it was better than to face dismissal, certain to come his way within six months, if not earlier. It was better to part with dignity. After a few sleepless nights, he took the final decision, although he managed to put up a straight face at home.

Samir was convinced that Vivek was a victim of racist discrimination, and he considered it an eye-opener regarding the autocratic manner corporates functioned in the US.

Both Samir and Vivek consulted lawyers who pronounced it a slam dunk, assuring them a favourable outcome. However, the amount to be spent on litigation, coupled with the adverse publicity—possibly extending to coverage in the media—held them back. Bagging alternate jobs would be simpler, which both were able to do within a couple of months. The brighter side of the United States of America.

◆

From An Undisclosed Location

December 2019

What bothered Samir while he was stuck in a dense forest, was his reluctance to disclose the incident to Neelu, to operate from Starbucks for a month furtively. He had not committed a crime, nor was he asked to move on, and losing a job carried no stigma for corporate executives in the US.

It was in stark contrast to Vivek, who had been frank, open, and transparent with his spouse.

His mind flitted back to his sixtieth birthday week.

WALKING THROUGH FIRE

17 May 2014

Ruplu entered the lounge around eight. 'Take your evening bath, Baba. Could you catch up on lost sleep?' she asked him.

'Nope, most of my time was spent on stupid official work. Thankfully, it is now completed and I feel relaxed like after a scintillating yoga session.'

'You and your yoga!' she said. Not that she intended to hurt her father, but the comments flew unthinkingly.

Irritated at the remark, he decided to strike back. 'Ruplu, where have you been?'

'Starbucks. Why?'

'With whom?'

'Did I not tell you at the lunch table?'

'Ruplu, since you joined college, I have never intruded into your personal life. But today I am compelled to. I felt sleepy in the afternoon and dropped into the café. It was not your supervisor there with you.'

She did not even take a moment to respond back. 'Yes, he came in late. Angela was also there. He had asked her to drop by because we are jointly presenting a paper on Tuesday. I mentioned it yesterday. So, it was the two of us till he arrived. But what I fail to understand is why you did not walk up to us.'

'I was embarrassed. Moved on to another café.'

'Embarrassed by what?'

He was unable to describe what he witnessed. What appeared unnatural to him was perhaps normal to her generation. It was unlikely that she did not understand the situation. She was not dumb, not by a stretch. Was she planning to come out of the closet? Or was he getting unduly suspicious?

'Nothing, just the thought that you lied.'

'Baba, I am a grown-up, why should I lie? I went there to meet my supervisor. Who else was there is not of any consequence. That is why I did not mention Angela's name.'

'Fine, let's dump the topic.'

'A possessive father is not what I particularly dislike, so it's cool. Shall I call Apu and Ma?'

'Give me half an hour.'

He still believed there was much more to it, but what she said also seemed plausible. He relented.

Neelu entered after a while with tea, cookies and a couple of pastries arranged in perfect symmetry. 'The tea has turned a tad cold. Joyita called at the wrong moment. Tell me if it needs to be reheated.'

'All well?' he asked her.

'Oh yes! She was inviting us over for their anniversary this Saturday.'

'Not another of those goddamn events! I detest them these days. Meaningless chatter, back-biting, stale humour. Anyway, I'm glad that the tea has turned cold. If we do not start right away, it may once again stretch into late hours.'

'What is so sacrosanct about our bedtime, Samir? Tomorrow is a holiday for us.'

It was lack of sleep after all. Poor thing had lost the habit of staying up ever since they dumped their fast life five years back.

The session resumed thirty minutes behind schedule.

♦

'I treasure memories of Adesh after so many years, although I no longer subscribe to his ideology. This happened in October 1970, a few days after I joined college. To me, it is irrelevant whether Adesh was right or wrong. I knew him from close quarters, and he was a sincere, brave and dedicated person who sacrificed his life for a cause close to his heart.' Samir's voice was palpably heavy.

'We went to school together till the eighth standard, lived close by and frequently visited each other. Kept in touch even after I left that school, sometimes for a chat, at other times, for a game of cricket or soccer. We lost touch after his family moved to their ancestral home in north Kolkata, bumping into each other after a few years in the queue to collect forms for college admission. He narrowly missed a berth in the physics department at Presidency, and was forced to settle for another college a couple of miles away. We frequently caught up after classes at the café across the road. He initially limited his activities to participating in study circles and penning articles under a fictitious name, but the Party persuaded him to play a more active role. Although convinced of the inevitability of an armed uprising, he believed in mass agitations culminating in a violent upheaval and not isolated terrorist attacks by partisans. A fierce ideological debate was raging at that time.

'It had been his idea to organize street hawkers and petty shopkeepers of the locality against a band of fierce lumpens owing their allegiance to the ruling party, operating hand-in-glove with the police and led by a vicious individual by the name of Pagla Keshto. Massive and sinister, the guy was famous for all the wrong reasons. Cold-blooded murder and rapes were second nature to him, and he managed to evade arrest, thanks to his contacts within the establishment. He had a round face, punctured with pock-marks, overshadowed by a pair of dark and cruel eyes, one larger than the other, and the gaping holes between his teeth resembling dark caves. His visage was sufficient to send shivers down anybody's spine. He put his frightening features to full use while extorting 'donations' from shopkeepers in the vicinity, an amount most could ill afford, yet were compelled to pay to be allowed to continue doing business.

'Adesh and a group of students from the college located within the heart of his theatre of operations decided to oppose the practice and managed to mobilize the harassed shopkeepers. It snowballed into a mass movement, restricted to open rallies and deputations to the local police station, as they refused to partake with the fixed amount demanded at the end of the week, shared equitably between Keshto's gang and local cops. The practice had been in existence since Adam's days and it was unprecedented to witness hundreds of shopkeepers downing their shutters. For the first time in his twenty-year-long career, Keshto was compelled to compromise. But he refused to take it in his stride. It made him desperate to strike back at Adesh, despite the looming fear of the Party he owed allegiance to, compounded by the adulation from co-students and residents of the locality, extending to the disinclined.

'Keshto made up his mind on a crisp fall morning. The season is called "sharaat" in Bengali and resembles the American fall. The smell of white flowers from chhatim—the devil's tree—and sweet-smelling shiuli pervade parks and gardens; white-petalled, orange-stemmed, seductive night-flowering jasmines and majestic kaas flowers lend a melancholy charm. The flowers symbolize wistful nostalgia for the better part of the year that has gone by and there is melancholy at the thought of the imminent shortening of daylight hours. The sky bears a traditional azure blue with spotless white clouds that glide majestically across. Rays of sunlight assume a golden hue, and the doel bird sings a magical tune to proclaim the onset of the festive season.

'The annual carnival, Durga Puja, is celebrated during this season. Educational institutions close down a week before the actual festivities commence, and the entire populace soaks in the festive environment. Those who can afford to splurge, relatives and workers are generously gifted, and retail therapy is normalized. This ends with five days of the festival when volunteers set up makeshift structures to offer homage to clay images of a goddess who is comfortably lodged inside. Cultural events are organized, rituals are performed with religious zeal, and poor residents of localities are fed. As the fable goes, the goddess Durga, accompanied by her children, visits her parents during those five days, leaving her husband Shiva to fend for himself in his abode up in the mountains, smoking his favourite pot.

Ruplu said, 'Sounds far more exciting than the stuff here in LA, although we too enjoy our share of fun, like staging plays.'

Apu quipped. 'Yes, like Ali Baba and the forty thieves.'

'With the dialogue scripted in Roman.'

'Come on, Baba. You never took time off to teach us the Bengali script. You lacked the patience.'

He reminded them of those futile sessions, and the room erupted in roaring laughter. Neelu, for a change, joined in.

'So pujas in Kolkata is a treat unmatched!' Apu conceded.

'Yes, it is. How often have I asked you to schedule our vacations around that time? To return to the story, Keshto was seething in a fury that year. The pomp and grandeur associated with his trademarked Durga and Kali Pujas, celebrated within three weeks of each other, necessitated millions of rupees. "Donations" had substantially decreased, thanks to Adesh and his compatriots, and the greedy man was desperate to re-establish his authority.

'Two days before the puja holidays. It was like any other day for Adesh, who was concentrating on a thermodynamics lecture with rapt attention, when he spotted a bunch of toughs loitering outside the classroom. "They have come for me," he whispered to his close friend, Joy.

'"No tension, Adesh. We are well-equipped to resist them. Do you think we will allow them to take you away?" Joy said.

'"They are devilish, possibly armed, stronger than us, Joy. I have no doubts that you will fight for me till the end, but you will be overpowered."

'"Let's buy some time then." Joy, a close friend and a comrade, responded after deliberating. Joy proceeded towards the podium to whisper in the professor's ears. "Sir, a few goons are loitering outside. They are presumably here to pick up Adesh. You must be aware of the happenings in the locality; we fear they are here to extract their ounce of flesh."

'Nurturing a soft corner for Adesh's intelligent interventions during lectures, a sidelong glance convinced him that Joy's fears were not unfounded. He whispered back after a moment's thought. "One of you rush to the Principal's office and ask for police protection."

'Although peeved at the professor's naivety, Joy retained his cool. "Sir, it is futile. You must be aware the Principal himself is a supporter of the ruling party. The only way is to slide him through the door at the top so that he can escape through the lab."

'The professor displayed an extraordinary presence of mind. "Just do as I say then. Fetch me the projector. Hurry."

'The goons waited for the lecture to end in a display of uncharacteristic courtesy. The professor now yelled at the top of his voice. "I'm now going to present some slides and I need the doors closed and the lights switched off. Nikhil, please do the needful." The statement was intended for the ears of the goons.

'Smelling a whiff of conspiracy, one of them barged in to bellow at the professor in a typically crass voice. "Sir, we want to speak to Adesh."

'The baritone admonition from the Professor failed to deter him.

'"It's urgent." The tone was cruder now.

'"Just get lost. How dare you disturb my lecture? I am running late and I need to project these slides. Can you please close that door, Nikhil?" The goon, caught unawares, decided not to confront a respected professor.

'Adesh moved swiftly to the top left corner of the auditorium. All the students, some supporters of the ruling Party, had gotten the hang of what was transpiring and sincerely wished that Adesh would manage to escape. The knob gently slid open, and that action was replicated through a few adjacent lecture halls, until he reached the laboratory at the end of the corridor. The lecture carried on.

'Peeking through the laboratory windows, Adesh noticed a few guys standing right outside. Barua, the laboratory assistant, hailing from a family that lived for generations in the locality, was snoozing. He had no laboratory session scheduled for the day. Woken by a gentle nudge, Barua asked Adesh to hide under a worktable, moving immediately out with his water bottle, ostensibly for a refill. Alerting the student community, the lackadaisical stroll back to the lab stoked no suspicion.

'Word about Adesh's hunters spread like wildfire, and hordes of students collected outside the lecture room. Discovering that Adesh had left the lecture hall, the goons suspected that he was in the laboratory and punted loudly on the door. Adesh had the sudden idea that he could slide down the thick water pipe, but it was abandoned after a stern rebuff from Barua.

'"Then let me fight, Barua da. I need a few sharp screwdrivers and slide calipers from the lab," Adesh said.

'Barua, a mature and down-to-earth person, dismissed his request. "Adesh, you have been watching too many action movies of late. I have a far more sensible suggestion. Why don't you hide in the cupboard there? It's empty and can be locked from outside."

'"I suffer from claustrophobia, and for how long? They will discover me."

'By the time the cordon formed by students outside the lab was dispersed by the more muscular thugs, a desperate Barua managed to persuade Adesh into the cupboard with a reasonably large hole at the rear that allowed a stream of oxygen.

'After five minutes, Barua unlocked the doors of the laboratory to a horde of abusive goons, armed with hockey sticks. A few hard smacks landed on his face. "Why the hell did you lock the door, and where is Adesh? We will not spare you."

'"He jumped out of the window and slid down that water pipe."

'Not spotting Adesh out the window, they pounced on him.

'"No human being can escape so fast. Are we a bunch of assholes?"

'Barua lapsed into loud sobs, his skills as an amateur thespian were put to good use. "Just listen to me. We reside in this locality for generations, everyone vouches for our family's allegiance to your Party. You may ask Keshto da. The bastard escaped ten minutes back after threatening to knife me on the roads if I dared open the door before he escaped. You know how vicious these people are, they butchered a police informer across the road only a few months back. Have heart, I'm the father of a two-month-old child and the sole bread-earner in my family."

'"Spineless coward!"

'That was followed by choicest cuss words, and the smashing of bottles and scientific equipment, followed by a few more slaps on Barua's face. The closet door was banged hard, not because they suspected Adesh was in there, but to vent their frustration.

'"I think he is speaking the truth," Adesh could faintly hear one of them. "These bastards are capable of such stuff."

'After the lab fell silent, Barua da could hear Adesh's faint whisper. "Barua da, it's intolerable in here."

'"Sshh! They just left, will unlock only after a few minutes. What if they return? Take continuous deep breaths. It will not take long."

'Soon the cops arrived and, sensing the defiant mood inside the college, advised Keshto's followers to disappear for the day. As the information reached Barua, he opened the closet door. Adesh was a tough sportsman and was soon able to breathe normally. The empath in him surfaced. "I heard them slapping you. Are you hurt?" he asked Barua.

'"Just shut your trap for some time and consume this bottle of water while I plan your escape."

'The plan was neatly chalked out. Barua would switch off the lights, lock Adesh inside the room, and go home to confuse the goons. After spending a good hour at home, he would hire a cab, keep the vehicle waiting outside the rear gate of the college—usually deserted after dark—come back and escape with Adesh. Barua was to alight at a distance, and Adesh would proceed home with him in the same cab.

'"But they could bash you up on the road."

'"Don't you worry, nobody can dare to touch me inside my para. Our family goes back five generations, supports the ruling party, and the locality stands as one to protect each other."

'The plan worked without a glitch. After reaching home, Adesh learnt that his father had left town on an emergent official assignment, a tired sister had gone off to sleep, and his mother, under the weather, was requesting an early dinner. It does not require creative imagination to conclude that he would have wrestled through the night, wondering about the next steps, but what is known for a fact is that the entire locality woke up a few hours after dawn to a cacophony of loud expletives. A posse of cops arrived to arrest a 'dreaded' extremist charged with the murders of eight policemen, despite the only 'crime' actually attributed to him was the organizing of innocent shopkeepers against harassment by musclemen. The police physically lifted him into the van after tying his limbs with iron cuffs. All said and done, Pagla Keshto was a generous contributor to the Party coffers!

'The incident took place a few months after we had both joined college. We were woken up by his mom's calls early in the morning; Baba buzzed his contact man in the establishment, who expressed his apologies since orders had come from the top. Unaware of what transpired at the college, I rushed to inform his friends. I was certain that Adesh was not capable of committing the crime for which he had been charged and would be absolved. He was a decent human being with whom I had spent my childhood, and he was incapable of swatting a fly. Barua da briefed me on the details. He knew me as Adesh's friend, and only the two of us were privy to the manner in which he hid him from the goons. For others, it was the anecdote of a student sliding down a water pipe right under the noses of a bunch of ruffians that held on.

'Killed in cold blood, Adesh thereafter transformed into a legend. The ruling dispensation spread the fake news that he had been arrested on purported charges dating to a period before college, unconnected to the happenings that day.'

Neelu, inspired by Miss Marple, fond of playing an amateur sleuth, blurted out. 'Why do you presume charges were trumped-up? The two of you were not even in touch during the period.'

'The coincidence was stark. His arrest followed the confrontation, plus Keshto was a powerful pillar of the ruling Party.'

'There is another implausibility in your thesis. If they wished to kill him, couldn't they have quietly picked him up from the roads? Why in the presence of the entire student and teaching community?'

'You have a point there, Neelu. Either they wished to send out a stern message or were plain stupid. I cast my vote for the latter. Imbeciles of the highest order.'

As he battled the rage that had resurfaced, he was reminded of another momentous incident in his life. It haunted him. Could he draw an analogy from quantum mechanics? If a subatomic particle could co-exist probabilistically at different points in space, why could a man not believe in a Hindu ethos and a violent revolution simultaneously? Why can't one be gay and a Catholic simultaneously? Why can't an Islamist enjoy an occasional pint of beer? For a few moments, he stood committed to the violent revolution he passionately believed in once upon a time along with Adesh, Utpal, Atanu da, and others alongside the metaphysical path to salvation through spiritualism he now swore by.

Apu, unaware of the cross-currents inside his father's mind, pulled him down to earth. 'Well guys, my take is different. If you believe in violence, be prepared for the consequences.'

'Apu, you speak like a dumbass at times. Neither Baba nor Adesh believed in violence. It was thrust upon them,' Ruplu defended her father.

Apu's rejoinder was inoffensive, 'You fail to understand their ideology then.'

The last thing Samir wanted at such a late hour was a heated argument. He did not like how Ruplu denigrated her elder brother.

'Let me apply my whip as the head of the family. We now move on to your story, Ruplu. If you need more material for your paper, we can have a one-on-one session tomorrow or the next weekend. Incidentally, don't you feel like you owe an apology to

Apu?' It was a rhetorical comment that prompted her to walk over and clasp Apu in a tight and elegant hug.

Caught unawares, Apu sat with a deadpan face, but Neelu's eyes welled up. The sight of the hugging siblings struck a chord in her, but for Samir, her tears bordered on melodrama. At a loss for words, he conveyed his earnest desire for dinner through an awkward gesture of his fingers.

The somber-faced Neelu took a while to comply. Samir was not smart enough to understand that her hesitation was an act of defiance.

REPLACING CRACKED PANES

17 May 2014

The serenity of the resplendent backyard was no match for the stillness inside the lounge. Ruplu had requested that she be provided with some time to assemble her storyline.

This provided him with an opportunity for some meditation. He was reminded of the days his family enjoyed their annual vacations to India. He often had to return earlier or differently time his visits due to problems in obtaining leave.

Initially, both his children had hated their annual trips to India. On her first visit as a grown woman, Ruplu expressed dismay at the multitude of individuals thronging the roads. She was incensed by the creepy youngsters, beggars extending their hands for alms, Indian-style toilets, and forced feeding by relatives. Over time, blessed by doting grandparents, uncles and aunties, and expectations of novel exotic experiences, they started looking forward to their annual visits.

Satyen replaced the Indian-style toilet, refusing to accept a penny from Samir. 'It is for my grandchildren, not for you. How dare you offer me cash?' he had said, accompanying the comments with a pat on his back to ensure his son would not misunderstand him.

His children found the food distinctive, the folks intriguing and the cultural differences amazing, replacing the lenses through which they viewed their country of origin. They started loving modern Bengali movies, were amazed at unending streams of folks scampering after buses and trams on gridlocked roads, ignored the smoggy winter air, gingerly walked down cracked sidewalks and were intrigued by pedestrians and stray canines, curious at the never-ending processions.

They appreciated the beef steak at Oly Pub on Park Street and were tickled by stiff upper-lipped senior members of the Calcutta Club, with its roots in the colonial era.

They loved watching plays adapted from Ibsen, Brecht or Sanskrit playwrights at the Academy of Fine Arts. However, Samir wished they could witness the fiery political plays of the seventies that had faded into oblivion with time. They loved family weddings and get-togethers, and not just for the delectable cuisines.

On those holidays, Samir would religiously purchase kurtas from a particular shop in Gariahat. Upmarket shops had come up by the tens, stocking reputed brands, but Samir would insist on visiting the same shop—located at a stone's throw from a restaurant that had once influenced the trajectory of his life on a sunny Sunday morning. The owner of the shop was now a tottering old man.

Samir felt relieved that his children's initial disgust at the perversities of an alien culture had given way to excitement of exoticism. He still believed that the brutalities of third world poverty had sparked Ruplu's left liberal proclivities, which had led her to meander into identity issues later on in life.

Back in LA, on some nights, he pined for the time at his nondescript Kolkata home. Nights that were peppered with the sounds of a persistent smoker's cough, friendly arguments prolonging into the dead of night, noisy youngsters chatting away till wee hours, clamorous beats of the roving watchman's stick, occasional stormy exchanges between neighbouring couples, azaan from adjoining mosques piercing the hush of the cockcrow hours and the unabated howls from indigenous breeds of canines incensed with 'illegal' migrants violating demarcated lines of control.

He otherwise detested a misplaced nostalgia for the past from the core of his heart. This was to ward off loneliness.

In this American jungle, he often forayed into the darkness to capture the ongoing chatter of boisterous neighbourhood kids and the heavy sounds of delivery trucks zooming past the freeway, and bumped into neighbours on leisurely dawdles, chatted up with the salesman at the 24/7 grocery shop before gulping a cold can of soda or apple juice. If he was still not in a mood to sleep, a longish trek would lead him to mountain trails under starry skies, the chirping of crickets triggering intimate conversations with nature in its multifaceted mystique, despite looming dangers from dense thickets covering its slopes.

An old Bengali adage: *'Jekhaney bagher bhoy, shekhaney sondhyey hoy'*, roughly translated as, 'Darkness descends wherever there is a fear of tigers', came true one night when a curmudgeonly vagrant emerged from the shadows.

A presumptuous Samir concluded that the guy was begging for alms and tossed a crumpled dollar from inside his inner pocket. He was shocked when the guy threw the tattered note back with veritable contempt. Then came the vitriolic outburst, 'Don't need your fucking bucks, just get off our backs.' It made him skip a few heartbeats. Samir scampered to safety, but it took longer for the horror to dissipate, and he had locked his bedroom door for the first time in his life.

Later, he had even spotted a pair of toxic eyes contemptuously staring at him from the cover of darkness. On the verge of buzzing the cops, a mournful purr from the neighbour's cat had yanked him back to his senses.

The tranquillity of his thoughts was momentarily interrupted when Neelu excused herself, requesting to be called from the kitchen the moment Ruplu was set to go.

Samir glanced at his daughter. He could empathize with the traumatic churns that were likely happening in her mind, insensitively cajoled to reconstruct a bitter episode. The impulse to call off the session was withheld when he was reminded that Apu had articulately advocated for this the previous evening.

He preferred Ruplu's chirpy or rude behaviour because it was tough to discern what lay beneath the icy veil when she turned thoughtful. She stole sly looks at them while she worked on her Mac, and her shifting eyes revealed either a scheming conspirator or a confused, pinched and flaky individual, unable to navigate her life.

His son's life, on the contrary, was an open book, extending to stories on peccadillos described to the last detail, or his first experience with marijuana. Once, on a balmy afternoon, while narrating particulars of his first break-up, he got so carried away that Neelu had to wink furtively at Samir. He was jejune and naïve, despite excelling in academics and sangfroid with a chronically nettlesome sister.

The pregnant silence ended abruptly with a brief statement.

'I'm good to go,' Ruplu said.

Neelu's teary eyes had not escaped him as she emerged from the kitchen. 'I understand your feelings,' he said to her, 'but the least we can do is encourage her to venture out of the closet.'

It did not occur to Samir that the tears had nothing to do with Ruplu.

Neelu gently wiped her eyes with a touch of feminine grace, and she promised to join them in three minutes, as soon as the oven's timer went off.

Ruplu began. 'Let me not waste time with a prelude. Incidentally, Apu is aware of the episode, and I am confident it was he who broached the topic last night after I stepped out of the room. Not that I hold it against him.'

Still, her expression conveyed that she had not taken it in the right spirit, although she was not in a mood to take up the gauntlet. She took another minute to resume her narration, avoided eye contact with the rest, and stared vacantly.

'The mention of a buddy by the name of James will likely not sound familiar to your ears. If an artist was commissioned to sketch him, I would visualize a charismatic and genial personality with a pair of sharp eyes, a taut and short physique and a majestic dispensation. In one sentence, he had in him what it takes to turn the head of a woman. Boasting consistent good grades in college, James was also a decent sportsman, a distinguished orator and a tender soul with a willingness to stand by friends without expecting anything in return.'

Her roving eyes traversed the room, and fixed for a while on Apu's downcast face. Samir wondered why.

'The guy was an African-American. You would recall that we visited the east coast six years back—I guess it was the summer of 2007—on a study tour. James's folks were visiting New York during the inter-semester summer break and he tagged along, after wrangling a short project from Columbia University. There were openings for ten scholars, and I persuaded him to part with his supervisor's contacts.'

Samir mumbled softly. 'Yes, I vividly recall your project in Columbia, although the existence of James is a revelation.'

'It was a great project. We had to slice and dice reams of data. Our objective was to analyse whether affirmative actions for blacks needed to continue or be altered in scope and amount.

'The first two weeks were hectic. Our supervisor, Dr Smith, a strict taskmaster, kept us on tenterhooks, discovering a fresh perspective after every round of analysis. The work was not frustrating because of the synergy. There was no time to breathe on a weekday till six, and we would escape immediately to the pub round the corner, or watch late-night baseball matches at the stadium, plays, or stand-up comedy shows off-Broadway. Dinners were had at quaint joints, but not the tony ones as we could not afford them. I stayed in a dorm at the Morningside Heights Campus; he and his folks stayed close by with his dad's buddy. We worked through Saturdays. The group would persuade me to join them on sight-seeing trips on Sundays, but I usually opted to go to the fabulous college library.'

Samir's loaded statement escaped her notice. 'I would have expected as much. You always nursed an affinity for libraries.'

Ruplu was running a mild fever on the second Sunday during the project and had planned to return to the dorm with a couple of weighty books from the Butler Library, unexpectedly bumping into James at the main exit.

'Hey, we are lucky to cross each other. Thought you planned to stick to the library this evening.' James remarked with a pleasant and vibrant smile.

'Not feeling too well. How did the sightseeing go?' Ruplu responded.

'The Statue of Liberty was amazing, but I liked Ellis Island better. Missed you, Rups.'

'Visited the place two years back with my family.'

'Indians are addicted to travel. My folks moved out of California for the first time after fifteen years and this is our maiden visit to New York.'

'You've told me this once, James. Don't have to rub it in.'

James noticed her struggling under the weight of the books and snatched them away, dropping a book and grazing his hands against her palms. She thought it was deliberate. She almost gave him a stern glare, but the broad smile on his face disarmed her as he bent forward to lift the one lying on the floor.

There was a lull in her narration, and he dared not steal a

glance at her, only to find Neelu and Apu gaping at the cuckoo clock. She continued.

James was in the mood for a date that evening. 'Are you familiar with the name Pete Seeger?'

'Not quite. Who the hell is he?'

'A mass singer. An eighty-eight year old guy who retains the strength and quality of his voice, renders numbers articulating the voices of oppressed blacks, unemployed, workers denied fair wages, indigenous people and soldiers sacrificing their lives to satisfy the greed of warmongers. Tonight, he is to perform at an outdoor auditorium near Central Park, roughly fifteen minutes away. Checked up on passes, they are available. What are we waiting for? Let's dump the darned books at the dorm and rush.'

'James, I am slightly under the weather and was planning to catch up with these books.'

He nodded after a moment's hesitation. It was not in his nature to push, and Ruplu sometimes wished he was more assertive. They strolled through the centre of the campus and exchanged not too many words, staring at various campus towers, each an architectural marvel by itself. Philosophy Hall, Pupin Hall—where Fermi accomplished the first fission of a uranium atom—and the famous alma mater statue against the backdrop of a moonlit sky. They converged on the 'steps', a regular hangout for students, which appeared mystical on a Sunday evening.

There was a pleasant breeze, pregnant with the fragrance of hibiscus and amaranths, and it fluttered the leaves. The urge to relax inside the claustrophobic dorm disappeared after a while, but it was not in Ruplu's nature to yield ground easily, conscious as she was of the price to command.

'Are you sure you are keen to hear the man sing? I've not even heard his name. A long walk followed by a dinner at Friday's joint would enthuse me more.'

REPLACING CRACKED PANES

James offered her a quid pro quo if she joined him for the concert.

So they hurriedly packed devilled eggs, ham sandwiches and lemon tarts from the campus café. The café was short on plates, which troubled her.

The concert was a novel experience. The numbers like, 'If I had a hammer', the famous Woody Guthrie composition, 'This land is our land', 'Guantanamera', 'Which side are you on?', 'Where have all the flowers gone?' and 'We shall overcome' were all hard-hitting, triggering awareness that oppressed humanity, possessed capability to craft its own destiny.

Aimlessly meandering on the way back, with no inclination to hop onto the subway, Ruplu noticed a linguistically incorrect signboard. 'Caution. Fines double inside the construct zone.' They took a slight detour. The diversion terminated at a yawning staircase leading into a subway station.

'Feel like jumping on the tube, Rups?' James asked her.

'I'm good to keep walking. Unless you are exhausted.'

'No, no. I have not forgotten what I promised you.'

A while later on their walk, he stopped in his tracks. The sheer intensity of his expression and his swagger was scary.

The tone was aggressive. 'Martin Luther may have delivered the song, "We shall overcome", forty years back, but it still inspires us.'

A tad nonplussed, Ruplu mumbled. 'It is not relevant anymore.'

The remark instigated him, and he flared. 'No? They have built a façade of racial equality, and the truth is harsher. Your ancestors were not shipped like cattle from Zanzibar and you will never be able to place yourselves in our shoes. Does the name Rodney King ring a bell?'

'Cool it, James. Unless you relax, I'll return to the dorm alone.'

He paused. 'Sorry, Rups. Got carried away.'

Ruplu accepted his apology. 'Rodney King. Yeah. He left an impression on my tender mind, although I watched the brutal video many years later. I was just a kid when it happened, and it was so close to where we lived those days.'

He went on. 'The world would not have believed that Rodney was unarmed if a bystander had not secretly shot the video. That was a decade ago, but only last year, Darryl Green, while returning from a nightclub, was shot dead in Brooklyn at four in the morning. The jury was unanimous that the shooting was unwarranted and the fellow had no criminal record. This reminds me of another Rodney. Rodney Reed. A friend of the fiancé of the lass he had purportedly killed submitted an affidavit a few years later. He declared that it was his friend who had murdered the "nigger-loving" girl out of jealousy. He was jolted when it dawned upon him that an innocent African-American had been convicted of the crime.

'My mother witnessed the shooting of her cousin during the riots that followed. The vision still haunts her. Her chest tightens, her breathing gets laboured and an unending stream of sweat spills through her pores. She needs help during those bouts. They last for a few minutes, but are pretty frequent.'

Ruplu smiled sympathetically. 'James, I genuinely feel sorry for your mother, but please try to appreciate my contention. The situation is far better today thanks to your struggles. Secondly, it is not unique to your community. What about the indigenous Indians dispossessed of their lands and butchered long before you guys were shipped in? Such incidents occur throughout the globe, including in India where grotesque caste oppression continues. There are innumerable stories from the country of brazen, ludicrous atrocities, like a lower-caste guy hammered for riding a horse, sporting a moustache, or refusing to stand up when an upper-caste man passes by.'

'You're kidding. These things happened way back in this damn country.'

'I am not kidding. Violent riots are also common in our country. Sixty Hindus, including women and infants, were burnt alive in a railway compartment while returning from a mission to construct a temple. In retaliation, seven hundred Muslims were butchered in cold blood. A far more serious genocide of Sikhs occurred in 1984. We suffered a horrendous partition; our neighbouring country, Bangladesh, faced genocide—mostly Hindus. And it happens here too. After 9/11, Sikhs were mistaken as Muslims and brutally assaulted. Balbir Singh Sodhi was shot dead inside a gas station while six Sikhs were butchered in Wisconsin. They do not understand the difference between Sikhs, Muslims and Hindus or between Indians and Arabs. Hindu techies were beaten up in Silicon Valley. A Sikh guy in Arizona was shot at because the assassin confused his turban and beard with that of an Arab's; the guy had told his pals that he was "going to go out to shoot some towelheads". It was premeditated. My terrified dad shaved off his goatee to avoid such a fate.'

She went on, a little aggressively herself. 'Not that I recall African-Americans standing up for hapless South Asians, and many of you were accomplices those days. Long before 9/11, the "Dot busters" in New Jersey derived pleasure from bashing up Asians, and quite a few of us died of cerebral damage. Rednecks brutally bashed up my dad in Memphis. I'm not even mentioning instances of discrimination at the workplace. Corporates blame us for offshoring white-collar labour to India even though the real reason lies in cost arbitrage for profits. Even Hillary Clinton once joked that Mahatma Gandhi owned a gas station, and Joe Biden remarked that it was impossible to enter a Dunkin' Donuts without encountering an Indian.'

James reached out and squeezed her shoulders tightly. It

caused some discomfort, but she ignored it, more curious about the direction the night was meandering into. 'Do you realize that this is the first time we have engaged in a stimulating intellectual discussion?'

'And why the fuck do you think I opted for this project? From a fondness for boring number-crunching at the university?'

Buses, cars and trailers zoomed by, oblivious to the two unconnected souls bonding together. At that moment, he was her perfect man, worth sacrificing her aspirations for. To James, she was the epitome of perfection. She was concomitantly intellectual, warm and reasonable.

He nudged her, then pulled her down the subway stairs that ended at the ticket counter. The man behind the counter was snoring. The station was tiny and deserted. There were just three directions to move: up the stairs and back to the sidewalk, into the platforms, or towards the bathroom, where he dragged her.

Ruplu's previous sexual experiences were vicarious. Erotic movies witnessed with friends, bumping into a promiscuous couple in the gymnasium after a basketball match and pornographic literature.

It was tender. It started with a deep kiss and a brutal hug, then subsequent caresses triggered libidinous hormones, reaching its acme when one of his hands ventured into her panties to trigger an orgasm. She had never experienced one before. She ran her hands over his cropped hair, clammy neck, thick shoulders and strong arms, down to his brawny back, sucking his nipples through his unbuttoned shirt. James picked her up, catching her gingerly on the rebound, punctuating the acrobatics with kisses at sensitive spots.

The interlude barely lasted five minutes, and they stopped when Ruplu remembered the punctilious strictures inside metro stations.

It ended with another deep kiss, as they sucked the last drops of saliva from each other's mouths.

They sat cuddled next to each other outside the ticket counter, sharing the first smoke of her life. She started coughing violently, but seemed to enjoy it. His torso provided not just comfort, but security. He gently rubbed her shoulders and kissed her neck. The guy at the counter chose the wrong moment to wake up and threatened to hand them over to the cops for smoking inside the station.

Their kisses continued on the sidewalk. Only one passerby, a South Asian, dared to look askance with a contemptuous stare; others never bothered.

James abruptly descended to reality. 'Hey, confused about our coordinates, where the hell are we?'

Ruplu responded. 'Don't expect me to be more knowledgeable than you, asshole.'

They followed Google Maps towards the Hudson River. Not a word was exchanged, since they were unwilling to trivialize such a sublime experience. The stillness of the narrow lane evoked bizarre feelings, and she decided to break the silence. 'Let us not pigeon-hole Pete. He talks about overarching oppression across classes, colours and nationalities, he talks about worker unions, war and strikes.'

'I understand where you're coming from. It just helps us relate to our context. We have indeed travelled some distance. I am told that during the sixties they had segregated toilets in a city like Boston.'

'Incidentally, Dalits, the moniker by which the lowest castes in our society are known, forged working relations with Black leaders. Dr Ambedkar, their leader in India, was called India's Martin Luther... The discussion is turning stale. Let us conclude by agreeing that your situation has improved substantively, and residual issues will hopefully sort themselves out in ten or twenty years. Come on, dumbo, cheer up. I feel now that you regret whatever happened a while back.'

'Want me to prove you wrong?' he said, grabbing her slight frame and picking her up like a rubber ball, flinging her higher before settling her on the sidewalk.

She was surprised and annoyed, and it showed. Yet she was reluctant to spoil the beautiful evening.

'Who the fuck do you think you are, a WWE wrestler?' she said.

'Sorry sweetheart, I thought you asked for it.'

It took some time to regain composure while he looked the other way, regretting his savage display of strength.

'I spot an open bar at that corner. Let's get a couple of drinks. It may calm you down.'

The sole customer, a middle-aged person, wore a red shirt that seemed incongruous with his pair of blue trousers. He sat at the corner table enjoying his drink. James felt as if his behaviour was erratic.

After settling down, they ordered a couple of Doom White beers.

The man alternately gaped at his device and ogled at James, head jerking like a cartoon character. The eccentric behaviour culminated in an abrupt request for the check, although he had consumed only a quarter of his drink.

The bartender, a dark, handsome, and cheerful person from Ecuador, was bewildered.

'You came in just ten minutes back. Any problem? Was the drink cool?'

'Loved every drop of it, my boy. It's just that my damn wife texted me. I need to go.'

The bartender laughed. 'No way am I ever getting married!

Do take care of her though, and do not look so terrified. She'll be all right.'

'An insane weirdo,' exclaimed James as he saw the last of him. Ruplu was still absorbed in savoring the memories of what she had experienced a while back.

The bartender sauntered up to them. 'Hi, I am Enrique, the bartender here. Why do you think we keep our outlet open till late hours? Just for drunk duds like him, and lovers like you.'

James laughed. The three of them were in a mood to let their hair down.

James cheered up after a couple of pints. He was blabbering with a loosened tongue until he was interrupted by a screeching noise from the worn-out tires of a heavy van.

'Guess we have more guests,' Enrique said. 'Business has been exceptionally good today.'

'Well, let's hope they are heading in another direction. We want a peaceful bar,' James said.

'I appreciate your needs, bro. And since when has an Ecuadorian been lucky?'

'I thought you told us that business was good today.'

'Yup, but I need to save enough to return to Ecuador, get married and settle down. This place is rough, man.'

Then he provided them with a few rounds of nostalgic tales from back home, talked about the girl he had left behind, pulling a photograph of a little girl from his wallet.

'Cool,' James said.

'She's pretty,' Ruplu blurted.

Enrique's face lit up.

After ten minutes, six well-built white guys trooped in. The senior guy was the first to comment. 'The guy looks like the one on the video.'

Ruplu was terrified at the thought of criminal gangs stalking the streets of New York at night. Then she spotted their uniforms.

Relieved that it was not the Ku Klux Klan, her words came in torrents. 'Look here gentlemen, there is a mistake somewhere. We were at a concert in Central Park. We are from California, working on a project at Columbia University...'

The bartender interrupted Ruplu. 'Sirs, you have not yet told us what the matter is.'

The senior guy replied. 'There was a break-in on the Tenth Avenue three hours back. A shopkeeper and his security guard were shot dead. We have shots from our cameras of three guys running past. Our fellas in plain clothes spread out. Martin was the one sitting here. After comparing the faces and heights of the two men, he was certain that this is it. So am I now.'

The Ecuadorian tried his best to protect James. 'Can you please show us the image on your device?'

'Who do you think you are—a blasted judge or an FBI veteran?' the officer shouted.

After a brief discussion with his colleagues, the senior officer softened his stance. 'If you guys can provide me with an alibi, maybe passes for the concert, I will consider letting you go.'

They searched desperately for the tickets, reminded they had used them as holders for tarts and sandwiches. The shortage of plates at the café had turned disastrous, luck deserting them rather cruelly that night.

'I will have to take you to the police station. Trust me, if you are innocent, nothing is going to happen, but you need to spend the night in prison and be produced in court tomorrow. You will be released by the judge if forensic experts pronounce that the image captured is of a different person. Let us not waste time, folks. Handcuff him.'

They pinned James's arms back till they hurt.

A cop blabbered from the manual. 'You have the right to

remain silent, but any statement will be held against you...'

The dazed James had not spoken till then.

'Look here, before you handcuff me, these are my social security and credit cards. You can photograph me if you like. If you find a resemblance with the picture on the video, just pick me up from this address. It is just twenty minutes away. And this is my cell number, you could call to verify right away.'

Ruplu butted in. 'You can also speak to Professor Tony Smith. We are jointly working on a project under him at Columbia University. At the time mentioned by you, we were in Columbia University. We have an alibi in the café, a guy who sold us grub to eat at the concert.'

They were in no mood to listen. They had made up their minds.

'Oh, come on! Neither the café owner nor this Smith guy is germane to this case. If the images match, you're done.'

'Rups. Did I not speak to you about Rodney Reed? A nigger has to pay the price for the colour of his skin.'

Ruplu, on the other hand, was reminded of Rodney King. 'James, listen to me. Do not lose hope. You have not committed any crime and I am a witness. I will call Professor Smith right away and am sure he can help us. If he is unable to, it's just a night in prison.'

The officers cuffed him. 'Escort him to the van. I'll join you after a glass of water.'

As they pulled James away, Ruplu attempted to speak to the police officer and add a human touch, invoking his mother's condition and what she had gone through.

It backfired. 'So there is crime in the family background. By the way, where are you from, and are you a visitor to this place?'

She blanched. 'We are from California, classmates working on a project at Columbia University. Told you, sir, a while back.'

'Look here, young lady. If he's innocent, nothing will happen to him. This is the United States of America. The world speaks about our judicial system. Don't worry. He'll be alright, if he is genuinely innocent.'

◆

Ruplu was discreet, skipping the raunchy details.

There was pin-drop silence in the lounge. Her family was riveted, the suspense in the air resembling that of a Poirot climax.

Ruplu had tears in her eyes as she continued.

'Suddenly, I heard a cacophony of noises. "Stop, stop, will shoot!" A handcuffed figure sprinted, with a cop in close pursuit. Both of them were fast, but it was tough to beat a young black man. Although he was within the cop's taser gun range, the gap kept increasing. Unlike your Dhruva Roy, they had no plans to kill him in cold blood. The taser was directed at his legs and was intended to incapacitate him. He fell with a loud bang. He was later diagnosed with a heart attack and a spinal cord injury. For James, running had been a knee-jerk response as it reminded him of the pervasive images of police brutality.

'He lasted till the hospital and collapsed before I could call his parents. He wished to tell me something...'

'What happened afterwards?' Samir asked.

'Due processes of the asinine law were followed. The law goes by the printed word, it lacks spirit. I am certain the situation would have been different if there was a privileged person in his place, not from a disempowered racial minority or a poor white family.'

Neelu responded for the first time. 'What happened to the officer?'

'A case of justifiable homicide was registered and he was let off on bail. Must have been acquitted later since he had not technically violated the law. The case was forwarded to the State

Attorney's office and the FBI. Then a civil rights investigation was independently launched. I visited the court on camera a couple of times before leaving New York. I stressed two aspects, that the arrest had been arbitrary, and that they had detained him based on a CCTV image that later proved to belong to a different person. And why did they have to shoot the taser? How far would he have managed to sprint in handcuffs? Later in a video conference from UCLA, I appeared for the civil rights folks. I had requested for my identity to be kept a secret. I did not want you guys to be stressed out, and at home, you could not see through my sullenness. Apu could, and I needed someone to confide in.

'James's brother advised me after a few months to not visit them since it was affecting his mother. They lived in a rundown, tiny apartment in the suburbs, two brothers sleeping with their father and two sisters with their mom. James had been her favourite son because he was the only one who cared. A couple of years later, she passed away, unable to recover from the double whammy—although the family received hefty compensation having hired a renowned attorney.'

'Ruplu, how come the case did not receive publicity? I do not remember reading about it in the newspapers.' Samir queried.

'It did receive a lot of publicity. You may not have noticed.'

As silence descended on the room, Apu escorted a sobbing Ruplu out. Samir resumed his musing. In his opinion, she should have raised a storm across the country. She was a first-hand witness but she had chosen to remain in the background, perhaps fearful of repercussions.

She was indeed a complex personality, but did he have the right to act holier-than-thou?

◆

Samir was reminded of a depressive Sunday afternoon. Two months after a critical day in his life, barely a week after landing in London in 1971. He was with his cousin, bored of him and his overbearing wife, whom he had to put up with for a few days before moving to the accommodation provided by the college. He decided to visit Oxford on a Sunday afternoon to escape the drudgery and stifling atmosphere inside the house and obtain a glimpse of the hallowed institution he had heard of from his childhood days. On a sultry day, after a short walk from the bus stop, he remembered spotting a small, hidden outlet, its windows covered by tinted glass.

Samir went in and settled on the stools of a plain-looking bar. His eyes strayed towards a young girl at the counter wearing a black T-shirt and a pair of white shorts. She was sensuous. There were only a few customers and she was serving draught beer, approaching him after she had finished.

'Hello,' she greeted. 'From India?'

His response had been daft. 'How did you make that out?'

'Oh, come on, there are so many of you here.'

'I see.'

'What can I serve you?'

'A coke, perhaps?'

She was in splits. 'This is a bar.'

He had been introduced to beer by his Ashim kaku a month back, and he had developed a fondness for it. But he did not wish to waste the precious pounds he was holding on to. 'Okay, but I normally don't drink,' he agreed.

Her blue eyes gazed at him for a couple of seconds, following up with a coy wink. 'A beer will not do you any harm. A cold beer on a Sunday afternoon. Just try one.'

He focused on a bowl full of peanuts. The bus ride had been long and tiring, and Samir was hungry, but held himself back at the thought of Satyen and the pains he had to go through to organize the cash for his sudden departure and studies.

'Why don't you try the peanuts?'

'No, a beer will be just fine.'

'It is on the house.'

Once again, laughing her head off when the expression on his face betrayed that he had not the foggiest understanding of what she meant.

'It is free of charge.'

'Oh!'

He gulped down the first beer, immediately requesting a second. Soon, they started a conversation about where and what he planned to study, his life in India, his family, interests in life and many other topics. She was a student of anthropology, her dad belonged to the middle-class and she had to work to earn afford her education even though she was on a scholarship. He was astounded that a college girl was working part-time as a waitress.

When her duty hours ended, she volunteered to show him around the place.

'By the way, the beers are on me,' she said.

'Thanks, Martha.'

It was a Sunday, and most university facilities were closed, so they strolled the cobbled streets, listening to her drivel on the quaint buildings that dotted the space. After some time, they settled next to the Magdalen Bridge Boathouse on the banks of the Thames to watch white ducks float lazily and rowers punt hard at the oars, the sedentary ones settling for sailing boats, their fingers kissed by the silky, gently flowing waters.

They saw a band of youngsters picnicking on the bank. Samir stretched on the green grass to absorb the moist breeze. It was peak summer, brightly sunny at 6 p.m. and Samir's snarky comment, 'The sun never sets on the British Empire', sailed over her head. The late sunset, serenity and orderliness of the surroundings soothed his nerves, and he wished to lie down for a while.

He thought of the rain-swept parapet at his Kolkata home, lashed by monsoon rains, the ghash phool that blossomed after the downpour. The plants bending sideways in his mother's tiny garden, the pots that dotted their terrace and the waxing and waning of the moon that he loved to keep track of. The squirrels darting in and the pigeons who took shelter under the asbestos shade, their tiny drawing-room that sported a decent look after many years.

He was lapsing into a sullen mood when he realized that he was not permitted to visit home for another two years.

And then the inevitable happened. The thoughts that had chased him relentlessly for two months, thoughts that he had managed to suppress for the last few weeks, resurfaced with a vengeance. The memories were dark, and he scrambled up, intending to catch the bus back home.

Just then, he noticed Martha turning edgy. He suspected her intentions when she requested he join her at her apartment for sandwiches and ice cream.

He followed.

A putrid odour of stale cheese pervaded the one-room tenement. The room was large enough for a double cot, a bookshelf and a wardrobe. They settled for bracers, the worktable in the kitchen serving a dual role. A shameless pinch on his crotch with barely concealed lust was sufficient to titillate.

He had recently started to experience a void after a period of celibacy and this opportunity was a godsend for him.

They lay silently on the mattress in pitch darkness. Martha requested a couple of drags as he lit a cigarette.

'After a long time, I feel as if I'm on the top of the world, Martha. I will tell you later what I went through before being forced to leave my country,' Samir said.

Samir was baffled by her indifferent silence. It was a different Martha.

He could feel the hormones flowing through his veins. In no mood to return home, he resolved to call his cousin to inform him that he had bumped into an old school friend and planned to stay with him.

'Do you have a telephone in your apartment?'

'No.'

'Is there a booth close by?'

'You are running late. The last bus leaves in half an hour.'

The message lacked ambiguity. He hurriedly gathered his clothes that lay scattered on the floor. When his hands strayed towards her bra lying in a corner, she screeched indignantly. 'Please do not touch those.'

Hastily dressing up, he rushed towards the door. 'Close it behind you. It's self-locking.'

'Bye, Martha.'

Once again, there was no response.

The sound of the click on the unoiled lock reverberated across the long corridor, resembling the corridors in hospitals. A black lady darted out of another apartment. Almost bumping into him, she turned her face away and walked away briskly. He was not sure whether the curse was directed at him.

Later in life, a counselor identified that Samir suffered from a syndrome where he churned delusions of romance even when a lady courteously smiled at him. He did not have the ability to distinguish a one-evening stand from a deep-seated romantic relationship—stemming from an abnormal craze for love and affinity.

When he realized on the bus that he had not satisfied her, that the act lacked adequate foreplay and that the climax had been too quick, he spun into a bout of depression. The thought reinforced that he had turned into a gigolo for a couple of draught beers (likely managed and not paid for), ice cream and smelly sandwiches. Bereft of a suitable outlet to vent the frisson of frustration, he descended into a deep slumber, overshooting his destination by a couple of stops. He was forced to walk the distance back through deserted streets.

His cousin and wife had left the door unlocked with a pasted message, asking him to warm his dinner in the micro-oven, but Samir had no clue how to operate one.

Ruplu had shed genuine tears for James. Whether they were out of remorse or because she was disturbed by haunting memories was not pertinent; that she copiously shed tears was all that mattered.

That afternoon, there was no drop in his eyes; he was not reminded of another girl who could be stuck in an airless dungeon huddled with prostitutes, streetwalkers, smugglers, robbers, fraudsters or swindlers. Perhaps the girl had been locked at home by her parents, unable to overcome the trauma. Or she had started to attend college, repeating a year, departing by early afternoon— face pointed downwards, a lonely soul scrambling into a crowded 2B bus where horny gropers waited for their prey.

Or perhaps she did not exist anymore. The thought was instantly dismissed but he had a faint hunch that it may be true. Difficult to trust those bastards!

At a time when she had needed him by his side, he had disappeared into thin air. Her face had not flashed, not while lazily exploring outlets on Oxford Street, savouring lovely sights of the first world or on the evening he went to bed with Martha two months after an episode that transformed the lives of two individuals, supposedly bound together by an irresistible force of attraction.

Back at home, at the sight of her daughter's tears, Neelu, as always, was blunt. 'I did not appreciate the need for this farce after so many years.'

'Why don't you say that to Apu? He brought it up.'

'Is Apu her father? You should have put your foot down.'

'I believed the catharsis would do her good. And why did you not voice your misgivings at the onset?'

'I did not concur with your decision but was not in a mood to express my opinion. Try to understand, the memory will haunt her for days. You have exhumed a well-preserved mummy.'

When pushed into a corner, Samir had the uncanny ability to turn aggressive, like a trapped cat. He altered the focus to suit himself. 'What shocks me is that as a mother you failed to perceive her condition at a time when I was bogged down with long working hours and extensive travelling.'

She gave him a disgusted look and exclaimed, 'As always, my fault,' accompanying the statement with an unusual wringing of her hands that left him a tad bemused, reminding him of similar arguments that took place once in a blue moon between his parents. The experience was novel because he did not recall her displaying such stereotypical Bengali masochism.

Apu entered the room to announce that Ruplu was now fast asleep.

'Great. I suggest that you sleep in her room for the night.'

'No need to, Baba. She will be fine by the morning,' Apu said, placing a pair of reassuring hands on his dad's drooping shoulders.

'Will take your word for it and plan my tête-à-tête for breakfast. Well, my estimate was spot on. It is ten past eleven. Chalo, time to retire.'

'Apu, you carry on. I have something important to discuss with Baba.'

He was surprised by this sudden twist, but what disconcerted him was the underlying insensitivity.

'Can't we do it tomorrow? We have the entire day. And why here? Let's start the conversation in the bedroom. I need to lie down.'

'Not the right environment. This is not an informal chat by a long shot and in bed, you will instantly go off to sleep.'

Apu had never heard his mother demanding a chat in confidence, and the lingo was unfamiliar. They had grown up in a transparent household, despite a nagging suspicion that Samir had always had a couple of secrets to hide.

'*Apu, kathata kaaney gelo?* Could you hear me?' she repeated.

The loud noise of the banged door was meant to convey Apu's anger. Like other millennials, he hated subordination.

THE CLOSELY GUARDED SECRET

17 May 2014

'Neelu, I had a disturbed sleep this morning and did not get a wink in the afternoon due to the official assignment. You slept like a log.' Samir still pleaded.

'I never stand between you and your sleep, but this is important.'

'How can a domestic matter be so urgent?'

'I like the word domestic. *Ta botey*. What you meant was that anything concerning Neelu cannot be urgent. I'm merely a doorknob. I may have been showered with all, everything a human being can perhaps long for—a cozy home, a closely knit family, vacations to exotic locales and an exclusive car. You did not cheat on me or neglect the children. Yet you have been parsimonious in according me love and respect, the vital components of a conjugal relationship.'

'What's wrong with you tonight? I suggest you reserve your litany of woes for tomorrow after Apu and Ruplu leave.'

'It is not possible. An encounter has been planned for eleven in the morning and we need to be on the same page.'

He could not restrain a sarcastic remark. 'An encounter! Is it Armageddon, doomsday or the last judgment tomorrow at eleven?'

She was smarter in her response. 'Could be all three. Although it affects just the four of us.'

'Although you keep your feelings to yourself, you are so transparent. From your behaviour at the lunch table, I suspected that something was troubling you. Now I know. You concluded that I am still in touch with the girl who accompanied me to the nursing home. But I have neither seen nor met her after leaving college.'

'All I can say is that you are a poor student of human behaviour. Incidentally, what is her name?'

'Oh god, give me a break. Anyhow, since you are so interested in trivia, her name is Runa.'

Her voice almost choked. 'Yes, I am always immersed in trivia.'

'I didn't mean it in a derogatory sense. You like to get into unnecessary details, like most ladies of your ilk.'

'Is that all you have to say about Runa? That she was a batchmate?'

'Absolutely.'

'Nothing more to it?'

This one stumped him. 'What makes you ask this question?'

Samir was confused. 'What the hell is she trying to drive at?'

'Bear with me then. Let me retrace to the time I left you before Apu was born. I was not certain of my course of action, even though I was mentally set on divorcing you. You turned out to be aloof, a disinterested and detached person. I was unable to communicate with my partner. It was not the ideal situation to be able to sustain a marriage. My parents, grandfather, uncles and aunts tried their best to persuade me. Divorce was not very common after all. My pregnancy was confirmed the day before leaving Cincinnati, but I kept it to myself. Fortunately, symptoms were not apparent for the first few months.'

Samir interrupted her rather rudely. 'Oh! Not again, Neelu. I know it by heart. You bump into this school friend of yours, a classmate from your primary school, with whom you had lost touch after she moved to a boarding school. She was on a short visit to Kolkata, you bumped into her on the road, she was the one who recognized you and pulled you into a restaurant near Deshapriya Park for a cup of tea where you caught up with each other. You opened up, but after a while, she empathized with you, unlike your folks at home.'

'If you are so impatient, let's call it off and proceed to bed,' Neelanjana retorted.

'Okay, darling. Carry on. But try to desist from the superfluities of language.' Samir was trying to be as gentle as possible.

'I practice brevity in my communication more than you, I can narrate episodes more interestingly. Even your friends say so.'

'I apologize. Carry on,' said Samir, being curt.

'The portion that will render you speechless has not yet been disclosed. When I mentioned your name, college and batch, the expression on my friend's face changed. Guess why?

'Anyway, she had come to Kolkata on an official assignment. She worked for an NGO in Bangalore. My parents were adamant about not going for a divorce, but I was pretty sure the tables would have turned if I disclosed the piece of information she had conveyed to me. So it was not an easy decision. It would be a point of no return. I decided against it. I was carrying Apu and could not reconcile myself to an abortion. I decided to bury the secret deep, but controlling the human mind is not easy. It keeps cropping up. I am now requesting that you make your confession after Runa drops by tomorrow, Samir.'

He sprung up from his chair. 'Runa drops by? What the hell are you talking about?'

'Eleven is when I have invited her.'

'And how the holy crap did you get to know her?'

What was equally puzzling was how her friend knew Runa and how she had learnt about that sordid episode in his life. Samir was pretty sure he knew what was being referred to. He had been smug under the belief that it had remained a closely guarded secret for so many years. It was credible because none of his friends ever mentioned it. They would have asked him if whispers were floating in the air, at least in confidence. They had mocked him so many times for escaping the country!

The loud laugh was rather unbecoming of her. 'That's another story. I had taken the call last night. The caller introduced herself as Runa Ganguly, an old batchmate of yours. The name rang a loud bell. The name and the incident after all remained etched inside me, waiting like a time bomb, for thirty years. I always wished it would disappear, but it was merely dormant. I guess it imploded yesterday.'

'I never expected this from you. Calling Runa over! This is chicanery.'

'You can call it by any name you like. The three of you were waiting for me, so I jotted her number and address, promising that you would call later since there were guests at home. I needed to be sure that it was the same Runa Ganguly.'

'So you did not just betray me, you lied to her too.'

Neelu was in no mood to interrupt the flow. 'While you slept soundly in the morning, I called her and sought to visit her. Initially reluctant, she succumbed when I appealed to her as a woman. I was accorded a warm middle-class reception at her apartment. Her son was there but walked out when the topic came up, and she refused to divulge a word on the episode unless explicitly permitted to do so by you. But neither did she deny it.'

'Deny what?'

'An incident in your life. You know what I am referring to. Her face expressed distaste at what I mentioned, but she never explicitly voiced her feelings. She is a smart woman with character. She encapsulates whatever I have missed out on all these years. She has agreed to drop by tomorrow morning, but only if she is personally invited by you.'

'Holy shit, what a scheming kind of woman you are! Never realized it in thirty-two years.'

'It is your decision, but my advice would be to grab this opportunity and come clean. You need catharsis more than Ruplu does. Be fair to Runa and us. As far as my knowledge goes, the incident was unacceptable in the eyes of the law, but you were driven by a political ideology. I fail to understand why you kept it under wraps for so many years. You could have divulged it yesterday. It was an opportunity but you lacked the gumption.'

He restrained himself with a lot of effort. Screaming was not desirable, and the kids should not come to know—not so soon after yesterday's narrative. Ruplu not disclosing that Angela would be with her in the café was a trifle compared to what he had hidden from the family for so many years.

'You have committed a felony that I will not take in my stride, Neelu,' he threatened.

Her pitch was louder this time. 'I have been ignoring your comments for so long. Did you just call it a felony? What an audacious statement. After festering such a dark secret for so many years. I lied to her, I told her that you had guests. I visited her without your knowledge. I lied about the time-share company and about meeting an old friend at Starbucks. But I have come clean in twelve hours, not after twenty-seven years.'

'The incident occurred well before our marriage. I do not understand how you enter the picture.'

'Did I allude to infidelity? Every individual has to be honest in a relationship and cannot leave a portion of himself by the wayside. We all have containers within which are stored innumerable episodes from the day we acquire consciousness. You presented yourself minus an unsavoury episode in your life.'

'You are ignorant. There is a concept called privacy. Think

about Ruplu. Would you like the world to know about the incident that scarred her tender mind? Is there not a possibility that a prospective employer may consider her potentially unstable if they come to know of the trauma that had once scarred her? Or the incident with James? Life requires constant erasure.'

She responded after a few moments of thought. The argument seemed strong on its face and Samir had managed to place her on the defensive.

'Her experience needs to be erased. I could not agree more on that. And your chapter too needs to be closed. And that is why I am asking you to come out with the truth. But am I saying that you should mention it in your CV or talk to Fox News or CNN? Perhaps we could even consider hiding it from the kids, but there is a possibility that they may come to know from someone else, which will lower your esteem in their eyes. It is better to come clean in one shot. What is relevant here is that you hid it from me. I feel cheated and have kept it under wraps, but it came up out of the blue yesterday.'

'I do not see any merit in your argument. Moreover, it was not a purely political act. You are mistaken.'

'That's what I want to know from you. In Hindu philosophy, karma extends as a continuum beyond generations. An individual, they say, is constituted not just by the contexts of his existence but his genes.'

'You seem to be an expert in Hindu philosophy. It is not the genes, it is the aatman.'

'You appear tired,' she finally conceded.

He sighed.

'I will conclude in a couple of minutes after disclosing the decision I have taken. You may have noticed a change in my behaviour since the evening because by then my course of action was charted out, ending a day of indecision. Today, I feel I have regained my amour proper, after so many years. Self-actualization of sorts,' she said softly.

'Why don't you elaborate, leaving out the frills?'

'No amount of sarcasm will provoke me tonight, Samir, but let me come to the point if that's what you desire. If you decide not to honour my request, I quit this marriage. Apu is established in life, and I am concerned about Ruplu. She has gone through harrowing incidents and needs monitoring and guidance, but I say that that is your responsibility from now on. My parents plan to shift to their new residence at Salt Lake in Kolkata since our ancestral home has gotten cramped after quite a few additions to the family. I will go and live with them, and visit you guys once a year.'

Samir stood dumbfounded. 'You're blackmailing me. This is atrocious.'

'Perhaps. But my decision is made, the ball is now in your court. Good night, Samir. I'm mentally exhausted.' With that, she started walking away, rather abruptly, only to return shortly to say, 'You need to inform Runa by ten since she requires an hour to powder her nose. And here are her contacts. She said she normally goes to bed after one.'

◆

The world suddenly upended for Samir. The terrible chapter had popped up like an inchoate infant. He had been complacent all these years, despite an inner voice asserting that it would tumble out one day, tumble like those spilled packets of condoms falling before his mother at their Kolkata home.

Human lives are driven by vicissitudes. The naïve get caught like unsuspecting fish in nets.

What Samir felt was not a gentle tremor but a volcanic eruption, spewing lava and ash under a placid surface. He felt a tight grasp on the guts and beads of sweat, trickling down his spine. He experienced vertigo.

Even in his fraught state, he recognized the absurdity of his situation. This was a development he had never anticipated, even in his wildest imagination. It was pregnant with the potential to churn into a mid-life crisis. He needed to keep his faculties in working order.

He swallowed a concoction of sweet, bitter-sweet, melancholy and macabre reminiscences from the past. He thought of the transfer from the hospital, joint marches, sprinting through pouring rains, the riverbank in a sleepy town called Santiniketan, expressionist plays on Saturday afternoons at Curzon Park, naughty kisses stolen in dark corners of auditoriums, rendezvous in seedy restaurants where waiters pulled the curtains as soon as guests settled in. The days when they were not on speaking terms. She had been the one with an olive branch, waiting patiently for him at the college gate.

He was reminded of the dreadful afternoon that had altered the contours of his life. Even as he was eager to sidestep it, it only reappeared with sharper clarity. The afternoon turned to be a blessing in disguise, but a possible malediction for her, an impression he still retained despite her sudden appearance from obscurity. Surreal, spooky, magically realistic. Forty-three years of conundrums converging into an unexpected conclusion.

He gazed at the contacts Neelu had left on a piece of paper, peering at the digits from varying angles as if the piece of paper was multi-dimensional. Finally, he decided to tiptoe towards the phone.

THE WIND BLOWS, BUT I FEEL NOT THE BREEZE

17 May 2014

Her phone kept ringing. Perhaps she had gone to bed early? Or was she reluctant to speak to him? To be embroiled in an unpleasant controversy?

The polished voice that answered the call set his veins on fire.

'Samir here,' he said.

'I guessed as much.'

Her voice was sweet, her accent impeccable and the unmistakable timbre and cadence made him shiver. She said, 'At the onset, let me beg your forgiveness.'

'There is no reason to do so. Neelu told me that you refused to divulge a word.'

'I have not transformed at all, Samir.'

'Perhaps I have. But tell me where you were for forty-three years. And where did you disappear that day? We considered you dead. "Missing" in official parlance. We were unable to ascertain the facts.'

'My life has been fairly uneventful. I'll narrate the facts when we meet face-to-face. Incidentally, I live in Dublin these days.'

'Are you aware of my life's history?'

'Yes. From Utpal, whom I keep meeting. Now do not ask me why I did not contact you earlier. But now I am in LA to meet my son, and it is difficult to resist the temptation.'

'How long do you plan on staying?'

'I leave town on Monday evening and have the entire weekend to spare. Have been buzzing you since the day before unsuccessfully. I had decided it would be the last attempt when your wife responded. I even contacted Utpal to verify the number. He said he spoke to you on this number a few days back. Why do you guys not respond to your landline?'

'The instrument is located in a corner of our house. The first time I heard it ringing was the day before, but my legs were aching and I had just returned from the office. In any case, I was not supposed to be at home at that hour. At night, we were sitting on the lawn outside. By the time we heard it, it stopped ringing. Yesterday, it got disconnected before I could reach it. And then she picked it up. You lack patience.'

'On the other hand, I believe I have held on longer than I should have.'

The mellifluous voice had turned croaky with age, and a futile attempt to conjure her appearance resulted in blur. He visualized her sepia-toned lips, fair complexion, mischievous smiles, and azure blue eyes. He was reminded abruptly of the day they locked tongues for the first time, her soft fingers caressing his stubble with finesse.

He was baffled at the ease with which he was propelled across time to an antediluvian era. That time, its mysterious people, bustling processions, smoke-belching buses. He was back in a flooded city, a gentle-flowing river, a tranquil lake. They ate phuchkas at street corners, shared intimacies. His emotions were overpowering him. Myriad thoughts were compressed into a few seconds, a fantastic illustration of the Einsteinian concept of compression and expansion of time.

'When did you reach LA?'

'Thirteen days back. My son, Kallol, works for an IT company and is in town on a three-month project. I decided to drop by for a brief visit.'

'Why did you not contact me earlier?'

'We went gallivanting last weekend to Disneyland, Hollywood and the beaches. Did not wish to trouble you on a weekday and Kallol's hours are weird. He leaves normally after lunch and returns by ten.'

She resumed after a brief pause. 'The main reason is... different. I wished to surprise you on your birthday. I came to know from Utpal that you planned to be in town.'

'Utpal's unexpected call a few weeks back! I should have smelt a rat. He had made tall claims about his son. The next time we meet, Utpal should only expect fire and brimstone for his devious behaviour!' It was as though things had suddenly fallen into place and Samir could see each moment play out before his eyes. Finding his way back to the conversation, he said, 'Are you in regular touch with Utpal? It is strange because he never mentioned the fact.'

'Whenever my husband and I visit India. He was under strict instructions not to disclose my whereabouts and he honoured my request. I buzzed him for your contact just before leaving Dublin, requesting him to discreetly enquire whether you planned to be in town.'

'Every time I meet him, the topic of you invariably comes up. I am amazed at the manner in which he has lied through his teeth for so many years.'

'He was just being faithful to me.'

He ignored the reference to his birthday. 'Which organization does Kallol work for?'

'An Irish software company.'

'That's great news. The young man has an amazing career ahead. Where are you putting up?'

'At Disneyland...cuddled in an apartment provided by his client. With two of his colleagues, South Indians from Bangalore.

Sincere guys. They make me feel at home every moment.'

'That's not very far from our house.'

'Great. Tell me when can we meet? Neelanjana was telling me she would try and convince you to come clean about your past before the family, but, given a choice, I would like to skip the encounter. It is embarrassing and does not concern me.'

'Frankly, I have not yet decided. She told me a while back. If at all, I will disclose the incident only in your presence. What a coincidence, Runa. Just yesterday I was narrating the story of that day in college. The day I was bashed up and you accompanied me to the nursing home.'

'Yes, she told me. But why were you talking about it after so many years?'

'Neelanjana knew about it before, but I did not wish to expose my children to the gory facts. They are brought up differently here, in a peaceful environment.'

'But why did you hide the second incident from your wife? You committed no crime, at least in my eyes.'

'Guess I'm made that way.'

'Not an excuse, Samir. I remember telling you so many times to be transparent.'

'Have not changed much, I fear. Anyhow, either we meet at eleven tomorrow and follow her plans, or I meet you wherever you have put up, or at a café. I am dying to meet you.'

A pedestrian dialogue followed about common friends he had met at the pub back in Kolkata, the happenings in his life, his family, his career, the manner his parents passed away a few years back and his new commitment to spiritualism.

Finally, she said, 'I did not wish to say this but I have not forgiven you for not getting in touch. I waited and waited. I respected your wishes and spoke about the incident to just one person besides my husband. That too, many years later. I'm certain that he has not leaked it. Kept it a secret for the last so many years, but look at you! You visited our city multiple times, not bothering to drop by at our place. I have followed up on your progress from Utpal. Despite how you have ignored me, I am delighted by what life has offered you. Not that I have lost out in life but, as my husband says, the lack of ill-will is a manifestation of the concept of 'mudita' in Yogic literature. Selfless pleasure at the success of loved ones.'

Samir replied with a touch of arrogance. 'Yes, Runa, I'm aware of the concept.'

What followed was an unwarranted outburst from Samir.

'I'm shocked that you condemn me without bothering to enquire into the circumstances under which I left the country. My situation was not a happy one. I requested an uncle to drop by at your residence, but he overturned my request with powerful arguments. It would have been rash.

'I do agree that the circumstances were different after 1977. Still, I was unsure of your whereabouts and sceptical whether my presence after so many years would be the cause of emotional stress. Though your memory remained forever etched in a corner of my heart.'

'Samir, face the truth, you consciously wished to avoid the past, you wanted to turn to a new page. Once again, you are fooling yourself.'

'You are mistaken, Runa. Lastly, slightly unrelated, let me tell you that I was disillusioned with the Party. Other than a few members, we were all a bunch of single-tracked, delusional individuals incapable of relating to human beings. Drowned in dogma, irrational like Abrahamic self-righteous fanatics, devoted to sacred texts and an abstract concept of a collective identity, unmindful that the whole is constituted by individuals of flesh and blood. We chased a Sisyphean myth. I am not belittling the sacrifices and noble mission of our comrades, but somewhere down the line, they lost the power to introspect, surrendering their intellect before a supreme intangible authority along with the ability to emote. I am convinced that I still suffer from a hangover from the past, unable to relate to folks around me other than perhaps my children.'

'Your soliloquy does not impress me.'

'Why did our ideology collapse? Have you ever bothered to introspect upon it?'

Her voice was gentle yet persistent. 'I'm not interested in a polemical chat right now, Samir, nor on whether you stored me in a corner or the centre of your heart, or your long-winding analysis. It is plain drivel. You opted to join voluntarily. I requested that you think it through. Once you subject yourself to the rigours of an organization, individual agendas are subsumed into a larger discipline. That is the way an organization works. Lastly, there was another unforgivable act that I do not wish to elaborate on now.'

He withheld his simmering rage. 'Unforgivable?'

'Do mull over it. Samir. I'm told by Utpal that your convictions have transformed over time. Ours have not. Even though I do not live in the country anymore. Call it fanaticism or naivety, I do not care a damn. I see no point in analysing the past. Merely intended to chat face-to-face, an occasion to savour nostalgic memories. Tell me what your decision is. I'm game to spend the entire day tomorrow. Monday you may have to go to work, and I plan to complete my shopping. Besides, I am carrying a small birthday gift from Dublin, in remembrance of a bittersweet day.'

Yes, the bittersweet day! The day they met for the first time under normal circumstances. He had not told her that it was his birthday. He hardly knew her then.

Her logic was impeccable. He had not been forced into activism, he had opted to join on his own, to gratify his ego, to taste the excitement, ride the high horse, and most importantly, gain her acceptance. Initially, it had been because of a desire to avenge the death of a close friend, but it had metamorphosed into a strong urge to work with her.

Runa had valued the relationship and cherished his birthday after so many years.

But still, the last comment had been uncharitable, and he had no clue as to what she was hinting at.

He was stirred at the click of the receiver because his mind had drifted. He was trying to remember her date of birth, but couldn't. What they call hard formatting in technical jargon. He was neither emotional about it nor penitential at the inability to recall a day she held so close to her heart. The strings failed to vibrate as they should have when a friend he was once in a relationship with, given up as dead, was now turning up like a phoenix.

Perhaps he had called her out of curiosity?

His life would move on even if they did not meet the next day. Her existence would morph into an imperceptible and ephemeral subatomic particle. But in that case, was it not imperative to meet her?

Why did he hesitate? Was it his baggage from an ideology he believed in the past, or were the spiritually inclined and woke activists inherently insensitive because they strove towards a distant utopia? A counsellor may be able to analyse hidden facets in his persona. But he was lost.

Switching on the table fan, he consumed a bottle of cold water from the icebox and preened for a few minutes in front of the mirror before strolling back to the lounge.

Thoughts churned once again. He was engulfed by waves of ecstasy, breaking on the shores one after the other on a stormy day by the seashore; memories segued one after the other—mostly sweet, a few bittersweet. Runa was alive and kicking.

He was repentant with respect to the rude utterances at the end, but simultaneously excited at the thought that he could meet her if he wanted to. He had taken Utpal's hint at her passing away at face value since rumours rarely turned out to be without substance. There was a saying in Bengali, '*Ja rotey tar kichu botey*', or 'a rumour is seldom without basis'.

Yet, he had broached the topic, recalling Runa many times and each time Utpal had feigned ignorance. But it was unfair to blame a person bound by an oath of secrecy.

He was no longer in love with Runa, but dormant feelings had burst forth from him like a butterfly from its cocoon.

It did not take long to travel back in time to another birthday, forty-three years back. 15 May 1971.

◆

Samir was a young lad of seventeen. He bumped into a girl, a couple of months older while rushing for classes. His dad had left after a brief meeting with the Principal. He could deduce who the sprightly girl was. She was walking towards him with brisk, bouncy steps. He planned to thank her for displaying camaraderie and empathy on a day few had dared to reach out, for accompanying him to the nursing home, showering feminine affection and volunteering to stay back for the night despite the discomfiture at the memory of the naughty giggle in the car. She was like a ray of fresh sunlight peeking through a corner of the drapes on a cold wintry morning.

She laughed loudly. 'Samir, are you aware that I visited your residence twice, and was dragged into an argument with your mother since I felt she was being unreasonably cautious? Nonetheless, I am so happy to see you hale and hearty. Gosh! What a scary situation! Does it still hurt?'

'Off and on. The brutes had every intention of killing me.'

'I know. All of us were beside ourselves till the doctor declared you out of danger. Are you aware that we called for a two-day strike in college? And that it evoked a spontaneous response? Just look...up there.'

His otherwise unobservant eyes strayed towards a handwritten slogan, composed in flawless handwriting and large characters decorating the plaster: 'Salute our brave Comrade Samir.'

The self-effacing Samir was not particularly exuberant at the sight. He was neither a paragon of bravery nor a desperado, and he regretted their display of panegyrics because it was hollow to the core.

He could only hope his father had not noticed it.

'We have not had the opportunity to be introduced as yet,' he said, changing the topic.

'Runa. History. Lots to discuss. When do we catch up? After lectures?'

She noticed the trepidation in his body language.

'Where do you stay, down south?' he asked her.

Despite astonishment at his irrelevant query, it did not show up in her response. 'Yup, close to the Gariahat junction.'

'Would love to meet you outside college. Reaching Gariahat is not a challenge for me.'

'Nor is it an issue for me, but why?'

'I will tell you the reason when we meet. How about Sunday morning?'

'What I wished to discuss was urgent. Have promised Atanu da to touch base the day you join.'

He continued imploring. 'Sorry, it is not possible, Runa. Try to understand. Please.'

She gave him a reluctant nod, a shrug of the shoulders and

a mystified look. Then she said, 'Let us catch up on Sunday then. Cannot confirm the time right now since my sister and her husband plan to drop in over the weekend.'

'Can I jot down your contact? I will call you.'

Suddenly, Runa had solved the mystery. She almost jumped in delight. 'It's crystal clear now, baby! Petit-bourgeois pushback from home. You must tackle it all by yourself, comrade. I have done it with my folks. The middle-class has opted to keep the status quo throughout history, despite their myriad existential issues. They have no qualms cosying up to the bourgeois and betraying the revolution at crucial junctures.'

The didactic jargon-mongering was not a novelty for Samir anymore. He had been exposed to a radical ideology over the last few months. Though it was trademark speech for most fellows, it was more pronounced in fresh converts. Samir had noted this aspect over the last few months in college, it reminded him of his kaku each time. Dogmatic polemics, quotations from classics at the drop of a hat, recruits positing themselves as the saviour of mankind. Unyielding, unswerving and rigid. Unwilling to learn from the very masses they set out to liberate. For them, the proletariat was a mass of imbeciles with no minds of their own, requiring guidance at every step. Their religious faiths were mocked, petty aspirations ridiculed. Activists donned the role of enlightened hegemons, as a bunch of white missionaries sent to 'civilize' natives. Cynical, bombastic and clichéd.

He had looked forward to a carnival of ideas, a transcendental worldview, but his expectations were dashed after every meeting of their student body. He had planned to voice his reservations at the first available opportunity because, in his opinion, without a radical transformation in attitudes, their organization faced inevitable doom. The prognostication was validated over the next year.

The woman in the corridor wore a light green cardigan and a

yellow saree that blended into a yellow rose hem. Runa's features were sharper than that of the average Bengali girl. She was well-endowed with an aquiline nose, a complexion on the fairer side and a voluptuous figure. She was not beautiful in the conventional sense, but had been gifted with a magnetic aura and a mysterious persona.

She flashed him an innocent smile out of the blue. 'Why are you staring at me?'

The second awkward situation.

'*Aagey kokhono meyeder shongey kothai bolishni money hocchey,*' she joked. 'Looks like you have never spoken to a young girl before.'

His denial, expressed through vigorous shakes of his head, left her in squeals of laughter. She quivered in spasms to expose an unsullied, innocent soul, bereft of malice because the cheer was not at his expense but at the awkwardness of his situation.

He deemed it fit to beat a hasty retreat without noting her contacts, necessitating her to dash behind him with a tiny piece of paper, barely covering the length of her fingers.

Although Samir's name was by then on most lips, few recognized the low-profile individual talking to Runa near the entrance. When his classmates spotted him, he found himself at the circumcentre of curiosity, bombarded by a volley of bizarre questions he had no option but to respond. He finally managed to steal a moment to remind them that AKR was renowned for his punctuality.

The following Sunday, he asked his parents at the breakfast table about going out for a couple of hours to catch up on missed lecture notes. Satyen's poker face conveyed the message that he had taken Samir's statement with pinches of salt. Ma was more forthright. 'Hope you honour your commitment. It holds for three more years.'

Samir was itching to snap back that her husband had committed once earlier, but he desisted since he was not in a mood for unpleasantness. On its face, the occasion was commonplace: a trip to a corner restaurant to meet Runa and convey his intention of withdrawing from activism for some time. But the thought of a date with a girl whose affable personality and appearance had bowled him over was tempting. He was simultaneously aware that he lacked the requisite skills to appreciate Cupid and his mysterious style.

Samir arrived bang on time to find her seated at the table, relishing her lebu cha—a concoction of lemon and tea. She seemed a tad paler than her usual self and was wearing a pair of thick spectacles. She looked different. He had not yet been exposed to the concept of cycles when it came to a woman's body, and her looks were unfathomable.

The familiar scent of the aguru did not escape his nostrils. At a loss for words, his gesture of apology for arriving late was met with a burst of hearty laughter—the third such laugh within a few days. He was not late; she was early. She had been unaware that a particular outlet was closed on Sundays. It was followed up with a reassuring comment that, having studied in a co-educational school, she was familiar with gauche guys like him interacting with members of the opposite gender for the first time.

The first salvo came from Runa after a round of pleasantries. 'What is the secret you wished to divulge today?'

'Nothing much—just that my parents do not wish me to continue with my activities. You see, I am the only child of my parents and they depend on me. However, I have decided on a break for a month or so.'

'These are your personal issues and you need to deal with them.'

She made a gesture as if she was planning to leave the table.

'Just a minute, Runa. Is there any way we could operate outside the college?'

'Well that is exactly what I came here to disclose. But you need to decide.'

'Any legal activity outside the college is game for me.'

Her voice was soft this time. 'Fine, let me tell you then. Atanu da wishes to create a mini cell consisting of just the two of us. It would be covertly associated with the Party and situated outside the boundaries of their college since we have been branded after the incident that day.

'At a clandestine party conference, the leadership has recently decided to tactically focus on the exposed layers: youngsters with their boisterous slogans, posters, class boycotts, and open forms of agitation in various colleges and universities, keeping a safe distance from the core. Militants would continue as the core layer. Folks like you and me would populate the third layer with tenuous links to the core, working for open democratic institutions like the Association for Protection of Democratic Rights or agitprop drama groups performing street plays. These platforms, populated by sympathisers, would confine themselves to innocuous non-violent activities, like rallies and open protests.'

The clarity with which she explained the structure, tactics and strategies through a brief presentation lasting half an hour left him spellbound. Every single sentence was impromptu, rattled off from the mind as it was forbidden to pen seditious stuff on paper. Her oratorical talent and a keen aptitude for the liberal arts were discernible. After concluding her speech, she gave him an intimidating stare that lasted for a few seconds. It threw him off-guard before she changed gear with an enchanting smile.

'Only if you agree, comrade. We do not operate a criminal gang, nor do we believe in compelling a reluctant individual.

Your baba requested Dr Mukherjee to keep a close watch on you, hence Atanu da felt that you should be left out for the time being. Vacillating comrades are dangerous to our safety. I managed to convince him, arguing that my parents with their middle-class expectations would not have behaved differently. Despite pretending to agree, I am certain he was confident you would not agree to join us since I was advised not to spell out detailed plans before obtaining your concurrence. I have disobeyed him... well, Samir, don't ask me why.'

Her voice turned a shade mellow. Though the tiny teardrop he seemed to spot in a corner of her eye was a figment of his fecund imagination.

He realized it was pointless to deny what he had naively expected would remain a closely guarded secret. 'I never expected Dipak da to betray me like this.'

Her smile revealed a set of sparkling, white, well-proportioned teeth.

'Samir, you have miles to travel. It was an intentional leak from the Principal himself. This is how the ruling class operates. They utilize every available opportunity to foster mistrust with the avowed intention of splitting our ranks. They are smart guys,' she said, then resumed after a brief pause. 'I'm in a bit of a hurry. My advice would be not to respond impulsively. Mull over it. I look forward to working with you, but the final decision can only be yours. Let me be candid. There is a selfish reason. If Atanu da has his way, he would nominate another individual, but I rarely get along with boys. Take a week and let's meet up next Sunday at another location.'

Calling for the waiter, she promptly paid for two cups of tea and gave him a wink. 'A word of guidance for a novice. When with a girl at a restaurant, do offer to pay up. That's what they call chivalry,' she said, laughing heartily. He did not appreciate it.

'Listen, leave the premises after ten minutes. You never know, someone may be watching us. Sorry, there was another point. Noticed you wearing a sacred thread that day. Please throw it out of the window. We do not relish comrades displaying their caste to the world at large.'

She made a final gesture before she left, gently pulling at his unkempt beard and brushing her hand over his overgrown bushy hair, ruffling both. He did not mind, although he was not carrying a comb.

Then she strolled down the long corridor of the restaurant in a relaxed and unselfconscious stride. Her slim physique faded into the sunshine. Her unoiled, dry hair fluttered in the breeze as she negotiated her way through gaps between sluggish trams sauntering in opposite directions.

The physical distance metamorphosed into a metaphoric chasm for Samir. His world was covered by a layer of candyfloss. Delicate strains of Madhuvanti, the famous classical raga of love, played in his mind.

He took his decision. It was an opportunity to work outside the ambit of the Principal and his espionage and the assignment would involve minimal risk because he would be positioned outside the core of the Party. Tantamount to eating the cake and having it too! The final reason was his excitement at the prospect of spending time with Runa, a comrade-in-arms. They would strive together for a better world, debating ideas, ideologies, strategies, tactics and plans-of-action. Her fondness for him was the clincher—she had made it amply clear. There was no second opinion that she would refuse to maintain contact with him if he rejected her gracious offer.

He concluded that she found him agreeable and convenient, and had expressed it in as many words. Perhaps, she hoped to dominate a mild-mannered man like Samir. Samir had recently read an elementary book on psychology which depicted the behaviour of authoritarian personality types; she arguably belonged to that category, a class of individuals who could not work in a team unless they were dominant.

Her pompous comments, though, left a bitter taste.

The sacred thread, his poitey, was worn by most Brahmins as a signifier of their celestially-ordained hierarchy within Hindu society, and he too had one wrapped around his torso, noticeable on his bare body that evening. Not that Samir believed in caste hierarchies, but for him, the thread was a reified expression of gratitude to his parents who celebrated the ritualistic ceremony with a dash of grandeur, despite not being too well-off. Her prescriptive comment sounded like a commandment. It made him believe that her dogma scored above everything else. She was intelligent and more experienced than him, and having studied at a co-educational institution, she could perhaps sense his infatuation as well.

Yet...he was determined not to entertain negative thoughts. He finally concluded that she was pure, unblemished and virtuous. 'The future's not ours to see,' he thought.

She proved to be both pure and virtuous in the days that followed, far more than Samir could ever hope to be.

Samir glanced at the blue sky outside.

It was a feeling of...
Liberation.
Freedom.

◆

Many years later, he had bumped into Atanu da outside a mall in South Kolkata. The man had greyed, was barely recognizable and he hurried past with a stern look on his face. A lady and two kids followed at a distance—a happy family. Samir, in his heart of hearts, could guess why he avoided him. But how much did he know?

◆

Famished despite a heavy breakfast, Samir ordered an omelet and a cup of steaming, sugary coffee, reaching home by noon to audible sighs of relief from Ma and ill-tempered frowns from a grumpy father. For a change, the typically sumptuous Bengali middle-class Sunday lunch of mutton curry and fine rice to the accompaniment of sweet yoghurt failed to enthuse him. Perched on a different planet where stars twinkled from proximity, he hated it when his mother affectionately asked if anything was the matter.

◆

Back in Orange County, he had to pinch himself hard to ascertain that this was not a nightmare. Clumsily grabbing the Balvenie, he was delighted to discover that a quarter had been left unconsumed. He gulped it like a bottle of cold water on a muggy LA summer afternoon. The mind soon churned the liquor like a washing machine, and he slumped into the divan as a jumble of images, of lizards and cockroaches and piles of murk, lacking neither logical nor chronological sequence, crashed into him.

It was only after he recognized an image of his father, of Baba lying prostrate on a narrow cot with closed eyes and a wide-open and toothless mouth, surrounded by smouldering incense sticks and gargantuan garlands made from white rajanigandha flowers, that Samir felt as if he had transcended into a world that belonged to the realm of virtual reality.

The memories tethered him to hard reality.

QUIETLY REMEMBERED DAYS

2008

The news had hit Samir like a bag of cement. He left the office by lunch to drive Apu into his college basketball match at Pomona College, a place not too far from his office. After the game he picked Apu up from his game to take him to dinner. In a reflective mood on the return trip, Apu's immodest chatter on his panache in basketball was getting on his father's nerves. He yearned for silence, and Apu's constant haranguing on various aspects of the game did not interest him. His son kept talking: about the pat on the back he had received from Kobe Bryant, the adulation from his trainers and friends, the short lecture on the criticality of the angle and velocity of the throw at the basket.

Samir's sarcastic response—'Then robots should qualify as the most prolific scorers, what do you say?'—did not resonate well with Apu but it bought Samir a few minutes of desired silence.

Neelu's call came in at an odd moment. It was unusual because she usually avoided calling him while he was driving.

'On the freeway, Neelu,' he answered.

'Is it possible to take an exit and park?'

He parked and called back within a few minutes.

'It's a call from Kolkata... I am afraid it is bad news,' she said.

Although Samir sensed the worst, her casual-sounding voice offered him a glimmer of hope.

'You can tell me now, but it's better if you hold on till we reach home.'

'Baba...' she had already begun her sentence.

There was no reason to shoot the next question.

'Yours or mine?'

'... Yours.'

'When?'

'Around an hour back. They got through just now. A sudden cardiac arrest.'

Although Samir had been mentally preparing for the news of his father's death for six months now, he had not expected it so soon.

On his last visit to Kolkata, Samir was stunned upon witnessing a once-active persona condemned to a vegetative state. Satyen displayed a pair of sunken eyes, emaciated skin and a sullen face. He was supported by colossal oxygen cylinders and salbutamol nebulizers. His excruciating walk from the bed to the dining table culminated in a series of gasps for ten odd minutes before he could eat a meal. The doctor advised Satyen to walk to the dinner table to prevent bedsores. Appointments with the best doctors in town had borne no fruit. He was diagnosed with an incurable chronic obstructive pulmonary disease (COPD). Satyen's pair of lungs were operating at just 30 per cent efficiency. It was the inevitable outcome of a life-long diet of heavy smoking and self-prescribed medication. The disease had been detected too late. Although the disease was terminal, some patients miraculously managed to survive for ten or fifteen years. Samir was neither optimistic nor desirous that his father endure such torment for fifteen more years.

His nurse, Mongola, was constantly at his side, sponging his body, changing his bedclothes thrice a day, cleaning his bedpan, feeding him—despite not being a trained nurse. She had joined their household when Samir was a child, a few years elder than him, and had stood by the family like a rock.

Once, Mongola's mother had had to undergo an operation,

and upon her request for financial help, Satyen, then a man of meagre means, could only partially assist her. Samir chose to provide the balance from earnings generated through private tuition. The day before she was due to leave for the village, he had withdrawn money from the bank, hoping to surprise her at night.

To his dismay, the purse had been empty!

He had confronted her and curtly mentioned that the money she had removed from his wallet was actually meant for her. Although he desisted from informing his parents, he had warned her that this better be the last time. Weeping bitterly, she vowed never to leave their home so long as his parents were alive and stuck to her word.

When the visit came to an end, a few hours before his flight was to take off, Samir's mama pulled him into the corner room to plead that Samir take up a job in Kolkata for a few years. As a US citizen, he could return any day, and acquiring another job should not pose a challenge for a professional as experienced and qualified as him.

'*Dyakh Khokhon, baba jiboney ekbari aashey,*' he said. 'A father comes only once in a lifetime.'

Since the man had spoken from a lack of awareness, Samir took pains to explain the implications of uprooting his family right now. It would be too difficult to obtain an assignment in a city like Kolkata and then find another suitable one back in the US at his age. He cited the example of his friend, Shubho, who was even unable to fly down for his mother's cremation.

Before departure, while bending to touch Satyen's feet as per Indian customs, Samir had felt a couple of roving fingers on his skull. The truth was revealed to him as he was dozing off on the flight. Baba had spoken through his eyes, his gently stroking fingers and through his brother-in-law. His bangal pride had stood in the way of an explicit appeal.

Samir soaked in the news, gently placing his device on top of the glovebox, and stared vacantly at the passing vehicles and the vast expanse of greenery. The car remained precariously parked on the freeway with its streamers flashing.

Apu, rejoicing in the glories of his basketball match, had not quite understood the situation. Only after a while, he exclaimed, 'Anything the matter, Baba?'

'Your Dadu is no more.'

The response from his son was initially muted but after a while, he spotted tiny droplets of tears and was reminded of his son's bond with his grandfather during vacations and his only visit to the USA.

The silence was interrupted by Apu's smothered voice. 'Are you okay? Let us call Ma and ask her to reach this place in a cab.'

Samir grabbed his phone. 'Not necessary, Apu. I just need to introspect for a while.'

Later, he was stunned by the compassionate hug he received from Neelu when they entered home. He could hardly recall their last embrace. It had been many moons. But this was hardly the occasion to speculate whether it was their loveless marriage or her inherent reticence that was to blame.

Without wasting time, he called his kaku for the details. Early in the morning, his mother, Sulekha, had gone to the kitchen to make tea, and Mongola was warming the water for Satyen's daily sponge bath. Out of the blue, Mongola heard Satyen loudly wailing for Sulekha. By the time she arrived in the room, Satyen was gone. As a neighbour aptly expressed, he had walked gracefully up the carpeted staircase to heaven, a replica of the Pandavas' journey to Mount Sumeru from Indraprastha.

Samir's focus was on the last rites habitually performed by the son. 'Kaku, there is a Peace Haven close to our Kolkata home where bodies are preserved. We can keep him there. Expenses will not pose a challenge.'

He did not feel like eating. He sat in his resplendent puja room, reciting a few immortal shlokas he had been taught in his childhood, and the transcendence of spiritualism provided him with a glimmer of relief.

> *Na jāyate mriyate vā kadāchin*
> *Nāyaṁ bhūtvā bhavitā vā na bhūyaḥ*
> *Ajo nityaḥ śhāśhvato 'yaṁ purāṇo*
> *Na hanyate hanyamāne śharīre*

(For the soul, there is no birth nor death.
Nor, having once been, does it ever cease to be.
It is unborn, eternal, ever-existing, undying, and primeval.
It is not destroyed when the body is destroyed.)

He meditated a bit, cried a lot, and then got ready to drive to San Francisco.

Neelu stared at him crying, and put a glass of water near the door. With hands on his head, she said, '*Jai Ma*, Samir, please drive carefully. You know the departed souls may come back in the first few days.' They hugged each other. 'Step out with the right foot first.' That was a sure shot way to have all obstacles removed.

Neelu was not initially superstitious right after their wedding, but had caught on after a lifetime with him.

Around 2 a.m. the same night, after a long and relaxing shower, he commenced the drive towards San Francisco. Generous doses of sugar were added to a flask of tea to help him stay awake until the wee hours of the day. The flask was neatly placed in the holder, a few water bottles placed horizontally on the side seat, visa papers stashed inside the side chamber and a jacket hung by the side since early hours in SF could be chilly. Instead of the customary Tagore songs, a few Ganesh Vandana CDs were hurriedly collected to shower him with divine inspiration during the journey. They were Baba's favourites.

The early hours of a Saturday dawn. Having travelled sixty miles through a sea of darkness, Samir felt as if the persistent drone from the speeding engine pierced the silence of the night. It was imperative to reach the Indian consular office in San Francisco by early morning to place himself ahead of the queue. It had dawned on him at the last moment that his Indian visa had expired. Although the agent assured him of instant renewal, it was imperative to be personally present at the consular office. He could have travelled in the morning if he could fix a slot, but they had closed down by the time he called.

Twelve-and-a-half hours across time zones, coupled with eighteen hours of travel—that would ensure that he would land in Delhi two nights later, in time for the early morning flight to Kolkata.

He heard echoes from a distant past. The phantasmagoric flares of the fireflies through dense darkness were triggering memories of an entire family perched on the terrace across a large sleeping mat to beat the intense humidity of Kolkata.

Samir remembered discarding the pillow, preferring to lie on his dad's arms. Despite Satyen's persistence, the Great Bear was all Samir could identify in the sky. The stars were like goblins from his stories—not lifeless gaseous substances.

After an hour of driving, Samir woke up with a start as a rear light flashed a few feet away. He managed to slam the brakes at the nick of the moment. He was reminded of his friend's fatal car crash on the east coast a few years back, and he hurriedly parked the car on the next available emergency lane.

He gulped a few cups of hot tea and recited the multiplication tables, taught to him by Satyen at an early age. These helped to do

...y with the last traces of drowsiness, and Samir could sense the benign presence of his father waving at him from the bonnet. He almost heard his voice. 'Khokhon, you'll get the visa, see you soon.'

Satyen was a pillar of strength who had stood by Samir solidly, like a rock.

◆

When Samir was a child, they would ride on alternate weekends from Kolkata to Ashoknagar, a suburban town bordering the then East Pakistan, by bus. They had settled there after emigrating from East Pakistan. Samir was born a few years after his parents migrated. After obtaining employment at a printing press in Kolkata, Satyen had brought his younger brother and Samir along. Kaku got himself admitted to a mediocre college, and Samir joined a playschool. They put up at a working men's hostel, popularly known as a 'mess', the moniker unwittingly pointing to the chaotic state of affairs. The hostel boasted of a shared ten-by-eight-foot room with a filthy toilet, a deep well to draw bathing water and a cracked dining table that could accommodate four persons at a time.

During the journey on weekends, Samir would demand to be seated next to the driver's cabin, impressed by the man's deft handle over the massive steering wheel and the darkness outside. He would think of an alternate world, replete with ghosts and goblins from Baba's never-ending tales.

These thoughts were occasionally interrupted by flashes from headlights and he often slumbered on his father's arms. He would recite multiplication tables as a respite from the monotony of the journey, and Satyen also bought him a piece of chocolate if he recited them correctly.

He caught himself murmuring '*Ek Okkey ek, ek duguney dui*... one times one is one, one times two is two.' And he shed copious tears.

Surprisingly, he never wept for his mother on the way back to Kolkata, perhaps because the separation was just for twelve days. Or perhaps because he was closer to his Baba.

He suddenly recalled a dark and desolate night, the night they reached Ashim kaku's place at 4 a.m. They had dropped Satyen off at their house, and not a word had been exchanged during the journey. It haunted him till the limits of his forbearance were breached. Satyen had to suffer a lot in life for his son!

◆

The remaining portion of the journey to the consular office was as uneventful as the process of obtaining the visa. Despite a longish queue, the formalities were completed swiftly.

There was a mild reprimand from the office. 'Can we request you to apply well before the expiry date in the future?'

Samir had not responded.

He reached for his phone when reminded that he needed to call his boss. Leave was instantly granted, but not before his boss expressed his incredulity that Hindu rituals lasted for more than two weeks. The fellow's lack of familiarity with Indian customs was understandable, but the absence of compassion reminded Samir of a white junior colleague who had casually requested half-a-day's leave to attend his deceased mom's funeral after enjoying a sumptuous lunch at the office.

◆

During the return journey, memories flickered one after the other in quick succession, each spanning decades. After escaping to Kolkata as a refugee, Samir's family had survived hand-to-mouth for several years until Satyen had obtained a more generously paying job, thanks to a friend who had migrated along the same time. The family was reunited, graduating from the 'mess' to a

-roomed apartment. Relatives reeling under the horrors artition were often accommodated inside their cramped rtment, and there were no implicit hints to move on. Baba as generous to a fault, a true sannyasin in the Vedic sense, earnestly believing in the concept of renunciation. Concomitantly a karma yogi. Despite his involvement in trade union activities, the management at Satyen's office appreciated his hard work during office hours and his appeal for others to follow suit. 'On what basis will we demand our dues if you shirk work?' was the common refrain made to his colleagues.

He had been a faithful adherent of the Bhagavad Gita, and was rarely ever interested in rewards or increments, promotions or bonuses. Samir's mother bore it without complaint, except when financial stress turned unbearable towards the end of the month.

Satyen's combination of conscientious dedication to work and his innate intelligence was rewarded with a promotion to the managerial grade with a hefty raise after a few years. The family was able to afford basic comforts in life, including purchasing a two-storied house on the eastern outskirts of the city and a piece of land at a nominal price. This was the prudent purchase that enabled Samir's higher studies abroad.

Satyen had kindled Samir's interest in the great Indian epics, narrated tales of the nation's struggle for independence, studded with heroic anecdotes of national figures like Surya Sen, Pritilata Waddedar, Matangini Hazra, Khudiram Bose, Bhagat Singh, Ashfaqulla Khan and countless others. As a voracious reader, he forayed at an advanced age from literature in the vernacular to novels by Charles Dickens, Victor Hugo and Alexandre Dumas, borrowed from their well-stocked office library. He often acted like the weeping protagonist in *Les Miserable* and *Don Quixote*, tilting his sword at the windmill with a distinctive flourish. Samir was driven to tears by the travails of *Oliver Twist* and inspired by Anna Zalomova, the immortal character from Gorky's *Mother*, and tales of both the Russian and French Revolutions had left indelible marks on his impressionable mind.

He was interrupted by a call from his cousin, Babu, that the corpse was lying inside Peace Haven and would remain there until he arrived.

As the landscape of LA appeared on the horizon, recollections of Satyen's last letter, sent by regular post, were sufficient to trigger pent-up emotions. He wailed inconsolably until his handkerchief was sodden with a toxic cocktail of sweat and tears.

> These days, I can barely walk and I just pray and pray. Do you pray too, or find it below your dignity as a domiciled American? My piece of advice: do not ever forsake our Goddess Durga.
>
> I can sense the shadows of death in the furrows of your mother's brows when she keenly observes my movements as I inch to the dining table, and in the tenderness of Mongola's hands on my spine when she assists me when I need to sit. Both convey the poignant message of Death. Yet I am inexplicably confident that I will make it to California to meet my grandchildren one last time.
>
> I visualize the godhuli bela of my life as the divine cattle trudging their way, raking dust in twilight. Despite my agnosticism after initiation into leftism during my student days, you are aware of how the seeds of my faith germinated in a flash. When I peek into the next phase of my journey, my faith in the Supreme goddess keeps growing exponentially.
>
> Do try and make it to Kolkata along with Neelanjana, Apu and Ruplu. How I wish to meet them! I know it contradicts my earlier assertion, but an inveterate Pangloss resides deep down!
>
> Incidentally, we visited Ashim last Sunday without a prior

appointment. Sulekha tried her best to dissuade me, but you are aware of my bangal obstinacy. I was confident that he would be at home on a Sunday morning. The journey was refreshing despite the fumes from passing vehicles that pierced my battered lungs! Ashim was initially furious. 'Why do you want to kill yourself, Satu?' but his subsequent cordiality dispelled my misgivings that he may not have liked our unannounced intrusion into his private space on a Sunday morning. Remember the night at the nursing home? He vividly remembers how I refused to accept his gesture of friendship. We switched to subsequent incidents, which I am sure you would not like to be reminded of. I apologize if I have offended you by mentioning the topic. That was not the intention, Khokhon.

An uncanny dream may be worth narrating before I close this letter.

A few nights back, while passing through what the Chandogya Upanishad describes as the second stage of sleep, dream-studded yet conscious of the difference between illusion and reality, I visualized Adesh gesticulating at me from a distance. He was there, yet he was not there. Waking with a start, I found Sulekha caressing me with her characteristic affection, not realizing that I was overjoyed at the thought that Adesh's spirit lives on inside my soul. As my life withers into death, everything seems fuzzy, including the right path to salvation for humanity.

Love you, Khokhon and I hope to see you soon.

Baba.

He lasted barely three months after composing that letter.

Upon reaching home, he was reminded of Satyen patiently waiting for them at the window, disappearing like a child as the cab halted on the narrow lane outside their house to rush downstairs to be able to catch them before Sulekha could.

Surprisingly, he never wept that much for his mother when she passed a few years later. Perhaps it was because he was closer to his Baba. He carried the guilt for a long time.

◆

The last rites were complete in the funeral ghats near Hooghly River. He shaved his head. There was a sense of closure with the long, winding rituals that took place with due solemnity. Prayers were offered, and Satyen's mortal remains were flung into the holy river of Hooghly, a tributary to the Ganges. In a haze, he obeyed every command from the priest like a droid, convinced that the soul could only liberate itself from earthly bondage if every ritual was followed to the last intricate detail. He spent fourteen days at home, reminiscing about Satyen's last days with his mother, relatives, family friends and Mongola, consoling and being consoled by others. Relatives from across the city visited them, leaving them little time to attend to themselves. He enjoyed their presence.

Unlike the urban custom of handing over snack-laden packets at the end of the ritual memorializing ceremony, Samir treated the guests to an intricate five-course vegetarian lunch with care and affection. The mourning period came to an end after close relatives were treated to six varieties of fish a day later.

Neelu and Samir requested his mother to join them in the US for a few months, but she declined the offer, promising to make the trip later. It was a trip that never materialized.

◆

Back in Los Angeles, Samir woke to a splitting headache. He was unable to gauge his coordinates. Was he in his tiny room at their Kolkata residence or the larger one at Runa's brother-in-law's ancestral home?

Dreams were ephemeral, and he was able to recall only a few later on: an incomplete graduate degree with three days left for his last shot; the sullen face of his father, locked in an elevator with no power, and a few others. Smothered by claustrophobia, he would wipe the sweat and proceed to the lawn for a stroll. He would gaze at the start-studded sky for a while, light a cigarette and gulp half a litre of water at one go. He was advised to keep lights switched on and read a book, not be in a hurry to get back to sleep, but he was apprehensive that the glare of the bulb might disturb Neelu, so he would lie quietly in darkness for a while till sleep got the better of him.

His panic attacks remained a well-kept secret for a long time.

But these were not dreams, they were reminiscences. His current headache was far more intense than the one he had the previous morning, and he instantly realized that he needed aspirin tablets and a head massage. His guru was never tired of reminding him that spiritualism and yoga do not fit hedonists. Struggling on his way to the kitchen, he noticed the empty bottle of Balvenie staring nastily at him, as if mocking him.

He could not make it. Slumping back into his cot, he slipped into another round of nostalgia.

THE MAGIC OF FRESH CHAPTERS

September 1973–December 1977

After a couple of years, Satyen and Sulekha voiced their desire to visit London. Samir did not have the heart to stand in the way of their journey outside India for the first time in their lives despite his keenness to visit his home town.

They stayed for ten days, reluctant to park longer at Satyen's nephew's house. They had heard gossip of the wife's inscrutable manners. However, their hosts were warm and cordial, driving them all for a weekend visit to the Lake District, not to mention sites in and around London. As a family, they enjoyed every minute of those ten days.

He remained aloof from politics for another year until his graduation, despite the vivacious anti-war movement raging on the campuses. He had only once participated in a procession commemorating the second anniversary of independence of Bangladesh, but that had been a pretty uncontroversial event.

He returned to India at the end of three years. He had heard blood-curdling stories about the northern and eastern regions, following the promulgation of a national Emergency in the country. Samir was paranoid and stayed mostly at home, rarely visiting friends and relatives. He met Ashim kaku, to whom he would perpetually remain obliged, and a couple of close friends from his first school.

He often landed at Chitpur Road, a locality he had nursed a soft corner for since his college days. It boasted a tradition that could be traced back to a few centuries, when the Bengali bhadralok was at its opulent best, scornful yet obsequious to 'gora sahibs' of the East India Company. It was situated on the banks of the Hooghly, a stone's throw from Tagore's abode at Jorasanko, and the northern stretch of the road was flanked by the largest red-light district of Asia.

In its heydays, Chitpur Road transformed after sunset, and the sidewalks were populated by perfumed babus, their faces glowing with cream, as they searched for voluptuous belles, courtesans, lustful ladies, prostitutes from diverse ethnicities and a kaleidoscope of social categories. The burlesque evenings in palatial rococo mansions preceded dense nights when desires intensified, eyes turning misty as the liquor sunk in. The babus considered themselves refined and immune from premature consumption.

Samir went to the locality twice a week, wandering around the banks of the river to witness moderately sized boats sail by, pahalwans enjoy oily massages, or bathers dressing after a quick dip in the holy waters of the placid river kissed by a setting sun. He would settle in a quiet corner of one of the innumerable joints dotting the quaint street to savour his favourite Old Monk rum with beef rolls and chicken kababs. The utilitarian wooden tables, covered by stained tablecloths, were waited upon by liveried waiters carrying their tiny notebooks with pencils stuck gingerly behind their ears, fulfilling the orders accompanied by white nuts served on the house in a jiffy—all with a smiling face. The restaurant priced their items ridiculously low, perhaps to compensate for the incessantly loud chatter and unhygienic surroundings.

Back in London, he jumped into the political fray after completing his graduation. A scholarship reduced his father's financial burden, and he was now determined to campaign against the curtailment of democratic rights in his country of origin, reminded of countless friends and associates rotting in prison.

He began with a rally before the Indian High Commission, chased by bobbies on horseback. Later, he even accepted a request to address a crowd from the soapbox at Hyde Park. Besides debates at the English-medium school a few years back, speaking publicly in English was a unique experience for him, and he thought it went reasonably well, both in cadence and content. A group of Indonesian activists, eager to know more about Indian conditions, offered to take him for dinner at a tony restaurant close by. They too had faced brutal genocide ten years ago and had been compelled to take up asylum in the United Kingdom. Their friendship was religiously nurtured for many years.

On the verge of completing his post-graduation, he was convinced that a career in research required more rigour and commitment than he was capable of. He changed his direction in life, planning to settle down with a fat salary.

An initial round of interviews with software firms ended unsuccessfully, but luck descended upon him on a bitterly cold winter afternoon. He was exhausted after the customary aptitude tests, interviews and group discussions with a US-based organization, and planned to proceed towards the hostel when the placement coordinator gently tapped him on the shoulder and announced that the recruiters wanted him inside. The organization was neither blue-chipped nor massive, but it boasted a host of niche, state-of-the-art software applications. They were headquartered in Cincinnati but had offices elsewhere too. There was no looking back.

The few months he spent at home in early 1977 coincided with the humiliating defeat of the dictatorial regime led by its then authoritarian Prime Minister. Two months later, a moderate left regime captured power in the state of West Bengal. Comrades were being released in batches, and Samir longed to meet old friends and whack the daylights out of lumpens of the likes of

Pagla Keshto. After a crushing defeat, they were in disarray—and to Samir, it seemed like an opportune moment to let go of Adesh's soul and Runa's memory. But his strong desire to act was thrown out of the window when he was reminded of Satyen and Sulekha's sulking faces before his departure for London.

One evening, at the Chitpur bar, he bumped into Utpal. For an inexplicable reason, the police had not targeted him. After completing his graduation, he had qualified for an executive role at a nationalized bank, and was now enjoying life to the brim.

Before Utpal could broach the topic, Samir asked him whether he was aware of developments in his life.

'Meshomoshoy told us that you had gone off for studies to the USA. We were worried when neither you nor Runa appeared for the annual exams. What he mentioned sounded incredible—you left the country out of the blue and avoided encounters with friends to avoid embarrassment.'

'Did you ever visit her place?'

'Her father was reticent. He just mentioned that she had been sent outside Kolkata for her safety. We presumed your parents acted in conjunction. Many months later, another rumour made the rounds.'

'What was it about?'

'Forget it, Samir. It was unconfirmed. Why should her father lie? I'm sure she will surface one of these days now that the worst is behind us.'

'Please, I need to know.'

'That she had been bumped off and her father was scared to reveal the truth because he was afraid for his other daughter.'

'What?'

'*Patta dish na*, I do not believe a word of it. I'm confident that Runa is alive and will make an appearance one of these days. Tell me, have you ever attempted to contact her?'

'It was not possible, Utpal. Believe me.'
'Fine. Let's change the topic.'
Utpal was a sensitive soul. He was aware that this was painful for Samir.

◆

Strange thoughts surfaced that night after his meeting with Utpal, and Samir resolved to visit Runa's residence the next day. A few clothes, left to dry on clothing lines on a listless balcony—those were the only signs of existence. There were clothes and a few undergarments of either variety. He focused on the sarees. They were not ones she would wear—far too flashy, bright, striped. Had her tastes altered during these years?

The locality seemed to have dozed off for an afternoon siesta, and a stray dog inched itself towards Samir, eager for a pat on the head.

After strolling for a few minutes, he turned away, engulfed by fear, reticence and an unwillingness to disrupt the emotional stability he had acquired. As he proceeded towards the main road, he spotted a man lazing around with a burning cigarette in his hands and betel juice overflowing from his mouth.

Samir instantly recognized him as the person who had once stalked Runa. She had pointed at him from a distance years ago. The man, too, must have seen Samir earlier because there was a glimmer of recognition on his face. All Samir now needed to do was to step up to him and enquire about her whereabouts, but he failed to muster up the courage.

He once again enquired about Runa from Utpal on his next visit, but there was still no news. 'One of us visited her father but he was distinctly rude this time. Let it not bother you, Samir. You need to move on.' Utpal kindly told him.

He had moved on, both metaphorically and physically.

During those months, one morning Samir received a call from the director of a British multinational corporation based out of Kolkata. After a couple of long chats with the vice presidents and the CEO, they offered him an assignment the very same day. Not that he was overly keen, but Satyen vehemently opposed the idea.

'Khokhon, your past will haunt you here. Maybe you can consider returning after ten years.'

Having idled at home for a few months, he set out on the next phase of his journey, armed with a suitcase packed with brand new clothes, mishti, stocks of medicines, toiletries, books, journals and bottles of cologne. A relative who was settled in Arizona advised him on the perfumes; stale body odour could make or mar one's reputation in the United States. After travelling cattle-class for more than twenty-four hours, and a longish stopover at Frankfurt, he was over the top when he finally landed in the country of his dreams.

The flight terminated at New York, from where he was scheduled to catch a flight for Cincinnati the next afternoon. He was to spend a night with Sankar, a doctoral aspirant he knew from college, a year senior to him. They shared one feature in common; they had both deserted the Party at a crucial point of its existence.

With a bagful of hopes and fantasies, he leisurely made his way through immigration and customs. He strangely remembered the mighty processions in Kolkata against the Vietnam War and the World Bank President, rebuffed by a city reverberating, 'Go back!' Guilt engulfed him, although he had secretly nursed the desire to study in the USA even during the heydays of their movement. It was surprising that he was not here as a doctoral aspirant but as an employee of a software firm, and a strange feeling gripped him as he ambled down JFK airport.

He had been in London for a short period, and it had never

crossed his mind to settle down there. On the other hand, the US had been a long-standing dream, an aspiration.

His socialistic beliefs persisted even in the USA, despite being fascinated by the other side of the country, its massive campuses, comfortable standards of life, the unpolluted countryside, various opportunities, white blankets of snow, red and yellow forests, and broad highways. He knew it had given birth to Albert Einstein, Fermi, James Watson, Alexander Graham Bell, or Dr Hargovind Khurana. It had nursed Noam Chomsky, Bob Dylan, Paul Robeson, Bob Marley, Angela Davis, Joan Baez, Malcolm X and Pete Seeger. This country offered unfettered freedom to express all shades of opinions.

Sankar had committed to meet him at the airport. He hailed from a middle-class family and had topped the state in his school-leaving examinations. As an individual, he commanded attention whenever he rose to speak, and he held an eccentric posture that amplified his tall and erect physique. His pleasant smile endeared him to students, and his voice left goosebumps among audiences. He was slightly taller than Samir and bore an off-kilter look, but he was also frail. Intrinsically brilliant, he had instantaneously transformed from a political thinker into a physics scholar. The transformation was the talk of the town.

Samir remember that Sankar was a part of the gang that had hurled explosives on the police, the same day Samir was beaten blue by cops.

Sankar was close to Utpal, and had agreed upon his request to provide his apartment to Samir for a night's sojourn.

The sight of a few nuns at the luggage bay reminded him of a discussion he had had with Sankar in college. Sankar, an unrepentant atheist, had once ripped him apart when he had brought up the topic of the existence of God. Later, more politely, he had said that as an agnostic, he found it challenging to step into the shoes of a theist. But the explanation lacked credibility, and he had been countered with a simple retort. 'Then why do you argue?'

His massive yellow suitcase on the sluggish conveyor belt interrupted his daydreams. Unmindfully, he pushed the trolley into the ladies' room, and scampered out after loud threats to call the cops. He exclaimed to himself, 'Gosh! What a way to start living in this country. I did not do it on purpose.'

He hurriedly rushed into the pleasantly warm climes of New York. The rumblings of homesickness immediately prompted him to consider returning to India after saving a considerable amount of money.

Unable to locate Sankar, he searched for a public telephone booth but, bereft of coins, was attracted by a gentleman offering them at a premium. The other face of capitalist USA—entrepreneurial to some, blood-sucking to others!

Having gotten through to his friend who was in the laboratory, their conversation commenced with long-forgotten profanities.

'*Ki rey gandu, tor na airport eh aashbar kotha chhilo?* I thought you promised to pick me up, you dirty lump of ass,' Samir shouted.

'Oh! Samir, I am dreadfully sorry, there was an urgent lecture I had to deliver here. Did Air India not convey the message? Typical public-sector behemoth.'

Sankar had evidently not taken too long to adapt to a fresh set of convictions. Samir realized later that it had been daft of him to request Sankar to pick him up in a city like New York.

He asked around and directions to the university were provided with meticulous clarity, and it was easy to locate the coach. Enveloped by fatigue, he fell asleep, and was woken by the driver's screams.

He spotted Sankar, standing next to a sleek and deep blue car. He had a slight paunch and was wearing dandy clothes and the quintessential symbol of Yankee decadence, a pair of jeans. His misdemeanour was soon forgotten as they sang paeans to their past, snacking and reminiscing through early hours on pleasant, pungent and epochal experiences. Sankar admitted to retaining his convictions at a broad level, but he wished to leave his past behind; he was more inclined towards particle physics. He did not bother to interrogate Samir on his sudden disappearance, accepting his account at face value.

A hired car waited for Samir at Cincinnati airport the next morning. The organization was well-funded and it operated in a niche sector. He was put up at a hotel for a month (as per company policy) but he struggled to get accustomed to the intricacies of the coffee machine, electric razor, locker, television, showers and the bathtub. By the time he began to relish the luxuries, it was time to move out to an apartment.

A distant relative of theirs lived in Cincinnati. Ma had taken special care to tuck a tiny piece of paper with their contact numbers inside the inner recesses of his suitcase. The family had visited India a few years back on the occasion of Durga Puja, and Supriya, their daughter, had enjoyed the festival to her heart's content. Her father happened to be his mother's first cousin, but as an orphan, he had spent a significant period of time with his mother.

When he called, Supriya instantly recognized his voice and it startled him. He was unaware that Ma had already called them.

Her mother called in after some time. 'I was in the washroom when you called. I want to invite you to our home this weekend. That does not mean you cannot drop in earlier. You are related to us, so treat our house as your own.'

The kind-hearted family entertained him at upmarket restaurants and took him along on long drives to the countryside during the weekends. He made a couple of visits with Supriya to the theatre and the baseball stadium, and surprisingly they were interspersed with soft hugs and a kiss, sparking the desire for an emotional relationship in Samir. She disclosed a secret one evening; she was committed to an American guy and hoped to marry within a year. Her parents were not yet aware of it, but were of a liberal predisposition. She proceeded to educate him on the difference between love and friendship, symptoms that manifest at the tipping point. After her speech, Samir ventured to inform her that he too had fallen in love at the age of seventeen, and that the feelings had been reciprocated in abundance. She did not believe him.

He was greeted one morning by a call from Hirak, a student of chemistry and a batchmate, hailing from a well-to-do family in central Kolkata.

'Where did you obtain my contacts, boss?' Samir asked.

Hirak's patrician voice roared through the wires. 'Sankar.'

'But he never told me you lived in Cincinnati.'

'Because he was unaware, dude. I bumped into him at the cafeteria when I visited their university last week to present a paper. Unfortunately, I will leave this city after a few months. I have completed my MS and plan to move to Dayton, Ohio for a PhD.'

Samir offered, 'Let's meet regularly till you leave.'

'Why the fuck do you think I called you? To hear your pansy voice? Come on, let us paint Cincinnati red.'

He concluded that Hirak had done an excellent job of learning Yankee lingo. He provided Samir with tips on living conveniently in the city, introducing him to shops where necessities were priced at a steal. He also made an insinuation that was intriguing, but Samir treated his opinion with scepticism. 'The past is not yet distant. Let us not forget that until the thirties they hung blacks and denied voting rights to women. This is a conservative religious country, Samir, not yet reconciled to desegregation. The Midwest is worse.'

He had not experienced any discrimination until then, but his colleagues' cold and distant behaviour was not something he was used to. The absence of warmth exasperated him. None invited him home or enquired whether he was facing problems settling down. Nor were they curious about his culture and background. There was no concept of a free lunch. When colleagues joined him for meals, separate checks were called for, each person religiously met the cost of his consumption and spent not a dime more. He was once greeted with nasty stares when he left his wallet behind. They hated being touched, unless it was for a formal hug. Thus, his visits to Supriya's family on the weekend and meeting with Hirak offered some solace.

Once, he met an African-American pastor while travelling for business. Their conversation commenced with Elvis, they then migrated to theology. The man was overjoyed upon hearing about Samir's Jesuit education and on learning that his devout Hindu mother had taught him to recite Christian prayers as a child as well.

His parting words confounded Samir. 'A piece of advice, Sam. Do not harbour high expectations from this country. You may be in for a rude shock.'

The prognosis did not take long to take shape.

♦

Samir raised his eyelids to meet the darkness. The lights had been switched off. Who could have done it? He had an excruciating headache. He felt the concoction of fluids inside him ebbing like the tides of a receding sea. His throat and lips were parched, like sandpaper, and he recalled the golden rule that vomiting toxic compounds before they settled inside the blood was a certain palliative in such situations.

Jumping out of bed, he noticed the meticulously wrapped duvet. He was confident that it had not been there when he had gone to bed.

A gas balloon seemed to throb inside as he swung his bare feet and found the carpet. An uncontrollable feeling of nausea hit him, bile spouting from the depths of the intestines. He struggled to hold on to the flow, but switching the lights on posed a challenge. Clutching at the soup bowls on the table, he puked into them, choking on the vile stew that poured in torrents. His stomach gurgled with stifled noises of protest. It was not a disciplined stream of puke.

The floor was soon spattered, and the bed and duvet were smeared. The soup bowls were relatively cleaner.

Samir saw shades of red. It was scary, but recalled that there had been a generous amount of tomatoes in the curry he had eaten. Determined, he thrust his thick fingers inside his throat; the sensation activated distant memories of passionate sex.

He slept soundly for the remaining part of the night, wrapped in the colourful but dirty duvet, overwhelmed by lofty flights of imagination, fleeting thoughts refusing to linger in his conscious memory.

The nauseating stench failed to penetrate his subconscious.

Apu was the first person to enter the room in the morning. His son was instantly reminded of a similar sight he had witnessed at a down-market bar he had gone to as a teenager.

WAKING TO REALITY

18 May 2014

Samir woke up and felt a certain mindfulness that had eluded him for so many years, despite the yoga. He was not in a mood to raise his head from inside the covers of the stinking duvet, and his initial urge was to sleep through the day. It was not unusual for him to crash in the lounge after a late night.

The putrid odour drew his attention to the stained floor. He realized that it required to be mopped and the duvet would have to be dispatched to the cleaners. The eerie stillness of the surroundings were in stark contrast to the unpleasant conversation he had had the previous evening with Neelu.

He took a couple of baby steps to the bathroom after the cuckoo chimed seven times. He was lucky enough to locate the mop tucked away in a corner, and wiped the floor clean, but the odour persisted. He rushed to the guest washroom and noticed that a white cloth had been dumped carelessly by the commode.

The phone was perched in its cradle. That was the clincher. He regained control of his faculties and was able to reconstruct the night's conversation, piece by piece.

Apu was waiting for him outside the room.

He stated, 'Had a few drinks too many last night.' But his body language was inadequate. He seemed to convey nonchalance, like a child who had spilt a glass of hot milk.

Apu nodded calmly. 'I visited the room an hour back to witness you snoring away to glory. Was in half a mind to clean the floor, but I could not stand the odour.'

'It is toxic, Apu. My sincerest apologies.'

'Not a big deal. But, I have to ask you, Baba. If it is not too personal, I would like to be briefed on what exactly was the matter with Ma last night.'

'Let me fetch the deodorant first, splash my face with water, dump the smelly bedsheet and duvet and change my clothes,' he said, dashing to the washroom.

For the second time in his life, he was decisively able to decide on the next course of action. He looked forward to relieving himself of the cross he had borne for a few decades.

He ordered Apu. 'I have something to discuss with you guys. What time is it now?'

'Around seven.'

'Let's assemble at the breakfast table around nine. Convey the message to both Ma and Ruplu.'

'Baba, I can feel something sinister looming in the background and I sincerely beg you to keep me on tenterhooks for these two hours. I'm not mentally prepared for this.'

He gripped Apu's shoulders reassuringly.

'Let me assure you, it is not what you suspect. Certain incidents from a distant past came up last night and I have decided to disclose an untold anecdote.'

'What anecdote?' Apu was startled.

'Something that happened during my college days in Kolkata. I have kept it a closely-guarded secret for many years, and was caught red-handed yesterday. Come to think of it, a lot depends on how the two of you take it. The ball rests in your courts a few hours from now.'

After an unnatural period of silence, an accidental glance at Samir's gimlet eyes unsettled Apu.

'Can I have the next hour to myself?' Samir asked.

As Apu's tall outline walked away, a queer feeling possessed

Samir. He seemed to have lost the Apu he had known for so many years.

◆

From an Undisclosed Location

December 2019

As he lay battered and helpless on the cot, Samir stared into the moonlit night. The stillness did not bother him. He had experienced many such nights before. Their neighbourhood in LA was not boisterous and he had often imagined hearing the sounds of the planets. The creepiness of the listless night had haunted him once upon a time when his family had gone to India for their annual vacations. It persisted for many years till yoga came to his rescue.

Neelu and her parents must be spending sleepless nights. Apu and Ruplu would be going through worse back home in LA. They were young, prone to giving up. For them, rationalism overshadowed optimism. Especially for Apu.

He remembered that they had planned to meet Runa today. She had a day to leave for Dublin. Surely Neelu would have called her to join in the search. In case they were unable to get in touch with her, would they suspect a twist in the narrative?

A wry smile escaped his lips. It was impossible to trust Neelu; she was capable of imagining the wildest things. Perhaps his children would trust him more. Perhaps.

Would the bytes have hit the newspapers? Unlikely, it had been close to ten or eleven when they kidnapped him last night, as far as he could remember. But the television would have been abuzz by now. There should be a splash in the Indian newspapers tomorrow. Non-resident Indians are the cynosure of the Indian population—a species viewed with ambivalence. Uprooted guys, yet people who are doing their bit by contributing to the country's foreign exchange resources.

He gazed outside the window. Darkness could be enchanting, especially when the darkness inside his mind felt so dense. He was now certain that he was near a river. If he could just escape! Surely there would be a few boats sailing by! Pushing the curtains aside, he stood near the window, staring into the vast dark landscape.

He thought he could hear the sound of rustling leaves. Perhaps a wild animal. Glancing outside through the iron grills, it was a spectre that he witnessed, the spectre of a living human being skulking into the night. It was not an animal. He had noted the faint outline of a man with two legs, running away as fast as he could.

Initially, he thought he was hallucinating. But the mind started ticking and the spectre transformed into an angel of hope. It was unlikely to be a member of the gang because there was no reason for the guard to run away if he had been stationed to keep watch.

Samir was like a drowning man clutching at a piece of straw. It was imperative to remain awake—the man may alert the villagers, who could inform the cops. What else, other than hope, could keep him going considering the desolate and desperate situation he was in?

But how would the man know that Samir was being held in captivity? It was naïve to think that someone, anyone, would come to his rescue.

Samir turned back to his thoughts, returning to his student days, to Runa and his friends.

A CONFLICT WITHIN

'It was the best of times, it was the worst of times'

—Charles Dickens (*A Tale of Two Cities*)

May–September 1971

Samir had conveyed his decision to Runa the next Sunday. The joyful expression on her face was discernible.

He soon grew frustrated. The wait for the next two months was excruciating and Samir was desperate, but the Party wished to confuse the powers that be that Samir and Runa had decided to quit politics and they were under strict orders not to interact with one another openly.

The Party had moles inside the corridors of power and they were waiting for Samir and Runa's names to be struck off the list, updated regularly by the ill-famed detective department.

Despite their clandestine rendezvous on alternate Sunday mornings at her brother-in-law's vacant ancestral abode, the enforced separation from Runa was agonizing for Samir.

The message finally arrived in the form of a tiny slip tucked into his palms while he was engrossed with Schrodinger's wave equation in the library. There was to be a gathering, followed by a protest rally scheduled for the upcoming Thursday. Details would be conveyed later.

The Association for Democratic Rights had organized the rally. The organization was ostensibly committed to a one-point agenda: the release of all political prisoners. The police would not have to intervene as the gathering was to include renowned luminaries, playwrights, intellectuals and physicians with no apparent links to the Party; none were batting to violently overthrow the government. They felt for the thousands of young men who languished inside jails, incarcerated under a draconian Act, subjected to brutal torture. Other organizations participated in demonstrations, staged subversive plays, sang mass songs and participated through democratic forms of agitation. The core members of the militant agitation were all but destroyed, rotting in confinement, butchered, in hiding or they had surrendered. The death knolls were ringing, loud and clear, like the chimes at the temple that Samir visited as a child with his father.

Samir and Runa were due to assemble at a park in the heart of South Kolkata. She repeated myriad dos and don'ts. Don't recognize her publicly, don't hover around the park before mingling into the mass, do stick to the script as far as slogans were concerned, and avoid speaking to others. Do not pose as a sympathiser of the Party but as a citizen, appalled at the unjust confinement of well-meaning youngsters.

Samir was alarmed when he saw the phalanx of uniformed policemen guarding the park and was disappointed with the low attendance. He was soon pleasantly surprised when the gathering swelled to a few thousand as the clock struck six. Activists emerged from obscurity, even the usual luminaries—including a renowned left-wing film director and a top gynaecologist of the city. Earlier, while Samir was sipping tea from an earthen bhar at a corner of the park, two middle-aged persons, sporting spotless white shirts and dhotis, had strolled up to him at a leisurely pace. They were clean-shaven and suave, reminding him of Thomson and Thompson.

'Waiting for the procession to start, comrade?' they asked him.

The query caught him unawares, and he replied with

hesitation. The gentlemen slyly looked at each other from the corner of their eye.

'We plan to join in as sympathisers, but can you throw some light on the organizers?'

'It is an organization fighting for the release of political prisoners,' Samir said.

'A left-extremist organization?'

Samir was surprised at his presence of mind. 'I dare not speak for others, but I am not a sympathiser. I am participating only because it is my opinion that the prisoners deserve a fair trial. I have full faith in our Constitution that guarantees fundamental rights to every individual.'

Before they could respond, a bespectacled and chubby middle-aged gentleman appeared on the scene. 'Look here, I know you guys. Please do not interrogate an innocent participant. Ask me whatever you wish to know.'

They turned around and disappeared, leaving their earthen bhars on the grass. Samir's rescuer placed a gentle hand on his shoulders, and said, 'Never speak to strangers. Your first lesson. They are police informers. We call them khochors.' He then swiftly moved away before Samir could delve into introductions. Runa told him later that he was famous: an erudite thespian, renowned intellectual and an authority on Shakespeare.

The procession, consisting of a few thousand dedicated activists, marched across the southern stretch of the city for a couple of hours before dispersing. The procession reminded him of a similar afternoon two years back, when he had participated as a detached observer. This time, he was an active participant. Runa stuck by him all through, just a couple of yards behind. By the time he reached home, he realized that his orientation into the sect was complete, and he felt euphoric that he had marched for a cause with his potential life partner.

♦

There were a string of hosiery units located in the city's southern suburbs. They employed a few hundred workers whose wages were abysmal. The factories would often close down, leaving them to fend for themselves. The Party planned to organize the workers, but not immediately. Instead, a night school was to be started right outside their slums, popularly known as bustees. Most of these workers were illiterate, and their children engaged in labour without the opportunity to go to school. An NGO involved in social causes, inclined towards a left-leaning philosophy but desisting from overt politics, offered them their banner for display.

Samir was slightly shaken. 'Will it be considered subversive?'

Runa explained. 'The police here are referred to as the Scotland Yard of the East, but we believe otherwise. This city is subdivided into zones, and each zone is unaware of what the others are up to. There is a possibility that the cops in the central zone may recognize us, but there is not a ghost of a chance that the southern zone police will. Even the central zone is now convinced we have quit active politics. The Party kept us inactive for some time with a definite purpose. We are smarter than the cops, Samir.'

'Interesting.'

'You will understand these intricacies as you go along. So you have been assigned to teach arithmetic while I will cover basic reading and writing.'

He hated the thought of teaching basic arithmetic, but he reluctantly agreed. The classes were scheduled to happen twice a week. He wouldn't meet Runa as she had been assigned two other evenings. The most challenging part would be convincing his parents as the classes would drag on till 8 p.m., starting late after the students completed their day's labour.

Samir spun a story at home that he was finding it tough to cope with the papers on light and electricity and needed private tuition. It exacerbated his guilt.

The following month, as Samir started teaching, he experienced how the 'other' lived and survived. The salaries they earned allowed them to eat enough for twenty days; their diet consisted of insufficient quantities of rice, salt and an apology for a vegetable curry. Sometimes, there was puffed rice. They were not able to afford medicines and nutritious food. They never enjoyed any leisure. As far as sanitary conditions were concerned, the less spoken of, the better. The children of the workers laboured in tea shops or as domestic servants to supplement their income. Wives often resorted to prostitution, and the men were adept at breaking railway wagons for extra income; they intermittently landed up in police custody and would be released the following day after paying a bribe.

Samir's family, too, had faced deprivation once upon a time, but such poverty was a world apart from his own. His students' innocence and respect for their 'mastermoshai' touched soft chords within him, and he would carry inexpensive chocolates for the children. On a few occasions, when he ran short of cash, or it slipped his mind, they merely revealed their disappointment through downcast eyes.

The initiative lasted a few months. One afternoon, on his way out of the laboratory in a hurry, he did not recognize a guy in his early teens jumping out of a corner of the corridor.

'*Apni Samir da toh*? Are you Samir da?'

'*Hyan, keno*? Yes, why?'

The boy's vibrant smile exuded childlike simplicity. 'I live just across the road. Atanu da had called, I am a cousin of his. Tiktikis are there today, so do not venture to the night school. That was the message.'

Samir had imbibed the codes by then. Tiktiki was a colloquial term for the cops.

He decided to play it safe. 'I do not understand. I teach arithmetic for an NGO and have nothing to do with politics.'

'Samir da, I am just a messenger from Atanu da. I waited patiently for your lab session to end because I did not wish to disturb you. The lab assistant came out for a smoke and identified you through the window.'

He was still wary of the youngster's identity. 'I have still not understood what you are talking about. Anyhow, you have conveyed whatever you were asked to, so let me be.'

A terrified Samir rushed home. There were strict orders not to contact Atanu da on the wires, so he called Runa. She was not at home, and it aggravated his trepidation. He was relieved when she called back. She had accompanied her parents to a recently released Satyajit Ray film. They spoke in an encrypted language.

She had received a couple of calls in her absence, but she was clueless as to why. They met the next morning at college. Apparently, it seemed like an insider had betrayed them, but there was no cause to worry since their assumed names as Party members were not known to the cops. They were greeted after a while with the scary news that a senior comrade had been arrested late at night.

With exams around the corner, students of the college were reluctant to call for a strike, and they restricted the protest to a deputation with the Principal. The future of the Party appeared increasingly dismal to Samir—like a fading star on the horizon.

Fiery debates raged within the Party, and some were reported by newspapers. One section was in favour of continuing with acts of individual violence while the other advocated a change in tactics. A struggle for Independence was being waged in neighbouring Bangladesh after the genocide launched by the state authorities of Pakistan, and the Party had split on this issue also. One group, led by the supreme leader, wanted to support the movement, but another group dubbed it a secessionist movement, inspired by imperialist agents. The nature of these debates, coupled with Samir's distaste for certain individuals, disillusioned him more and more, although he remained committed to the ideals of equality and an exploitation-free India. He would continue with them so long as Atanu da and Runa remained.

SANTINIKETAN

July 1971

The university at Santiniketan, Visva Bharati, set up by Tagore in the semi-urban locales of Bolpur, had grown on Samir from his childhood days. His mama's modest tenement, located on the banks of the Kopai River was framed by bougainvillea tendrils, and it served as a second home for their family. They paid quarterly visits to Santiniketan. Situated at an elevation, the undulating plains of Bolpur, termed in local dialect as the khoai, were conspicuous with an expanse of red soil.

Ma's artistic talent blossomed at Santiniketan. Samir, on the other hand was more carefree there. He was permitted to explore the landscape studded with sal trees, madhavi creepers, mango trees, stunted jambolana, flame-orange palash, blood-red simuls, free-flowing creeks and the shallow Ajay and Kopai rivers. They always made it a point to visit the famous Kala and Sangeet Bhavans set up by Tagore, discovering a fresh perspective each time. They heard the mellifluous chorale from the adjoining villages inhabited by Santhals who drowned themselves in locally brewed mahua as night fell, and strains of Rabindra Sangeet from students of the university; there were songs that contained insightful philosophies proclaiming universal love for humanity, sung in the high-pitched tone of bauls, singers inspired by the Sufis, who accompanied the lyric with the sweet strains of a single-stringed instrument called the ektara.

Samir would gently descend into his world of dreams at night, unmindful of the endless chats between parents and the relatives who invariably accompanied them and the neighbours permanently settled there. Their trips to Santiniketan provided him with a few days of freedom away from the rigid discipline and roughness of Kolkata.

When Runa proposed they visit Santiniketan for a weekend escape, Utpal and Srimati willingly agreed to join. He was surprised by her suggestion because she had once dubbed Tagore a bourgeois poet along with the startling piece of information that Tagore's grandfather had purchased land for the university at throwaway prices from poor Santhals. Brought up in a family that iconized Tagore, Samir had opposed her statement, noting that Lenin too admired Tolstoy and Pushkin more than Gorky and Mayakovsky—despite their feudal upbringing. Some of his friends supported him. After all, Tagore was firmly ensconced inside the psyche of the average Bengali, and it was difficult to negate his influence.

By then, Samir was successful in hoodwinking his parents that he had quit activism. When he requested their permission to spend a weekend with Utpal at Arghya da's palatial bungalow, Satyen approved without batting an eyelid. He did not mention Runa and Srimati, and the nagging guilt magically disappeared as the train chugged lazily out of the station that morning.

Arghya da was the district magistrate based out of Bolpur and, as an alumnus of the college, surreptitiously maintained links with erstwhile comrades; he had even provided shelter to a few militants active in the district. It was an ideal breeding ground for young revolutionaries since poverty was endemic in the district. The land was not half as fertile as the neighbouring districts, and starvation, malnutrition and deprivation were ubiquitous among the Santhals.

The two of them sat at night on the banks of the Ajay River as the breeze softly kissed the sal trees. It was a full moon night.

Sitting lazily on the banks, Runa expressed her apprehension that the clouds may soon cover the bright moon, spoiling their fun. It was just the two of them, and in an impulsive moment, they had ventured out of the bungalow, despite the guard warning them about the snakes that Santiniketan was famous for. Arghya was a bachelor, and after a tiring day at work and a bit of sermonizing had crashed. Utpal and Srimati went to bed in separate rooms. Samir suspected that there was a platonic slant to their relationship.

The sudden appearance of a flock of peacocks startled them. They beat a hasty retreat, deciding not to intrude upon the couple's privacy. Time stood still.

'Close your eyes for a while, Runa, then open them and stare at the moon,' he said softly.

She took off her spectacles to wipe them. 'I have this strange feeling that the moon recognizes me.'

The unperfumed, piquant smell from Runa's armpits carried a whiff of titillating promiscuity. It was even more intoxicating than the inexpensive aguru perfume she usually put on.

She continued, 'Let us absorb the stillness of the night. Feel the rustle of the leaves. Experience freedom through oneness with nature. Do you recollect Sankar's lectures during our last study session on the essence of unity with nature?'

Samir lit a bidi and did not seem too interested. He gave her a gentle kiss instead and said, 'To our eternal love.'

'No, to the revolution,' she said. Her response disappointed him.

'At this moment, only you occupy my mind,' Samir cajoled.

What followed was a distasteful stare. 'It can never be. We have vowed to dedicate our lives to a cause. We have dreamt of a new world.'

With no desire to enter into an argument, he hurled his weight at her, pinning her down, leaving meandering kisses. Like any teenage girl, she succumbed after some initial resistance.

Unable to set herself free, her gentle note of protest was, at best, half-hearted. 'Samir, can we not do it at the bungalow? We have a room and a cot to ourselves. What if the locals come?'

'Fuck them. This is a sublime experience. I am not willing to forego it.'

'Fuck the proletariat?'

'Can we shun jargon for a while? Why do you have such a one-track mind?'

'It pervades every vein and artery of my anatomy.'

'And where do I feature in all this?'

Her toothy grin gleamed in the moonlight. It reminded him of their encounter at the restaurant. Her soft voice penetrated the stillness of surroundings, and she said, 'A tad below on the pecking order.'

Perhaps Samir had loosened his grip in a bout of absent-mindedness, but what happened next was unimaginable. She showed off her prowess, and he was not just overpowered but rolled across several yards on the grass. His male ego was unwilling to accept defeat, and he mustered the strength to overthrow her after a while.

He wore an expression of primal passion as he pinned her firmly to the ground. 'You asked for it. We now go the whole hog,' he said, lifting her saree and petticoat with savage intensity. The buttons of her blouse had given way.

They had confined themselves to fellatios earlier and this was his first experience of consummation. The first orgasm, aided by a warm flow permeating her anatomy, generated an electrifying sensation. She visualized a rainbow of colours, and heard the soft strains of the shehnai. He turned limp in her arms and Runa kissed his forehead, which was drowned in beads of dewy sweat.

She was now confident that she could control him.

The moonlight lit up the overbearing casuarina trees, and the gently flowing Ajay bore witness to this pair of disparate souls—lying naked on the sandy bank, blending into a single entity, merged in a tight embrace. The beating of drums and cymbals from the Santhal villages was faintly audible, but it seemed eons away.

His eyes drifted to the blossoming buds of the mango tree, and he had a desperate urge to enjoy the delicacies of his favourite summer fruit, but the season was still a month or two away. He realized he had crossed a threshold, attained the heights of a summit and experienced a transcendental event.

An inscrutable, undefinable sensation brought stirrings within him. The oft-repeated three words heard in American movies were too gross, too trivial for the occasion they had just shared. Lighting a bidi with trembling fingers, Samir slipped into a trance.

The precocious Runa let him be. All to himself.

'It was a feeling of...

Liberation.

Freedom.

Like a flight of white storks sailing by on a clear spring afternoon.'

A fit of panic engulfed him as the implications of his impulsive act dawned upon him. What would be his next step? How would he manage the situation? Would he face a scandal? And how could she afford to be so unruffled? Perhaps it had not struck her.

He was in no mood to express his forebodings.

He lay gently on the grass, gazing at the vast expanse of the sky and the stars sparkled like fireflies in the darkness. He abruptly stole a glance at her body, barely covered with a crumpled saree. He was too close to miss the bloodstains.

'Runa, you have hurt yourself. Trust you to start wrestling here. Let us get back. We should manage some first-aid.'

She laughed uproariously.

'What exactly is funny now?' he asked gruffly.

'You are so innocent, darling,' she said, pulling his cheeks hard, accompanied by an order to unzip his pants.

'But why? Have you gone bonkers?'

When he reluctantly agreed, he noticed the bloodstains on himself. It resembled stains of betel juice.

Her brusque comment came after a few minutes. 'You think I would have let you...otherwise? I am no ordinary girl, Samir. You will realize it soon.'

It was time to proceed back to Arghya's bungalow, but before he could express his desire to do so, she suddenly jumped up like a spring. She had a flustered look in her eyes.

'Samir, something dreadful has happened.'

'Now what?'

'My golden chain has fallen off. Please, we have to locate it.'

He had noticed it at the station while helping her climb on to the train. It was a necklace made of heavy, twenty-four-carat gold, stuff one wore during weddings or occasions. It was somewhat unusual on a woman who never got tired of proclaiming her disdain towards an ostentatious display of wealth. And she had worn it on a short holiday. It had been deftly hidden under her traditionally-drawn saree, and he had desisted from commenting in the presence of others. The topic had slipped his mind after they arrived at their destination.

They were not carrying a torch, and it was pitch dark. Samir proposed they rush back early in the morning, but she wept like a two-year-old infant.

'It is risky, someone may stumble upon it. It's better for us to spend the night here, waiting for dawn to break.'

'But how can you be so sure it fell off here?'

'I checked it once before.'

Samir pulled her affectionately towards himself.

'Let us forget it. I am here for you, why do you need the necklace?'

'Samir, please, I beg of you. My mother will be heartbroken.'

'Okay. It is difficult, but let us run to the bungalow and fetch a torch. I'm sure the guard will have one. Otherwise, we can wait here till dawn.'

'Let us search once. Then you can go and fetch a torch while I guard the place.'

'Are you crazy? How can I leave you here alone?'

They kept looking through the ground. To Samir, it seemed to be a wild goose chase. He was certain that she had dropped it elsewhere. He protested, weighed down by exhaustion and inclined to abandon the futile search. 'Listen, Runa. There is no way we can find it. You might have dropped it elsewhere. I am certain.'

Just at that moment, before she could respond, he felt a heavy metallic object scraping his feet. It was beneath a tall patch of grass at a spot far from where they had lain. He was surprised that they had rolled so much of a distance.

He placed the necklace where it belonged, lifted her gently and rocked her while she held on to him.

'The necklace passed through generations on my mother's side,' Runa explained. 'It is, by custom, bequeathed to the eldest daughter or the eldest son, if there is no daughter—who in turn passes it on to his daughter or once again to his son, until there is a daughter born to a future generation.'

'Sounds like the mitochondrial-DNA, although slightly different in the way it works,' he joked.

'I never knew that you were well-read when it came to genetics.'

'I've only read a smattering from the library. Why did you

wear the necklace on a trip to Santiniketan of all places?'

'I never wear it. Have you seen me in it in college?'

'Then why today?'

A pregnant silence greeted him. He heard the whisper of the leaves on the ground as they were ruffled by a gentle breeze. The sweet scent of palash accosted him.

She asked him to wait, and soon, they had both dozed off to sleep, soaking in the taste of salty sweat as the night dissipated into morning. The stars disappeared from the sky and the moon hid behind a thin layer of clouds. They were woken by cuckoos, screeching monkeys, and peacocks set to welcome the dawn. The couple scampered towards the bungalow through the thick forest, eager to reach before the sun rose.

They occasionally paused in their frenzied run, enchanted by the animals running helter-skelter, the birds singing the moon to sleep, the squirrels scampering to their abode in the trees—nature was revealing its glory to a pair of city-bred lovers.

Their return did not escape the trained and experienced eyes of the guard who promptly complained to Arghya, and was utterly disappointed when instead of displaying an interest in his juicy story, he was instructed not to speak on the topic—neither with him nor anybody else.

The promiscuity continued through the morning until the cook knocked to announce that breakfast was on the table. According to his compatriots in college, Arghya was not, by nature, a person prone to mincing words.

'Why did the two of you spend the night outside the bungalow?' he demanded to know.

Samir decided to be smart. 'Well, we wished to enjoy the splendid night.'

Runa opted to keep a discreet silence.

'But why were you in a distraught state when you returned?

That's what the guard told me.'

They remained silent.

'Your behaviour is unacceptable,' he scolded. 'You could have caused problems for me if a cop had spotted you. They keep patrolling the riverside at night.'

The sincere apologies that followed failed to mollify him.

'That apart, you have insulted the Santhals. This land belongs to them. They are remnants of pristine humanity and, although you may consider them prudish, their prudishness is based on a rational approach to life. You violated the intrinsic purity of their surroundings.'

He recalled Utpal tersely remarking on the return journey that any other person in Arghya da's place would have stripped them naked in the public square.

Samir was absorbed in sublime thoughts and preferred not to offer a rejoinder.

◆

Runa said nothing but her cheeks had turned flaming red.

With just three days to spare for a short honeymoon, Samir and Neelu left for Santiniketan. A close relative of Neelu's had cordially invited them there, and he too happened to be the District Magistrate at Bolpur then. Arghya had gone places in his career and Samir dared not meet him.

Samir was overjoyed at the thought of visiting the same bungalow after so many years with Neelu and her relatives. The bungalow had been painted and renovated. The DM, a typical family man, polite and hospitable to a fault, received them at the station. Samir found him dull and anodyne compared to Arghya, who had not just been interesting but was a thoroughbred intellectual.

Coincidentally, they were offered the same bedroom he had once shared with Runa, and thoughts of her occupied every moment of his stay. He found it tough to control his tears when he was reminded of the incident by the river.

For old time's sake, he requested Neelu for a nocturnal trip after her relatives retired for the night. He was warned by the guard with familiar stories about snakes before they set on their brief journey.

It was the same riverbank, the sal trees, another moonlit night.

Neelu's cryptic refusal cut short his audacious attempt. 'This is a public place, Samir,' she said roughly.

He had tried to joke on the way back, tickled by her hysterics at the sight of a long rope lying portentously on the grass.

'Human snakes are far more dangerous, Neelu,' he said.

She did not bother to counter the inscrutable comment.

◆

From an Undisclosed Location

December 2019

The urge to crash addled Samir's tired brain. His eyelids kept alternately opening and closing despite his desperate attempts to stay awake.

The night seemed even more toxic than before.

Optimism was Samir's forte. Both Neelu and Runa had thought so; Ruplu and Apu believed otherwise. Now, he tended to agree with the former. Samir was hopeful that help would arrive. However, he also thought that he should have yelled at the top of his voice to draw the attention of the man who had run away. He was not famed for his presence of mind, other than on rare occasions.

He decided to steer his mind back to the weekend that had changed his life.

BREAKING THE FAST AND FACING THE MUSIC

18 May 2014

Ruplu woke him at 8.30 a.m. She was as demanding as ever.

'You are a spoilsport, Baba. I had planned to sleep in. Trust Apu to wake me with the news of a family meeting at nine. Now that I am up, let me express my gratitude for providing the opportunity for a catharsis. I feel like a different person this morning. What do you plan to speak on?'

Samir realized that she had presumed it would be a pep talk.

'Ruplu, I have similar feelings this morning. A stone has been lifted off my back... Can I request thirty minutes for a quick bath, baby? Let us catch up at nine at the breakfast table.'

The headache had lessened. His nausea had abated, but out of abundant caution, Samir gulped a couple of aspirin tablets before helping himself to some earl grey teabags, soaking them in boiling water, puzzled that Neelu was not in the kitchen. Possibly there were leftovers from the previous night for their breakfast, or she had a quick omelette in mind.

At the table, the mood appeared gloomy. Neelu wore a saturnine expression, Apu looked as if he was waiting for doomsday and Ruplu was not half as cheerful as she had been a while back.

'Well, guys,' he began, 'let us get to the topic. What you heard over the last three evenings was the tip of the iceberg. I have kept the other events a secret for many years, although

Neelu happened to know most of it. It was kind of her to keep it to herself. I received a call yesterday early in the morning from a lady by the name of Runa, my comrade-in-arms with whom I had once fallen in love. After forty-odd years of silence, she had been trying to call me for the last three days. Neelu picked up the call last night and spoke to her in the morning before I could.'

Ruplu, having made an assumption, jumped to his defense. 'That's not fair. A friend of forty years calls up and Baba maintains that they have not met for so many years. Why are you so upset over it, Ma?'

Possibly Ruplu had a deal in mind, a quid pro quo? Was yesterday's incident at the café uppermost in her mind?

Apu's smile conveyed relief. The news must have appeared anti-climactic to him.

Neelu was dying to wade in, but Samir cut her short. 'That is not the point, Ruplu. The issue is not that she called, but her call led to unravelling a secret Ma has been privy to for many years.'

'And what is that secret?'

It was a breathtaking effort to go ahead and select the right words. Still, when the words left his mouth, Samir was surprised. They flowed effortlessly, like a gentle stream. 'The secret I have withheld for so many years is that I was once upon a time implicated in a murder charge, and that led to my abrupt departure from India.'

Apu was perhaps looking forward to another juicy story. 'Like Adesh was? I'm dying to hear the rest of it, but what foxes me is why you left this portion out yesterday.'

He hated disappointing him. 'It was not similar, Apu. I committed the murder.'

There was pin-drop silence. The cutlery stopped clanging and all hands were still. Ruplu did not know how to react, but Apu managed to stutter a few words.

'Was it political...or personal? Were you convicted?'

'No, I was not convicted. I was let off the hook. Yet another story. It was a demi-political murder, not cold-blooded, and not political in its entirety. There was a personal component. But listen, Runa is currently visiting LA and she expects us at eleven. The appointment was fixed by your mother last morning and I plan to pick her up. I will narrate the full story in her presence and leave it to you to pass the final judgment. I'm willing to walk out if you guys disown me. Neelu volunteered to leave, but why should she? I will rent out a small apartment, bequeathing this dwelling to all of you.'

Neelu butted in. 'Do not try to stroke cheap sentiments, Samir, like those B-grade Bengali soap operas. All I wished to know was the truth. I threatened to walk out if the truth was not disclosed, otherwise, life continues as before.'

Samir stopped her. 'As adults, they are entitled to speak for themselves. But I have a small request. I don't want to disrespect Runa since she will be our guest. I plan to leave by 10.30 a.m. with Neelu to pick her up.'

'Why do you want me to join? I need to cook for them.'

'I do not want you to suspect that I have tutored her on the way.'

He expected her to decline, but she consented after a moment's thought.

The stillness in the room was mind-numbing. Samir could sense that the words had had an impact, and he remembered that they both had strong views regarding homicide. Both of them were in favour of retaining capital punishment, despite Ruplu's liberal posturing on other issues. This factor had contributed to his reluctance when it came to divulging the details of the incident.

The siblings rose and left the room. They had locked themselves up in their rooms long before Samir and Neelu left.

A LONG LOST SWEETHEART

18 May 2014

Runa's apartment was tucked deep in the backwaters of Disneyland. In the midst of utilitarian concrete towers, all stashed side by side; the blocks were painted in a uniform, unimaginative shade of white that screamed for a fresh coat. The lawns were in disarray, the grass in need of pruning and the bushes were untidy heaps.

Samir requested that Neelu not be snobbish; Kallol was on an H-1B visa.

The visitor's parking lot was at a distance, and despite walking the stretch, they were ten minutes early. Neelu smiled graciously while they waited for the elevator, sensing his predicament.

They were greeted at the door by a slim, unkempt, reticent young man with a curly mane that needed taming. His eyes were languid and entrenched, and they bore the distinctive stamp of a techie. He didn't look like Runa—he was darker and not half as sharp, and distinct Mongoloid slant dominated his features. But Runa was present in the manner Kallol carried himself—confident, humble, sincere.

When he bent to touch their feet, his flawless Bengali did not escape his notice. *'Ma snan korchen, aapnara boshun.'*

Settling on the wooden dining chairs surrounding their tiny dining table, Samir initiated conversation. He did not wish to lose the opportunity to extract information before Runa barged in. The conversation, in chaste Bengali, pleasantly surprised Samir.

'When did you arrive at Los Angeles?'

Kallol was prompt in his reply but not too excited. 'Two

months ago, uncle. I will pack up in a month. This was a short stint as a replacement.'

'A pure IT project?'

He noted the lucid manner in which Kallol responded, reminding him of his encounter with Runa at the restaurant. 'Python with a bit of Data Analytics thrown in. Interesting, despite the back-breaking pressure of deadlines. I feel as if I'm running a race against time, having lost two months to my predecessor's goof-up. I have found the time, though, to explore the city during weekends. I love the eating joints here.'

Samir was persistent. 'When did your family move to Dublin?'

There was a bit of hesitation. 'Oh, my parents moved there... thirty years back, I think? A year after they got married. I was born there. My father is a doctor and works at a government hospital.'

He noticed that Neelu was listening attentively to the conversation, eyes alternating between him and Kallol.

'Dublin is an amazing city. I visited once when I was a student in London.'

'Yes, but hardly a first world city.'

'Are your grandparents alive?'

His eyes brightened. 'Yes, on both sides. They are not in the pink of health, but they keep travelling to Dublin every alternate year.' He seemed quite attached to his grandparents.

'And...is your Ma well-settled?'

He smiled radiantly for the first time. 'She has still not adjusted. Her heart is still in Kolkata. She keeps pestering Baba to return home. No denying that Dublin is not a particularly exciting city for her.'

'Hmm. I expected her to be homesick.'

For a few fleeting seconds, before Neelu turned round to spot her, he thought that the woman who entered the room was the mother of one of Kallol's South Indian flatmates. He stood corrected when she spoke. 'Sorry, *ki kore bujhbo bol tui aagei eshey jabi?* Sorry, how was I to anticipate you arriving early?' Her croaky voice reminded him of her old melodious tones.

Samir wanted to laugh. He had been notorious once upon a time for his lack of punctuality. Neelu smiled but Samir was in a haze.

He was not naïve enough to expect Runa to not have aged, but he was surprised that her spark was missing. It was not because she was tanned and darker complexioned or because of the fat clinging to her waist. So much was different: the missing spring in her steps, her jet-black hair was grey, and she wore a set of hideous dentures.

It seemed to be a puzzle that he would perhaps never be able to solve. The change was not cosmetic but almost a mutation of her genes. The enzymes and proteins had undergone an irreversible chemical transformation.

He recognized that he was having a far more intense response to her presence than when he had listened to her voice, even though their conversation through the wires had brought back long-lost memories of a sweet, albeit brief, star-crossed romance. They had detached many moons back on a torrid afternoon before they could enjoy life to the fullest; at a juncture when he had barely sensed the stirrings of pure romance, untainted by selfishness. The indomitable barrier of time now occupied the space between the two souls.

He never considered himself worthy of her generous outpourings of love. She was an irrepressible free spirit, a dreamer, a romantic. He had initially been in the relationship to satisfy his emotional needs, to relieve the self from abject loneliness, and because he was enticed by carnal pleasures. But for her, it had been selfless, she had surrendered from the beginning, despite her simultaneous affair with the revolution.

Samir had redefined himself during those eight months they had spent together. Shamelessly amorous on numerous occasions, gutsy to the point of stupidity on another occasion, until he was hurled into an abyss from where his folks extricated him.

He was able to perceive what he had lost. She was no longer a young lass who activated his hormones like vasopressin.

He was abruptly stirred by Runa's remark. 'Congratulations, you look great these days! *Aar tor mohilader dikey phyal phyal taakanor obhyas gelo na dekhchi.* You still retain your habit of blankly staring at women.'

Neelu broke into splits of laughter and Samir felt uneasy. Kallol was in two minds about whether to stay in the room, and was persuaded with a nudge that did not escape Samir's eyes.

The sparkle in her eyes was unmistakable. 'Don't I deserve a hug after so many years?' she said.

This time, things were easier. The bear-hug left traces of dopamine; a forty-year-old circuitry switching on at an incredibly low voltage. He almost smelt the concoction on her: aguru with the odour of unperfumed armpits, menstrual blood, spilled semen, the raw smell of probiotic curd, shutki fish, onions, raw mangos, papayas, sweat, and talcum powder, on a hot summer afternoon.

Many years after Shakespeare's pronouncement on the scent of the rose, scientists stumbled upon the truth that olfactory sensations meander through compartments, storing memories and emotions before reaching the thalamus; the expensive perfume she had sprinkled on her saree today smelt like the aguru of yore.

The next few minutes were devoted to pleasantries. Samir proposed after a while that they move on, extending the invite to Kallol, who only accepted after a sidelong glance at his mother.

She left to pick up her purse and his birthday gift and returned with something wrapped in fancy paper. He stole a hasty look at the framed picture on the side table. It portrayed a contented family: a stocky and dark husband with blunt features, and Runa and Kallol beaming with unselfconscious joy. He was surprised when he felt happy, 'mudita', as she had described. It engulfed him and he was bereft of envy.

Their garrulous talk on the way back were all hogwash. His thoughts kept swirling, and he was aware that it was pointless to brush the harsh truth under the carpet. Nonetheless, Samir had to put up a brave face. He turned ponderous on the journey, and started believing that Apu and Ruplu would not go to the extent of breaking up relations. But he also knew that he would never be able to regain their lost respect.

He reflected on their relationship. His audience had been so stiff, detached, and aloof; those indications were amply present at the breakfast table. They had locked themselves in their rooms. More than his act, his lack of transparency would have annoyed them. His only hope lay in the prevalent adage that over time, animosity dissolves.

He learnt more about Runa on the journey. Runa worked as a modern history teacher at a local school on the outskirts of Dublin. The rest of the time she devoted to pro-bono activities. When she analysed the nature of poverty in Ireland, Samir felt tempted to make a snide remark. But he decided against it. 'Not on such a complicated day!' he thought.

While climbing the stairs to their home, her encomiums on their abode shed lingering doubts that this was the same Runa he knew. It was the opportune moment to fulfill an insatiate desire from their last meeting, but Kallol was following right behind.

They settled in the drawing-room. Neelu directed them there. He himself would have preferred the lounge, with its touch of intimacy. But Neelu, like most homemakers, was more perceptive on such matters.

Neelu took on the role of a familiar Bengali host as they settled down. 'Tea or coffee?'

'I deprive myself of the elementary pleasures in life, although Kallol is a compulsive coffee drinker.'

Samir laughed. 'A quintessential techie. I survived on coffee once upon a time.'

'Coffee before sunset and whisky afterward,' Kallol joked.

Samir did not quite appreciate the comment. They had been introduced only an hour back, and Kallol was so much younger than him. It stirred in him silent admiration for Apu and Ruplu. It would be unthinkable for them to be so intimate with his friends. Maintaining his poise, he responded. 'Not to worry, we will get some cold beer before lunch.'

Runa was able to read his mind. 'Samir, I keep reminding Kallol to forget his ex-pat identity when speaking to folks from our culture. Somehow, it fails to register.'

Kallol apologized, and Samir found himself in a quandary on who to side with. Finally he said, 'Forty-three years have passed, Runa. We need not stick to traditional values.'

The intervention was uncalled for since Runa, a mother, was using this opportunity to instill some sense in her son.

'*Tui aar paltali na, Samir*. Samir, you have not changed one bit,' she said.

Her exasperated sigh reminded him of the lady who, once upon a time, had attempted to transform him and make him more mature.

The trio chatted for around an hour. Neelu was nowhere to be seen, except when she briefly appeared to serve coffee and nuts. Samir felt that her behaviour was unacceptable. Even though the three of them thoroughly enjoyed the intimate conversation, the absence of Neelu and the children would not go down well. It was discourteous in Indian culture for the hostess to absent herself from guests. And it was Neelu, not he, who had invited them. It would be fine on other occasions if Apu and Ruplu dropped by just for a few minutes, but in this instance, Kallol was here too. They were usually scrupulous on such matters. Apu, if this were a normal day, would have ungrudgingly joined in and Ruplu would have made conversation without appearing bored.

Excusing himself, he was pleasantly surprised to witness a well-laid-out table. Neelu would have had stocked ingredients; there were three elaborately cooked dishes, two of them were meat preparations. The dishes were freshly cooked. And he had planned on bombarding her with a piece of his mind for not joining the conversation!

He heartily complimented Neelu when she appeared with the dessert plate.

'Wow!' she laughed. 'Your personality has transformed after an hour with an old flame. This is the first time in living memory that I have heard a word of appreciation.'

'That may be your perception... But I promised cold beer to the youngster. I will rush and get it. Can you provide them company till then?'

'I overheard your conversation. It should be here in the next ten minutes. Never mind, it is only one. Let us plan for lunch at two and let me set the warmers on.'

'But home deliveries take longer.'

'Apu has gone to fetch them.'

'Apu? How is he feeling now?'

'In a mood to be patient. Ruplu initially adopted an uncompromising stance but I managed to bring her around through a bit of cajoling. It is more your lack of transparency than the act itself, Samir. Anyway, she is taking a bath. The beer and the three of us should rendezvous at the drawing-room fifteen to twenty minutes from now. How long do you think your story will last?'

'Difficult to estimate.'

'Then let us commence after lunch. They are not in a hurry, so time is not a challenge.'

The family assembled around 1.15 p.m. Contrary to Samir's apprehensions, Ruplu developed an instant fondness for Kallol, or at least pretended to. Apu was delighted to meet a professional from his industry and soon, their conversation veered in an unexpected direction.

Drowsy after a sumptuous lunch and a can of beer, Samir toyed with the idea of a power nap, but the demand for the story surfaced with vehemence when they settled in the drawing room, and from an unexpected quarter.

'Samir, there is a reason we have assembled today,' Runa said. 'I suggest you begin the narrative. Assuming all of you are still in a mood to listen.'

'Certainly, Runa. Certainly. That is the reason we are here,' he said.

He gave them a self-conscious smile, and he was set to go. It was all planned—the point he would start at, when he would take a break, when he would rise to draw curtains.

There was silence, like the lull before a Cincinnati tornado. And then the words poured like a stream, flowing effortlessly down the mountains.

THAT FATEFUL DAY

October 1971

Things changed a few months after their trip to Santiniketan. There were twenty days for the annual examinations. These exams were not so serious, and were conducted by the college at the end of the first year, unlike the university exams that were held at the end of second and third academic years. Samir was still hell-bent on scoring well and was motivated by his senior comrades who had scored well last year. The joke doing the rounds was that you had to be a radical to excel in academics at Presidency College.

It was a typical morning. Dawn had broken an hour back and the bright sunshine filtered in through the windows. Samir had not drawn the curtains last night. Kolkata had been blessed with untimely rains at night, and he had woken at the stroke of dawn by the beep of the alarm clock, distressed that the black clouds that permeated the sky a few hours back had disappeared. He had planned on spending the day at home reading, enjoying the pattering raindrops, the sight of pigeons resting in their garden for respite from the rain, the calm and moist breeze, fluttering leaves, the aroma of petrichor, khichuri and fried aubergines for lunch.

He had not quite absorbed his lessons on Light and he had spent most of the lectures doodling. He couldn't understand the maze of straight and curved lines with their weird trajectories; his mental block was tough to overcome. He planned to dedicate the day to overcoming the block and catching up, assisted by a highly recommended book obtained from the library.

After completing his morning constitutionals, he grabbed

his jhola, precariously hanging on a chair. He was momentarily concerned when he realized that it did not contain the heavy book he had borrowed from the library but instantly recalled that he had placed it inside Runa's jhola and although she usually remembered to hand over his belongings at the end of their days, this probably slipped her mind. The bus to take her home had arrived out of the blue.

He did not know how to contact Runa because their telephone was not working. He toyed with the idea of going to her house, but her father—a civil servant with no compulsion to reach office in time—rarely left bed before eight. The rings of the calling bell at such an 'unearthly' hour would not be appreciated; in one instance, Samir had been subjected to his biting sarcasm. He had two alternatives: he could either study a different subject or doze off.

He chose the latter.

His mother woke him and handed him his morning tea. Upon hearing about his predicament, she requested that he first finish his breakfast before leaving. But by the time he reached her house, Runa had apparently left for college. She seemed to have pulled a fast one at home because classes had been dissolved to allow students to prepare for the exams and very few students of their batch were expected to be there. She had explicitly mentioned her plans to study at home. Samir was a trifle suspicious and thoroughly disgusted with the situation, and the only option he had left now was studying for another subject and holding on to the library book for an extra day, incurring a penalty.

Runa called around eleven. The book was with her; she was studying at the college library and planned to drop by Samir's residence on her way home but would be able to reach him by seven or later. Tempted to share a quick cup of black coffee at the café with her and gain a few extra hours with the book, he left hurriedly for college.

When he reached there, Runa told him that a message had reached her early in the morning that Pagla Keshto's goons had brutally attacked the students of another college, and the female students of that college planned to lay a siege on their principal's office, demanding enhanced security for their male compatriots. The college was the same one Adesh had enrolled into, and they needed at least twenty girls to bolster their protest. By the time he reached, she was about to leave but agreed to a quick cup of coffee, vociferously expressing her disapproval when he volunteered to accompany her.

'I think I need to be with you. Pagla Keshto's toughies control that college. They are scumbags of the highest order, the ones who orchestrated Adesh's murder,' he said.

'I'm aware of the incident but I'm also sure that they will not dare to touch us women. For tactical reasons, male activists have been advised not to venture close to the college. No cause for tension.'

Despite there being a strong cultural taboo when it came to assaulting the fair gender, respected in local culture as a mother and a goddess, multiple breaches had occurred in the recent past, and Samir could not be as certain as she was. Cultural transformations were often incremental, not discernible to the naked eye.

'Let me spend some time with Barua da while you chant your slogans. I have not had a chance to meet him since Adesh's murder.'

'But Samir, boys have been specifically asked not to venture anywhere near the college today. And what about your plans to study?'

'I will catch up at night, darling. Or sneak in an hour if Barua da is busy with his students. I am neither planning to participate in your demonstration nor do I belong to the students' organization of that college. Can I not visit an old friend?'

It was a reluctant surrender. Runa was aware of how difficult it was to persuade Samir once he had made up his mind. Walking to the college was pleasurable yet discomfiting because of the humidity, and both of them sweated profusely. Runa sprayed her saree with perfume twice to mask the stink, and Samir did not let go of the opportunity to poke fun at her for the bourgeois habit. She, in turn, reminded him of his earlier remark on sweat, bordering on snootiness. These were the two issues he typically teased her about. The other concerned the gold chain she had misplaced at Santiniketan. He had dubbed it a remnant from her feudal background, a residue from a period when her ancestors, feudal landlords from the western part of Bengal, had oppressed the peasantry. The gold chain was an epitome of wealth accumulated through the sweat and toil of poor peasants. She had flared up when he mentioned it the first time but stopped reacting when he reminded her of the remark she had made about his poitey.

The last five minutes of their walk were devoted to academics. Runa had been studying the history of the Mughal period in the library and she sang paeans about their generous sponsorship of the fine arts and literature, annoying Samir. He believed that the period represented a dark chapter in Indian history when Hindus were victims of genocide, forcible conversions and an oppressive jizya—a tax imposed on non-Muslim citizens. Their argument remained inconclusive until they spotted the outline of the college.

After confirming that she would meet him at the physics laboratory by six, she crossed the road to join a bunch of girls assembled on the opposite footpath. Before leaving, she had squeezed his fingers gently. 'Samir, you made my day.'

The warmth of her touch conveyed more than her words,

and he recalled the night they had spent together in Santiniketan. He stood silently for a few seconds, unable to move, and gazed intently at her eyes. They seemed to have changed their colour within the past few minutes. It was not customary for boys and girls to embrace each other under the public glare during the seventies; so Samir restrained himself with difficulty.

Barua was effusive. He was yet to come to terms with Adesh's murder, and Samir's presence sparked memories of the young boy he had assisted a few months back. Despite being busy helping students with their apparatus, he joined him immediately.

'What a pleasant surprise! I'm overjoyed to see you after so many months, Samir. You should come more often to meet your good old Barua da,' he said, slapping him rather forcefully on the back.

Samir replied: 'I have wanted to for a long time. Today, however, I plan to be with you until six—if you permit me. You carry on with your class for the time being. I will catch up with my studies.' Then he briefly explained why he was there.

The man's face turned sombre.

Samir immediately backed off. 'I'm sorry if I have disturbed you. Never mind, I shall wait at the canteen. Just need to send her a message. Can you help me with that?'

'You have misunderstood me, Samir. I can provide you with the company until 10 p.m. if that is what you demand. I'm disturbed for a different reason. Let me request my assistant to take charge before we settle down in the corner room.'

Once they settled, Barua explained. The news from the grapevine was that a few goons from the locality planned to disperse the protest violently. 'She must be a good friend otherwise you would not have been here. If you tell me her name, I will arrange to send her a message. The three of us can then sit here and chat over tea,' he said to Samir.

Samir snorted. 'I will be roasted alive if I were to do that. She is a devoted individual, not like me, and she seriously believes that they would not dare attack girls.'

'She is naive. The goondas do not fall into the category of normal human beings. Allow me to request someone to send word the moment they sense trouble.'

'Brilliant. The same old Barua da who once hid Adesh inside a closet.'

'Shh! Are you in your senses?'

Samir buried his head in his elbows; he felt like slapping himself.

'Just be cautious in the future. Let me now arrange assistance for your friend,' Barua's expression bore a worried look before leaving. He returned after fifteen minutes to announce that the girls had confined the Principal to his office, and the man was willing to discuss the issue only if they called off the protest. The silver lining was that Pagla Keshto's bunch of ruffians were not around yet. Perhaps Runa was right, or the Principal had wished to handle it in his way.

'You never know, Samir. One should not trust these bastards.'

The topic veered to Adesh thereafter. A glass beaker was converted into a makeshift ashtray and it had to be upturned and cleaned several times. Barua was keen on knowing more about Adesh's family, his childhood, interests in life and a million other details. Samir was touched when he found a passport-size photograph wrapped in cellophane paper inside Barua's wallet, a copy obtained from the college office a month after Adesh had passed away. The portrait churned bitter memories. Samir had managed to come to terms with the death only by stoking the fires of revenge inside him.

He suddenly felt uncomfortable at the thought that he was sitting inside the same room where Adesh had once hid inside a cupboard. That had been a day before his arrest. Barua was called out of the room by a colleague, and Samir made use of the opportunity to reminisce about his childhood with Adesh.

The laboratory assistant soon entered with the news that a few infamous lumpens had been spotted entering the principal's room, armed with knives. Samir jumped out of his chair, but he was pushed back. 'Do not behave impulsively. Just sit tight inside this room and do not create complications. Do not forget that you are not a student of this college. Let me check up on it.'

He waited patiently. Five, ten, fifteen, twenty minutes passed in intense agony. He had no desire to disobey the man, but he accidentally overheard a conversation between two students that girls were being molested. It set his blood on fire and he decided to disobey Barua. Walking briskly towards the principal's room, he soon found himself unable to wade through the numerous voyeurs standing ten yards outside. From a distance, he could spot a few wailing girls and he noticed that a couple of protestors were seriously injured, lying prostrate on the floor. Others were dispersing.

His eyes wandered, but Runa was not to be seen. The only other person he knew was a male student, Joy, but he would not have come to college today.

Barua was not visible. Samir felt glimmers of hope...perhaps Barua and Runa were waiting at the laboratory. The jog was tiring since this college compound was far more expansive than theirs, and he hated trampling over the green grass mowed with care. After reaching the laboratory, he was dismayed. The empty room stared nastily at him. He hung around for ten minutes before sprinting back, making it to the crowd in less than three minutes. It was hot and humid, and he was panting like a mongrel.

A posse of cops were stationed outside the room. They had dispersed the voyeurs, and the crowd was now situated at a distance. Samir barged in after ungraciously pushing away a pot-bellied constable stationed at the entrance. The bunch of goons around the cops mistook him as one of their own and let him pass into the room.

The gruesome spectacle he witnessed lingered like an apparition for many, many years. It was later diagnosed as PTSD. It led to panic attacks, and he was often compelled to leave bed, quit the golf course or stroll out of his cubicle for a walk in the sun; he would even blank out during official presentations. He would prematurely ejaculate on the few occasions he went to bed. He had sought the help of a clinical psychologist a few months before his marriage, and had been substantially cured but old passions failed to resurface.

Samir noticed Runa. She was pinned to the floor, a pack of scums lying on top of her. Their pants were unzipped, and they were groping and smooching her in a manner that reminded him of wild American movies. Her blouse was torn and the saree was in a sorry state. Their jouissance was being expressed through exuberant laughter and it reminded him of a pack of hyenas. He was not sure where the Principal was.

The primitive savage in him leapt out. He was no longer an introverted puppet belonging to a civilized generation, bogged down by niceties. The eyes strayed to a knife on the chair and he lost sense of time, place and context. It was not that he had acquired the skills of a professional warrior, but he felt the innate force of passion and was driven by spontaneity. The act would have appeared choreographed to a casual bystander.

Samir spun the knife round and round in an elliptical motion, like a discus, and the initial idea was to scare them. But he stuck it close to the stomach of an unsuspecting man. It hit the man, striking him with an intensity that generated a snapping sound.

He turned his eyes away and only after a few minutes stole a glance at the body that lay in torrents of blood. There was a listless face, spilled intestines, blood vessels draining through creases; he heard popping sounds of small firecrackers as innards fell like dry leaves. The disassembled human body appeared ghastly, yet he had no feeling of repentance. He was overjoyed at his own display of athletic prowess.

When the truth dawned on him, it hit him like the force of lightning. The body on the floor was not of any of the goons, but of the principal, who had been trying to pull them off.

It sent chills down his spine when he realized that a split second's carelessness had sealed his fate. He would never be let off the hook. In all likelihood, he would have to pay through his life or be confined till the last breath of existence.

The body did not groan in despair or try to cling on to the dying vestiges of existence. A still pair of snow-white eyes simply gazed at the ceiling as it lay on the blood-soaked carpet, taking on the appearance of a cheap rug. Rays of the dying afternoon sun were faintly visible through the solitary window situated in a corner of the room. The summer heat was stifling; air-conditioned rooms were rare those days.

Runa lay huddled in a corner. She had covered her face with a torn blouse and was crying: a terror-stricken aria with discordant notes. She shivered out of fright. Her skin had turned as pallid as that of a leukemia patient. But her bare eyes spewed intense hatred.

The cowards disappeared at the sight of gore. He could hear her feeble voice, begging for him to escape from the room that consisted of just the two of them and a corpse now. His hands were reasonably clean and, if he walked away insouciantly, not a soul would recognize him inside the college. He could escape into the mild darkness of the twilight city.

It skipped his mind that the cops were standing right outside the door. They chose the right moment to troop in. The goons were accompanying them and, after Samir was identified, they disappeared. One of the cops in plain clothes bent forward to examine the blood-spattered chest of the corpse while the others glanced as if admiring a parquet floor.

A guy with a stethoscope barged in after a few minutes. He was the college doctor. 'Not an iota of life left. There is no point rushing him to hospital,' he said and covered the corpse with a white tablecloth.

Samir noticed Runa's moving lips but he could not follow what she was muttering.

Slaps and punches landed on his face. They were not half as painful as the ones he had faced months back. These guys were trained to ensure that they left their victims alive. Moreover, for them the boy that was Samir not only held the key to critical information of the murder but deserved a slow and painful death.

The beatings and curses continued intermittently for half an hour till a senior officer tottered through the door with a slew of constables.

'No physical injuries here, please. This is an educational institution. We need to move him fast. Never know, his friends, the illegitimate children of Chairman Mao may be around,' he said before turning towards Samir.

'*Bejanma, bokachoda, khankir chheley,* how much did Mao pay your Ma to fuck her?'

It was regular shop talk. Policemen usually spoke in a dialect similar to that of the underworld, peppered with profanities. The two reinforced each other. Samir suddenly felt like a transformed person, permeated with chutzpah. He was now almost an audacious revolutionary tempered in steel—a Che Guevara.

'Why are you dragging my mother, you coward? Speak straight or listen to what I have to tell you. Look what they have done to her. You did not bother to enter the room earlier. I was just trying to protect the hapless girl and threatened them with the knife. They snatched it from my hands and one of those goons pushed the sword. He was trying to get me, but in the melee, it hit him. The ones who just walked away,' he said while pointing in the direction of the door.

The room burst into a boisterous laughter, and he felt a kick that landed a few inches away from his crotch.

'Take this piece of turd away. Do me a favour, call for female officers from the Entally Police Station. The nearest station with lady constables.'

'But what has she done? She was molested, groped, and scratched. I am the witness. They just ran berserk,' Samir pleaded.

'That is none of your business, you motherfucker. You are a fool if you think you will be treated like a revolutionary. We will shove you into a pit and pour piles of dirt on you, shovel by shovel, until your mouth is full of muck. Slow, painful suffocation. Not a soul will come to know,' they threatened.

He could barely hear the conversation a few feet away. 'Arrest the whore so that she does not get the opportunity to speak to those assholes, the bleeding-heart intellectuals. She will be charged as an accomplice. Please don't goof this up.'

'Sure, sir. Trust me,' the officer responded, following the statement with an unctuous salute.

'Have you informed the mortuary?'

'No sir, the official procedure is to take him to a hospital for a death certificate. Have called for the ambulance.'

That was the last Samir saw of Runa, and he could not even bid goodbye while they roughly dragged him away. At the gate, he spotted a sullen-faced Barua, a solitary figure standing innocuously near the college gate, pretending not to notice the nod directed at him. He was more concerned about his safety, apprehensive that a few students in the lab may have identified Samir as the individual who had chatted with him until a while back. He was nervous that he would be implicated, incarcerated, subjected to third-degree torture and lose his job.

Fortunately, neither Samir mentioned his name nor could any student identify him as the man sitting inside the laboratory. Perhaps some did, but they chose not to divulge the information to the cops out of love and respect for their Barua da. Perhaps they too harboured sympathies for radicals, typical of students of that era.

Barua's sleepless nights ended after a month. The authorities never came to know that Samir had sat in his room for an hour before committing the murder.

SORTING OUT THE MESS

October 1971

It was like any other evening for Satyen. He had been diagnosed with high cholesterol and a mildly high blood pressure and advised to take hourly evening walks along with the usual dietary restrictions and a host of medicines. He religiously returned from work at 6 p.m., and slipped into his sneakers before proceeding to the Park Circus lawns for five brisk rounds. Sulekha would drop in at a neighbour's house for a round of gossip during that time.

He was surprised that evening to find Sulekha at home when he returned.

'*Aarey bolo na,*' she explained. 'Our absent-minded professor has forgotten to take the house key along. The friend who had the book was at college, so the poor soul had to rush. He called from the college library, promising to return by seven. Should be here any moment.'

'Studying at the library, my foot! Must be chatting there with his girlfriends!' Satyen roared.

'He studies sincerely these days. I have noticed.'

'I'm unable to comprehend young people and their ways. Thoroughly unfocused. Wasted a whole day running after a book. Phew! You carry on if you wish to.'

'Just tell him there's food in the refrigerator. I will be at Swapna's place.'

Satyen had dozed off when the phone started screaming. Not in a mood to take the call, he ignored it once, but mustered the energy when it rang again.

'Speaking from the Detective Department, Calcutta Police. Is this Samir Chattopadhyay's residence?' a gruff voice yelled.

'Yes. What is the matter?'

'Who is on the line?'

'His father.'

'Your son is in our custody, indicted on a murder charge. The call was to inform you.'

'Are you trying to fool around? My son? He is incapable of murdering anyone.'

'Isn't his name Samir Chattopadhyay and doesn't he study at Presidency College? First year, physics department? He was charged with murdering the principal of another college.'

Satyen could only respond after a few minutes of stunned silence. 'I do not believe you one bit. Either you have committed a mistake, or you are pulling a fast one.'

'My job was to inform; whether you believe me or not is your prerogative.' The curt comment was followed by an abrupt disconnection.

Satyen had never felt so clueless. Not even on the day he had received a call that Samir was lying in the hospital. He believed the policeman had been a prankster, and the calling bell would buzz in a while, and the door would open to a beaming Samir with his familiar smile.

Perhaps it was an instance of mistaken identity, and Satyen would need to pull a few strings to figure it out.

The worst scenario, however, haunted him within minutes, and he felt a torrential rush of adrenalin that disintegrated his mind. He was plagued by indecision, and he surrendered to the superior force that he had always believed in—only a divine power could offer solace during such moments.

His mind drifted to forebodings on what the future held in store for his only son. Had he not woven countless dreams around him? It seemed to be the end of the journey, and he was soon drenched in torrents of sweat. He was not in the mood to fetch Sulekha, gossiping just two minutes across the road. He thought he would let her enjoy the evening, perhaps for the last time in her life. He needed space to focus on what had to be done.

It was common knowledge that only a few returned alive from the Detective Department Office. Their Kafkaesque interrogation chamber was notorious and the lucky few who left the chamber alive spent their lives battling mental disorder or crippling physical disability.

A conversation came to him in a flash. With Ashim the evening they released Samir from the nursing home.

Ashim had told him, 'Satu, let me warn you. Samir is sliding down a slippery slope. We were student activists in our days and are aware of its addictive nature, despite the situation being far less ominous then. I, for one, will be pleasantly surprised if he manages to extricate himself. What I am going to disclose right now is a closely guarded secret, not to be shared with anyone. Not even Sulekha. Suprio Ray, perhaps the most influential politician in Bengal today, is a patient of mine. He is suffering from a neurological ailment that only a few of us are privy to. Although cured for now, it needs perpetual monitoring. He relies on me and our relationship extends beyond a medical consultant to a friend with whom he would not mind sharing an occasional drink. To repeat, do not discuss this with anyone, but do not hesitate to call me if you ever need assistance.'

Ashim was prescient. Not half as credulous as himself, a bumbling idiot.

It was close to seven, and he could be expected at the chamber unless he was visiting a patient. Thankfully, the receptionist responded to Satyen's call. 'Yes, he is in town, but with a patient. Cannot disturb him right now.'

'That is fine, but I need to speak to him before the next patient walks in. I am his childhood friend, Satyen, and it is an emergency. Need to speak to him urgently.'

'Can it not wait till eight? There are just two others in the queue.'

'Please, it cannot.'

'Sure. Will sound him, Satyen babu. The tenor of your voice conveys a note of desperation.'

Ashim called back after ten minutes.

'Anything the matter, Satu? Hope it's nothing serious,' Ashim asked.

'Very, very serious, Ashim,' Satyen began. There was no scope for garrulity, and he kept it brief.

'What are you saying? I heard about the murder...but I never imagined... When did Samir leave home?'

'Apparently around noon to pick up a book from a friend.'

Ashim took a while to respond, his mind whirling in cycles, working fast. 'Didn't I tell you once, Satu? He was doomed. Anyway, let me send my patients off; it is not fair but I need a few minutes to work out the next steps.'

Ashim called back after ten minutes. 'I remember telling you once that I am quite close to Suprio babu. He is fortunately in town, visited him only yesterday. Since he will not appreciate speaking on the topic over the wires, I will drop in at his residence. He is normally back by six, but I will wait there in case he is late. I will call you after.'

'It could be a prank, Ashim. I do not wish to embarrass you.'

'That's unlikely. I heard about the incident from two different sources. It may be on the radio also. Do check up. When did he say he will return home?'

'By seven.'

'It is half-past seven now. Still, let me check through my

sources. I will call you.'

Satyen rushed towards the radio, but could not gather himself to switch it on. There was a flicker of relief, leading him to light a cigarette. A faint ray of hope permeated his being. What else could he do but hope that Ashim would sort this out at this hour? He now started believing in the probable scenario that Samir just happened to be at the scene of the crime. After all, he knew his son. Samir could not even kill a lizard.

Such is the human mind. Fickle. The worst apprehensions resurface like spasms before the bursting of an appendix. Satyen remembered that homicide was punishable under the Indian Penal Code with hanging. Life imprisonment was granted only in rare instances.

The gentle click on the lock indicated that Sulekha was back. She was upbeat; she would have consumed ample stories.

'Our hunch is right, bujhley?' She chirped. 'Sharmistha officially announced the marriage of her son. To the same girl.'

The pallor of her skin and the tone in her voice altered as soon as she noticed him. 'Why are you so pale? You are sweating profusely,' she asked, scared that he was passing through an attack.

The tables were turned after the contents of the conversation were disclosed. She stood still like a statue for a while and slunk into the sofa like a sack of hot potatoes.

'Ashim is on the job,' he said. 'You have to take charge of yourself, Sulekha. I cannot tackle two situations simultaneously.'

The call from Ashim came through in fifteen minutes.

'Satu, my contact spoke to Amherst Street Police Station. They could not record the culprit's name because before they could do so, he was bundled off to Lalbazar. However, the description seems to match Samir's. And your son has not yet returned, has he?'

'No, Ashim.'

'It is good that they have not recorded his name. It would have spread like wildfire by now if he had been taken to the local police station. Lalbazar is a black box and information seldom leaks out, although you never know. I have to be fast. I'm leaving for Suprio babu's house.'

◆

Satyen had recently decorated their modest drawing room with a panoply of artifacts and decorative pieces. He had changed the upholstery on the sofa, bought an elegant table lamp, a couple of paintings and a massive idol of Lord Ganesh. He would religiously switch off the tube lights every evening, light the table lamp and admire the ambiance before reading the evening newspaper. He was a disciplined person and never permitted time to gain the upper hand. He followed a regulated schedule to the last few minutes. Concluding his evening walk by half past six, he would follow it with a quick bath; occasionally take a short nap and devour the evening tabloid *Ganashakti*, the mouthpiece of the moderate and dominant left party. By eight o'clock, he would have completed his dinner, caught up with a novel, the news, or listen to a favourite classical music recital on the radio before landing up in bed by 11 p.m.

He experienced a disorienting sense of timelessness today while discussing the implications of Samir's act—blaming others, analysing what went wrong. The stream of conversation was punctuated by Sulekha's sobs and bouts of menacing silence. She loudly recalled innumerable episodes from Samir's childhood. As a child of ten or eleven, he had once accidentally swung the cricket bat at the wicket-keeper's nose, oblivious that he was standing close to the wickets. The boy had started bleeding profusely, and terrified by the sight of blood, Samir had rushed home. The boy's mother, who visited them after an hour, seemed to be more concerned about Samir than her son, who she knew would be alright.

Today, the same Samir had been accused of murder!

When the doorbell rang, they realized it was close to eleven o'clock. 'Who could it be at this hour? The news must have reached relatives. Perhaps they disclosed his name on the radio,' Satyen blurted out loudly.

It was Ashim. He did not appear too grave.

'A glass of cold water, Sulekha. It's been a long day,' he said and began speaking before the glass reached him. 'To ease your tensions, Satu, I will start off. The good news first. Two pieces of good news.'

Satyen's heart leaped.

'Samir will be released after twenty-four hours under the cover of darkness. At least, that is what has been promised. It goes like this: the two of us will pick him up from Lalbazar Detective Department at three o'clock in the morning. Not a soul should know where he is other than the three of us. You or Sulekha are to confidently tell anyone who enquires after him that he is not at home. Be it a relative, your friend or his friends. Even your brother, if he drops in. Smartly, without procrastination.

'He will be subjected to interrogation throughout the day at Lalbazar. They, perhaps, suspect a few leaders are behind the act. There is no cause for fear because an explicit instruction has been passed on to not torture him. They only want information. That is the clear condition for release. You will visit him before ten o'clock in the morning to impress upon him the gravity of the situation. If you are unable to convince him, I will visit him again around four in the afternoon and instructions have been passed that they will allow us entry. Let us hope he agrees.

'The second piece of good news was that other than a few officers, Suprio babu and the three of us, not a soul should get to know of his identity. Lalbazar Detective Department is insulated from the outside. By god's grace, his identity remained hidden, not just at the college but even with the policemen who arrested him. The official version circulated to the press states that the identity of the assassin was being ascertained. With a host of preventive detention laws in place, prisoners may not immediately be presented before a magistrate. Do you remember the guy indicted for murdering the Vice-Chancellor? His name is Tapan Bose, and he is presently pursuing an engineering course at a US college. It was tougher because his dad, a doctor and a good friend of mine, approached me rather late in the day, and by then, his name was all over the press.

'Suprio babu is not doing this for the sake of our relationship. He unwittingly revealed this after consuming a couple of drinks, and I could gauge that he was paranoid that I may blackmail him. Although he has been cured of that disease, it will prove disastrous for his political career if news leaks out. Not that I mind, so long as it works for me.'

Satyen protested, 'But the Principal's family may raise a ruckus if they come to know that his assassin has been freed.'

Ashim nodded. 'That is why I emphasize that not a soul should know. Samir will be immediately rearrested if that happens. You must be cautious to a fault. After a few days, they will tell them that he has been eliminated, which is not a rare occurrence in our times. Now the bad news. For obvious reasons, he cannot continue to live here, nor attend college here. If the news ever leaks out, the paparazzi will hound him.'

'You mean he has to give up his studies?'

'This brings us to the second piece of bad news for you, though in my opinion, it is a blessing in disguise. He must leave the country within two months, failing which, he will be rearrested. He has been given a moratorium of two years before which he cannot return. I remember you once telling me that your London-based nephew has assured admission to colleges there, and you can sell off your land to organize the fee and living expenses. I have lived in the UK for three years. If you have the dough, admission even to a good college is not a challenge, certainly not with the marks Samir obtained in his school-leaving exams. If the process takes longer, he can cool his heels on a tourist visa there, which will be converted to a student visa the moment his admission is finalized. If you cannot organize the sale in two months, I will loan you the money. Samir is, after all, a son to me.'

'You have put me in a spot. Ashim. I will never be able to reciprocate what you have done for me,' Satyen said with tears in his eyes.

'Reciprocate? How long have we known each other? And let us keep our fingers crossed. I hope everything works out smoothly.'

'What exactly happened today?'

'I'm not aware of too many details, but I was told that there was a protest demonstration organized by a few girls of the college. Samir appeared out of the blue, pounced on the principal and butchered him with a sword. As straightforward as that. That is the official version. Now do not look so put off. The facts are not that simple. Don't we know your son? It is poppycock. Bullshit. Suprio babu spent half an hour, enquiring through his parallel channels, although he did not divulge the details for obvious reasons. The mainstream press will carry the official version. So... god's in his heaven, and all's right with the world! Was it not Robert Browning who said that?'

'I wonder whether I will even recognize my son, Ashim.'

'I'm sure there is more to it. He will stay with me till he leaves the country. I have promised Suprio and there is a selfish reason too. With age, I have started experiencing the pangs of loneliness.

Two months of an interesting company for me. I'm keen to know more about their movement and engage in contentious ideological discussions. My apartment will also be safest for him, as long as he does not turn adventurous. Sadhan will monitor him through the day; he is my trusted Man Friday.'

The silence that pervaded the room was uncanny. Ashim could tear through it only after a while.

'Satu, I vaguely remember you telling me that your boss gifted you a bottle of scotch, from one of his trips outside the country. Don't tell me even you have started boozing these days.'

'You know me, Ashim. You know me,' he agreed. 'Sulekha,' he called for his wife, 'it's in the cupboard in our room.'

Although the news should have put them at ease, the impending uncertainty cast a deep shadow on the ageing couple.

LALBAZAR

September 1971

The tight slaps on the short journey to the police van were not that painful, but the humiliation before a bunch of onlookers, who had gathered on either side, was tougher to bear. Samir held his jaws tight, a tactic taught by others to avoid pain. The news spread like wildfire, as it does—a rule rather than an exception in Kolkata.

When he was pushed into the van's rear, he saw a spacious unit capable of accommodating close to twenty individuals. It was insulated from the driver's unit. He was reminded of his transfer to the hospital, even though that had been a qualitatively different experience.

He heaved a sigh of relief when the van started moving. He only had two emaciated constables as companions, who were not trained to hold their rifles gracefully. They were keen on chatting about the incident. Unable to extract much from him, they offered him a cigarette, which he gladly lit, more as a diversion. He realized that he was being audacious when he enquired where the van was heading.

The constable politely responded. 'To the local police station. Should take fifteen minutes, given the rush-hour traffic.'

Their constant chatter about the erratic ration supply lines in the city did not disturb his concentration, busy as he was conjuring a tale that he considered not just foolproof but brilliant. He had designed it to shield both Runa and Barua da. He felt a tinge of satisfaction through his arteries, and it charged his ego.

He reminded himself that he had stood fourteenth among half a million examinees. Such a line of thought was rather unusual for the self-effacing Samir.

The van screeched to a halt outside the police station. No official proceeded towards them nor did the constables attempt to open the broad doors at the rear. Through the grilled windows, he could hear a bunch of enlivened cops in animated discussion.

'The principal was patiently negotiating. I am told he had already accepted their demands when the scoundrel rushed in with a girl in tow and, out of the blue, stabbed him. Cold-blooded, unprovoked.'

'The fucker needs to be hung upside down.'

'After dripping his face in hot, boiling water.'

The constables moved away, rendering themselves inaudible. Samir realized that he could be saved a lot of pain if they decided to eliminate him like Adesh was. He was reminded of a horrific experience as a child at a religious festival in a village, where he had witnessed a sacrificial goat clinging on to its last breath. It had left a lasting impression on his mind and made him consider vegetarianism, although he continued to eat chicken and fish.

The door sprung open to reveal a tall, bespectacled officer with a bulging paunch, displaying a pair of handcuffs. Not bothering to acknowledge Samir, he directed the conversation at the constables. 'There are orders to transfer him to Lalbazar. Are the two of you capable of dealing with a dangerous criminal like him?'

Their faltering gestures prompted him to call for a guy who held a rifle that resembled a carbine. It dawned on Samir that he had been accused of homicide, an extraordinary crime in the eyes of the law.

The city resounded with tales of third-degree methods employed at the police headquarters in Lalbazar, where they extracted information from accused prisoners. Prisoners were water boarded and cigarettes were burnt and shoved inside the anus. Samir needed a diversion; his mind veered to the book at the core of the disaster, currently lying on Barua da's table. The enclosed library card bore his name. He sincerely hoped that the man would have hidden it for his safety, although it was irrelevant to Samir at the moment.

A wave of despondency enveloped his mind at the thought of not being able to appear for the ensuing exams.

The city descended into darkness—although Kolkata is never dark in the true sense of the word. The city's bright neon lights coloured even the bleakest of moments. He gazed at the headlights from passing vehicles, brightly lit houses on either side of the road, and traffic lights emitting a thousand lumens to animate the pulsating city that rarely sleeps. The darkened interiors of the van, in sharp contrast to radiant city lights, sparked memories of his childhood trips to Ashoknagar. If only he could reach out to Satyen.

He felt a rush of serendipity that his father would be the only person in the world who could rescue him from his predicament. Could he not take the help of his innumerable friends, refugees like him, some of them doing well in life? There was Ashim kaku too. All Samir pined for was a fair trial and protection from physical torture.

Satyen was capable of bigger things in life, but after spending his early years fighting for workers' rights, tending to refugees in distress and meeting family commitments, he had been left without the means to bolster his qualifications. Whatever he had achieved could be attributed to his sincere and single-minded devotion to the jobs assigned to him.

As the vehicle entered Central Avenue, one of the city's busiest thoroughfares, he could not fathom the reason for the darkness outside. Power cuts were unusual those days. His mind ultimately strayed to the strange occurrences of the last hour. He tried to tighten his chest muscles to hold back his tears, but it was ineffective, and he collapsed like bags of sand before a tsunami. His male ego was unwilling to reveal his soft side before three strangers, but when the tears came, it was like the first rainfall of the season. First as droplets, then trickles and finally, as torrents. Then the random thoughts in Brownian motion. While attempting to hold on to the grills on the side of the van, he realized that they had already handcuffed him.

He had grown up in Santiniketan barely a few months back, transitioning from companionship to love. A swarm of locusts pierced through his heart at the thought that his relationship would now collapse like a pack of cards. The stoic constables stared at one another, forbidden by protocol to offer solace, but disinclined to slap him into silence. They were men of flesh and blood too, and perhaps, they reserved a soft corner for him.

A gentle nudge on his shoulders indicated that the van had reached its destination.

The interiors at Lalbazar were adequately lit and brightly painted, different from normal police stations. Nonetheless, it was dirty to the core. Samir was led into a room where his meagre belongings—his watch, handkerchief, moneybag and clothes—were taken away. He was made to sign a list of inventories and ordered to change into a uniform and put on a badge bearing a number he was able to recall after many years. 1463.

The accommodation was meant for prisoners who stayed back for nights between interrogations. They were ultimately transferred to local police stations. They brought only top leaders and dangerous 'criminals' here.

He heaved a sigh of relief when he was informed that the interrogations would commence the following day.

The evening was devoted to reports: they recorded his version of the incident, captured it on a sound recorder, and simultaneously noted the details on hard copies. After this he was asked to affix his signature to their jottings. They refused his request to contact his folks—the facility was not made available to criminals.

'But how will my folks ever know that I am in custody?'

It was a futile attempt. 'You should have thought of this before murdering a man, bastard.'

Entreaties invoking his father's health condition evolved no sympathy. Only when the Inspector moved to the washroom, the constable standing near the wall behind, bent forward on a conspiratorial note.

'How much dough do you have in your purse?' the man asked.

He had withdrawn his Science Talent scholarship a few days back and he could boast of the princely sum of a hundred rupees.

'Offer him the amount, he will allow it to you. That's the unwritten code here.'

It worked. Although he was not allowed to speak to Satyen, but permitted to hang on to hear the conversation that lasted less than a minute.

'The prick was under the impression his son is incapable of murdering a human being. Fucking dumbass,' the Inspector laughed as he hung up.

Samir's well-thought-out defense was scornfully rejected.

'I cannot wait for the Deputy Commissioner to react to this. The guy will just bugger you till your ass hurts,' the Inspector said.

'It is the truth and nothing but the truth,' Samir commented in a feeble voice.

The other officer added. 'A fucking idiot, you claim to be a student of Presidency!'

Samir's narrative went like this: He was walking down the road to visit his aunt. Attracted by the commotion, he had walked into the college out of curiosity to witness a few young girls in torn sarees. Inside the principal's room, a bunch of wretched goons were molesting a hapless girl. Spotting a sword lying on the table, he had lifted it to threaten the goons, but they had managed to snatch it away from him, and in the melee that followed, it had accidentally penetrated the principal's stomach.

Needless to state, it was a sleepless night.

Satyen arrived sharp at nine o'clock and presented his credentials. The constable who guarded his solitary cell through the night conveyed the news that his father was here.

'Hurry, boy, you will be dragged in as soon as the Deputy Commissioner arrives.'

He was overjoyed. By then, he had completed the morning ablutions in an unclean bathroom and eaten a breakfast consisting of two loaves of half-toasted bread, a smattering of butter, a tiny banana and a cup of weak tea.

It was not that Samir had not expected to see a pair of sunken eyes; no father worth his salt would have been able to snatch a wink after such an incident. Nor was his unkempt appearance unprecedented, since Satyen would often skip his morning shave when he was unwell or relaxing on a holiday. What was unbearable was the transformation of a man whom Samir had last met twenty-four hours back.

'Don't stand there like a zombie, I have been allotted just fifteen minutes and need to convey something important. Sit down,' Satyen said.

'I am very sorry for whatever happened, Baba, but it was not my fault.'

'That's not what the newspapers say.'

'They are lying, Baba. Have they published my name?'

'No, they have not. What an opportunity lost to a potential Bhagat Singh!'

'Please listen to my side of the story.'

'There is no time for it, nor am I interested in it. That's not why I am here.' The ageing man lowered his voice to a whisper. 'Listen carefully with full concentration to what I have to say. Ashim is pulling a few strings at the highest level. You could be released tonight, but it is not a certainty. It will happen only if the information they desire is provided truthfully. You will not be tortured, but there are no guarantees if you choose to act tough. I'm certain you are aware of the extent they can go to. Do not try to defend your friends. This is your only opportunity to be spared the gallows. Is that clear?'

'You are not listening to me. My friends had no role in yesterday's incident.'

Satyen lost his patience. It was rare for him to raise his voice or utter words that hurt people's self-esteem. 'I'm not interested in listening to your side of the story, idiot. It is not relevant. What do you think of yourself? Super-smart? You have let your family down again and again, and yet you have the arrogance to talk back. Do just what I ask you to if you wish to be freed.'

The constable rushed in, attracted by the yelling. He was taken to task by Ashim later. 'Satu, you should not have lost your cool. He is in a distraught state. A lot more patience was required.'

◆

The Deputy Commissioner was an impressive person. Tall, slim with penetrating and sharp eyes. He bore a calm, innocuous and sympathetic exterior; he was suave, handsome, flamboyant, yet physically fit. His chamber was huge, well-decorated, with a teak table at the centre, a few revolving chairs, three or four huge cupboards, a few portraits of himself—one of them depicting him receiving an award—and a set of revolvers on a side table. The man ordered the armed guard to leave the room.

When he was politely requested to grab the chair, Samir had a strange feeling that the man was there to help him.

'Samir Chattopadhyay, I presume,' the man began.

'Yes.'

Yesterday's police report was lying before him.

'Tea or coffee?'

The reply was hesitant. 'Would like some coffee.'

'I will take ten minutes to go through your papers,' he said. He spoke in a soft and melodious voice. He gently buzzed the bell on his table. A constable rushed in, greeting his senior with a full-throated salute.

Samir's eyes got fixed on the name plate on the table. Dhruva Roy!

He felt a shock wave running through his spine. The saliva seems to be drying up like drops of water in a hot pan. He nearly fell off the chair. This was the man who had murdered Adesh. The embodiment of evil. A psycho, a devil. He would rather hang than talk to this man across the table.

'I understand the feelings that are flooding you. The intense hatred shows in your expression. I expected it. But you should also understand that it is a job that I do. Most of my relatives these days refuse to visit us socially. Not a soul appreciates that I am just a cog in a machine. If my throat is slit tomorrow—and I am aware that I figure in your hit-list—some other Dhruva Roy will take over, and he may turn out to be more ruthless. Do read up your hero's thoughts diligently. He has somewhere stated that it is not individuals but the system that is at fault,' the man said.

Samir understood that the guy was pulling a smart one. He was an expert in interrogation techniques, and his initial strategy was to shower Samir with kind words and torture him later. The sweet talk was meant to inspire confidence and disarm him at a vulnerable moment. If it failed to achieve the desired objective, there were third-degree methods he could use.

The man could transform himself into a ravenous wolf within minutes, but he was under strict instructions not to inflict physical torture. Although, after a cursory look at the boy's face, he was reasonably sure that third-degree methods were unnecessary. He, too, was sick and tired of pushing long sticks down the dirty anuses of the bastards!

'Give me a few minutes to peruse your statement. The coffee should arrive by then.'

Within five minutes, the man had managed to scan through the pages. He pulped it to shreds, furiously targeting the bundle of torn sheets spectacularly into a waste-paper basket.

'I'm told your father was here this morning. Did he disclose anything?' the man asked.

Samir suddenly felt the desperate urge to escape—no price was too high an amount to achieve this. He wished to pursue his studies, lead an everyday life, to go back to Runa and his parents.

But Satyen had instructed him to be honest and he would follow his instructions to the hilt.

The only option he had left before him was total surrender, but he was keen to protect Barua da and Runa. The former came from a humble background and lacked Satyen's contacts. He was not culpable, but he would be harassed, and they would suspect him of links to the Party if they came to know that Samir spent the afternoon in his room. Even without evidence of complicity in the murder, the usual Preventive Detention Acts were in place. Last evening's conversation between the cops flashed through his mind. They were planning to implicate Runa too, and she would, in all likelihood, be in their custody by now. Revealing the truth would facilitate her freedom since the law was sympathetic to violated women.

The revised confession took fifteen minutes. He told him

everything. From the time in the morning when he realized that his book was missing until the time that he committed the act. The only fabrication in the statement was that he had waited for Runa at the college canteen. This was fortunately not disputed by Dhruva because he had no reason to.

A few close friends had requested Runa to support them in their agitation, and she had reluctantly agreed.

'You are surely aware that students protesting yesterday belong to a particular persuasion,' Dhruva asked.

'I have never bothered to interrogate her on her ideological proclivities.'

'Really? Interesting.'

He soon realized that it was an attempt to catch a flying arrow. 'In today's world, the two of you, friends studying at Presidency College, rarely discuss politics?'

The Deputy Commissioner looked at him intently with piercing eyes. A trapped Samir moved his gaze away. 'I will return to this aspect during the second half of our interrogation. Your story otherwise sounds plausible. Do me a favour and jot it down on this sheet of paper. I would prefer it if you compose it in English, but Bengali is fine. Normally, my clerk jots down the contents while I verbally interrogate, but I have kept him away due to the confidential nature of today's discussions. As far as the murder goes, just state that you did not commit the murder. It happened before you entered the room—write that. Young man, do you realize that as far as the actual murder goes, it is your word against the ruffians? There was no other living individual in the room other than them, a dead man and your friend.'

Samir gaped. His eyes were wide open. He was unable to trust his ears.

'Are you surprised by my statement? Dhruva Roy is here to help you, young man.'

'Baba asked me to be honest,' Samir said.

A burst of raucous laughter followed. 'An obedient but radical son; does it not sound like an oxymoron?'

'I have already told you that I am not a radical.'

'Wait till I fix you in the afternoon. Till then, focus on the confession.'

Unable to control the currents of thoughts and counter-thoughts, Samir descended into a trance. He was interrupted by a stern bass voice and jolted by the sudden transformation of a convivial person to a diabolical personality. Dhurva's mocking, ugly pupils gaped at him like a dragon spewing fire. 'We have not called you here to cogitate. Do you wish to be hung on the noose? Or shot to pieces at the Victoria Memorial like a street dog? Have you forgotten the fate of your friend Adesh? I shot the bastard with my own hands, and I do not have all the time in the world for an insignificant person like you.' He lowered his voice. 'Did you understand? Will be back in an hour to commence the critical portion of our interrogation. Complete the confession but do not sign till I have a look.'

He had not used a single foul word. He was different from low-level officers Samir had encountered earlier. He was certainly a shrewd interrogator, well-versed in the art of playing hot and cold, with the right mix of brain and brawn to add to the cocktail. Samir felt drained of the mental strength required to lift his pen.

Dhruva's mission in life was to uproot the dissenters as if they were trees, cut the wood into a thousand pieces, burn them, dump the ashes in the ocean for the rough waves to scatter, and leave no trace for posterity. He had no qualms about employing unsavoury means, if that meant he could achieve his objective.

Samir was intrigued. He seemed caught in a thriller that was fast unravelling. How on earth had Dhruva learnt that Samir was a friend of Adesh's?

The man barged back in shortly, back to his original self like a chameleon, patting him gently on the back. 'Need to visit a police station. Another bitch has been apprehended. Just wanted to tell you to place the sheet inside my drawer after you complete the composition. They will call you for lunch, but do not leave this room until it is placed safely inside my drawer. I find you have not yet begun writing. Never mind, it will take some time to get over the spell. But do not forget to complete the confession before I return, because I will not have much time afterward.'

Samir took around forty-five minutes to complete the piece. He placed it in the drawer and went to eat syrupy gruel consisting of low-end pulses and vegetables mixed in thick-grained rice. It reminded him of how they had eaten for the years after migrating from East Bengal.

He found himself wobbling towards Dhruva's office, unable to gauge what further shocks lay in store for him. What was the objective of the second round of interrogation? Satyen had told him they were interested in some information. What could that be? Despite being tormented at the thought that the man may reveal his darker side again, he could faintly see a concomitant ray of light at the end of the tunnel. The conversation seemed to be heading in a favourable direction for him.

Dhruva was intently reading a whodunnit penned by a famous author, Saradindu Bandopadhyay, when he entered. Samir had read the book long back. It told the story of a man who aimed poisoned needles at his victim's heart, triggered by bicycle bells.

'Have you read this novel?' Dhruva asked.

'Yes, quite a few years back.'

'I too read it in school, but Saradindu novels need to be read multiple times to discover the underlying twists. Don't you agree?'

'I guess you are right.'

'Tell me something about your background. Your father, folks at home and so on.'

Samir told him.

'What?' Dhruva's expression conveyed incredulity. 'The only child of your parents! And a father who struggled to establish himself after migrating as a refugee? You should not have traversed the path you chose. Look at me, I am the only son of a widow who struggled against all odds to bring me up. I initially hesitated to join the police force, but did not have an alternative when offered a job. We needed it desperately because my father had passed away when I was twelve years old.'

'Yesterday's act was not premeditated, it was impulsive,' Samir said.

Dhruva smiled mischievously at him. 'You are an intelligent boy. You stood fourteenth in the state school-leaving exams. Do not pretend that you have not yet got the hang of the bigger picture.'

'Of what?'

'Of the fact that we know a lot more of you than you imagined before you met me.'

'You mean about Adesh? Yes, I heard you, but have not applied my mind to it.'

'You have, and I could read it in your eyes before walking out of this room. Samir, do not try to outsmart me. I may not boast of an enviable academic record, but I'm known to be an intelligent person. An expert on human psychology. I would have otherwise not occupied this chair.'

'I have no doubts about that.'

'Then do not compel me to lose my cool by coming up with ludicrous statements like this. Don't say that you are not aware of Runa's political convictions. I am not an ass sitting here. We need to conduct this discussion in a climate of transparency. It was committed by your father's friend, Ashim babu. Tied to a lot of stuff, including your future. Get this into your mind.'

Samir did not quite understand how to respond. The man had an enormous ego and had to be dealt with sensitively.

The man continued. 'Now, listen to me carefully. You appeared on our radar a year back when my men surreptitiously photographed you on the day of Adesh's cremation. Although some cops from my team believed you were a harmless school friend, the act of running after a bunch of jokers who sang the Internationale betrayed your proclivities. We enquired and got to know that you studied at Presidency and flirted with the radicals.'

Samir interrupted. 'Adesh was my childhood friend. We were also family friends. My parents were there at the funeral. He was not a criminal, but a decent person shot in a fake encounter.'

'But your parents did not run after the guys singing the Internationale. And why don't you unambiguously state that I shot him? I thought you guys have guts. Come on, it does not matter to me in the least.'

Samir preferred not to reply to this, satisfied that he had managed to communicate what he had intended.

'Shall I resume?' Dhruva said. 'You get beaten up by CRPF personnel. We operate independently of the police and CRPF. Our man was on the spot and followed you to the hospital and nursing home. The boy who accompanied you was the son of a leading barrister, and we were not overly concerned—one of those fashionable radicals who run away at the first sniff of danger. We watched the girl. Your current girlfriend, Runa Ganguly and you. I agree that the Party was smart enough to keep you away from activism for two to three months. But we were more intelligent. We made it appear like we have deleted your names from our files. You were right there on our radar.

'Why suddenly the two of you? Because you fit into the mould. A boy and a girl, hooked together in a clandestine affair. It is the usual honey-trap. It is old hat, Samir. We spotted you at the APDR rally; that was, for me, a personal moment of euphoria. Why do you think two guys approached you of all persons? There were many others. I did not, of course, expect a rookie to smell a rat. To cut a long story short, we traced you subsequently at several APDR processions, Curzon Park, Mohammed Ali Park, masquerading as teachers at a night school, and so on.'

Samir was amazed at their capabilities. The Party had underestimated them.

'Not for nothing do they call us the Scotland Yard of Asia.'

'Why did you follow two greenhorns like us?' Samir asked, denying nothing.

'Good question. We have better things to do. I would need to employ tens of thousands of informers to follow every single extremist. We have close to five or six thousand guys on our watch list. On occasions like the APDR rally, Curzon Park and so on, our men swarm the place. The informers are specialists in recalling faces up to a hundred each and keep them at the back of their minds. They carry photographs also for quick reference. Khochors, as you call them. One of them spotted you. We obtained information about the night school through our sources and our men recognized both of you. You should not have backed out; we had no plans to arrest you. We wanted your school to continue because we had information that there were sinister plans to form a militant cell, a plan you were unaware of. It was a false alarm and your leaders chickened out. The two of you were like hens laying golden eggs. We wanted you scot-free so that you could lead us to your leaders. My department opines that yesterday's incident is a setback, but I do not concur with them and am hopeful that the narrative will reach its conclusion today.'

Samir protested, 'But we were associated with frontal organizations. Legal and above board. Both Runa and me.'

'Let me teach you the Party's methods. Some compare them to the mafia. It is a one-way street, the only difference is that they do not harm you if you leave the Party, not unless you spill the beans. That much I can credit them for. After all, you are not a gang of bandits. You follow an ideology that conditions your mind and targets the underlying emotions. It sucks you in, you get addicted like a junkie is addicted to his daily shot of morphine, and you are made to believe that you are on a grand mission to liberate the oppressed. Don't you feel far more committed today than when you joined?'

'Perhaps. To the ideals. I am disillusioned with the Party to a great extent,' Samir said.

'That is because it is in a state of disarray.'

The man was genuinely incisive, Samir thought.

'Yesterday's incident has nothing to do with the Party. It was an impulsive act. I was unable to control myself when I witnessed what Runa was passing through. I had no intentions to hurt the principal. I thought he was one of the goons,' Samir finally said.

Dhruva smiled. 'I admire pure, unadulterated love. Even though have never fallen in love myself. Could not afford it. The first movie I saw in my life was *Devadas*. We are aware of your relationship... Bloody scoundrels.'

'Who are you referring to?' Samir asked.

'Pagla Keshto and his gang, who else? Will act against them, sooner rather than later.'

Samir knew it was bluster, but did not tell him. They dared not. Pagla Keshto's apron strings were tied to his political bosses.

'Not to digress, but we possessed information that the Principal would be confined and outsiders would be joining in. Our men waited in the hot sun, thoroughly disappointed at the non-appearance of any familiar face. Then we noticed you and Runa ambling down. Your presence was unexpected; they realized later you were an escort. You maintain you hung out at the canteen, I believe you. Rather, I have no option but to do so, because they did not follow you inside. I have pulled up my guys for not doing so. But that is not important. They could not believe their eyes when they saw you being dragged away. It was not compatible with the impression we had. I immediately instructed you to be brought here, much before Ashim babu pulled his strings. Perhaps we would have even released you without his intervention.'

While he was relieved that Barua da's name had not cropped up, he did not believe a word of the other portion of the statement.

'We do not have much time on our hands. The only name I now require is that of your conduit to the core of the Party. You were not acting on your own. We need the name of the person. In writing. Period. You will be released by early hours tomorrow, the unearthly hour only to ensure the news does not spill to the world outside. You have no fears of a fake encounter, your father and Ashim babu will escort you. And they will inform you about the plans. Just follow their instructions to the hilt. Do not even attempt anything funny, because you will be rearrested. This time, the consequences will be brutal. In any case, the Party is on its last legs in its present form, and you lose nothing.'

Samir stared. Satyen had once taught him the meaning of the adage: between the horns of a dilemma. He had faced multiple dilemmas before, but this one was qualitatively different. Atanu da's coy face blinked like a fluorescent light on its last legs. He was a boy universally loved and respected for his sincerity, honesty and commitment to the cause of liberating oppressed humanity. He was a selfless person with compassion. His father was a migrant like Satyen, and he had brought up three brothers against heavy odds. How could he possibly let him down?

Samir's determination oscillated—not like a pendulum but like particles in random motion. He required an external force to let them take a particular direction.

'I can provide you with half an hour to decide,' Dhruva said. 'Think about your parents. They are of advanced age. If you refuse, the *law* will take care of you.'

The emphasis on the word did not escape Samir.

There was no point in procrastinating. He thought of his father's grim face in the morning, the expectation of a reunion with Runa, a future career, a mother who must be going through suffering.

There was only one condition that he would impose.

'I have just one request. Runa is to be released. The poor girl had no role in the murder. She was just a victim.'

Roy laughed his head off. 'Are you crazy? Are we a bunch of duffers? Arresting her would stir a hornet's nest. She would testify in court and the media would pick it up. That was what the asses at the local police station were planning to do, but they were shot down within minutes by the Commissioner. Our men visited her house last night to communicate that we do not plan to arrest her, but that any mention of the incident to the outside world would not be conducive to her safety. Her dad promised to cooperate, claiming ignorance of where she was. My guys could make out he was lying. Not that it matters as long as she does not sing like a canary.'

It took him ten seconds to disclose Atanu da's name, an hour to jot down the man's dictation, blindly like a stenographer, and a few more minutes to sign at the bottom of every page. Dhruva insisted he read it again before signing.

It implicated Atanu as their conduit to the core Party and accused him of hurling explosives from the college terrace, including the day they had bashed up Samir. It also mentioned his plans to organize hosiery workers and slum-dwellers into an armed militant cell, and implicated him in a couple of other incidents Samir was unaware of.

Dhruva finally said, 'Thank you. Do not ever repent for what you did today. You have done it for your country. We have been targeting this man for a long time, and have been unable to do so in the absence of concrete evidence. Preventive arrests have been kept at a minimum due to global outcry, which in any case, was not advisable for someone like Atanu, a bright student of an elite college. And lastly, believe me, Runa will remain safe.'

He suddenly lifted the glass of water from the table, forced it between Samir's fingers, and boisterously raised a toast. 'To your love. I sincerely hope you unite once again. But after two years, not before.'

It was apparent that he was not mocking him. Every tyrant perhaps has a soft spot tucked away in a corner.

'Last, nobody will ever come to know that you signed on this piece of paper. Do not even nurse the thought that you will be harmed by your erstwhile comrades.'

Samir spoke honestly. 'I do not fear getting bumped off. Our Party does not indulge in killing erstwhile comrades, but you have played havoc with my self-esteem. And I did not do it for my country. I did it for my freedom. Atanu da and others fight for the people of this country, not that of some other country.'

Dhruva exploded with a ferocity greater than the one Samir had witnessed earlier during the day.

'Bullshit! You do it for that son-of-a-bitch, the man across the borders, the man who appears like a fucking, fat pig! Have you ever had a close look at his portrait?'

Samir suddenly did not care. 'Your statement reflects your racist temperament.'

'Fuck off! Do not throw half-baked jargon at me. They do not impress me. As for your self-esteem, guys of your ilk never had one.'

'I am at your mercy today. I am not in a position to retort.'

'Cut the crap,' Dhruva calmed down. 'I was recently diagnosed with high blood pressure. Which reminds me. Promised to call Ashim babu.'

The call with Ashim kaku was short and sweet, confirming plans for the night.

As they shook hands, despite the benign look on Dhruva's face, Samir felt like smothering him, the least he could do to avenge Adesh's brutal and lawless murder and for compelling him to throw Atanu da under the bus.

They reached Ashim's place at 4 a.m. Neither Satyen nor Ashim spoke a word during the journey. Ashim was at the wheel and informed him about the plans for Samir to stay incognito at his house for the next two months, minutes before Satyen was dropped off. He refused to delve into further details, promising to speak the next morning since it required time and mental calm. He had driven fast as there were no speed restrictions at that hour. The desolate morning was depressing. For a few minutes, Samir felt like running away and joining the radicals at some remote corner of the country, one of those liberated zones the Party kept talking about.

His mother had packed and left his belongings in the car with matronly affection, and it did not take long to change, brush his teeth and crash. Ashim dropped in with a packet of biscuits just in case he needed some sustenance.

TURNING A NEW LEAF

September–October 1971

Samir was woken by bright luminescence. He was freezing, burdened by nightmares, convinced that he was running a fever till he registered the humming noise of the air-conditioner. A year and a half ago, before his school-leaving examinations, he had spent a few nights in this room when his parents had gone off to Puri on a pilgrimage; Mongola too had to visit her village in an emergency.

Samir swiftly brushed his teeth in the attached bathroom, was reminded of the hellish bathroom the previous morning, and rushed towards the dining room where Ashim was perusing the morning news intently.

'Good morning, Samir. Slept soundly?'

'Oh yes, but I prefer the air-conditioner off. I'm not used to it.'

'That's a matter of personal choice.'

Tea and toast followed, served by Sadhan, Ashim's domestic help for thirty-three years. The very mention of food turned his stomach.

'I have sent my part-timer off for a week. Sadhan is reliable. Let us see how it shapes up. Hopefully, a clearer picture will emerge.'

'I still have no clue on what is going on.'

'I can describe it briefly now before I leave for the hospital in an hour.' He then patiently explained his commitment to Mr Ray, the quid pro quo of his release, and how important it was to maintain confidentiality.

In the end, he dropped the bombshell about Samir's education.

'I am in no mood to leave the country now, Ashim kaku.'

'You should understand that the discovery of your release will result in tremendous embarrassment for the government. Very few may be aware of your identity at the current moment, but there is a possibility you would be recognized by someone somewhere if you stick around.'

'I am unable to accept your decision.'

'Your other option is to go back and surrender at Lalbazar today. I leave it to you.'

'I would have won the case in court,' Samir argued.

'Samir, sometimes I wonder how you scored such high marks in your school-leaving. You have not even understood the gravity of the situation. You should have seen your parent's faces the night before. I was dead tired, nonetheless provided company till well past midnight. You need to be more considerate towards your ageing parents. Do whatever you wish to. But remember, that it will be a terrible loss of face for me personally, and a devastating experience for your parents if you refuse to abide by whatever I have committed to on your behalf. I must leave now. My patients are waiting. Just one point. Whenever the calling bell rings, lock yourself in your room. And a final request, give it a day, and let's discuss it in the evening. Till then, do not call anyone. It is a sincere request.'

After he left, Sadhan fetched Samir copies of the previous day's newspapers. The murder was a front-page news item, but it ended on the note that a person had been detained, whose identity was not yet established. Neither was the suspect named nor mentioned in the incidents leading to the murder. Samir had no illusions about how 'free' the media was in the world's largest democracy, but there was no way they would have known in this instance. Runa's face kept surfacing like a phantom. Twice, he picked up the receiver to call her father, desisting at the last minute. It may lead to unforeseen repercussions; the news may leak. Their phone could be bugged.

Suddenly, he was reminded that Runa's phones were not working two days ago. It offered him some consolation that they would not have repaired it so fast.

Opting for a quick nap, he dreamt of their night at Santiniketan, her soft hair tickling his cheeks and soft breasts dangling on his chest. Then followed a series of nightmares, as if a hyena was chasing him, he saw a ball of lightning, an avalanche, a tidal wave. He woke up to gulp a glass of water, pouring from the jug meticulously kept on the side table by Sadhan, desperate to ward off sleep and take control of himself.

Only two days back, he had been a typical youngster, enjoying a carefree life, studying for exams, a papa's boy, an individual committed to a cause, yet inclined to achieve a scientist's fame. He had no desire to analyse the events; he merely wished to drown himself in random thoughts without coherence. It was one of those rare occasions when staying awake was preferable to sleep.

Samir shelved the plan to call their residence for a few days. A rash act could harm both him and Runa and circumspection was needed.

It was worse at night when the Principal's face appeared in ghoulish forms in his dreams. True to his upbringing, Samir never considered living beings as bodies bounded by the physical contours of their appearances; as mere statistical entities, cogs in a machine. This man had a past, a present, aspirations for his own and his children's future, a desire to be surrounded by loved ones and remain preoccupied with the small pleasures of life. Every individual was helpless against fatal diseases or accidents, but homicide was an avoidable act. The individual had not even been a participant in the assault, he had just tried to drag the goons away. Samir was enjoying the comforts of his father's friend's plush home, awaiting a career satiated with infinite possibilities. At the same time, a grieving family was skipping their meals in another part of the city, perhaps close by. His kids were hopeful that their daddy would appear from nowhere, and his wife and parents yet to reconcile themselves to the harsh reality of his death.

Reconciliation comes from resilience. But grief is a human trait. Animals recover faster; humans take longer. He had witnessed stray dogs near his residence losing their offspring to speeding cars, returning to their daily struggles for food after a while.

But soon, Samir too started enjoying the company of his host and eagerly awaited his return from work. He was even graciously offered a bottle of beer twice a week before dinner. The after-dinner discussions were gratifying to his intellect. Ashim's breadth of knowledge and repertoire of literature provided Samir with an opportunity to study and analyse the philosophy he claimed he believed in without delving into its intricacies. Before leaving for work, he would assign him a book to read and discuss in the evening. He was not into harangues; he listened patiently to his interpretation, offering his comments at the end. A brief discussion would ensue.

He listened to Samir when he narrated the various events of his life over the past eight months, both the political aspect and the romantic. He interrogated the Party's philosophy; he was brutal in his criticism, yet appreciative of their dedication and valour, quipping in with his experiences as a student leader at Dhaka University. Satyen too had once been actively involved in politics and had even been in jail for a few days. Samir was unaware of this, although he always suspected his father was as opaque as he was.

Samir scanned the newspapers each day for more news on the day's incident, but there was a gradual blackout. It had arguably been directed from the top echelons. A small news item appeared after a few days, stating that the murder occurred before the detained person entered the room, and so, he had been released. The fingerprints on the sword corroborated their theory. The name was not mentioned.

Satyen dropped by surreptitiously at the house three or four times to obtain Samir's signatures on a few sheets of paper required for his transfer certificate, passport, visa and college admission, but he carefully avoided the topic. Samir went out of the house only once to the Deputy High Commissioner's office for a visa interview after Ashim obtained permission from Dhruva Roy. For those few hours, it was an enchanting experience to witness the hectic life of a city bursting at its seams.

Sulekha visited him independently. He could understand the low frequencies of their visits and the reason why they met him separately, but their curt behaviour was heart-numbing.

One morning, Satyen came over and triumphantly displayed the transfer certificate he had obtained from the college, although Samir could not gather himself to look at it for more than a few minutes.

'Did you meet Dipak da?' Samir asked him.

'Yes. He was puzzled at our decision. Incidentally, for public consumption, you are proceeding to the USA, not the UK. I hope Ashim has informed you about that. Those are the instructions from the top.'

'Did he convey any other information?'

The expression of despair on Samir's face was far too evident for Satyen not to understand what he hinted at, but he limited himself to a curt no.

His parents came together a few days later with his visa.

That was the day they disclosed that Utpal had turned up at their residence, puzzled by why Samir and Runa had not appeared for the annual examinations. They told Utpal that Samir had been sent off to the USA after a warning from the police, that Samir had left without meeting his friends to avoid the embarrassment.

'Our relatives are under the impression that you are attending the National Science Talent summer camp, and will be informed after you leave the country. Maybe a day or two earlier,' Satyen said.

Samir had just one thought: why did Runa not appear for the annual examinations?

His detailed memories of the forty days he had spent at Ashim kaku's home were patchy after so many years. Only bits and pieces appeared, like the day it dawned that, by nature, he could block his memories easier than many others. Runa's memories will hardly haunt him once he managed to stow them away. He hated it, but that was the stuff he was made of.

One evening, he decided to have a heart-to-heart chat with Ashim kaku since the days for his departure were numbered. Sadhan had called him in at 9 p.m. for dinner with the news that his employer planned to meet up with friends at the club.

Returning after midnight, he was surprised to see Samir perched on the sofa.

'Not feeling sleepy tonight?'

'No, I require half an hour of your time.'

'I'm sozzled and sleepy, Samir. Still, if you insist...'

Samir requested that Ashim visit Runa's house to find out where she was and what she was going through. He wanted her to be told about his whereabouts and the compulsions for proceeding abroad. Satyen, in his place, would have exploded, but this man was an epitome of patience and, in a chatty mood, powered by rounds of spirit, he narrated his stories of his own love and how he had to leave his sweetheart behind after the partition. His lover, a Muslim woman, was under no compulsion to migrate, yet she had been willing to join him in Kolkata. But Ashim had been aware of the hardship refugees were going through back in India, and had dismissed her proposal as unfeasible.

'It took me a few months to erase her from my memory, but there was no option. Samir, I do not see the two of you getting together soon. If she is incognito, why would her father disclose it to me? He does not even know me. And how could I possibly tell him about your whereabouts? It will be risky even if one person comes to know. Samir, you must efface her from your memory for two years at least. It is tough, but you do not have an option. For our sake. And the little that I have understood you, it will be easier for you than for many others.'

It took a few more days to accept it. Samir could feel Runa's presence leaving him inexorably, step by step. He wished to grab her, lift her in a gentle swing and flood her with kisses. But the distance kept widening every night.

An ugly thought surfaced a couple of times—Samir wondered whether they had eliminated her—and it sent shivers down his spine. But he admitted each time the fallacy of such a thought. No, she was safe. It would take her a while to overcome her trauma, but she would bounce back, sooner rather than later.

Soon, luminous images of himself making an earth-shaking discovery inside a well-equipped laboratory, with pots of money and palatial mansions where he would shift his parents replaced memories of Runa and the spectacle of red flags dotting the horizon.

He would meet Runa, if he could locate her after two years. And if she was willing to forgive him.

He managed to bury her deep in a vault. He did not erase the memory, but he stored it in his heart. The rare occasions that she managed to ferret her way through the heap were painful.

His kaku and mama joined his parents to bid him goodbye at the airport—exactly forty-five days after the incident. They were unaware, and for them, it was a departure for greener pastures. Kaku was nevertheless, slightly suspicious. Ashim could not bid him goodbye at the airport as he was stuck with a complicated surgery that took longer than he had anticipated.

He found himself seated next to a hefty Welsh gentleman on the Air India flight to London. Noticing tears in his eyes, the gentleman tried his best to console him. 'Sad to leave home, young man? Never mind, London will embrace you in its arms. It always does.'

THE AFTERMATH

18 May 2014

Samir was surprised that he was able to narrate these incidents before Neelu and the kids. He suddenly felt like he had reached adulthood at sixty.

Not a soul stirred in the room. It seemed like every person expected the other to interrupt the uncanny silence. Samir was not that concerned about Neelu or Kallol's reaction, it was Ruplu and Apu who mattered to him. Their relationships had stood the test of time for more than a quarter of a century, and he would hate to witness them crumble like a pack of cards.

His excitement at catching up with Runa had overshadowed the trepidation earlier, and his apprehensions had grown while narrating the story. The first person he managed to steal a glance at was Ruplu. She sat, leaning towards Apu like the tower of Pisa, her face immersed in her palms. Whether she was suppressing a smile or intense anger was not perceptible. Apu was fiddling on his device, like a seasoned sudoku player. Looking askance at Runa, he noticed her observing him intensely; she seemed like a leopard on the verge of jumping at its prey.

It was like one of those off-kilter novels, where the aftermath has greater suspense than the main plot.

Here, however, it became anticlimactic, making the whole episode sound like a shoddy novella penned by a rookie. His children had burst into fits of roaring laughter. He could only guess who started it because both were rolling over by the time he turned his eyes. Kallol sported a smiling face too, hesitant about whether laughter was the appropriate reaction, and Neelu's sad face conveyed confusion.

Runa chose the opportune moment to stare the other way.

Unable to trust their reactions, he stared at them in turns to ascertain whether what he thought he heard was real. He simultaneously pinched himself, a technique taught to him as a child by his mother.

He finally shot at Apu. 'What's funny?'

Apu spoke between giggles. 'Why did you hide this story for so many years? Your story did not live up to my expectations. I was expecting something sleazy, something erotic,' he managed to utter, still rolling over.

Neelu was acerbic. 'Apu, please mind your tongue. At times, you forget how to speak with elders.'

Ruplu's remark was, as usual, childish. 'You have gone up in my esteem, Baba. Just wait and watch. I will now compel you to join our rallies.'

A self-deprecating stance was appropriate under the circumstances. Samir was unsure whether sarcasm lurked underneath her comment.

He finally said, 'I killed a human being, dammit. A father, a husband, a son. A life was extinguished like a candle in a few moments.'

'It was an accident. You did not realize he was not one of them,' Ruplu said calmly.

Apu reverted to his analytical self. 'It's like a road accident. If a man suddenly jumps in front of your car, would you feel remorse if you ran him down? Perhaps sympathy, but no remorse.'

It was the right time to score a few brownie points. 'It has battered me all my life. That was the only reason I could not disclose it earlier.'

Runa butted in. 'As a witness to the entire incident, I vouch for every word of what Samir has uttered, as far as happenings inside the principal's room are concerned.'

'You came to the rescue of a girl in distress. The scums had no right to exist,' Ruplu said.

'Oh, come on. You carry it now to the other extreme,' Samir said modestly.

Runa interjected once again in her scholarly style. 'After the incident, I read up several books on the topic. In most countries, perpetrators of hot-blooded murders are let off with a few years of imprisonment, less if the victim was indulging in a lawless act. In this case, it was the worst possible crime, they were violating the modesties of a defenseless girl like a pack of hyenas.'

Neelu supported her. He pinched himself once again.

'But... I killed the wrong person, Runa. What do the boys have to say? Apu has already expressed his opinion but does he have anything to add?' Samir said.

'No, Baba.'

'Let us then hear an unbiased voice. Kallol?' Samir turned to him.

'How can I be unbiased? You rescued my mother. Come on, uncle. Give me a break. I have heard this story multiple times, and have always nursed a desire to meet you.'

'One of the reasons I was keen to drop in on this visit, Samir,' Runa added.

Apu interjected. 'Now please don't say no to what I have to ask for. You have to treat all of us to dinner at that Mexican joint.'

Ruplu detested Mexican food and made no bones of it. 'No, the veggie place, they serve prawns made of veggies. Au Lac. But we got to be quick. We leave by six tomorrow.'

Samir protested, 'You guys are rude. Runa and Kallol are our honoured guests. I leave it to them to decide.'

Runa responded, 'Samir, you have forgotten. I don't care about food. In my mother tongue, they would call me a sarbabhukh. But a veg dish masquerading as a non-vegetarian one sounds exotic.'

'Kallol?'

'Given a choice, I would vote for the vegetarian joint, Au Lac. Have been freaking out on Mexican food with my Mallu roommates for the last month. Was not aware such a joint existed.'

'Done. Apu, you are the odd man out.'

'Would have normally battled it out. But not today.'

'Baba, I have a question for you. Did you ever desire to establish contact with Runa auntie?' Ruplu asked.

Samir had anticipated such a question and from her. She was immature and insensitive, as always. As he fumbled for words, Neelu jumped to his rescue.

'Ruplu, you must appreciate the intimate nature of the sentiment and leave it for the two of them to share their views, if they ever wish to.'

Samir said, 'Guys, we need to hear Runa out on what she has been doing all these forty-three years.'

Runa blushed. 'A small request. My life has been unexceptionable in comparison. I prefer to send an email later. It will be less anecdotal and more redolent of fine sentiments. I feel constrained to narrate it right now, not because it is confidential. You are free to share the mail with them.'

Samir nodded before interjecting. 'I have a small query before we move on. I was fairly confident that not a soul was aware of the incident. I met many of my contemporaries in Kolkata. Started taking Neelu along after I was certain that they were unaware of the true story. If it had been leaked, at least one of my friends would have asked me about it in confidence. They were under the impression that I was pushed out of the city because the police were troubling my parents. Runa's whereabouts were shrouded in mystery because her father was less forthcoming. A few believed she had been killed and that her father was constrained to come out in the open because the other daughter was under threat. This was what Utpal told me. Yet, someone mentioned the incident to Neelu's friend. Did you check on the name of her contact?'

'No, that was not disclosed. As I mentioned to you earlier, she was leaving town the next day. She called me before leaving, and I have not met her since.'

Runa said, 'Dhruva Roy made full use of your lack of knowledge on legalities, Samir. When you charge an individual based on disclosure, his lawyer has the right to summon the informant as a witness. However, I am unaware of what happens if the witness lives abroad. They had no video conferences those days. Atanu da declined to pursue your interrogation when he came to know the name. He was certain that the litigation would stutter on for years, and dragging you to the witness box would demoralize other comrades. We met after many years, and till then, he had not spoken about it to a soul. I was informed only after I prodded him many times.

'I smelt a rat when Atanu da mentioned the date of his arrest,' she continued. 'It was the night after the incident. He was away from Kolkata and tried his best to contact me after reading about the incident in the newspapers. Our phone was not working, so he rushed back to town and was arrested when he set foot inside his home. After many years, I mentioned the incident only to him and my husband. I am confident they have not spoken about it to anyone. Even Utpal does not know. But when did your friend tell you this, Neelanjana?'

Neelu did not take long to respond. 'In 1984, two years after our wedding.'

Runa shrugged. 'Then it can neither be Atanu da nor my husband. They learnt of the incident only during the mid-nineties.'

Samir sputtered, 'But he may have guessed it.'

Runa countered him. 'No. He was under the impression that the lumpens did it, and the two of us were implicated because I happened to be there, and you as the other member of the cell—which he believed they found out—was forced to sign on the dotted line in exchange for agreeing to allow you to go abroad, and me outside Kolkata.'

'Then it must be one of the other police officers, the ones who conducted my interrogation on the first evening, or the plain-clothes guys who spotted us entering the college. Dhruva and Suprio, for obvious reasons, would not have talked about it.'

'I doubt it Samir. Cops are normally discreet. But you never know.'

The thought of Atanu da being aware that Samir had thrown him under the bus was devastating. That was why he had avoided Samir at the mall so many years later.

Stealing a glance at her watch, Neelu expressed concern that Apu had a flight to catch the following day.

'Not before we drink some coffee,' Apu said.

'I will prepare it. Give your poor Ma some respite,' Samir offered. 'She's been slogging since the morning. Which reminds me, we need to uncork the bubbly.'

Ruplu volunteered.

Runa commented in a soft, slightly sarcastic tone. 'A historic occasion for your family.'

Samir replied. 'Now that you tell me, it could be one of the reasons. There is another one.'

Apu interrupted him. 'You cannot even imagine the reason, Runa auntie. Nonetheless, do try.'

'A promotion at work?' Runa said, playing along with the banter.

'Wrong. What about you, Kallol?'

'....an award?'

'Wrong. The victory of that despicable bigot in India.'

Kallol was bitter. 'Oh shit! Do not tell me. Baba calls him the Genghis Khan of India.'

Runa looked at Samir with piercing eyes. The expression conveyed scorn and anger. She was not angry with the man resting on his victory laurels in India, but at him, the turncoat who was once close to her.

He remembered her statement. *'You have transformed over time; we have not.'*

Samir chose to be combative. 'Why do I always have to toe the line, Runa, even after so many years?'

'You need not, Samir. Just respect this request of mine. Uncork the bubbly at home after dropping us,' Runa's comment was toned politely.

Samir tried to defend his decision. 'Apu and Ruplu may not be awake, they are travelling early morning tomorrow.'

'Never mind, they don't care. Drink it all by yourself.'

This one from Runa was below the belt.

Apu was more discreet. 'Or keep it for my next visit, I will concoct a gob-smacking mimosa for you.'

Samir reluctantly agreed for the sake of the evening.

Runa recalled the birthday gift, and dug deep into her spacious purse, gingerly unwrapping the paper to reveal a smiling portrait framed in a gilt-edged jet-black frame. Samir instantly remembered the occasion. The photograph had been clicked at Santiniketan by Arghya da. Even in the black-and-white era, he had been a brilliant photographer managing to capture Samir's sharp features, bushy Beatle-like mane, his cheerful smile and a pair of innocent eyes to their last details. Even the tiny mole below the left eye that he operated on later was in the frame. He dared not remind Runa that it had been taken just after they were hung to dry for their indecent behaviour.

Those were the days of Kodak films, and one had to complete

the entire roll before developing the snaps. Arghya da had sent the negatives through his driver to Runa's place during an official visit to Kolkata, three days before fate intervened. She had promised to print two sets of copies, but life turned topsy-turvy.

The others were effusive at the sight of this unexpected gift. The frame was classy, the embedded photograph was solidly welded into the frame and each component appeared coterminous.

Neelu was the one who thanked her. 'I promise you, Runa, it will find a pride of place on our mantelpiece. I cannot recall a similar portrait of the young revolutionary.'

The gift reminded Samir of an object preserved for forty-two years, safely embedded inside his locker. There was a copy of the key in his office; the other one was stashed in his carry bag. Neelu had once requested him for some space in the locker for a short period. They were proceeding to Kolkata after three days, there were a few weddings to attend and she wished to withdraw her jewellery from the bank locker and keep it there a few days before flying off to India.

He had flatly refused. 'I have my official documents and certificates inside. Cannot afford to lose even one.'

'But why will I misplace them? Don't you trust me?'

'Sorry, Neelu, not this one request. There is no space inside the locker. Please do not make this request. Our flight is at night, and you can pick them up in the morning.'

Neelu had worn a saturnine expression for a couple of days but she could do very little.

Samir suddenly got up, saying, 'I need five more minutes. I have something for Runa.'

'Oh! Come on, not a take-home gift, Samir. I have crossed that stage in life,' Runa joked.

'It is not a take-home gift, Runa.'

Samir was known for such anticlimactic detours, but all eyes turned when he entered again with a red jewellery box. Ruplu sported a perplexed expression; she was apprehensive that her mother may not quite appreciate the idea of presenting an old flame with a necklace or a pair of earrings.

'This is what I have preserved carefully for decades. I was confident that someday I would be able to hand it over—either to you or your parents or a close relative of yours.'

It held the necklace they had almost lost in Santiniketan. It took a while to sink in.

Runa gasped. 'But where did you find it? How, Samir?'

'It was lying on the floor of the principal's room. One of the goons must have snatched it from your neck and dropped it while rushing out. I picked it up before the cops entered. It escaped the attention of the cops at Lalbazar. I have never let it out of my sight. I purchased a locker at the first opportunity. A heavy load is now off my shoulders, and Neelu can freely share the locker with me.'

Runa was unable to restrain herself. Kallol consoled her as she cried, but Samir withheld the gentle touch of solace. The day was so complicated.

At the restaurant, Samir ordered a bottle of expensive wine and asked everyone to drink at least a glass each, although Runa drank it in teaspoons. The food was delicious, and all carefully avoided the burning topic of the day. The conversation instead veered towards a comparison of life in the States with the less prosperous country, Ireland. Samir flaunted his knowledge of their country of domicile, based on a recent reading of Tana French's page-turners. He soon learnt that Runa, Apu and Kallol too had read quite a few of them, and the discussion enlivened.

After clearing the check, he proposed that Ruplu and Apu proceed home in Neelu's car while they drop Kallol and Runa in his car, but Neelu opted to join the siblings on the pretext that they were to leave early in the morning.

THE CONVERSATION

18 May 2014

Once in the car with Runa, it took him a few minutes to locate a romantic Tagore number, not the devotional ones he was habituated to. Samir was sure those songs would drive her bananas.

She chose to limit the discussions in the car to the hectic plans she had for the next day. She had to mail the study material to her school since she would be landing a day late. She would also have to make a visit to a friend she could not find time for earlier and purchase stuff ordered by her husband and friends back in Dublin, procure another piece of luggage since the suitcase was not spacious enough.

Kallol's boss had let him report in the morning and leave by three, after which they planned to visit the shopping centre nearby.

Mulling the idea of accompanying them, he remembered his own hectic plans at office.

Kallol was quiet until the car took its final turn into the complex. He sought Samir's assistance in exploring opportunities in the States, disgusted with the shoddy treatment meted out to non-Irish employees in Dublin.

'Strange. I thought they were only against Protestants. It is the same story here but could be a shade better since your domain is hot at the moment.' Samir was his usual cynical self, nonetheless requested Kallol to drop in for lunch on Sunday. Kallol got off at the entrance.

After Kallol alighted, Runa said, 'Drive the car around the corner to the parking lot.'

Samir was wary. He was in no mood to speak to her one-on-one and needed time to get used to her freshly-minted avatar as a friend.

'Why?'

'For a simple reason, duffer. They do not allow parking here for more than a couple of minutes. My, my, Samir, I am not intending to pounce on you like a sex-starved woman.'

Perplexed at the unexpectedness of the comment, he blurted out. 'Nor did I harbour such a thought. You remain as presumptuous as before.'

Her gentle smile and matronly pat on his bald head were perhaps intended to smoothen ruffled feathers.

'Are you okay?' she asked.

Although he smiled back, he was unsure what she was trying to drive at. 'As fit as a fiddle, Runa. Any doubts?'

'Not anticipating trouble back home?'

'Frankly, I do not know. I'm yet to understand Neelu after thirty-two years of marriage. Will face the consequences. I was more concerned about how Ruplu and Apu would take it.'

'Oh, yes, you can have my word for it. They have taken it in the right spirit. I understand human beings better than you do.'

'That you do,' he said, following it with a yawn.

Her fingers gently slid below his belt.

He flinched. She said, 'I was just checking if it is well-behaved these days. Have narrated the episode of our first encounter with countless friends. The sexual fantasies of a severely injured person en route to a hospital. Don't worry, I have never mentioned your name, not even to my husband, but folks found it hilarious.'

'You and your friends have no better topic to discuss?' Samir blanched. 'So what, I was young and horny those days.'

Runa switched the topic. 'You seem to be sleepy. I have a couple of queries.'

'Shoot. I am always at the receiving end with you.'

'We lived through a tumultuous era in Bengal's history, at a time when the last embers were dissipating to gentle ash. We endeavoured to rekindle the flames by pouring cans of fuel, and were forced to end our journey barely after it began. But we would not have made much difference in any case. There are numerous attempts to record episodes of those years but in my opinion, most lack depth. I visited the Kolkata Book Fair a few years back and procured quite a few publications. There were recorded experiences, some focusing on the personal, some on the political, but what I missed were scholarly analytical treatises. Where do we go from here? Wallow in right-wing politics, remain aloof like Sankar and Atanu da, or bleat on social media like many others? We have experienced the zeitgeist, the subsequent earth-shattering changes and the opening up of different perspectives. I need to express myself. Santanu, despite his academic brilliance, is not a thought-leader by temperament. As an activist, he fought fearlessly at the barricades, and is disillusioned today like many others, yet not bereft of the occasional spark. Utpal has beautiful anecdotes to narrate, and you are a capable author. A potent and invincible combination. Incidentally, have you retained your old habit?' Runa was on a roll.

Samir quipped. 'Yes, on topics like project management, artificial intelligence and big data.'

'Don't joke, Samir. Let me be candid. There were just two reasons I wished to meet you. Kallol was keen to be introduced and I wished to bounce this proposal off you. Are you game?'

'I am touched that you remember my written contributions under a fictitious identity for a journal whose name I now forget. Only you and Atuna da were aware of the author's identity. I recall the maturing of convictions within a few months—despite gradual disillusionment with the Party—but more pertinent was how I honed my skills in Bengali.'

'The journal was named *Aagun*. Your skill lay not so much in your style, but in the passion, conviction and clarity of thought. You displayed inner radiance. You were a source of illumination. I'm not undermining the literary quality, but the well-researched content shone like a bright ray of light. You also composed a couple of them in English for the journal called *Threshold*. Are you aware that Atanu da still nurses a soft corner for you and believes that you had no option but to sign the confession under duress and leave the shores of India? He bears no grudge or ill-will.'

'He was smarter than me. He was my icon, but the manner in which he once avoided me at a mall hurt me! Do tell him this when you meet him next.'

'We do meet. But I do not have the heart to speak to him on this topic. He is a human being who lost six years of his life behind bars. Perhaps they would have still got him, but you were the catalyst. I am slightly more sensitive to the situation than you are.'

'What does he do for a living now?'

'He works for a private organization. Completed his graduation and went for an MBA.'

Samir decided to be candid. 'I would be less than honest if I say that your offer does not appeal to me, but I would also like to clarify that I am no longer your fellow traveller nor intend to become one in a hurry. It is just the temptation to start meaningful writing once again.'

'I'm aware of your worldview, but that I am still requesting you to write only shows that I hold your writing style in high esteem.' The clarity in Runa's voice was unmistakable.

'The decision will not be a hasty one. Not like the one I made at the restaurant forty years back, Runa.'

'Nor will I order you to throw your sacred thread out of the window.'

They laughed till their jaws ached.

'You retain your photographic memory,' Samir said. Inching towards her, he placed his thick fingers on the nape of her neck. Despite attempts to set herself free, his grip was steadfast.

'Samir,' she pleaded. 'Let us not even attempt to traverse down that path. Let us move in a different direction. We have left behind a chapter in our lives. Inexorable changes have taken place and I live a happy family life. Your children, at least, adore you, even if we leave Neelanjana out for a moment.'

'I'm not so sure,' Samir admitted.

'Take it from me then. Incidentally, can you seriously consider removing your fingers from my neck? It hurts.'

'And what you did a while back was appropriate?'

'I would have taken this in my stride if you had been gentler. This is torture. Sadism. Power play.'

He let go of her neck only to pat her back gently. 'Your fondness for jargon has not waned in so many years.'

She said nothing for a while, then spoke softly. 'What I now plan to ask you is not intended for my emotional gratification. Your response will not make the slightest difference to my life. It stems from an academic curiosity and I expect a truthful reply. So... How long did it take you to get over my memories?'

Samir was taken aback, but he answered honestly. 'Since you insisted on an honest answer, it took me less than two months. But there is a caveat. The memories lay buried deep inside me, and threatened to take over at the slightest trigger. I'm a detached individual, not one who can easily relate to others. That is the reason I failed to develop feelings for Neelu after so many years. She wished to pervade every sinew of my being, for which I was not game. We were on the verge of a divorce, I'll have you know, but she returned to give our marriage a second lease of life. There were two kids to nurture, plus the lure of living in the States was tough to throw out of the window, I assume. I appreciated her compulsions later, but the decision to return from India is inexplicable, even after she came to know of the gruesome incident and your existence. Possibly she did not wish to abort Apu.'

Runa smiled. 'It is not tough for me to understand as I too am a woman. We are made that way; we rarely accept defeat when another woman is involved. Before she left the States, it was only you. She returned to fight both of us. Now she will accept me because she has seen me as a happily-married woman.'

'What you say makes a lot of sense,' he said.

The snort was typical of Runa. 'Were you not incapable of true love?'

'It took some time, but it blossomed at Santiniketan. It took less than eight months. This one lasted for twenty-seven years,' Samir said.

'It also took less than two months to erase me from your memory.'

'I consciously tucked it away, Runa, deep inside my heart. Try to understand that there is a world of difference between them. You were there, right there.'

'Samir, you say you have not understood Neelu. In my opinion, you have not even understood yourself. You are a confused soul.'

Samir tried to make amends. He proceeded to narrate how he had pined for her during his honeymoon to Santiniketan. He had made repeated visits to the places they frequented, and he even told her about his feelings when Utpal had conveyed the rumour of her demise. He told her that he thought of her as he lay inside the garbage can in Memphis and found courage in the memory.

'It was an association,' Runa explained. 'You stayed in the

same room at Santiniketan, you visited the kurta shop with me and you met me at the adjacent restaurant. Even after hearing from Utpal, you never felt the need to visit our house, and it was just half an hour away. Samir, let us change the topic. I am upset, but I have no desire to play the role of a jilted lover, not at this stage of my life.'

'I did reach the gate of your residence. What about the necklace? I kept it for so many years.'

'It is the only thing that has touched me, Samir. It did spark a desire to redefine our broken relationship. We can be friends. I have already expressed myself through my tears.'

'There are numerous other instances I will narrate some other day... I think it's time to split. I do not wish for Neelu to get the wrong idea.'

Runa added, 'Nor do I wish Kallol to think anything of it, though he is a liberal person by nature. This should be the golden rule for the future: we meet only in the presence of our spouses.'

'Done. I have just one last request.'

'Okay, but only because you saved the necklace.'

The kiss was superficial, lasted long enough and it was passionate, yet the bubbles of romance burst as bubbles invariably do. Their tongues penetrated deep, but the sensation was of a gentle touch. The mind floated only on the surface. 'This is the last time we touch each other, Samir. Goodbye, a mail will reach you tomorrow,' Runa said when they broke away.

Samir was not keen to drop her there. 'It is dark outside.'

'But the traffic is unidirectional.'

'Never mind, I will go round the circle.'

'Let us hope this drop does not turn out to be as eventful as the previous one.'

Her remark tickled him, but it had not been made in jest. Before bidding her good night, he did not forget to save her contact number, bridging the gap between two individuals lost in time and space.

Samir was in a mad rush to reach home, desperate to compensate for a fraction of the time he had spent in the parking lot with Runa. His apprehensions were unfounded, Neelu looked fresh and top-of-the-world and Apu was wide awake, waiting to wish him goodbye.

'You leave at six? When do you plan to visit us again?' Samir asked.

'Not later than a month, Baba,' Apu said, enveloping him in a tight hug.

The mood had detectably changed. Although Ruplu planned to return in three days, she was unable to hold herself back from giving her father a tight hug.

He skipped his bath. It was not that he was dying to go to bed, but he was desperate to catch Neelu before she slept. When he came in, he found her applying cream on her face.

'Tell me, how do you feel tonight? Honestly,' he asked her.

Her response was instantaneous. 'It is too early in the day. I need some time to absorb this. But there is no immediate thought of leaving you, and I am being as truthful as truth can be.'

He felt confident when he heard her.

'I have a long day tomorrow,' he said. 'Still, wake me before they leave.'

'If I manage to.'

She gave him a soft squeeze of the fingers, a tickle on the neck followed by a gentle kiss. Desire flowed like an aquifer. After twenty-odd years, as far as Samir could recall.

Both of them began to snore loudly in a while, but not before he had texted Runa his email address. They woke to find that the kids had already left, but he looked forward to the new day.

TYING LOOSE ENDS

19 May 2014

The first item on Samir's to-do list was to catch Mike. The best time to do so was during the first half an hour of work, when Mike was usually found playing games on his laptop, which he termed a 'tonic for the mind'. The door to Mike's office was perpetually open, but Samir habitually pinged Mike's assistant for an appointment before he met him. Unable to locate the assistant this morning, he barged in to meet a baffled Mike.

'Morning, Sam. Had a nice weekend?' Mike asked, slightly surprised.

'Yes, thank you, Mike. I have mailed you a document. Can we discuss this now?'

'I thought I sent you an invite for Thursday.'

'There may not be sufficient time if you ask for it to be reworked.'

'Cool. Fix an appointment with Alice. She should be coming in an hour late.'

Jenny was surprised by Samir's erect, confident and magisterial posture. 'Senior is in a confident mood this morning,' she noted.

'Yes, Jenny. Did you have a merry weekend with your grandchildren?' he politely enquired.

'Fabulous, Sam.'

Basking in his newfound confidence, he immersed himself into the rigmarole of a Monday morning. Things were complicated as a competent team member had just resigned. Mike called him in at 2 p.m., making it a point to peruse through the document before they met. His boss was effusive, and the alterations he suggested were cosmetic.

'I will push for this at the next meeting. Colin can keep bullshitting for all I care about. Do demonstrate the prototype to me on Thursday before showing it to the board on Friday. But tell me why you did not present this last Friday?' Mike asked.

'Well...I also expected a minimum trust in me.'

'Trust, like respect, has to be earned, Sam. You were procrastinating, you did not appear confident.'

'Perhaps, but that was the outcome, not the cause. I need to earn trust and respect a lot more than others.'

'Why do you say so?'

'Don't worry, Mike. Let us keep it at that and meet on Thursday for the prototype. Will retain your invite.'

Mike gazed at Samir. He wondered what could have happened during the weekend to make him speak so freely.

Finally, at 4 p.m., Samir found the time to check his personal email. Runa had sent him an email; its timestamp indicated that she had mailed it more than twelve hours back. He decided to read it after reaching home.

Neelu retained the chirpiness and warmth of the previous night and proceeded for her daily evening walk after serving tea and cookies. In certain respects, she was a quintessential Indian, enquiring whether the children had reached safely, conveying the news to him.

He switched on his laptop after a long and refreshing bath.

```
Dear Samir,

You must be wondering about the crazy
timestamp. This was the best I could do
given my demanding schedule today. I will
```

catch up on lost sleep in the air.

There was a book of letters lying on Kallol's table. I am absolutely not enamoured with Napoleon, but his love letters to Josephine were a pleasant read. I have no desire to hurl bombastic sentences like him. "I hope before long to crush you in my arms and cover you with a million kisses burning as though beneath the equator." I am not used to artifice. Napoleon was just forty-five. A lot of water was gone under the bridge since the days when I was captivated by you. As they say, love has no reason. Possibly, I still think of the sight of a battered young boy of sixteen, a pair of gimlet eyes and his innocence.

To revert to the fateful day in our lives, as a man it will be tough for you to perceive a violated lady's humiliation. To say I felt miserable would be putting it mildly. I even contemplated suicide or at least not return home because I was ashamed to face my folks. It is just because they insisted on dropping me that I reached home that evening. While being escorted out by a few kind-hearted ladies that day, it reached my ears that the nasty scumbags had 'raped us'. I was not in a mood to refute the rumour since the feeling of disgrace was as horrible as it would have been had there been forcible penetration. But still, I felt a selfish feeling of fulfillment at your daring act.

A senior professor, a woman, took me to the ante-room, just behind the principal's room. She offered to put me up in a cab and escort me home, but I refused. I thought I was in a more desirable and surmountable situation than you, and was dying to provide you some assistance by speaking to the press and later testify in court. There was no policeman in sight. Their absence remained a mystery for many years because I overheard their conversation that they were planning to arrest me.

It was clarified yesterday after hearing what Dhruva Roy had to tell you.

I never realized when they changed my tattered clothes. Humiliation and agony dripped from every fibre of my body as I returned home wearing a funny-looking blouse and a new saree. It did not take long for Ma to comprehend what the matter was. My heart and pulse rates had accelerated. It was tough to breathe normally. It felt as if my body and mind had been ripped apart, seemingly independent of each other; my breasts throbbed in pain. I sunk my face into her arms and wept, for how long I don't know, for I had lost track of time. Perched in a corner, Baba soon learnt of it and was left speechless for a few days. Years after the incident, I still puke at the slightest irritation. It could be triggered by the smell of an innocuous cucumber, an eggplant, or a fried egg; whatever reminds me of their sweaty, alcohol-drenched breath. It took me several years to return to consuming meat, although my parents and sister compelled me to eat fish and eggs much earlier.

My sister and her husband came home after an hour. After speaking with Baba, they decided to shift me to my brother-in-law's vacant ancestral home. My sister stayed with me. Baba, a civil servant, was confident that the cops would drop in to interrogate me, which he wished to avoid. I did not inform them that I had overheard a conversation that they planned to arrest me because that would only have added to their tension.

A couple of plain-clothed gentlemen trooped in minutes after we left. I was puzzled about how they traced me since I had been introduced to others in the congregation by my assumed name. It was a scary thought that they kept a tab on us for so many months!

Primarily, I was determined to defend you in court, the only person other than the goons to witness the happenings. I did not disclose my intention to my folks for apparent reasons, nor did I attempt to contact others in the Party. I would intervene at the right moment, I decided.

They arrested Atanu da the next day. But my state, roosting at a location, was agonizing. Despite our family doctor giving me a heavy dose of tranquillizers, the day's incidents kept reappearing. I kept scanning newspapers, including left-leaning publications, for weeks with no luck. Until I noticed the item stating they released the detainee because he had entered the room after the murder. I requested my brother-in-law to drop in at your place. Meshomoshoy reiterated whatever he mentioned to Utpal. Knowing your parents, I am sure they would not have mentioned this to you. The sheer joy of hearing that you were safe and outside jail overshadowed the hurt. It was not that incidents of departure for safer destinations were unheard of those days—Tapan Bose's name was still fresh in our minds. I was hopeful that you would contact me at an appropriate point in time, reappearing from ashes like a phoenix.

It was easy to obtain admission at Hindu College, Delhi, with the marks I had obtained in my school-leaving examinations. Baba flew me down there. Hostel accommodations were not available, and a relative offered to host me, but I moved in as a paying guest nearby, loving the anonymity of the new city.

Many boys entered my life, but they were like inert elements. I could not bond with them beyond a point. Some lost interest after a couple of months, while others persisted despite well-defined boundaries.

I did nurse a faint hope in the background that you would return, yet I gradually sensed that my emotions too were fading. I was desperate to hold on to them. I even planned to drop a note to my cousins settled in the US to try and locate you, a ludicrous proposition in the analog age. Not that it would have helped because you were in the UK.

Then, I consciously allowed emotions to fade on their own after a year as I was muddling through life. I fell in love with my books and the terrace adjoining my rented-out attic. I grew obsessed with the starlit sky and the ephemeral moon, and I spent the first few hours of the night soaking in its stillness and mysteries. I would be interrupted by the sounds of croaking frogs, chirping crickets and the occasional whizz of passing vehicles. The locality was situated far from the hustle and bustle of the capital city. It was cold, foggy and depressingly listless during the winter months. The temperatures often touched zero, and a severe bout of pneumonia once hit me. The landlady was affectionate and nursed me like a mother, treating me to hot soup, serving me medicines at the correct hour and gently rubbing my forehead till I fell asleep. She urged me to contact my folks, but I fibbed that my father was a heart patient, and it was better not to inform him. After I recovered, she started conducting surprise checks and arranged for a room heater and a spare quilt to be delivered to me. It was an emotional experience. It compelled me to forego the habit of lurking outside during the winter months, but I held on to it during the other seasons, barring a few rain-drenched nights. After a few hours outside, I would absorb myself in eclectic written material from around the world before my thoughts slowed down and I fell asleep. Some nights, I could only sleep after weeping on my pillows. It continued for five long years.

During vacations, my parents dropped in when I shifted to our relative's place.

I will not dwell too much on my first encounter with Santanu, my husband. It happened shortly after he was released from jail, when he was on a trip to Delhi to appear for the All India Institute of Medical Sciences entrance examination.

I was visiting a friend. There were elementary books on high school chemistry and biology scattered all over the cot. We had completed our post-graduations. The friend was my classmate, and both of us decided to continue living in our abodes until we obtained suitable employment. I almost finalized my appointment as a teacher at a convent school and was waiting for the appointment letter to arrive in a day or two.

Since my friend was not at home, Santanu requested me to wait. It was a casual visit, but there was an irresistible urge to stay back. Noticing my baffled look when he stated that he was appearing for an examination for admission as a first year student, he disclosed his situation. He was none other than the fabled 'Comrade Daktar', the name plastered across the southern stretch of the city during those tumultuous years. They arrested him towards the end of 1973.

Despite obtaining admission, he moved back to Kolkata after the announcement by the Government of West Bengal that incarcerated students would be permitted to resume their studies from the point at which they were interrupted. Since I could not overcome the possible trauma of visiting Kolkata, he would come to meet me in Delhi at every opportunity. We decided to get married after he passed out of medical college. He hailed from one of the southern districts of Bengal and was living in Kolkata alone, but he too promised to settle in Delhi after completing his internship, which as you know, is an imperative for medical students.

I made an impulsive decision to visit Kolkata after starting to work as a teacher. I was lucky to obtain a reservation on Rajdhani Express at short notice. Reaching late in the morning and after spending some time with my overjoyed folks, dropped in at Santanu's place around 4 p.m. That day, the heavens had descended on Kolkata, and the narrow by-lane leading to his tenement was inundated. He was forced to live there because he had not obtained hostel accommodation.

Putrescent garbage floated on knee-deep water, overflowing from choked drainpipes; it posed an affront to the olfactory senses. I had to suppress my urge to throw up by wrapping my handkerchief tightly around my face.

The first thing I saw upon entering his shack was a tattered mattress from a flea shop extending till the third quarter of an old-fashioned cot, a tiny study desk and a couple of plastic chairs with broken handles. Recesses in the walls served as cupboards, and they were packed with cheap hair oils, toothpaste and two brushes, a razor, half-used soap, a few clothes sandwiched between books of poems composed by revolutionary Bengali poets, polemic literature usually available at road-side bookstalls, a few thick books on medicine and the ubiquitous *Sanchaita*. On a makeshift clothesline, a couple of undergarments and an off-white shirt were hung and water dripped from them in a steady trickle. Exposed cement gaped from portions of the floor, the tiles pointing precariously towards the earth's centre. He shared the bathing space and toilet with a dozen families, and serpentine queues were regular during morning hours. He also treated dwellers from the slum who suffered from numerous ailments free of charge.

It was an embarrassing moment for both of us. I insisted that Santanu stay with my parents, but his self-esteem stood in the way. We signed on the dotted line on this visit, and I commenced living with him whenever I visited Kolkata, rarely venturing outside. My brief stints at his place toughened me. My parents relented a few months later after he obtained employment at the Dublin Government hospital, thanks to his academic brilliance. We were compelled to leave the country in a hurry, and did so without the customary celebrations since I had a notice period to serve and his dates were rigid.

My trips to Kolkata from Dublin were more frequent. Due to visa complications, I was unable to take up a job for the first few years, and then, Kallol was born. I bumped into Utpal sometime during the mid-eighties at a theatre, and heard about you, and I did not utter a word to him about the incident.

Why did I wear the necklace to Santiniketan? It was the custom in our family to ritually exchange it with one's fiancé as part of getting engaged. I could not muster up the courage to propose to you, and I realized it later that it was too early to do so. It was a childish impulse before leaving Kolkata for Santiniketan.

The reason I wore it on that fateful day is anodyne. If you recall, I had to rush for the bus the previous evening, and I forgot to hand over the book that changed our lives. I told you I had a wedding to attend, and it was late. Ma insisted I wear the necklace. When we returned, it was late, and I crashed in a fit of exhaustion. I was woken by the call early in the morning requesting my presence at the college, and, in a hurry, I forgot to lock it and was thus wearing it.

On the day I left for Delhi, Ma requested that I hand it over to her for safe custody. It then dawned that I was wearing it that day and it would have fallen off. She did not express disappointment, instead consoled me, but she would have been miserable. The topic never came up after that. I cannot wait to disclose yesterday's piece of news. My only worry is that the careless Kallol will lose it someday.

So much for my life. Unexceptionable, as mentioned yesterday.

After twelve years, regular trips to Kolkata opened fresh vistas while I went out exploring nooks and crannies that I had rarely visited earlier. I did not see architectural legacies, but I met human beings. Luckily, I never bumped into old friends, perhaps because they did not frequent the places I visited. I had the opportunity to experience the aspirations and dreams of the subaltern classes: epitomized in taxi drivers, hawkers, daily labourers and guards. Each person was eager to improve his material condition, educate his children and strive towards a better world. My brother-in-law's chauffeur religiously parked a tidy sum in his LIC premium account, hoping to cash in someday. The watchman in my sister's apartment saved money in a recurring deposit, going hungry for a few days a month if he was short. The carpenter who did sundry jobs at our house doubled as a cigarette vendor at night to supplement his income. During my childhood, the rickshaw puller who took me to school came to our house one day with a box of sweets to celebrate his daughter's first division in her school-leaving exams.

There has been a remarkable transformation. It is hard to miss.

Neoliberalism has spurred their urge to live a better life. It has inspired them to offer a better deal to their progeny. Not that their aspirations are close to being met, far from it, but what was striking is the strong desire to improve their conditions and not be content with what they were or had. They all want a brighter future for their children.

This aspiration is what we missed to cultivate. We failed to churn expectations, and that is where neoliberalism succeeded, digging its own grave in the process. We refused to engage with the masses during those tumultuous years, understand them and inspire them. We missed the trees for the forest and subsumed their identities into an abstract category called 'class'. We failed to perceive the deep-rooted influence of caste; we dished abstractions beyond their comprehension. We provided the vision of a distant utopia that they were unable to comprehend. We failed to articulate the vision of collective, integrated humanity living in peace and harmony. We spoke of a giant leap, overlooking the steps that had to be climbed one at a time, an accumulation of marginal improvements within the existing set-up. The experience of teaching at the night school was an experience to cherish, but it too fizzled out.

Any change needs to be prefigurative; it does not take place in one quantum leap. Dr Binayak Sen achieved wonders with his organization, Rupantar. I visited him once inside the jungles of Bastar. It was a fantastic experience that I will talk about when we meet next.

I remember you voicing such concerns on multiple occasions, but we did not pay heed and dismissed them as outpourings of an infantile mind. It is not that I accept your present disposition, but I do concede that once upon a time, you demonstrated an uncanny understanding of where we were going wrong and what lay in store for us.

The feelings that permeated those historical moments were infectious, they churned unprecedented levels of energy, and I am proud to have belonged to that generation.

My interpretation of the 'aatman' as the eternal essence of humanity would perhaps sound like a red rag to spiritual individuals like you. Along with karma, it represents the continuity of time, flowing as it does, seamlessly through generations, ages, centuries and periods. There is ample evidence in our scriptures to support my contention. As individuals, we migrate across borders, travel through time and space, witness the departure of friends, relatives and dear ones, progress in our careers and recapture and reinterpret experiences every moment. They return at odd moments to haunt us, to tear apart fixed ideas of our past; we are caught in the continuous rediscovery of our existence. A set of beliefs morph into another set, containing quintessential elements of the past. Such is the progression of mankind through the ages.

There is a verse in the Bhagavad Gita on the unequal distribution of wealth. This edict states that every man should retain only the portion required to satisfy his primal craving. 'Man is the power of only as much as will satisfy his hunger; if he aspires to possess more, he is a thief and deserves punishment.' Narada advised the rich to store grains 'sufficient for a year, six months, or three months' and to share the surplus with the poor.

The Indian tradition encompasses a

storehouse of materialist and egalitarian philosophies predating the Vedas. Back in its early stages it produces a society where man lived with each other as a community, with a dialogic spirit, enjoying the fruits of labour collectively. Lokayata epitomized the voice of the people. It was only at the later stage of the development of Vedas that we notice the stratification of society, sanctified by the Manusmriti, reified into caste and gender, although something bitterly opposed by the Nastikas and Lokayatikas.

It is time to integrate the thought processes of the early Vedas, Lokayat, Buddhists, Jains, the Charvaka, Sankhya and other progressive trends within our philosophies. Our medieval materialist philosophies predate European thought processes.

The predominance of idealistic and mystical trends coincide with the rule of the maharajas and upper castes. Manual labour was looked down upon in post-Vedic India, with the ulterior motive of stealing the wealth of knowledge acquired by the labouring classes who worked on the soil, reared buffalos, and cast metals into myriad forms.

The Rig Vedas were sceptical of the existence of a supernatural force.

> *But, after all, who knows, and who can say Whence it all came, and how did creation happen?*

> *The gods themselves are later than creation,*
> *So who knows truly whence it has arisen?*
> *Whence all creation had its origin,*
> *He, whether he fashioned it, or whether he did not*
> *He, who surveys it all from the highest heaven,*
> *He knows, or maybe even he does not know...*

Amartya Sen has clearly defined the various strains of atheistic thought in Indian tradition, dating back to Buddha and Ashoka. The concept of Prakriti was expressed succinctly in the Vedas, glorifying the integration of man with nature. It can be seen through the rising of the sun, the mountains, lakes, the sea, the silence of the night, plantations, animals and even micro-organisms. Remember? When we were overwhelmed by the full moon and its simmering reflections floating on the river Ajay, I remember attempting to inspire you to imbibe the beauty of the surroundings—the essence of our philosophy—but you were more interested in exciting stuff that night.

Tagore's Balaka was inspired by the dynamism of nature and the continuity of life. It encompasses the evolution of mankind from its pastoral, nomadic days to modernity. I see little difference between the struggle of the Blacks for social justice, the tribes of Africa struggling to maintain control over their resources or the tribal of Niyamgiri in Odisha waging battles against the primitive accumulation of their land and forests to mine bauxite for manufacturing fighter aircraft. They are all tied by a singular thread: the unity of mankind. From the Santhal rebellion to the struggle of Alaskan natives to retain their land.

Only Tagore could have allegorized the flow of time through the flow of a river:

Oh! Mighty river,
Your water is invisible, quiet
Unbreakable, continuous
Flowing ceaselessly.
In the thrill of pulsation, you move in shapeless fury
Vigorously hit by the naked flow
Heaps of foams rise.
The dazzling rays of light are reflected in the currents
From the fleeing darkness.
Revolving repeatedly in eddies
Layers after layers
The sun, moon, and stars
Rise like bubbles.

We commit mistakes, but that is a part of life, a process of renewal. Saplings planted below the soil will grow into trees someday, because they too contain within themselves memories of the tree that was uprooted. Like antibodies fighting viruses based on memories of past ones. If the sapling succumbs to pests, we need to plant them once again for life's eternal message to resound.

Do give my proposal a serious thought. I have no time limit in mind, but the momentum has to be sustained. This will be a team effort, which will involve Utpal and the two of us. We will hopefully be supported and motivated by our spouses.

I hope I have not sounded too preachy or upset your spiritual sensibilities. If I have, it is your turn to forgive me. Let's plan to catch up in Kolkata next May, but most importantly, let us keep in touch.

Please feel free to share this with your family if you desire to.

'*Aano bhadra krtavo yantu vishwatah.* Let noble thoughts come to me from all directions.'

Lal salaam!

Runa

P.S. The last two words were meant to irritate you. You deserve it.

Samir must have gone through the note ten times, reinterpreting it each time. With Runa, one had to be careful to read between the lines. She was skilled. He was convinced that the spiritualism was contrived to con him. What she did not realize was that it was not just the Indian tradition that fascinated him, but the spiritualism of the munis and rishis, the countless sadhus and yogis dotting the Himalayas and the motherland. He dwelt on the spirit of yoga, transcendental meditation, the cosmic unity pervading the universe, and the divinity of Rama, Shiva and Kali. His spiritualism was beyond her comprehension. She lacked the depth of understanding of the scriptures.

There could be a co-existence between two disparate visions, like a quantum mechanical phenomenon; however, excluding one for the other or allowing one to dominate over the other was ruled out. It was not a synthesis of two opposites but a coexistence of conflicting identities. It was tough, but it was possible. He would not permit her to dominate his mind. Even if she lost interest in him.

He vowed to reply to her note someday. At the right time and setting. There was no point arguing now. Upeksha—ignoring criticism with intelligence—is what he practices these days.

Neelu returned from her walk.

'I have forwarded Runa's mail to all of you,' Samir announced as she entered.

She did not show much interest; he would have been surprised if she did. It was too much to expect an enigmatic personality to transform as if by a sleight of hand.

He was in a mood for another round of confessions and he wanted to come clean.

'I wish to drop another bombshell,' he said to Neelu.

'Now what?'

'I was not as innocent a soul as I projected to all of you, but I was a part of a group that threw explosives from the college terrace that day...

'A few of us had sneaked out to the terrace. The others were experienced; they had perfected the art of throwing explosives so as not to hurt passers-by on the road. Atanu da, out of the blue, handed me an explosive, and I dropped it instantly without caring to look down. He shouted at the top of his voice.

'What have you done, Samir? You could have killed someone.'

A couple of CRP soldiers were hurt, grievously, but not fatally. The signal from the comrades downstairs conveyed that the forces had entered the college. We rushed down the stairs, but I slipped and fell. Others did not notice me, and by the time I could reach the second floor, the CRPF were right there. My friends, by then, were perched inside the classrooms, indistinguishable from other students. I proffered the excuse that I had gone up to challenge the guys throwing bombs, but it sounded so ludicrous!'

'Does Runa know this?'

'How could she? She was chanting slogans downstairs. Unless Atanu da has disclosed it to her later. She would not be bothered. There were six of us there: Sankar, Atanu da and three others. I was the youngest. Joined the core group a couple of days after they killed Adesh.'

'But how could the Principal let you off?'

'The young officer, an alumnus of our college, chose not to report me. There was no hard evidence.'

'The CRPF was right then when they claimed they spotted you coming down the stairs?'

'To the dot. And the officer was smart enough to understand.'

'Why did he then decide not to report you?'

'I obtained his contacts a few years after the change in government. When I asked him, he claimed it was mere compassion for a youngster lying helplessly in a pool of blood. It may not be true. I later learned that he was an activist in college, a few years senior to us and he had continued to remain a sympathiser. The story does not change from the point they started hammering me. Runa did pour water on my wounds, but that was just before they carried me to the hospital.'

'How many more surprises do you have in store for us, Samir?' Neelu said, chagrined.

He recalled the invitation to his friend's wife to spend the night, the experience in Philadelphia. His kissing Runa. Those were aberrations; he had generally been faithful to Neelu.

He decided to be funny but, as usual, it fell flat. 'This is the last one. From this life. Cannot vouch for my past life though.'

Neelu did not find it funny. 'Your life is messed up, Samir,' she quipped.

Since yesterday, he had been hoping that their relationship would turn a new page and he was still hopeful, but there was also the fear of hope. He barely managed to stammer out a few words with difficulty. 'You think so?'

CATCHING UP

May 2015–October 2019

The six of them—Runa, Santanu, Samir, Neelu, Utpal and Srimati—met regularly at Kolkata every May consecutively for five years, although the overlapping days were usually restricted to a maximum of ten. He loved the teamwork between them.

On the work front, he started enjoying his newfound importance in his organization. Alan, the Chairman, insisted that Samir henceforth attend all the Board and shareholder meetings. IT had, in the last few years, emerged as a transformative agent.

Samir also assisted Kallol, a regular visitor to their place, in finding employment in San Francisco. The boy was merely a bridge to Runa, although he was wary of Kallol's growing intimacy with Ruplu. Not that he held anything against him, but to enter into a new relationship with his mother—a kutum as they called it in Bengali—was not quite what he relished at this stage in life. It would only add to complexities, and he was still clueless about Ruplu's romantic preferences.

The initial request from Runa was that he compose a compendium of essays but, surprisingly, it graduated into a novel at Neelu's suggestion. It was agreed by everyone during their first common visit to Kolkata, but made little headway. He enjoyed bonding with the rest; it overshadowed the urgency. Neelu was a transformed individual and had integrated seamlessly into the gang. It was surprising to Samir, because they were not her type of people. On the one occasion that he and Runa met separately at a café, thanks to a last-minute ditch by Utpal, she commented that

Neelu's transformation was noticeable. Her expressions changed whenever he spoke, and it appeared that she was a teenager with a crush. He remembered twisting Runa's hands playfully.

Usually, the six of them would hang around till late at night during their visits to Kolkata. They would then head to one of the coffee shops of luxury hotels that dotted the road to the Kolkata Airport or at low-end dhabas that served food through the night. Their conversation ranged from the sublime to the ridiculous, and they regaled each other with countless anecdotes from the past, enlivening their rendezvous.

Ashim kaku was still going strong, although he had discontinued his medicine practice. He looked healthy, slim and trim, but he was suffering from the common ailments of old age. He would rarely miss his evening walk, and his walking stick was more a prop than a necessity. His mind was alert, and Samir left him with a copy of his unfinished novel. He seemed enthused after reading it and he provided Samir with valuable insights and expressed the desire to see it in print during his lifetime. Sadhan had expired by then, and an old lady performed the role of an attendant.

Sulekha passed away two years after Satyen, it was a sudden cardiac arrest. She was a diabetic patient. Samir had requested her several times to stay with them, but she was persistent in her refusal. It was another heart-breaking episode for Samir and it was totally unexpected. Feeling responsible for Samir after the demise of his parents, Ashim would send the car to the airport to receive his family, insisting that they stay at his home for a few days before shifting to the ancestral abode, which was well-looked after with Mongola as the caretaker.

His apartment was well-maintained and appeared the same as it had during the days when Samir spent a couple of months there. He held animated conversations, peppered with a host of anecdotes, not limited to Samir's brief sojourn at his place. He was now a father-figure since most of Samir's relatives from his previous generation, including his kaku, had left for their heavenly abodes.

He passed away a few days after Samir's sixty-third birthday. The news was conveyed to Samir by his nephew. It was the end of an era.

◆

Samir was surprised by an unexpected call one afternoon.

'Samir? I obtained your number with much difficulty. I did send you a friend request on Facebook earlier. Did you not notice it?'

'Pardon me. I'm not able to place you.'

'Your childhood friend, Subroto. I was visiting LA, so I thought it may be a good idea to catch up. I obtained your contacts from someone who knows you. I am here for another ten days.'

Samir had missed the friend request; he had not ignored it. He had too many these days. The initial impulse was to cold-shoulder Subroto, but he pulled himself together on second thought. Nonetheless, he was sarcastic. 'Tell me, Subroto. What reminds you of me after so many years?'

Subroto spoke softly. 'Samir, I behaved nastily once upon a time with you and many others. Success went to my head. Now, at an advanced age, I realize that these worldly successes are ephemeral and meaningless. I do not know what got hold of me. I now wish to renew our connection. My earnest request is to meet up just once. Anywhere.'

'Subroto, we are not kids and I am not the type who takes things to heart. That is not what my philosophy teaches me. Please drop in. Are you free over the weekend?'

Subroto dropped in for dinner; they dined and talked for a

few hours. His Canadian wife had split, taking away his children, who had been part and parcel of his existence once upon a time. The real tragedy was that they, too, were not too keen to meet him, and avoided the court-mandated weekends. Ten years had passed since they had last met their father, and he had no clue where they were or what they were doing.

'Successes in life do not mean anything, Samir. They lack depth, they are illusionary.'

Samir felt pity. He dished out clichéd spiritual advice and tips on retaining mental equanimity. He was not sure whether it helped him because, although they spoke regularly thereafter, the topic never came up.

Ruplu decided one morning to venture out of her closet, introducing her partner, Angela, to her parents. Samir feigned ignorance. He took it in his stride, albeit with a lot of effort. It took Neelu longer to come to terms with it because she was more conservative by nature and had no prior inkling. After reading copious literature about the phenomenon, he tried his best to convince Neelu that it was in her genes. Soon, Ruplu's partner started accompanying them on holidays and became an integral component of the family. She settled with them, despite Samir's hesitation and Neelu's vehement opposition.

Kallol continued to visit them.

Narendra Modi was re-elected in 2019 with a thumping majority. Samir was the only one among his friends who celebrated. Mocking comments from the other five of the group were responded to with a beatific smile whenever the topic came up.

Although the first few chapters of his novel were completed within a year, it assumed a concrete form only after five years. High-quality discussions followed, at times till early hours. Utpal and Runa visited the Jaipur Lit Festival once, but the publishers they met felt that it was still too early in the day.

After quitting his day job, Samir took pains to put in the final touches, although he was aware that incremental changes would continue even after he had mailed the manuscript to the publishers. More would follow. They would insist on alterations to cater to the market's invisible hand.

As far as his spiritualism was concerned, it was alive and kicking. He had however become less obsessive about it. Neelu no longer had any reason to fear the tantric part of his life. Samir soon realized that he had overdone it and promised not to wear it on his sleeves any more. By then, he had started believing in an innovative version of leftism that coexisted with spiritualism, 'indoctrinated' by Runa, deftly rationalized with the help of Heisenberg's Principle.

He travelled to India every six months against odds to acquire a couple of degrees in yoga and ayurveda, embarking upon the next phase of his life as an evangelist, an occasional activist, an active propagandist on social media and an author—all rolled into one.

After he decided to hang his boots at work, Mike tried his best to persuade him, but Samir was adamant. They hosted a massive farewell party for him, toasted him with accolades with respect to the digital transformation of their business model.

Samir was keen on incorporating their company's digital journey as a case study for Harvard Business School and he had sent a copy, but he crossed his fingers. This too was a long-cherished dream, as close to his heart as the still-unpublished novel.

AN UNSCHEDULED VISIT TO KOLKATA

December 2019

This visit was planned within fifteen days. They usually had their tickets booked months in advance but in this case, Neelu's cousin's daughter's wedding had to be finalized in a hurry because the couple was to leave for Germany. She had called Neelu the same night, but she refused to visit Kolkata at such short notice. They contacted Samir after that and pleaded with him to persuade her.

Samir agreed as he had another reason to visit Kolkata. Runa had informed him a few days back that after resigning from her teaching assignment, she had taken up employment with a British NGO that had donated a substantial amount to their Indian counterpart working in the border districts of West Bengal. They were sending her there for an audit. She was to spend considerable time at the site and the remaining at their Kolkata office. She planned to visit once again on their annual vacation two months down the line. Samir and Neelu were also scheduled to visit Kolkata during her second visit to finalize the structure and contents of their novel before sending it to prospective publishers.

It was a golden opportunity to complete the process two months earlier than planned and the temptation to meet Runa, without Santanu around, was compelling enough for Samir.

Neelu could not resist a snide comment when he told her of his plans. 'I never realized you were so fond of my cousin sister.'

'Oh, come on, I get what you are hinting at. Have long crossed that stage, Neelu.'

'Really?'

'Honestly. In any case, I would have met Runa two months later.'

'But Santanu plans to be around on that visit.'

'Come off it, Neelanjana. Unless you are pulling my leg. It is just that your cousin sounded sincere.'

Neelu burst out laughing. 'I do not believe a word of what you are saying, but let me tell you, I find nothing wrong in meeting her when Santanu is not around and I am busy with the wedding. It is quite natural. Why do you wish to deny the obvious?'

The first few days in Kolkata were spent in festivities, Samir thoroughly enjoying the Indian wedding. He called Runa after the rituals ended.

'What a surprise, Samir. Why did you not inform me earlier?'

'To surprise you. Cannot comment on whether it is a pleasant or an unpleasant one.'

'If you had told me, I would have completed my work in the border area a day earlier. I'm scheduled to return to Kolkata in three days. Let the five of us sit down and finalize the contents of the novel. We will still have a day before I have to leave for Ireland. Incidentally, a leading publisher expressed interest after perusing the latest draft.'

'That is terrific news.'

'Not something to be overly excited about, Samir. They have only expressed interest and it still has to go through a few more layers. Have you informed Utpal?'

'I plan to call him right away.'

'Where are you putting up?'

'At Neelu's place in Salt Lake.'

'Great. I will drop by on my way home. Incidentally, I'm at Taki, on the banks of the river Icchamati, bordering Bangladesh. I could pen a novel on my experiences here.'

'That would be interesting stuff. The topic of our next!'

'So three days from now? I'll leave around 2 p.m. and reach Salt Lake by five. We can meet the next day at my house for lunch. Do keep these hours free and let it be a kind of open-ended meeting. Let us make full use of your unplanned visit and send it to the publishers before the end of the month.'

'Incidentally, we have decided to stay back till your next visit.'

'Great news, but that should not become an excuse for delays!'

Runa reached Salt Lake around 8 p.m. three days later. Neelu had gone out to visit an ailing relative with her parents.

Samir said, 'I was worried because of the delay.'

'*Aar bolish na*. Typical British bureaucracy. Twenty different forms to fill up. Anyway, it is all over now. We can continue the day after, if required. My flight is late at night.'

He winked at her. 'Yes, then we shall positively meet that day. Let's finish the novel tomorrow and just the two of us meet. Preferably at your place?'

'Neelanjana's not at home?' Runa asked.

'Nope, but she is expected any moment.'

'No wonder you're so enthused. Look, Samir, we took a joint decision.'

Samir stared at her with a cunning expression. 'Did I hint at anything physical?'

'Even otherwise.'

'But we did meet by ourselves once before.'

'If you remember, that was because Utpal ditched us at the last minute. And you started touching me, pulling my hands, hugging me inappropriately.'

'Your sense of humour is atrocious, Runa.'

'You were not joking, Samir, I know you better than anyone else. Likely better than your wife does. I'm changing the topic. Okay? Something interesting happened the day before. The head of the West Bengal unit of the NGO here, Nandita Ray, out of the blue asked me whether I ever studied at Presidency College. I told her it had only been for a year. Then she inquired about you. I was taken aback. She is around Neelanjana's age, so she must have been ten years old at that time, studying at a boarding school. Her working life was spent outside Kolkata, and she had been transferred here by the NGO just five or six months back. She is not married. Mysterious, isn't it?'

'We are a famous couple, Runa. Icons of our generation,' Samir joked.

'She claims she heard about us from a cousin who studied at our college. But the name, Sarbajit, is unfamiliar to me.'

'Come on, we can't remember the names of all our contemporaries.'

'Possible, but it is a bit weird. I have informed her that you are in town. She said she would love to spend some time with both of us after she comes from Taki. I told her we will be busy. She said if you're okay with it, she will catch up with you after I leave.'

'Would love to. She must be one of those chroniclers churning out dozens of books on that era. Someone would have told her about us. I see it as flattering, please pass on my number.'

Runa abruptly got up from the sofa. 'Have already done so, without your permission. Relieved that it's fine with you. But presently, I am dead exhausted and need to freshen up. See you tomorrow.'

Samir protested. 'Wait a while for Neelanjana.'

'Is she not going to join us tomorrow?'

Samir remarked, 'Yes, she will.' But all the same pulled her down onto the sofa.

Runa sighed and waited silently. Fortunately, Neelu came in after a few minutes and after exchanging pleasantries, Runa left. Samir had a quick dinner and walked to the park for his usual after-dinner stroll.

He did not return. The police were informed after a couple of hours. Neelu went around the park several times and even traversed the nearby streets on foot. A roadside hawker remembered seeing Samir enter the park, but he did not notice him exiting.

Utpal and Runa came in early in the morning. The police were prompt, proactive and followed every single lead. It was only towards the night that they heard some good news. The cops had spotted someone locked inside a room in a remote corner of the state. The man looked like Samir, and rescue operations were planned for the night, but they refused to state the location.

But what if there was a shoot-out? Neelu and Runa shed copious tears at the police station despite the cops' assurance that he would be safe. Still, they were cautious and added that there were doubts about whether the person that had been spotted was truly Samir.

◆

From an Undisclosed Location

December 2019

Samir had fallen asleep. He woke to a pleasing sight, a police officer inside the hut. The entire operation had taken less than ten minutes. The cops had intentionally arrived after midnight, hoping to catch the criminals napping.

Breaking open the door, they managed to nab all three of them before the sidekicks could even comprehend what was happening. The revolvers remained tucked inside their pockets and were confiscated soon after.

The officer was courteous. 'Samir Chattopadhyay?'

'Yes, I am,' Samir cried. 'What a relief! Never expected this. Was waiting for certain death.'

'What have they done to you? Your face has marks all over. They will have to pay for this.'

'The tall guy was particularly brutal,' he complained.

'Here is my mobile. Call up your wife. She is at the end of her wits.'

Samir's next comment was vacuous. 'Thank you, sir. I have always held the West Bengal Police in high esteem.'

Neelu's voice on the other end was the sweetest thing Samir had ever heard. He could sense the relief, joy and excitement, perceptible through the wires.

'Let me find out from the officer what their plans are. I will call you in ten minutes,' he said, hanging up reluctantly.

The officers informed him. 'We can either finish the formalities right away at the station and drop you home, or you can rest at a guest house through the night.'

'I would love to snatch a few hours' sleep, try to efface the scars as far as possible, obtain a shave and a decent wash,' Samir told them.

'There is a government guesthouse fifteen minutes away from where our jeep is parked. We can walk to the jeep, shouldn't take up more than ten minutes.'

Samir nodded and asked. 'Where exactly are we at the moment?'

The officer paused, then said, 'Let us take a walk while I explain.'

Within moments, they had reached the banks of a gently flowing river. It was gleaming with a silver shade in the bright moonlight. After a few heavy showers, the clouds had cleared, but the grounds were still patchy.

It was pitch dark, and only a few streetlights were visible on the other side of the river.

'Is this the Hooghly?' Samir asked.

'No, this river is called Icchamati. On the other bank is Bangladesh. There is a gang that operates in this area. They carry their victims from all over the state to murder them—immediately, if they have been hired as contract killers—or they contact the relatives for a ransom. The relatives are afraid and normally pay the amount without informing us. In many cases, even after receiving the ransom, the hapless victim is brutally murdered, but in most situations, they are dumped at some corner of the state. If they are lucky, they get noticed by a passer-by. Depends on the gang. The unfortunate ones are killed nonetheless. They transport the body in a boat across the border in the dead of night and hand it to their friends on the opposite side. Burying a body in Bangladesh is not a challenge, and even if the body is recovered by their police, our police are not informed to avoid the hassle.'

Samir shivered. He asked, 'And what is the role of our Border Security Force?'

'They are in the league. Paid handsomely every month. Corrupt buggers.'

He felt another cold shiver running down his spine. 'Sir, if you cannot provide police protection through the night, I would request that you drop me home after the formalities are over.'

'That goes without saying. An armed constable will be posted outside your room,' the officer reassured.

Samir still had questions. 'But why did they target me?'

'That is what we still have to find out. They must have presumed you have lots of cash and were expecting a ransom. The interrogation will reveal the motive. By the time you are at the station tomorrow morning, we will be able to throw some light on the situation.'

After a relatively comfortable night at the guesthouse, Samir reached the police station at 7 a.m. The officer who had escorted him was still around.

Samir asked incredulously, 'Did you not go home last night?'

His innocuous, youthful grin was infectious. 'I had to complete the interrogations and finalize the report. After seeing you off, I hope to catch a few hours of sleep.'

Samir smiled back. 'There was a question I forgot to ask yesterday. How did you manage to locate me?'

'Luckily, we came to know from our informers that you were confined somewhere in the vicinity, but they were not aware of the precise location. Sent out several guys on recons last night. We were not even aware of this dilapidated house deep inside the jungle. That is why the kidnappers were complacent. Honestly, we were plain lucky. One of our men spotted you through the window.'

Samir felt a jolt of recognition. 'Yes, I saw the man and was hoping against hope that he was either a villager or one of you. Otherwise, why would he run away after seeing me? Did he recognize me?'

'Your picture is all over the media. He ran away because he thought you would scream, which would have alerted them and you would have been moved elsewhere. We did post two of our men a few yards away till we landed in full force. We chose the hour to minimize casualties.'

'Did the mastermind get away?'

'No. Their boss has been nabbed, just a few hours ago. The funniest part is that they claim that they were hired as contract killers by a senior and respected official of the NGO that operates here. A lady by the name of Nandita Ray. We did not believe a word of this story. They were out to extort ransom from your family and would have called in a day or two. But contract killing assignments are executed immediately.'

Samir was stunned. But he did not express it. He felt that it would not be prudent to reveal that the same woman had apparently had a conversation with Runa a few days back before delving deeper into it.

'But why would they needlessly implicate her?' he probed.

'She had stopped funding a local organization run by the goons after identifying certain anomalies. We got it verified by our sources. That explained it,' the officer said.

THE CLOSURE THAT NEVER TOOK PLACE

December 2019

Samir reached home around 3 p.m. He was hugged and smothered by Neelu and the family, and then he called Ruplu and Apu. He kept it brief even though his children were in the mood to hear the minutest details. Worse, he now had to ward off the many reporters who had come to the house. After responding to their queries, he disclosed to Neelu and Runa what the cop had said in the morning. They unanimously decided to confront the lady Nandita Ray without wasting time. Runa was due to leave for Ireland in a few hours. Luckily, she had dropped Nandita off at her house once and remembered the precise location.

It was Nandita who opened the door. She was wearing a deep blue nightgown. She was tall and fair, with long hair and eyes that appeared a trifle slanted to Samir at first glance. Her age showed, but she had managed to retain her petite figure.

They were greeted with a deep, unfriendly stare for a couple of minutes. She seemed undecided on whether she should bang the door on their faces or call them in for a whacking.

She had placed the two of them. Runa, of course, she had worked with just a day back.

'Why have you come all the way?' she demanded.

'To know the truth,' Samir said promptly and gently.

She sighed, then finally said, 'What truth?'

'No need to spell it out,' said Runa. Nandita retorted, 'I need to think about it. Give me a few minutes.'

They waited patiently as the minutes ticked by.

At long last, her face was visible. 'You can come in, but on the condition that you hand over your mobile phones to me.'

All of them consented and were allowed in. They settled down on the sofa. But she disappeared through the front door, only to reappear after a few minutes. 'Went to check up if the police was accompanying you.'

The statement that followed was unsettling. 'The reason I agreed to divulge the truth is because whatever I did was for a cause. It was not for money. As a matter of fact, I have lost a lot of money.'

She suddenly looked at Neelanjana, smirked and blurted out. 'Neelanjana does not seem to have recognized me.'

Neelu stared back at Nandita with a quizzical expression. Samir and Runa were taken aback and kept looking at both of them. Neelu's eyes showed a faint glimmer of recognition, but it was soon followed by a stupefied expression.

'Samir,' Neelu began to cry. 'She, she...she is my childhood friend...the same girl who narrated the incident to me thirty-five years ago. I am flabbergasted. But Nandita was not your name.'

'I changed my name through an affidavit ten years back. There was a purpose. Although my folks still call me Jayashree.'

Runa was enraged and uninterested. She had a flight to catch; she did not have time for trivia. 'We are not interested in your name. Tell us why you did what you did. Do not try to deny it because we are now certain it was you who organized the kidnapping.'

'Well,' Nandita nodded, 'I am not the kind of person to hide behind smoke and mirrors, and it should have struck you after working with me for the last ten days. The motivation was pure revenge. It is devastating to see that things did not proceed as per my plans.'

Samir stared back in shock.

She continued. 'I have been working with many characters in that area for the last few months and I knew who was capable of doing what. I stopped their club's funding on a pretext—hoping to kill two birds with one stone. If they were apprehended and spilled the beans, then there would be a discernible motive for their implicating me. I wouldn't be caught. I, however, promised to resume their funding if they did this for me. I did also pay them a hefty advance. All in cash. There is no money trail. I never even corresponded on the cell with them...'

She sighed and said, 'I believe I made just one mistake. I could have murdered you within minutes and packed off the corpse to the other side of the river...'

Samir was shell-shocked.

'...but I wished to mislead the police if they caught them because ransom killings are normally delayed. We had planned a ransom call this evening where we would promise to call back again by tomorrow morning. That call that would not happen and I had hoped it would thoroughly confuse the police.'

'But...revenge for what?' Samir finally asked.

The riposte came after a moment's pause. 'For killing my father.'

'What are you talking about?'

'You murdered him with your own hands. *The Principal*, remember?'

The entire room was silent for a few minutes. A grandfather clock on the wall ticked the seconds. An eternity seemed to pass.

Samir quietly tried to resume the conversation. 'But did you ever get to read the police report? I entered the room, searching for Runa. Your father had, by then, been murdered by the goons of the ruling party and his body was on the floor. They were groping Runa when I entered.'

Nandita screamed. 'Bullshit!'

'On what basis did you arrive at your conclusion?' Runa asked calmly.

'There were witnesses in the room. Unfortunately, they were part of Pagla Keshto's gang. They would have been hung upside down if they dared speak against the administration back then, but they confided with my uncle and advised us to investigate through our channels.'

'Where did you get my name from?' Samir demanded.

'Think, think. You are supposed to be a bright guy, aren't you?'

'I am in no mood to exercise my faculties after the trauma I went through yesterday. Let us be transparent tonight.'

Nandita raised her voice. 'I will disclose it after some time. Wear your thinking cap till then but first, tell me why you murdered my father. He was in no way responsible for Adesh's death. He was an educationist, a simple soul.' She pounded her fist on the table in the front. She was sobbing, her body was trembling.

Samir waited with his hands clasped. It was one of the most difficult situations he had faced in his life. He took a deep breath, lowered his voice, made a time out sign with his palms and said, 'Timeout please. Timeout. Look at my eyes please, focus! Please add a little bit of compassion to your heart.'

Nandita lifted her eyes, but they were still red with revenge.

'I am not a murderer. Do I look like a professional murderer? Look at my eyes, please. It conveys everything. This event has haunted me for the last forty-eight years. You are not aware of the circumstances leading to his murder. Do you think that the goons would have told you that they were in the process of raping Runa? Please think this through!' By now, Samir had started to choke and his face showed tremendous pain.

'The murder was not done to avenge Adesh's death. I would have not gone alone if that was my intention. And your father was in no way connected to Adesh's murder. And I agree with you...he was a professor and a kind soul.' Samir then added, 'See we are on the same page.'

Samir got up from the sofa and vigorously paced through the length of the room twice as the others remained seated, yet to get over the shock. Noticing sweat on Samir's forehead, Neelu wanted to tell him to calm down. However, Samir's dramatic gestures had had no effect on Nandita and had indeed fallen flat.

'That is the second fairy-tale of the evening!' Nandita continued with her pronouncements.

'This one is not,' Samir said gravely. 'Use your common sense. Murders committed by our Party were never surreptitious. We proclaimed it to the world. They were political assassinations; they were enacted with a purpose.'

'I never said your Party took the decision. You did it to settle a personal score. You concluded that my father was behind your close friend's death.'

'And I sacrificed my career, my future in the process? I murdered him inside his office with cops stationed right outside? Give me a break,' Samir scoffed. His frustrations were at the fore now that he was being held accountable.

She pondered for a few minutes. 'Then why did you do it?'

'It was an error. I never met your father before the act, how would I have recognized him?'

'So he looked like a rapist to you?'

'He was facing the other way. I turned him around and did not even look at his face. It was a costly mistake. Please understand that I am not and was not a professional killer.'

'And the knife? You carried it for self-defense, is it?'

'I did not. Look here, the bastards carried them, they were meant to scare away the demonstrating girls. One of them was placed on the chair, I was at that moment consumed with rage, I grabbed it, and...I...I lost control over myself. I lost all sense of context. How, how can I convince you of this after so many years?'

He closed his eyes in agony.

Nandita appeared confused but displayed certitude and determination when she spoke. 'I do not give a fuck. You were the guy who pushed the sword. I lost the person closest to my life. Neelanjana, do you remember that I lost my mother at the age of three? He had brought me up single-handedly. He fed me, bathed me, dropped me at school, bought toys and clothes for me and taught me everything I know. After college, he conducted private tuitions to provide me with the best of what life had to offer. I inhabited his world. After becoming the Principal, he put me in an expensive boarding school and visited me every weekend, loaded with goodies. I was the envy of my classmates. It was tough to accept his death, although my uncle and auntie treated me like their own daughter. I have not been able to get over the loss after so many years.'

'But you know the truth now,' Samir pleaded.

She flared up. 'Have I not said that, for me, the fact that you are the killer is enough? You can report me to the police. I will stand in the witness box and rake up a long-forgotten incident. The world has forgotten him. Let the case come to light after fifty years. Let the identity of a murderer be revealed. You are a killer leading a cushy life abroad after conducting mayhem in the name of a revolution. In the age of social media, be rest assured that the story will reach the world. If you can risk it, go ahead. Will you ever be able to prove my involvement in the kidnapping?'

'We have not yet decided what to do on that aspect. But tell us just how you got to know my name? Other than a few police officers, my parents, Runa and a close family friend, not a soul was aware.'

'Not yet been able to figure it out, Mr Brilliant?' she mocked.

He responded after some thought. 'Must have been one of the other police officers at Lalbazar that night.'

'We were led down a blind alley during the first few years before we came to know your name. I could not meet any officer other than Dhruva Roy, who stuck to the story. They must have replaced the knife because your fingerprints were not on the weapon. The police were very powerful those days. We moved heaven and hell after the new government was elected. I was grown up, nearing sixteen. The home minister was sympathetic, and he promised me his full support. Still, there was little he could do because the police report had already been deftly manipulated. Considerable time had passed, and Dhruva Roy and other officers who were present that night had already retired. The new government was not too keen to lodge a fresh case against an extremist when his party comrades were being released. We never got to know the names of the other officers. How much did you pay that man, Dhruva Roy?'

'Not a farthing. He sympathized with my situation.'

Runa chose to speak. 'Why don't you tell us and end this suspense?'

'There was one person who knew your identity that day. His existence has slipped your mind.'

'Who?' Samir asked again.

'Think, think. Your intelligence seems to have escaped you.'

'I have lost the capacity to use my brains. Try to appreciate what your hired goons did to me since yesterday.'

'Serves you right. You are a murderer. My only regret is that you are still alive,' she said with pursed lips.

'Okay,' Samir shifted. 'Let us leave then. I am not dying to have this information. Runa, Neelanjana, let's go.'

She spoke up at that. 'Do you remember an individual called Barua da?'

Samir was speechless for a minute. 'But...but...he happened to be a sympathiser. He kept Adesh hidden in a cupboard and he had disclosed this only to me. I kept his secret. Even today, not a soul is aware of it. I mean, other than my family members.'

Nandita scoffed. 'He did not subscribe to your ideology, and he merely adored Adesh as an individual. He hid him inside the cupboard but harboured no special feelings for you because he hardly knew you. He hails from a family who had sympathies for the ruling party then. So was my father. Barua da was responsible for cleaning the laboratory equipment. My dad liked him. He was trained and promoted to the post of a laboratory assistant. Both of them held strong opinions with respect to the criminals who operated in the locality despite their affiliations. Baba complained to the local legislator multiple times, but Pagla Keshto was so powerful those days!

'Barua da was scared to come out in the open with your name until the government changed. Samir happened to be in *his* room before the incident. He was worried about his own safety, but after the defeat of the then ruling party, shaken by rumblings of his conscience, he visited our house one morning. I still remember the day. It was a Sunday. It was raining profusely, and my school-leaving exams were due to start the next day. I do not know why I was remembering Baba that morning. Perhaps because he often spoke to me about the school-leaving examinations and his expectations for me.

'He came in and started weeping inconsolably. He showed us the library book that had been issued to you; it was still in his possession. He asked for our forgiveness, and offered his help to trace and indict Samir. He managed to obtain Samir's address from your college office. I visited your father and introduced myself as your friend. He was initially hospitable but, after a while, grew suspicious. He refused to divulge any detail other than that you were working in the States. Did he not tell you?'

Samir clarified. 'Now that you tell me, I remember bits and pieces. I had laughed his suspicions off.'

Nandita continued. 'Barua da was convinced that the two of you had gone to the college that day intending to kill my father. He had asked you specifically not to proceed towards the Principal's room.'

Samir immediately countered. 'But Barua da was not even in the room. How would he know?'

'Circumstantial evidence. He could not enter the principal's room, so he proceeded towards the laboratory to meet you. Despite his instructions to not proceed towards the principal's room, you were not there. He had to lock the laboratory and the ingredients, so it took some time. When he returned, he saw you being dragged away. What does it prove?' What Nandita said seemed to carry a lot of sense.

'Yes, he had told me not to. But I was not bound by his advice. I overheard two students discussing that girls were being molested by the goons, and I rushed. I could not initially enter the room due to the crowd that had gathered. I rushed back to the lab, but he was not there. It was still unlocked. Maybe, on my way back, we crossed each other. The crowd had dissipated by then, so I could enter. And then I witnessed the ghastly sight.'

'And why was Runa di part of the demonstration? She was not even a student of the college,' Nandita quizzed Runa, turning towards her.

Runa spoke up. 'Excuse me, I was invited by the girls of the college. There were several outsiders that day. They could not mobilize sufficient girls from inside the college. They believed that the principal would not be able to recognize us as outsiders. The goons appeared out of the blue and attacked us mercilessly. Some of us were bleeding, some had their clothes torn and others escaped. I was not allowed to leave the room. It was a horrendous experience. As a girl, you should place yourself in my shoes. If Samir had not barged in at that moment, they would have taken it to an extreme. Your father was trying his best to prevent the goons, but he was not able to...and the police did not even try to come inside.'

Nandita was unconcerned. Her motivations were still strong. She continued. 'Thirteen years after the incident, I bumped into Neelanjana while I was on an official visit. She was dying to narrate her personal sob stories and went on and on, treating me as her sounding board. When she disclosed your name and told me which batch you were in, it took me just a second to realize this was the same man. I took a day, pretending that I knew someone from your batch, and volunteered to find out more about you. Before leaving the city, I provided her with details of the incident and offered to introduce her to Barua da. She proclaimed that she had already decided to divorce you. It gave me some satisfaction; it would provide some solace to my father's soul. I rang her mother after a few months later and learnt that she was still married and was the proud mother of a son.'

Neelu pointed at her, 'And you kept calling my mother for so many years, each time asking about our plans to visit India. I wondered why, after all, we were only friends in primary school, and had just met for a few hours that day.' She seemed relieved that the mystery was getting solved after so many years.

'Yes,' Nandita agreed, 'but I gave up the idea of killing him after a few years. I was posted outside Kolkata, lacked the resources to hire a contract killer and I did not wish to get involved in a murder at such a young age. My father's spirit would have been disturbed. At first, I decided to approach the media, but my folks advised against it. They believed it would not garner much traction because the police report was foolproof. Then I mentally resolved to avenge the death after returning to Kolkata when I was older, if Samir was still alive. The transfer to Kolkata was a godsend.'

Runa asked. 'And so you settled on hiring contract killers from that locality?'

'Murders are routine affairs there, so it was not tough to identify capable guys. I had Neelanjana's number, and I was in touch with her parents. I even had their address. So when her mother informed me that you were planning to visit the city after a couple of months, I chalked out a plan. I was not aware of your schedule change, but as luck would have it, Runa di turns up in the role of an auditor. I am convinced now there is an Almighty upstairs. She told me that you were already here, so I got to work. My men kidnapped you from the empty park at night, everything was going like clockwork, but...anyway...there is no point crying over spilled milk now.' She hit her palms on the table in a fit of rage, unsettling the flower vase and spilling water all over.

Samir tried his best to sound sympathetic. 'Take it easy. We appreciate your sentiment.'

Nandita frowned and threw her right index finger at Samir. 'You understand *nothing*. I would do it again, even if am prosecuted this time. I have the right contacts now.'

'Providing you with Samir's contacts was a grave error of judgment on my part. But asking me for his contacts was another error on your part. We would not have suspected you otherwise.'

She laughed heartily, almost rolling over. This one puzzled all three of them.

'You really think I am that stupid? I am planning to write a book on those turbulent days, focusing on my father's death. I do not have writing skills, so there is a guy Sarbajit helping me. He was also a student of your college, writes exceptionally well in Bengali, and is hardly known because he was an unassuming character those days. A sympathiser, initially, but later hated the direction the movement had taken. He knew both of you—of course not your involvement in the murder of my father. So my alibi was strong.'

'So...you decided to take the law into your own hands?' Runa's statement seemed incongruous with the tenor of the conversation.

Nandita's anger was now palpable. Her tone was high and her hands were flailing. 'A commie is teaching me the nuances of the law? And did I not tell you that I had Runa's parents' address with me, their original ancestral home as well as the Salt Lake address? But yes, if I had not met you, I would have missed the opportunity this time because I would not have known of your sudden change in plans. I would have gotten around to it on your next visit.'

They were discreet enough not to tell her that Samir planned to stay in Kolkata for a few more months.

For a change, Neelu turned philosophical. The tone was friendly. 'An eye for an eye makes the world blind, Jayashree. It happened many years back and now you are aware that it was just an accident. Let us turn a new chapter in our lives.'

Nandita laughed loudly. It reminded Samir of the tall man at the jungle abode. Her contempt for Samir was as venal and intense—it pervaded her entire being.

Samir maintained his cool. He was also keen that the *red stain* in his life was washed away, now that he believed in another philosophy. But he was also apprehensive that the consequences of this revelation would stick to him like a leech for the remaining years of his life.

'The closure will never happen, Neelu. Right now, I do not wish to entertain my dad's killers for one more minute. Here are your phones, I request that the three of you get lost. Let me reiterate—I will be successful one day.'

Samir took the phones and got up. 'Before I leave, how is Barua da?'

'He passed away a few years back. He was suffering from cancer.'

'I am sorry to hear that, despite how he felt about me.'

On the way home, it was Neelu who broke the silence. 'Is this what is called karma, Samir?'

Samir said nothing. Runa instead quoted her favourite sentences from *Hamlet*.

'I am thy father's spirit,
Doomed for a certain term to walk the night,
And for the day confined to fast in fires,
Till the foul crimes done in my days of nature
Are burnt and purged away...'

They were quiet for a while, then Runa spoke again. 'I do not consider it a foul crime, Samir, do not misunderstand me. It is just that the spirit of every act committed during our lifetime persists, and by the spirit, I do not mean it in the spiritual sense but as a spectre, an image that keeps haunting us.'

Samir chose to remain silent throughout the journey.

EPILOGUE

December 2019–May 2022

Runa left for Dublin after a few hours. They decided not to pursue the case and left town on the seventh day, although the police provided them protection. For the next couple of years, they did not visit the city because of the pandemic.

The novel was published after two years—delayed due to the pandemic. By then, Samir had managed to mitigate the fear of further retaliation and he and Neelu, after procrastinating for a few months, decided to be present in Kolkata for the launch. Runa flew in from Dublin. It was well-attended. Some faces appeared vaguely familiar—perhaps they were long-lost friends who had aged with time.

Nandita was also there during the Question and Answer session. She was sitting unobtrusively in a corner. Samir was initially unnerved a bit and it perhaps showed but then he managed to overcome the fear, after rationalizing that she could not possibly do much, what with so many well-wishers around. There was also police protection that had been provided to him. And how long would he remain petrified? At worst, she may ask him a few uncomfortable questions. He talked to Neelu sitting beside him and then both walked down to Runa sitting on an adjacent table a few feet away. She had also seen her, and all decided to chill. Utpal, Srimati and a few of their friends were sitting on the front row. Utpal's presence bolstered his confidence.

The sessions started half an hour late as the publisher got delayed in a traffic jam.

'Samir babu, is this your story?' a journalist fired the first salvo.

'Well, to a large extent,' Samir laughed heartily.

'I mean: Samir the protagonist and Samir the author, are they the same?'

Samir did not answer directly. He pondered over it a bit. His gaze turned soft, and he stared at the picture of Tagore on the mauve wall of the auditorium.

'Samir in the story moves through the world of light and shadows, *alo andharer manush*. Samir, as a person, is treading the path of freedom,' he answered finally.

Samir glanced slyly at Runa. He then scanned the room for Nandita. This may be a unique opportunity.

Neelu, with her inquiring eyebrows and a smile on her face, winked uncharacteristically at Samir. They had discussed this topic in the past. However, she knew how uninhibited Samir could become when he started talking about his transformation.

'Have some of you pre-ordered and actually read the book?' he asked the audience.

A few hands shot up.

'That's good news. Thanks for doing this. There is so much to talk about. But I will be brief.' Samir chuckled. There was a peal of laughter that came from Neelu and Runa's table, as though they were questioning his capacity to be brief.

Samir nodded. 'I mean, I will try. I have learned over the years that brevity is wisdom.' He then smiled a *gyan papi* smile.

'*āno bhadra krtavo yantu vishwatah*,' he chanted. 'This means—let noble thought come from all directions.' His head moved gently towards the right.

Samir looked at Runa as well as Neelu. His face appeared as bright as a fresh lotus. As if he was looking through himself. 'Do I start from here?'

Runa smiled when she recalled that she had quoted this

sentence in her letter to Samir a long time ago. She never realized that Samir could chant it so mellifluously.

No one in the auditorium spoke.

Samir continued. 'It is one of my favourite hymns. So is the first shloka of Rig Veda. I will come to that later.'

Samir now looked straight at Runa with his penetrating deep eyes.

'Runa, you asked me to work together. You talked about Vedas. You talked about Charvaka. You talked about caste and Manu. But before I answer their question, let me ask you: have you tried to really understand the meaning of this mantra? Did you ever feel the mantra? Vedas are not just a tool to intellectualize, they are meant to be understood and felt. You may ask: "What are ideas and where do they come from?" or "Where do they (these ideas) evolve and where do they dissolve?" I can tell you that they don't come from the outside; they come from the deep crevices of one's mind.'

'Let me chant a relevant Shanti Mantra from Isha Upanishad,' he said and smiled. 'This is becoming a free meditation class, haha!'

Someone from the crowd murmured. 'This is expected from the Samir we knew in college. I could apprehend the transformation!'

Samir tried hard to recognize the face, but could not. He waved nonetheless. Then, he began to chant.

'oṃ pūrṇamadaḥ pūrṇamidaṃ pūrṇātpūrṇamudacyate |
pūrṇasya pūrṇamādāya pūrṇamevāvaśiṣyate ||
oṃ śāntiḥ śāntiḥ śāntiḥ, ||'

'In this ocean of infinity, no matter what you do, the unbound remains infinite. It remains full. This existence with its unlimited intelligence, it gives and takes, expands and contracts, creates and dissolves ideas, thoughts, galaxies and life itself. Some explode with the bright light of a billion suns, some disappear in the cold darkness of a black hole, where even TIME, KAAL, is frozen.'

Samir paused, looking down and closing his eyes 'Rising, falling, rising-falling as one and same.'

Neelu was listening intently. She rarely attended Samir's Pranayama sessions, but she had often overheard snippets of them. But this one was a tad different, she realized.

Runa seemed puzzled, but she too was listening intently. There was a complacent smile on her face, although she seemed defiant. The conflict was apparent in her face. It was like light and shadow.

'There is no classification. There is no my idea, or your idea,' Samir said. 'Charvaka and Shankaracharya are the same; ideas and intelligence manifest in absolute synchronicity. We, with our limitations, see them as "us" and "them", but my Vedic system has never held any such contradictions. It just speaks of continuous expansion, from quarks to the multiverse, from particles to waves. Have you studied the double split experiment? Your observation bends the reality, to express it simply.

'Runa, knowing you and your background, I know where you come from. The whole of western thought is mostly about classification and separation. Slicing and dicing. You see Newton and Einstein as different; I see them as one and the same. From one end of the spectrum to another.

'You cleverly insinuated as if we are the ones who divide and waxed eloquent on the universal unity and oppression, appealing to me to work together.'

There was another question from the audience. 'Can you explain further? How can atheism, materialism and spiritualism work together? I have not seen an answer in the book.' This was the same man who had recognized Samir before.

Samir nodded. 'Yes. I will give you my opinion and tell you

where the unity can happen in real terms. But let me finish my train of thought. Every morning, I utter the mantra you quoted in your famed letter, Runa. My chant predated your letter. I don't impose my meaning on it, but I chant it and let the meanings come to me. On rare and lucky days, I see the thoughts exploding. I see the Big Bang, even the edge of our universe, which even the James Webb telescope has not reached.'

Samir was in a state of altered consciousness. He looked as if he was half awake; his eyes were tearing up, and his left palm was trembling. He held on to the table in the front of him.

The room was absolutely silent.

'I feel this silence every day...*Kevala Kumbhaka*. Have you ever trekked the Grand Canyon, Runa? I bumped into my personal silence the first time there. It was a hot summer day, and I was resting on a rock after a few hours of walking. I realized something: not a single leaf rustled, not a bee buzzed, not an earthworm wiggled. The stillness outside beautifully merged into the calmness within me. In fact, there was no inside or outside. It was one single pure, omnipotent Existence. I somehow realized that all these worldly expressions are toys, they have been created by our intelligence to amuse ourselves. That is called *lila*, my dear friend.'

'Now, to come back to the practical question of how to work together. I need to ascend from my *anandamaya kosha* to *annyamaya kosha*,' he quipped. 'That's a yogic term. I am sure most of you know about it.'

He turned again to Runa and said, 'This is related to your letter, Runa, but let me give a Vedantic non-reductionist view. I have already tried to explain through my heart, but let me use my intellect now.'

He paused, then gathering himself, he spoke to the audience. 'Oh, by the way, for those who do not know, this is my partner-in-crime, Runa. And this is my wife Neelu—my real partner. Our friends here Utpal and Srimati are right here in the first row.'

The crowd clapped, and a few of them even responded with a loud "Namaskar".

'This was a nice break from all this heavy spirituality, I guess!' someone said.

Samir then continued. 'As Vedic people, we have had a policy of inclusion even to the detriment of our own identity. Colonization has imposed distortions in our thoughts and actions. I was part of that colonized, yet intellectually elite, class. But the Vedas and Vedanta have taught me the limitations of intellect, and they have advised me to use all my faculties: my intellect, emotions and supra-emotions. Initially, I admired the likes of Carl Sagan. I wanted to be like him to confirm the gloriousness of my roots. I read English and some Bengali, but I soon delved deep into my roots. I read scriptures in Sanskrit. My rishis, my Gautama, Bhardwaj, and my Vivekananda. I feel their blood flowing through my veins.

'Am I with all of you?' Samir was slightly uneasy with the silence.

He continued. 'I don't see the world as matter first or white, brown or black first, proletariat first or capitalist first or even human beings first. I believe that we are a tiny spot in the vast tapestry. We are all here to understand our true nature and the very nature of freedom. Communism, capitalism, any "ism", cannot give you mukti or kaivalya. Nor will quoting western writers make you a higher being. Even with Indian spirituality, there are a plethora of writers from the West who speak of the fusion of spirituality and matter, like Rupert Spira, Aldous Huxley, Edwin Bryant, Fritjof Capra, Jack Kornfield, Rupert Sheldrake, Gary Zukav and so on. While I applaud their work, I have started to let go of those limits and soar. I have let my practice guide me. My mantras show me the way. There is no point in walking from Los Angeles to New York, no matter how exciting it may be. I choose to fly and leave my mark on the tapestry. I leave myself in the hands of a pilot! It relieves me from my limitations, my colonized samskaras, and my all-binding impressions.

'Unity in Diversity is a limiting term. Unity is Diversity, Diversity is Unity. There is no difference. We, Vedic people, look at things in this holistic way. The other views, especially Marxism, comprehends things in terms of matter. Unfortunately, visible matter is only 5 per cent of the world. However, via quantum and qualia, modern medicine and ayurveda and yoga, we find ways to meet each other and discuss these differences.

'Nonetheless, there is one big cautionary note I must make. We, the modern Vedic people, must be aware of it. Don't steal our history. Don't let others steal our identity. Don't let them, in contemporary terms, steal our copyrights.

'Ask the colonizing minds: Who gave you the right to define us in your terms? We never gave it to you. Don't try to convert us and we will not convert you. We belong to different ends of the spectrum, and that is the way we like to keep things.

'I don't want to delve into the historic context of Manu and caste. One thing I know is that we have been under the foreign influence for more than a thousand years. I live in the West, and I know the mentality. Religion has been used by them to classify and dissect and divide. Even a non-entity like caste in the West has become a point of defining us in California School systems. My type of God. My path. Marxism has gone the same way. Karl Marx never knew the richness of our system! He replaced one dogma with a dogma of atheism! My system is the only way. Our Vedic system has been criticized; history had morphed it to suit their purposes.'

Samir couldn't resist, he was on a roll.

'In fact, Runa some of your comments and assumptions were viewed via the lens of the West. Natiskyavad means 'no to astikyavad', it has to come afterward. How can it predate the Vedas? You imposed your Marxist views of the origin of class society to change my history. Most "sophisticated" Indians have been taught that way. I was also enslaved, but surprisingly, my "Marxist" dad always kept the light of the Vedas burning. That is where the first shloka on Agni comes in. The unblemished fire of the unbound. My fire kept on burning. "*Agnimīle purohitam yajñasya devamṛtvijam, hotāram ratnadhātamam.*"'

Samir paused. 'But that's a debate for another day. We are here to celebrate the book launch. And we, all of us, worked together.'

The journalist prodded. 'Samir babu, can you talk a little bit about how you kept the fire going even in your environment?'

'I will be brief, as I promised to. My wife always smiles when I say that I won't say much. But your question can be a whole story in itself. In those radical days, back in the seventies, I had out-of-body experiences almost every night. I visited the refugee camps to help the downtrodden though our leaders made ivory-tower impositions of their thoughts in the real world. I meditated and asked Lord Shiva for forgiveness for not being able to serve them wholeheartedly. My dad was visited by nightmares since 1947 till his death.

'In America, I was a socialist for a long time. But then the Wall fell. I could not sleep for days.

'But things changed. I heard horrific stories from immigrants from Russia and Eastern Europe. I heard of the gruesome acts of inhumanity. Then, in the USA, I saw the naked face of "One God, My God" systems. I was asked to convert by my own boss, not just once, but a few times. In my mind the so-called West and that includes Marxism was reduced to rubbles.

'I began to search for a genuine purpose. I needed to do kriya as my toxins were deep-rooted. I started studying and practicing yoga and ayurveda. They became my identity. My healers.' Samir took a brief pause. 'Am I boring you? My friends are usually bored with my chatter on such spiritual matters.'

And then, he continued. 'Interestingly a lot of Marxists now have epiphanies when they discuss Upanishads with a western sadhu, with a glass of Merlot in their hands. Some even discuss how Marxism can be tweaked and M-C-M can be transformed to M-C-S-M. "S" stands for spirituality. These are of course the erudite all-knowing crowd. I avoid them.'

He laughed when he saw faces blanch in the audience. Some were smiling.

'Sorry. I am known to be brutally direct at times. I will stop here. As my rajas and tamas are taking over my satwa.' He laughed again and folded his palms.

Each finger perfectly matched the other. Pancha-prana in full balance. He grew silent and for a few seconds it seemed like the audience had gone numb, until there was a sudden roar of applause. There was a standing ovation, and many of them even had tears in their eyes.

When Samir noticed Neelu, her eyes were searching for Nandita. Samir also tried to locate her in the corner but she had left. Runa told him later that she had left abruptly and it seemed to her that Nandita was crying.

Samir addressed the audience, 'You think we can take this as a closure?'

'No, we wish to hear Ms Ganguly's views.' There were evidently quite a few non-conformists in the crowd.

Runa got up. 'My views are there in the letter inside the novel. However, much as I would like all of you to read the novel, I am aware that quite a few will miss out. So, let me conclude in a few sentences. I remain a dogged Materialist. I persist in my beliefs. I am situated at the other end of the spectrum. Dialectical and Historical Materialism continue to be my beacons of light. For me, what Samir mentioned, like seeing the Big Bang, is a subjective experience. A few years back, I would have passed sarcastic, snide comments but I have now become much more tolerant. It could be hallucination for those who claim to have experienced supernatural phenomenon, but that would be too offensive a word. All I can say here is that I personally believe in what can be seen, felt, smelt, touched, logically and mathematically proven. And I still believe in class struggle.

'Nevertheless, I loved Samir's exposition because I am dialectical by nature. I love arguments.' Having said this, she gently sat on the chair while smiling at both Neelu and Samir.

There was another round of applause.

'No more comments from me, Runa has to have the last word, and so be it. I am on my way to real liberation that I have always sought since childhood. How can liberation be attained in this grand illusion of the material world?'

There was further laughter from the crowd. They seemed to enjoy the show.

Neelu came close to Samir and whispered, 'You were at your best.' Samir lightly touched her back and said, 'You still look stunning.'

The novel was aptly titled *Fear of Hope*. However, the closure that Samir longed for remained elusive. The fear of hope pervaded his mind for many years, although they never heard from Nandita Roy ever again.